VE may 14

SCREAM FOR
ME

Also by Cynthia Eden

Die For Me: A Novel of the Valentine Killer

Fear For Me: A Novel of the Bayou Butcher

CYNTHIA EDEN

SCREAM FOR ME

A NOVEL OF THE NIGHT HUNTER

Montlake
Romance

Copyright © 2014 Cindy Roussos

Published by Montlake Romance
PO Box 400818
Las Vegas, NV 89140

ISBN-13: 9781477848463
ISBN-10: 1477848460

Library of Congress Control Number: 2013910017

Thank you so much to all the wonderful romantic-suspense readers out there! I really appreciate all the support that you've given to me.

PROLOGUE

His prey stumbled through the dark parking lot, teetering in her high heels, swaying as she tried to brace her body against the old sedan. Her blonde hair was pulled back into a ponytail, and her slender shoulders were slumped.

Voices and laughter drifted in the night. The last few bar patrons slowly staggered away.

They didn't acknowledge the woman. They were too busy trying to stay upright.

He was the only one who watched her.

She wasn't drunk. That wasn't why she swayed. The woman was bone tired. Lily Adams had worked a double shift, staying far later at Striker's than she normally did. She had to be so very weary.

She shouldn't work so hard. If she wasn't careful, little Lily was going to work herself straight into an early grave.

She finally got the car door unlocked. Lily slid into her sedan. Cranked the engine. It sputtered, then died. Lily tried again, obviously used to this routine.

It was a routine he'd watched before.

A few minutes later, after a few more false starts, her car backed out of the lot.

He waited a beat, then followed her.

When she turned on the old, long stretch of highway that would take her back to the little ranch house she had off of County Road 12, he was close. So close. His headlights were turned off, and sweet Lily Adams had no clue she was being hunted.

The hunt was always so much fun. Not the best part, of course, but still…

He enjoyed it. The hunt built the anticipation. Let him know of the pleasures to come.

He kept track of the miles as they passed. It was important to keep track because he'd planned this so perfectly.

Up ahead, her car began to slow. To sputter. *Right on time.*

When the sedan stopped completely, he smiled and flashed on his lights.

The road was instantly bright, the headlights falling straight on Lily and her car. She hadn't gotten out of the vehicle. Sometimes, they did. When their cars stopped, they would jump out. They tried to lift the hood, tried to see what was wrong.

Tried to fix what couldn't be fixed.

But Lily wasn't moving.

He parked behind her. Took a breath. Let the anticipation build even more. Then he slid from his vehicle and headed toward her. The road was empty. Stretching as far as he could see. No help in sight.

No help would be coming for Lily Adams.

His gloved hands fisted.

She would make such a perfect addition to his collection.

CHAPTER ONE

Dr. Cadence Hollow was beautiful when she slept. Her defenses were down, her body so relaxed. No fears plagued her, no desperation. All of that was gone in sleep.

Kyle McKenzie studied his partner as the plane slowly descended. Cadence's head rested on his shoulder. She'd hate that intimate position when she woke. She always tried so hard to keep distance between them.

Distance he'd like to eliminate.

His fingers skimmed over her cheek. Like touching silk. So soft and smooth. His head had turned toward her, and he was close enough to catch the light scent that always surrounded her.

Cadence smelled like flowers. Roses.

She was also the embodiment of every fantasy he'd had for the past year.

"McKenzie." She sighed out his name without opening her eyes. "What are you doing?"

Imagining you naked. Was that such a bad thing? Probably. Since they were partners and they were supposed to have a serious hands-off rule in effect. But a guy could still dream.

The plane jerked a bit. Cadence's lashes lifted. Her big, golden eyes were startlingly aware for someone who'd been asleep. That was Cadence. Instantly alert.

Always on guard.

"We're touching down," he told her.

Her head rose, a faint furrow appearing between her brows as she realized she had been sleeping on his shoulder.

Not that he minded being her pillow. Not at all. Especially because she'd been the one to move closer to him.

Cadence licked her lips.

Torture.

Then she hurriedly straightened in her seat. "I didn't realize we'd arrive so soon."

"It's been two hours." Not that he'd been counting. They'd left their base in Quantico early that morning, heading out on another case he already knew would hit too damn close to home.

Hell, he'd taken the case *because* it hit close. When he'd gotten the phone call from the police captain in Paradox, Alabama, everything had changed. It wasn't his first time talking to Captain James Anniston.

Because fifteen years ago, Kyle's sister had disappeared in that same small, southern town.

Vanished without a trace.

There had been no way he could have denied Anniston's request for assistance. Kyle hadn't told Cadence about his connection to the town, not yet.

He knew Cadence. She would think he was going to the town for the wrong reasons. *To find my sister.*

Cadence would be right.

As an FBI agent, he'd always thought he knew all about the evil in the world. Then, last year, he'd been transferred to the violent crimes division and specifically assigned to work with Cadence.

Her specialty?

Serial killers. She was a doctor turned profiler, an MD who'd taken to profiling not just killers, but also their victims. Her profiles were dead-on and had resulted in a case closure rate that had caught the attention of all the higher-ups at Quantico. Cadence's skills were in high demand at the bureau.

Killers weren't stopping. They were simply becoming more vicious.

Right then, he and Cadence figured there were between thirty and forty active serials hunting, just in the United States. All those killers were why Uncle Sam had recruited the agents to work specifically at serial apprehension, or SA as the bureau called it.

The pilot's voice came over the speaker, reminding them to secure their seat belts as they landed. It was a private plane, one the FBI let its agents use when they were going out on cases like this one.

When time matters. When a life could hang in the balance.

"Do you think she's still alive?" Kyle asked Cadence, unable to hold the question back.

Cadence hesitated.

She doesn't.

Cadence never seemed to have much hope. The victims were the ones she focused on; she got them to lead her to the killers, yet she never seemed to think she or Kyle could actually save anyone. Stop the killers, yes, but rescue a victim?

No.

"Lily Adams has been missing for less than twelve hours," she said, giving a quick shake of her head. Her gaze cut toward the window. "There's certainly a chance she could still be alive, but I don't know what to expect."

Such a lie. Cadence could actually lie amazingly well—to everyone but him. The longer they'd worked together, the more hesitant she'd become in telling him a direct lie. Now, when she lied, she didn't even look him in the eyes.

"This might not even be a case for us," she continued as the plane slid down the narrow runway. It wasn't exactly a commercial hub. The pilot hadn't even been sure they could land at the old place. Not at first.

Cadence sighed. "Why did you push so hard for us to come here?"

Here being a small spot on the Alabama map, just west of Huntsville. Most folks would probably never even hear of Paradox, but Kyle had never been able to forget the place.

Lily Adams's disappearance matches my sister's. Captain Anniston had called Kyle because the guy saw the link, too.

"I pushed because I think we can save her." Unlike Cadence, he actually *did* think they had a chance of helping victims, and not just finding their broken bodies.

Her gaze, so golden and deep, the most unusual eyes he'd ever seen, came back to him. Cadence was a gorgeous woman, no getting around that, with an oval-shaped face, high cheekbones, and a small, slightly curving nose. And those lips. Full, red. Bow shaped. Seriously fucking bow shaped. Who had lips like that? *Cadence.* Her skin was pale, her hair so dark it almost appeared jet-black.

Those golden eyes studied him with the same assessing stare she used on perps. He tensed beneath that gaze. "Stop." He hated it when she analyzed him. But then, Cadence had a tendency to analyze everything.

She didn't look away. "Saving Lily won't save your sister."

Hit. He thought he'd been so careful, never telling Cadence about his past.

But it looked as if he'd underestimated his partner. Cadence knew about the demons that had driven him to join her in serial apprehension.

His fingers tightened around the hand rest.

His sister. It had been fifteen years since he lost Maria. How much did Cadence know? The actual case files on Maria's disappearance were sickeningly slim. Just the barest of facts, because the sad truth was that there hadn't been much for the authorities *to* find. But over the years, he'd created his own files. He'd never stopped searching.

And dammit, he had to follow this lead. If there was any chance that Lily Adams could be connected to his sister's disappearance, Kyle knew he had to act. Protocol be damned.

All of these years. All of my searching. Finally, this could be the break he needed. Anniston had given him the tip on Lily's disappearance right away. If they found Lily…

Then I might find clues that can lead me to Maria.

His jaw locked. "We investigate the Adams case. If it's BS, and the woman ran off on her own, then we walk away. All we've lost is a day."

A day they could have spent on another case. Catching another killer.

"Just a day," Cadence said softly.

This time, he was the one to look away. He didn't want Cadence seeing the emotion that might be in his eyes.

Hope. He'd never lost it for his sister, or for any of the victims. He never would.

Cadence didn't even seem to understand what hope meant. To him, that lack of understanding was a real fucking shame.

After a few moments, his eyes cut back to her. Only Cadence wasn't studying him any longer. She was looking down toward her lap. The case file—bare bones at this point—was still open. Her gaze slid over the picture of Lily Adams. Thirty-two, blonde hair, green eyes. A wide smile.

Lily Adams looked happy. Full of life.

If he had his way, they'd find her—*and she'll look that way again.*

He settled back in his seat and waited for the plane to come to a stop.

***

Cadence hated Alabama summers. Hated them. Once upon a time in a life very far away, she'd grown up on the Alabama coast. Growing up here meant it was impossible to forget the heat that hit like a blanket when you walked outside. The sweat could drip and drip from your body because there was no relief in sight.

No, you didn't forget. But you sure tried to.

She'd tried hard enough to put those memories away.

Cadence lifted the hair from the back of her neck, attempting to fan her skin. Like that was going to help. The sun glared down on her as she and Kyle stood in the middle of a deserted, two-lane highway.

The middle of nowhere. She'd seen plenty of spots like this before. Perfect killing spots.

"Her gas tank was empty." The slightly drawling voice drew her attention. The local police captain had escorted them out to the old highway. The road wasn't *exactly* deserted.

"Why hasn't the vehicle been moved?" Cadence asked, frowning. The sedan, with its faded blue color and taped back taillight, sat on the edge of the road.

"You folks told me to leave it where it was," Captain James Anniston told her with a frown. "Don't worry, I had a guard on it at all times. It's been secure. When I called Quantico, McKenzie here told me—"

"I told him we wanted the scene as protected as we could get it," Kyle interrupted. He'd taken off his suit jacket. The heat had gotten to him, too. Kyle and his suits. The guy never seemed to dress right for fieldwork. Always too fancy. That was a rich boy for you.

He shouldn't have wound up chasing killers with the FBI. His family business and the family's big stack of money should have kept the guy busy living the country club life.

His gaze slid to her. A bright, glittering blue stare. The stare that always looked a bit haunted.

I know why you joined the bureau. Why you turned your back on everything waiting for you in Maine.

Guilt could sometimes eat a man from the inside out. From what she could tell, guilt had consumed Kyle for years.

If he wasn't careful, the guilt might destroy him one day.

Or send him back down to Alabama permanently, chasing ghosts.

But she was the one who'd agreed to travel with him, so she'd do her job. Even if the job turned out to be nothing. *Only missing twelve hours.*

She let her gaze shift back to the captain. A fit guy, maybe in his late forties, tanned, with faint lines near his eyes. Laugh lines? Or worry lines? "You put out the report on Lily very fast. Usually a missing-persons case waits for—"

"I wasn't waiting for forty-eight hours, ma'am. Not with Lily." His jaw locked and the sun gleamed off his bald head. "I'm not some backward hick, Agent Hollow. I know when I got suspicious circumstances staring me right in the face."

Cadence blinked. "I never said you were." If he only knew about her own roots…but few people did.

That life was over.

She cleared her throat and reassessed the captain. Something had set the guy off. *Handle carefully.*

He pointed to the car. "Lily Adams has a daughter. A nine-year-old girl who is her absolute life. There is no way—*no way*—Lily would wander off without her."

Cadence's heart beat faster. She'd only had time to learn the barest of details about Lily Adams before she'd jumped on the plane. Kyle had been insistent that they take the case, almost desperate, and she hadn't been able to turn him down.

It was his eyes. The echo of pain in his gaze pierced through her every time.

Kyle McKenzie was a good agent. A little reckless too often, and too prone to going with his gut, but he was dedicated to the job. Dedicated to saving lives.

He wasn't her first partner. She'd had several over the years. Some hadn't been able to handle the darkness of the job. One had been killed in the line of duty by one of the monsters they hunted.

When she'd first been paired with Kyle, Cadence had been less than impressed. Kyle was handsome, wickedly so with his flashing eyes and chiseled jaw. He'd come to her with a bit of a playboy reputation.

She hadn't been interested in joining his group of admirers. Cadence hadn't ever been swayed by a handsome face. Handsome was boring, easy. Not for her.

She'd soon learned there were plenty of layers to Kyle McKenzie. What you saw with him was *not* what you got.

Until recently, Kyle had been almost too perfect with his classic features. But on their last big case, he'd gotten into a vicious hand-to-hand fight with a killer. The result? A broken nose that now gave the agent a rougher, more dangerous appearance.

That dangerous edge of his had been coming out more and more lately. She was too aware of it—and of the growing attraction she felt for him.

They were supposed to be just partners, but lately—*I want more.*

She wanted him. And if the way he looked at her was any indication, the desire was mutual.

"Lily's kid has to be frantic about now," Anniston continued. "She's probably at home, crying her eyes out."

Because the girl just wanted her mother back. Cadence swallowed. Goose bumps rose on her overheated flesh.

Back home in Alabama.

The cases involving kids were always the hardest for her to handle.

She kept the emotion out of her voice as she asked, "Just what scenario do you think happened here last night?"

Kyle was walking around the vehicle, studying it carefully. He'd put on gloves as he bent near the driver's side. Sweat dampened the hair near his temples. His blond hair was so thick and heavy, no wonder he was sweating.

They were all baking out there.

"Lily's car ran out of gas. She probably started walking." Captain Anniston turned and pointed north. "Her house is that way. She must've started walking and some SOB picked her up. Took her."

Cadence glanced down at the road.

"Lily probably thought she could make it home. Just a few more miles, and she would have been safe." Anger rumbled beneath the captain's words.

Cadence walked to the edge of the road. The shoulder was covered by loose dirt. She glanced to the north, then back to the south before focusing on the captain. "No rain has come through here?"

Anniston shook his head. "Due for some later, but it's been dry here for the last week."

There were no signs of footprints, but Lily might have just stuck to walking on the road itself. Then there would have been no prints left behind.

Cadence headed around the car to take a look herself. She stopped at the gas tank. Frowned. There were scratches around the tank. As if someone had pried the lid open.

"You said the car ran out of gas?" She thought of how Lily must have felt as her car sputtered and coasted on this dark road.

Scared. So scared.

"The tank was empty. I checked around the vehicle, trying to figure out why it had stopped. The battery was fine. Engine, oil… everything else was fine. It was the tank that was desert dry."

"You said her purse was found in the car." Kyle turned away from the vehicle. His broad shoulders were tense. "If she was walking, don't you think she would have taken that with her?"

The captain didn't reply.

Kyle cocked his head as he studied the captain. "What about her keys? Where were they?"

"Still in the ignition."

Hell. Along with the purse, this put a different spin on things. Cadence put her hands on her hips. "She didn't start walking anywhere, Captain."

"But—"

"If she'd walked, she would have taken her purse. Her keys. Women don't leave their purses behind." Now she realized why Kyle had been so adamant about taking the case. An abduction like this…a fresh case…*we might even be able to find her alive.*

If they acted quickly enough.

Kyle opened the driver's side door and slid inside.

"My men already searched the vehicle," Anniston called out. "We recovered everything."

Kyle raised his hand. A cell phone was held in his gloved grip. "This had fallen between the seats."

Turned out Anniston's men hadn't recovered everything.

Anniston hurried toward him. "You think Lily tried to call someone for help last night?"

I would have called for help. On that long, dark road. The cell phone would have been the first thing Cadence reached for.

Some profilers tried to figure out the killers based on their actions and the clues killers themselves left behind.

Cadence didn't work that way. When she tracked killers, she became their victims.

She had the nightmares to prove it.

"Who was keeping Lily's daughter last night?" Someone must have been watching the girl.

"Lily's mother. Lily and little Carrie…"

She saw Kyle tense at the girl's name. She'd seen a similar reaction from him on other cases. He was always sensitive to the families.

She understood. Dealing with the families was often the hardest part for her.

"They live with Lily's mother up on Miner's Way."

"The mother didn't report receiving a call from her daughter?" Cadence asked.

"No."

Cadence considered that for a moment. Maybe Lily wouldn't have wanted her mother to rush out at night, no doubt dragging Carrie with her. So she wouldn't have called her…*but someone else.*

Who?

Maybe Lily had called someone for help…only that person hadn't been the savior Lily expected.

***

Tracking the last phone call Lily Adams made was an easy enough matter. A few touches on the phone and her most recent call list had appeared.

Curtis Adams. Lily's ex-husband.

Cadence and Kyle now stood on Curtis's doorstep, the captain just a few feet away. According to her recent-call list, at 2:12 a.m., Lily had called Curtis.

When the captain had questioned him before calling the FBI, the guy had denied hearing from her. Anniston had said that after discovering Lily was missing, his first stop had been the ex. Only Lily's ex-husband had sworn he hadn't heard from Lily in weeks.

Guess someone lied. Cadence knew far too well how often and easily people could lie.

It wouldn't be the first time an ex had gone after a former lover. Cadence had seen plenty of cases play out that way—most with sad endings.

Had Curtis Adams found himself in the perfect position to get a little payback against Lily? According to Anniston, Lily had full custody of the couple's daughter, and Curtis had been shut out in the cold by the court.

Did that make you want to punish her? When he'd found himself on a dark, lonely road with Lily, was that just what Curtis had done?

Cadence knew they were about to find out.

Kyle lifted his hand and pounded his tanned fist against the door.

Cadence heard the pad of footsteps inside. Only those footsteps weren't coming toward the front door.

They sounded like they were running *away* from the front of the house.

Kyle's bright-blue gaze slid to her. He gave a curt nod, then he shouted, "FBI! Curtis Adams, we need you to open the door!"

In the distance, a door slammed.

"He's running out the back," Anniston snarled as he turned to jump from the narrow porch.

Innocent men weren't supposed to run.

Cadence drew her own gun and raced after the captain. Kyle was right at her back.

She saw a blond male jump into a pickup truck, one that was painted fire-engine red. He revved the engine as Anniston pounded on the window and ordered him to stop and exit the vehicle.

"Get out, Curtis!" Anniston shouted. "*Now!*"

The guy wasn't exiting.

The tires screeched and the vehicle lunged forward, heading right for Cadence.

"FBI!" she yelled. The guy was coming too fast, the pickup fishtailing.

He's not stopping. Hell.

She lunged to the right just as she felt strong hands wrap tightly around her. She was thrown through the air and landed in a heap of bushes, with Kyle's hard body pressed tightly against hers. Cadence only had a moment to feel the hard thrust of his body. The ripple of muscles. The leashed strength.

Twigs scraped against her as she jumped to her feet, but Kyle was up first, aiming his weapon at the back of the truck.

"Stop!" Kyle bellowed.

That obviously wasn't happening.

But then Kyle fired his weapon, shooting at the back left tire. A damn good shot. It should have been. She knew her partner spent plenty of hours at the firing range.

The truck swerved, fishtailed again, and plowed right into a tree.

That was one way to stop him.

Only Curtis Adams wasn't done yet. He shoved open the driver's side door, leaped out of the vehicle, and started running down the old dirt drive.

Perps never made it easy on them.

Kyle raced after the guy, and Cadence was the one following this time.

Curtis wasn't getting away, not from Kyle. According to the stories at Quantico, her partner had been all-state back in high school. She'd sure seen him sack fleeing suspects before without even breaking so much as a mild sweat.

Kyle tackled Curtis, knocking into him with an impact that could have easily broken bones.

Cadence rushed to a stop next to them. Curtis had twisted around and lifted his fist, preparing to plow it right into Kyle's face.

"Don't," she snapped as she aimed her gun at Curtis's head. "In case you missed it the other two times, we're FBI, and you need to *freeze*."

He finally froze. Or at least stopped fighting. Flushed cheeks, wide, wild eyes, breath sawing out in a frantic rhythm—the guy's whole body trembled.

Kyle climbed to his feet. "Where is she?" Kyle barked.

Breath wheezing, the captain rushed over to join them.

Curtis still hadn't risen.

Cadence's eyes narrowed as she studied his pupils. *Pinpricks.* And that nervous gaze of his kept flickering over Cadence's shoulder. *To the house?*

She darted a glance back. He'd been leading them *away* from the house. What was inside?

Lily?

"Where is Lily Adams?" Kyle demanded as he hauled Curtis to his feet.

Curtis immediately stumbled, and Cadence didn't think the stumble was from the crash with the tree or with Kyle. She peered at Curtis, noticing the red sores on his face, particularly around his mouth and across his forehead. His cheeks had a hollowed look, and dark circles lined his bloodshot eyes.

"Curtis Adams," she said quietly. "You just tried to run down two federal officers with your vehicle. Do you have any idea how much trouble that's going to make for you?"

As soon as her words sank in, Curtis immediately attempted to lunge away.

Kyle grabbed him and hauled him back. Kyle's suit had torn, and dirt covered most of the expensive cloth.

His handsome face sure looked pissed.

"What drugs are you on?" Cadence demanded as she sized up Adams.

"Nothin'!" he spat. "Get away from me, you—"

Kyle's hold on the perp tightened. "You want to be real careful what you say to her next."

Like she hadn't been called plenty worse than what Curtis was about to say. But Kyle never liked it when anyone said a cross word to her. Protective, straight to his core. That protective streak could be damn sexy.

But then, so could he. Rumpled, sweating, fury straining his features, he looked like the lethal threat he was. Definitely dangerous enough to intimidate Curtis.

"Anniston." She directed with an inclination of her head. "How about you pull out your cuffs?" Curtis was running high, and he could attack again at any moment.

Meth. She'd bet on it. All of the telltale signs were there, and tremors were shaking the guy's body harder now.

If she went back into the house—*when* she went in—Cadence was sure she'd find drug paraphernalia.

Anniston began to rattle off a list of Curtis's rights. As the captain talked, Curtis just looked confused. *When you assault federal officers with your car, you're gonna get arrested.*

"Where's Lily?" Cadence asked once Anniston was done.

The handcuffs clicked as they locked.

"I don't know!" Curtis shouted.

"She called you last night," Cadence continued, undeterred. "Did you go and pick her up? Did the two of you fight?"

If he'd been riding high on meth last night, there was no telling what he might have done.

"I already told the cop." He jerked his head toward Anniston. "I ain't seen Lily! We ain't talked since the divorce!"

The woman had left such a fine catch? Hard to imagine. "She called you. We saw the proof on her phone."

"I didn't talk to her!"

Maybe. Or maybe it was just another lie. "Is she in your house? Did you *hurt* her?" Cadence stared right into his wild eyes as she waited for his response.

For an instant, she saw sanity flash. "Hurt Lily? No…never!" He shook his head and his shoulders seemed to slump. "Go look…go look inside…she's not there."

They'd definitely be looking. "Take him in," she directed Anniston.

The captain hauled the guy away.

Cadence turned back to the house.

Kyle was already heading for the rear door, a door that Adams had conveniently left wide open.

"You think she could be in there?" Kyle asked quietly.

Cadence heard no sound from inside. "No. He wouldn't have told us to go in if he was keeping her here." Curtis wouldn't be that stupid, would he?

Cautiously, she entered through the back door. Kyle had his gun out. Cadence took five steps into the kitchen and saw exactly what she'd been looking for.

Tinfoil, bent to look like a bowl. The telltale glittering residue shining on the foil.

Over on the counter, a spoon, its curving base darkened brown.

Meth.

They slipped from the kitchen. Their footsteps creaked against the broken linoleum tile.

The house was in shambles. Trash, old food scattered everywhere. And the stench in the house…Cadence swallowed.

The guy obviously didn't believe in cleaning, but when you were a meth addict, there was little you believed in, other than the drug.

Her gaze swept what passed for a den. No sign of Lily.

She saw a faint, flickering light on an old end table.

Cadence hurried toward it.

An answering machine. A very old, dusty answering machine that appeared to still work.

The red light indicated Curtis had missed a call.

He'd sworn he hadn't talked to Lily.

Could it be the guy didn't even realize his ex *had* called?

Yes.

"Kyle!"

He was there in an instant.

She pressed the button to hear the message.

A woman's voice, low, shaking, pulsed from the small machine. "Curtis? Curtis, are you there?" Her breath whispered out, sliding from the machine. "Look, I need your help."

Cadence glanced up. She found Kyle's gaze locked on her.

"My car stopped." Fear trembled in the woman's voice. Lily's voice. "I'm out on the highway, just a few miles from home. Please, Curtis. If you're there, pick up."

Silence. Lily had waited for Curtis to pick up. He hadn't.

"Someone's here!" More fear. Her voice was higher. "There are lights behind me. Curtis, please, *pick up!*"

Curtis had been busy. Curtis had never even heard the phone ring.

There was a rasp in the background. Someone else talking.

"I'm fine!" Lily's voice shouted.

Cadence saw Kyle's jaw harden.

"Help is coming," Lily said, her voice still a little too loud. Why?

Because she'd been talking through her window. And that was why they couldn't hear the perp's voice.

Cadence's heart beat faster. Were they going to hear Lily die on this recording? There had been no blood at the scene.

And no Lily.

There was another rasp, a murmur. Whoever was there was talking to Lily.

Silence. Then…

A grinding sound.

No, Lily, no! Cadence knew Lily had just lowered her window.

You let him in.

"What seems to be the trouble?" A man's voice. No accent. Hard. Rumbling. Carrying so easily to the recorder because he'd been right next to Lily and her phone.

Close enough to kill.

"I don't know, Officer. My car just stopped."

"Fuck," Kyle whispered.

Cadence's breath burned in her lungs. *Officer.*

The man was speaking again. "Why don't you step out of the vehicle, and we'll take a look, okay? If I can't get it working for you, I can always give you a ride." There was no threat in his words. He sounded helpful.

Don't get out of the car, Lily. Like the warning would do any good now. She could almost see Lily in her mind. Nervously reaching out to unlock the door.

"It's not safe for you to be alone out here," the man said. "You never know what's waiting in the dark."

Cadence knew exactly what waited. Monsters. A monster had been standing right beside Lily.

"I don't recognize you." It was Lily's voice, only it was harder to hear now. "Th-the light's too bright." The words were muffled. Had she put down her phone?

Kyle stood as still as stone.

"I thought I knew most of the cops in this area." Even muffled, the rising fear was obvious in Lily's voice.

Too late. She realized she might have made a mistake in trusting the man.

"Have you been drinking?" A sharp crack of demand, the words were more audible than Lily's had been. "Ma'am, I smell alcohol on you. Step from the vehicle, *now*."

So clever. The man had tricked her, intimidated her, and gotten Lily Adams to do exactly as he'd wanted.

"No! I—" There was a groan of metal.

She opened the door. She went to him.

"I work at a sports bar, Striker's. Some beer spilled on me earlier, and I—"

Lily's voice broke off. Just stopped.

Kyle's blue eyes glittered.

"I know just what you've been doing, Lily." The man's voice. Mocking. Satisfied.

Muffled cries broke from the machine.

Then…nothing.

Beep.

"Sonofabitch." Kyle breathed the words. "She was taken by a cop?"

Maybe. Or maybe that was just what the perp had wanted Lily to think. Either way… "We're going to need to meet with all of Anniston's men."

And they'd be questioning Anniston, too.

They had concrete proof now. Lily Adams hadn't just disappeared of her own accord. This investigation wasn't merely based on Kyle's hunch or gut instinct.

Lily Adams had been abducted.

Somewhere, out in the small town of Paradox, her abductor could be waiting.

We're going to find you.

CHAPTER TWO

They'd taken over the small police station in Paradox. Curtis Adams was in a holding cell, and Kyle hoped the jerk would hurry up and become more coherent for them soon. Trying to question a guy high on meth was useless.

Officers in three counties were now searching for Lily. Her face was being splashed across the news. Time was of the essence. They'd caught this case early, thanks to Anniston, and if they could move fast enough…

"It reminds you of her, doesn't it?"

He turned, not surprised to see Captain James Anniston standing in the doorway.

James looked over his shoulder, glancing back to where Cadence was hovering over an old computer. Then he crossed the threshold and shut the door behind him.

Since it was his office, the guy should have felt plenty comfortable heading inside, but judging by the look on his face, comfort was the last thing James felt. "The minute I saw Lily's car, it reminded me of Maria, too. That's why I had to call you."

Maria. His sister's name seemed to echo in his mind, but Kyle didn't let his expression alter. "The setup is the same." A car, abandoned in the dead of night on a long, lonely stretch of highway.

In the same damn town.

When he'd been out on that road, memories had burned through him. It had been all he could do to hold onto his control. Cadence never had a problem with control. He had to fight to keep his every minute.

Kyle cleared his throat and tried to stay cool. "The cases are sure similar, but my sister was eighteen when she vanished. Lily's thirty-two." It was a big age gap for a serial—not that anyone had ever tied his sister's disappearance to a killer.

No one had ever found Maria McKenzie. She'd gone on a road trip, determined to exert her independence as she headed down to Florida for a summer vacation. Her friends had been waiting for her in Pensacola, right on the beach. *White sand, blue waves.* That was what Maria had told him. *Pensacola Beach.* She'd been so eager to start her journey.

But she'd never made it to those sandy shores.

Officer James Anniston had found her car. Traced her tags. Contacted Kyle.

Then my world fell apart.

Because he'd promised his parents he'd go on that trip with Maria. Sworn he wouldn't leave her on her own.

He'd broken his promise.

"There were no signs of a struggle at Maria's scene," James said. "Just like with Lily."

Only with Lily, they had a lead. They had a voice. They *knew* she'd been taken.

With Maria, even James hadn't been convinced—not at first—that she'd been taken. They'd thought she hooked up with some man—that she went off to enjoy her summer.

And what? Just left her car behind on some Alabama road?

No. He'd never bought that story. When Maria hadn't turned up in a few days, weeks, or months, his parents had started to understand.

Their daughter wasn't coming home.

His mother had turned to the bottle. He'd always thought she drank herself to death. His father had thrown himself into his work. A heart attack had taken him away at just fifty-eight.

And as all of those long days rolled past, James had come to understand that Maria hadn't disappeared with her boyfriend. Evil had come to that small Alabama town on that long-ago night, and that evil had *taken* Kyle's sister.

Kyle had kept in touch with James over the years, calling just in case any new evidence had been found.

There had never been any news. Until now.

"Lily." James's voice was musing. "She kind of looked like Maria. That same long, blonde hair."

Kyle had noticed the slight physical similarity right away. It was another reason he'd busted ass convincing Cadence they needed to get down to Alabama.

"You know we're going to investigate every officer you have here." Cadence had already started to run background checks on the men. They'd interview them next, to see if anyone slipped up in interrogation.

"It's not one of my men." James was adamant on that point. "Two of 'em—Hollings and Wentworth—were breaking up a fight at Phillip Long's place. That dumb SOB is always hitting his wife." He ran a hand over his face. "She just always runs right back to him."

Because of Lily's phone call to Curtis, they had an exact time for Lily's abduction. An exact time meant it was easier to confirm alibis. Or break them.

"You've got other officers," Kyle pointed out.

"We know Heather Crenshaw didn't do it. She was with her partner, Jason Marsh, all night on patrols."

There was only a small number of officers in the Paradox Police Department, and Kyle knew he and Cadence would work their way through all of the alibis.

The problem was the guy they were looking for might not be part of Anniston's crew. He could work in another county. He could be a state trooper.

Or he could be some asshole who'd bought a plastic badge at a costume shop. It wouldn't be the first time a perp had pretended to be a cop to get close to his prey. Awhile back, the same thing had happened in Mississippi. A guy pretending to be a state trooper had raped four women before he was finally stopped.

If you want to make a victim trust you, become someone they can count on. Someone they need.

"A woman alone like that, in the middle of the night," Kyle sighed. "She would have been grateful to see a cop pull up and offer to help her."

On the recording, Lily had sounded relieved. *Officer.* But the relief had turned to fear all too quickly.

"We're the good guys," James said with a sad shake of his head. "Or at least, we're supposed to be."

Cocking his head, Kyle studied the captain. James was still in good shape. The lines near his eyes were deeper than they'd been, and while they'd been talking, Kyle had noticed James's hands shook.

"In all my years here in Paradox, there have been only two missing-persons cases." James eased into the rickety chair behind his desk. "Your sister and Lily Adams."

He'd have to tell Cadence his sister had disappeared in this town. No getting around it. He wanted to tell her when they were alone, not in front of a room full of avid cops.

His past was his own. Bloody, dark. Twisted.

"This is a quiet area," James continued. "We have drunks like that jerk Phillip Long, but we don't have crimes like this."

Yes, you do.

"The last time I saw you," James said, glancing up at him, "you were here asking me for help."

Begging, more like. He'd been so desperate, so wild to find his sister or any clue that would tell him where she had gone.

At first, he'd wondered if his family would get a ransom call. They were wealthy, and they could pay anything a kidnapper wanted for Maria's safe return.

No demand was ever made.

There was just…nothing.

"Now I'm the one who needs your help." James's voice roughened. "You hunt guys like this. I've followed stories about you, seen the headlines in the papers."

He didn't seek out those headlines. He just tried to help where he could.

"You got here so fast. Maybe we can find her alive. Whatever you need, whatever I can do, tell me." The captain's sigh was ragged. "And I'll do it."

A light knock sounded at the door.

Kyle glanced over and saw Cadence standing on the other side of the glass. She hesitated a moment after her knock, then swung open the door.

"Am I interrupting?" Cadence asked carefully.

Kyle shook his head. He'd have to tell her everything soon enough, but going through the hell of his past wasn't his favorite activity.

"It's time for the interviews, Kyle." She gave a little inclination of her head toward the captain. "I'm going to need to interview you, too, Anniston."

James flushed, but gave a grim nod. After what they'd heard on the machine, there would be no getting around the interviews.

Or accusations.

In small towns like this, it was easy for people to turn on each other. Kyle had sure seen it before. Fear was the worst kind of virus, ravaging everyone in its path.

"I'll wait outside," James said as he edged past Cadence. "Ma'am."

She didn't speak until the door closed behind the captain. Then she pushed back her shoulders and lifted one eyebrow as she faced Kyle. "We could have a really big problem in this town."

Yes.

"The sooner we figure out who was on that road with Lily Adams, the better."

Tell her.

"I called Dani at Quantico." Danielle Burton was Cadence's go-to girl when it came to information retrieval. "I asked her to pull all the missing-persons cases in the area for the last five years. This could be a one-shot crime, but just in case…"

Five years wasn't gonna cut it. "She might want to go back further."

Cadence frowned.

He headed toward her.

"Just how far?" Cadence asked as her head cocked so she could study him better. "Are we talking, say…fifteen years? That was when your sister vanished, right?"

Every muscle in his body seemed to clock down. It looked as if he was about to see just how far Cadence had dug into his life. Had she discovered his desperate searches, his—

"This isn't your sister's case." Sympathy was there, shining in her eyes. "Is that the real reason you brought us here? Because it was another disappearance, in the same town—"

"In the same way. With a car, abandoned, and a girl gone in the dead of the night," he growled as his hands fisted.

Get your control. Hold on to it.

Kyle's head bowed as he sucked in a sharp breath.

Then he felt a touch on his arm, featherlight. The scent of flowers deepened around him.

"What are the odds of that?" he managed as his head lifted, and he found Cadence standing less than a foot away, still touching him. Staring up at him with worry on her delicate features. She was close enough for him to pull into his arms. How many times had he wanted to do that? Pull her against him and use pleasure to make them both forget the nightmares waiting out there for them.

Don't do it. You can't. He cleared his throat, kept his control. "Another disappearance. Same place, same way. It shouldn't happen, Cadence. You *know* it shouldn't."

Her eyes searched his. "You think it's the same perp? After all this time?"

He'd clenched his back teeth so hard they ached. "After the case in Louisiana, is it so hard for you to think it *could* happen?" Kyle gritted out the words. "Look at the Bayou Butcher, look at how long he'd been killing." A fifteen-year span for the crimes wasn't impossible. Not if the killer had been careful enough.

Smart enough.

"I wondered...when you insisted we come down here...just how closely this could be linked to your sister."

Now he realized she'd come for him.

"I'm so sorry for what happened to her." The emotion in her voice was real. "Please know that I am. Sorry for what happened to her and for what her disappearance did to you. But Kyle, this case is about Lily Adams. Her daughter is at home, crying for her mother. We have to focus on Lily right now."

Not Maria.

"You're the one always telling me to have hope," she said. "We have hope in this case. We have a chance to find Lily."

Not Maria.

Maria wasn't ever going to be found. He'd tried to come to terms with that, over and over. "I know the job." His own voice was hard, grating, when hers had been so soft. "And I'll do it." He pulled away from her and headed for the door.

"Kyle!"

He hesitated, his fingers wrapped around the doorknob.

"I *am* sorry about what happened to your sister."

How far had she dug? Had she talked with the family he had left? His old friends? Had she learned how desperate he'd been back then as she discovered every secret he had? He didn't know her secrets, and that didn't seem fair.

I want them all. No, he wanted her, as exposed as he was.

"If I could help you find Maria, I would," Cadence told him. "Maybe after Lily, if we find new evidence while we're here—"

He yanked open the door. "They're waiting on us."

The cops. The perp.

All were waiting.

As for Maria…

He knew she'd stopped waiting to be rescued long ago.

***

"Officer Crenshaw, you knew Lily Adams, didn't you?" Kyle asked as he leaned across the small table in the only conference room available at the Paradox station.

Cadence sat beside him, still too conscious of what had been said in the captain's office.

He's hoping to find his sister.

She'd known that, though, from the minute he came to her desk back at their main office, his eyes shining with barely contained emotion.

We have to go to Paradox. A woman's missing.

"I knew her." Heather Crenshaw, a slim redhead with a steady, green gaze, gave a slow nod. "Lily was a few years ahead of me in school."

Cadence glanced at Heather's partner. "What about you?"

Jason Marsh. Tall. Dark. Handsome. He spoke with a faint southern drawl. A thin scar snaked out from the corner of his left eye, disappearing into his hairline.

"Yes, ma'am," Jason said with a nod as his eyes stayed on her. "I'd seen her at Striker's plenty of times. In a town this size, folks pretty much know everyone else."

True enough. But Lily hadn't recognized the officer with her. *Because it wasn't a cop at this station.* Her gut had told her it wasn't, but the interviews still had to be conducted.

"Where were you patrolling last night?" Kyle asked. His voice was smooth, low, emotionless.

She'd seen the emotions blazing in his eyes moments before. The past was haunting Kyle, tearing him apart on the inside.

"We were near the town's main street," Jason said easily. "Some kids spray painted the side of the school gym a few nights back, and we were making sure they didn't come back for another run at the place."

Kids and graffiti. Paradox wasn't exactly the crime capital of the world.

I'm wasting time with the cops. They weren't going to give her any information she could use. Sitting with them wasn't where she needed to be. She and Kyle both needed to be *out* there, joining the teams already searching for Lily. She'd immediately ordered for the searches to start, pulling in local and state help in the woods, even as she set up the interrogations.

It was the locals who would be of the most help. And since she had locals in front of her, she needed to ask different questions. More useful ones. "If you were going to dump a body in this area, where would you go?"

Silence.

Kyle turned his head slowly. Stared at her.

Her gaze cut back to the two cops. "Someplace secluded," she added. Hell, the whole town was secluded. Surrounded by miles and miles of forestland. Mountains, lakes, thick woods. But maybe the locals knew one spot that would work best for making a body vanish. "There's got to be a place around here folks don't visit. Some spot a hunter wouldn't stumble on when he was chasing game."

"*Cadence.*" Kyle's voice held a warning edge.

He'd realized she was looking for a body, not a live victim. *Lily could still be alive; I'm not saying she isn't.*

She was also covering as much ground as she could. "I need you both to think of areas like that. Get trackers out there. Get the county's canine unit, and give them some of Lily's clothes." They needed to start tracking right away. Cadence pushed from the table and rose to her feet. "Let's not waste any more time."

"Does that mean we're clear, ma'am?" Jason wanted to know. He'd risen too, cautiously unfurling from his seat.

"It means I'm not spending any more time in here. We *all* need to be searching the town, the woods, to see if we can find Lily." Cadence knew exactly where she'd start her hunt.

The last spot Lily had been seen alive.

She opened the door, marched outside. "I want everyone's attention!"

She already had it. All eyes had sprung to her the moment the door flew open.

"Canine units." She snapped out the words and gestured over her shoulder to Jason. "Officer Marsh is calling them in. We want them searching the woods for Lily. Start at the spot where her car was abandoned and work out from there. Check any"—damn, she hated to say it, but—"potential body dump sites you can think of. You know this area. Search it."

Kyle had come to her side. "We need a guard to stay with Lily's family, and we want a trace put on their phone lines." He knew the drill perfectly. After a year working with her, he should.

"Why?" This came from Officer Randall Hollings. They'd talked to the slightly paunchy, balding officer earlier. "Do you think whoever took Lily might call for some kind of ransom?" He shook his head. "Lily didn't have any money. Why else do you think she was working a double shift at Striker's?"

"It's not always about money," Cadence replied. *If only it were.* Greed was easy to understand. The sadistic motives of the killers

34

she had faced over the years? *Not so easy.* "It's possible our perp might want to taunt the family, or..." *Hate saying this, hate saying it...* "If he has already killed Lily, then guilt might grow in him. He may feel the urge to reach out to the family. Even to confess his crimes." She'd seen that happen, too.

Randall gave a low whistle. "That's messed up."

Killers often were. That was why they were killers.

"We'll all need to stay in close contact," Kyle said, his voice strong and hard. "If you discover anything, everyone needs to know. Lily Adams is out there, and we *are* going to locate her."

It wasn't a promise Cadence was ready to make. It was a vow Kyle shouldn't have made.

Cadence had checked the weather report earlier that day. A major storm system was coming their way. They needed to hunt, *before* that storm hit. Because once it did, the storm would wash away any trace that Lily's abductor might have left behind.

Mother Nature was going to work against them. That meant they had to work even faster, even harder, if they were going to beat her.

Then the doors to the station opened. A woman with graying hair and worried eyes stepped inside. A little girl, blonde, shaking, was at her side. Cadence recognized the girl from pictures she'd seen just a little while before.

Lily's daughter. Carrie.

"Please," the woman said, as she glanced around the station. "Please, tell me where my daughter is!"

Tears slid down the little girl's cheeks.

Deep inside of Cadence, something seemed to break.

***

"What happened back there?" Kyle asked as the car they'd taken from the station slid to a stop. It was a patrol car, so it wasn't like they were keeping a low profile as they headed toward Striker's.

"We got the officers organized and took control of the case. That's what happened." She wouldn't have thought the guy needed a point-by-point breakdown of a situation he'd seen plenty of times before. They'd talked with the cops, confirmed alibis, a very necessary step because they didn't want the perp working with them. Unfortunately, they'd been there and done that before, too. They'd cleared officers and then they'd stopped wasting time. They needed boots on the ground, needed men searching, and that was exactly what they'd gotten.

"I'm talking about what happened when you saw Lily's mother."

It hadn't been the mother who had gotten to her.

The little girl. She'd reminded Cadence too much of herself. She cleared her throat and said, "I didn't want to give her any false hope."

"You didn't want to talk to her at all."

No, she hadn't. Cadence couldn't afford to let emotion get in the way of her job. "The captain can interview her. He knows Lily's mother. He has the connection already established with her."

She climbed from the vehicle. A few other cars were scattered in the Striker's parking lot, along with some pickup trucks and two motorcycles.

"Sometimes, people need hope in order to get them through the day."

Careful now, Cadence glanced back over at Kyle. She made sure not to let any emotions show on her face. "Then you give them hope."

A muscle flexed in his jaw.

In the next instant, he strode around the car, hurrying toward her. Cadence sped up her pace and marched toward the bar's entrance. She didn't want Kyle digging too deep right then. *The case, the case.* It was what mattered. Not her. Not him.

She yanked open the bar's door. The interior of Striker's was dim, but on the far right wall, she saw a line of big-screen TVs. Pool tables were scattered to the left. Dining tables waited in the middle.

Kyle's hand closed around her elbow. "Why do you get to know all my secrets?" he demanded, his voice a low whisper in her ear. "But you never share yours."

She kept her past buried deep inside.

His hold on her tightened. "You're not going to get away with this forever, Cadence. One day soon, I'll know everything about you." A dark promise. One that sent a surging wave of sensual awareness through her.

Her head turned. He was just inches away. Big, strong, seeming to surround her. She'd tried so hard to avoid letting her personal feelings get in the way of their partnership.

But Kyle kept pushing her.

One day, she might push him back.

They were close enough to kiss then. She'd thought of kissing him before. Thought of a whole lot before. Late at night, when she couldn't sleep, he was what she thought of.

What she wanted.

Wrong time, wrong place. That was their story. She pulled away and offered him a hard smile, "No, you won't know everything, but keep dreaming." *I know I will.* Then she made her way to the bar. A waitress was there, one with her long, dark hair pulled back in a ponytail.

The waitress smiled when she saw Cadence and Kyle. "What can I get you two?"

Cadence pulled out her ID. "We need to ask you some questions about another waitress who works here."

The woman leaned across the bar. Her very abundant cleavage almost broke free of her small, white top. "You're FBI?" Her brown eyes widened into minisaucers. "What's the FBI doing here?"

"Lily Adams is missing," Kyle said as he slid onto the stool beside Cadence.

The brunette gasped. "Lily? She was here last night!"

And she was gone today.

There was no point keeping Lily's disappearance quiet. They actually needed to tell as many people as possible. The more eyes looking for Lily, the more hope they had of finding her. "Were you working the late shift with her last night?"

The woman, her name tag identifying her as Susannah Jane, nodded. Her gaze nervously flew back and forth between Cadence and Kyle.

"Did anything unusual happen here?" She gestured to the area behind her. "Did anyone cause trouble for Lily?"

Susannah Jane shook her head.

"Did any customers hit on her?" Kyle pressed. "Maybe some guy who didn't want to take no for an answer?"

Susannah Jane licked her lips. "Guys are always hitting on us here. The more they drink"—a bitter laugh slipped from her— "the prettier we become."

Susannah Jane *was* a pretty woman, but her eyes were hard and tired.

"Was there anyone in particular who liked to hit on Lily?" Kyle wanted to know.

"Lily was going through a divorce. She flirted, but she never carried it past that. There was no one." Her shoulders trembled. "Lily's *gone*?"

She seemed to have just understood how significant that was. Family and friends often had that delayed reaction as the pain and fear set in fully for them.

Susannah Jane's fingers were shaking as she poured herself a—whiskey? Yes, that was what it looked like. She knocked the drink back fast.

Interesting. "Do you have any security cameras here?" Cadence asked.

Susannah Jane shook her head. Her fingers clenched around the empty glass.

"Where's the employee exit?"

Susannah Jane pointed to the door on the right. "Lily parked her car out back, two spots over from the Dumpster." She swallowed and her voice dropped as she said, "Always in the same spot."

Cadence realized that would have been a pattern the perp could have easily noticed. "Were any other waitresses on duty last night?"

"Just me and Lily. Stacey and Leann are both sick. That's why Lily had to pull the double."

"If you think of anything else, call me, okay?" Cadence slid her card across the bar.

Susannah Jane stared at it a moment. Didn't take it. "There's nothing else." Her voice was hoarse.

Cadence left the card on the counter. "You never know. You might remember something later." She inclined her head. "Thanks for your help."

Cadence and Kyle headed for the employee door. Susannah Jane was already reaching for her phone as they left. The card was still on the bar top.

The door took them to the back of the building.

"No lights," Kyle muttered as he glanced around. "At night, this place would have been perfect for hunting."

Too perfect.

Cadence slowly walked from the back exit over to Lily's parking space. Her nose twitched at the acrid scent in the air. "Do you smell that?"

"Gasoline." The one word was clipped.

Yes. Just past Lily's parking space, long green grass grew in a wild tangle. She bent near the grass. "The scent's stronger here."

Kyle had followed her. "The SOB drained her gas, then dumped it here."

Sure looked that way.

Cadence rose. "He was out here, waiting for her." Or he'd even been in the bar, watching her.

Cadence turned around and stared at the long rear wall of Striker's.

Why did you pick Lily?

What was it about Lily that had caught her abductor's eye?

"He planned out every moment," Kyle said, and she looked over to see him glaring at the parking space. "He could have taken her right here, if he'd wanted. It was so late, no one would have even noticed what was happening in the darkness."

Cadence pulled in a slow breath. When she profiled, she used the victims to help her. She saw the killer through them.

But Kyle tried to get straight into the minds of the killers. Sometimes, he seemed to get into their minds almost too easily.

"He wanted her alone," Kyle continued, his voice deepening. "Far away, so it didn't matter if she shouted for help."

Goose bumps rose on Cadence's skin. She was conscious of the secure weight of the holster under her arm. "He was watching her out here." He'd had to be. He'd emptied her tank, made sure she would break down, and he'd followed her, waiting for the perfect moment to attack.

Waiting for that long, lonely stretch of road.

"He had it all planned out, every minute." Kyle faced her. "He's done this before."

She was very afraid he had. "We're already checking for missing persons."

"We're going to find them. Sonofabitch, we're *going to find them.*"

The clench in her gut told Cadence that Kyle was right.

***

Heavy rope cut into her wrists and ankles. Lily had been jerking and twisting against the rope, and she'd made the skin raw and bloody beneath her binds.

He smiled as he stared down at her. He'd been so quiet when he came in. She didn't even realize he was there.

Her blindfold was in place. Not because he didn't want her to see him, but because he didn't want her to see *anything.* Soon, Lily would learn he controlled her life. What she saw, what she heard, what she tasted.

What she felt.

Everything.

You're mine, Lily.

She would never be free of him.

She was on the bed he'd prepared, hunching and turning on the bare mattress. She still wore her clothes, and he'd let her keep them, for a time.

Breaking prey too quickly could lead to disastrous results. He'd learned that over the years.

He stepped closer to her. He pushed against the wooden door, letting it creak so she'd realize she wasn't alone.

At the faint sound, Lily stopped struggling. Seemed to stop breathing.

"Lily." He whispered her name. He loved her name. Delicate, beautiful. Like she was.

Lily didn't belong at Striker's, waiting tables and serving drunk fools. She sure didn't belong with the twisted SOB who cared about his drugs more than he cared about her.

Lily is mine. She belongs with me. He'd show her that.

Grunts and moans came from behind her gag. He could remove the gag, let her talk, let her scream. No one would hear her screams here.

No one ever heard the screams here.

In silence, he crossed to Lily's side.

His fingers trailed over her cheek.

She jerked back, shuddering. More grunts. Moans.

He shook his head. "You have a lot to learn, Lily." He bent and pressed a kiss to her temple. She tried to head butt him.

He smiled. *One free pass, Lily. Punishment will come next.* "It's okay, I have plenty of time to teach you."

Just as he'd taught the others.

If Lily didn't learn her lessons, if she didn't do exactly as she should…

She'd join the ones who'd disappointed him.

CHAPTER THREE

They'd spent hours searching the woods. Long, grueling hours of trudging through the heat. Chasing after the dogs.

They'd turned up nothing. Not even the faintest of scents had been detected by the canines. They'd searched the woods. Searched abandoned houses in the area. Old cabins. No matter where they went, they couldn't find a trace of Lily.

Night had fallen. The heavy, thick darkness that Kyle knew meant—

"We have to stop searching for tonight," James said as he ran a weary hand over his damp forehead. The captain had been alternating between checking in the town for Lily and combing the woods. The damn seemingly endless woods. "The men are exhausted, and the dogs are so worn out, they can't track anymore."

Not that there seemed to be anything to track.

Kyle figured Lily's abductor had taken her away in a vehicle. There were no scents to track around Lily's car. The guy *must* have taken her that way. After he'd gotten her in his car, the SOB could have just kept driving, leaving Paradox in his rearview mirror.

Lily's face was being splashed across the TV screens in the Southeast right then. The FBI had opened a tip line for anyone who had information on her.

They were trying everything they could to find her, but so far, they were turning up nothing.

No prints had been found on her car—well, no prints other than Lily's and her mother's. The driver's side door appeared to have been wiped clean. No one at Striker's remembered seeing anything unusual the night she'd vanished.

No one could remember *anything* that would help Lily.

"We'll be back out here at oh six hundred," James said as he inclined his head toward Kyle.

Right, 0600. As soon as light streaked across the sky, the search would start again.

But what would happen to Lily during those dark hours?

What had already happened to her?

James turned away. He took a step and stumbled.

Kyle reached out and grabbed his arm to steady him. "You okay?"

A muscle flexed in James's jaw. "Just a slip."

Was it? Because Kyle had just noticed that the captain's hands were shaking again, too. "Is there something you're not telling me?"

James shook his head. "It's been a long day, and I'm not quite as strong as I used to be." He gave Kyle a grim smile. "Don't worry, I'll be back and ready to go tomorrow. I'm gonna help you find Lily and the SOB who took her."

He knew James wanted justice. But the captain's speech was a little ragged, and Kyle couldn't help but wonder if more than exhaustion was weighing on the man.

When James left, Kyle stared at the twisted mass of woods. Voices rumbled behind him. Engines growled as vehicles drove away.

They were all leaving. *What if she's out there? What if we just need to search a little longer?*

"We can't find her tonight." Cadence's voice was low and steady. Almost soothing. He hadn't even heard her approach. "I know you don't want to stop the search, but it's just for a few hours. The men can't see."

We don't even know if she's in these woods. Cadence didn't say the rest, but she didn't have to.

The words hung between them.

"There's a small motel at the edge of town," Cadence said. "I booked us rooms there."

He turned away from the woods and saw Cadence standing there, with darkness all around her, lit only by the light spilling from the cars' headlights.

"We can't do anything else out here," she said. "Not tonight."

She was being so careful with him. Too careful.

"Don't," he bit out as he stalked toward her. The others weren't close enough to overhear, so he could lower his guard and let some of his fury out.

Cadence shook her head. "Don't what?"

He wanted to wrap his hands around her. To pull her close.

No, I just want to touch her. To feel her.

"Don't handle me with your damn kid gloves, Cadence." The words were snapped. "I'm not some victim you have to coddle."

He'd rolled up the sleeves of his dress shirt—like that had done much good. He was covered with grime and sweat and plenty of insect bites.

I fucking hate summers in the South.

Insects were chirping all around them, and he'd had to dodge snakes in the bushes for most of the evening.

"I never thought you were a victim." Cadence turned from him and headed for the car.

She knew he'd follow her. Wasn't he always trailing after her?

Wasn't he the one who *always* kept the need in check? The desire he damn well knew they both felt.

After today—after this hell—why couldn't they turn to each other for some comfort and release? Let that desire burst free?

Replace death with pleasure.

Cadence climbed into their vehicle and pulled the door shut behind her. Not a patrol car anymore. An SUV that James had arranged for them. Cadence was in the driver's seat.

Jaw locked tight, he jumped in the vehicle with her.

"How do you do it?" Kyle demanded as they pulled away from the scene. He couldn't help it, he looked back. Saw the darkness staring at him.

"Do what?" Her voice was soft, but when he looked back at her, Cadence's grip on the wheel appeared a little too tight.

"You just walk away, and don't look back." She'd done it, time and time again. He'd seen her do it. "I mean, you're supposed to be the one who knows the victims so well." A snap of anger heated his voice. "Don't you wonder what it's like for Lily right now? What's happening to her? How can you just give up?"

Give up.

The charge and the anger weren't really for Cadence, he knew that. The rage was his own. He'd given up on Maria.

Now I'm attacking Cadence. For no reason.

"I don't need to wonder." Her whispered words carried easily to his ears.

"Why the hell not?"

"Because I know." The vehicle picked up speed and rushed down the old road.

Past Lily's abduction spot.

They kept going. Going.

Past the spot where Maria's car had been abandoned so many years before.

"You don't know," he growled. Because she couldn't. Cadence and her fistful of degrees. She'd done case studies. Read victim profiles, but she'd never *been* a victim. "Maybe you should pray you never do." The words were low, vicious. *Don't do this to her. Not her.* He fought to pull in his fury. Kyle grabbed hard for his control. He took a deep breath. Exhaled. *In. Out.* The drumming of his heartbeat seemed too loud to his ears. *Don't attack her when the rage should be aimed back at you.* "Hell, I didn't mean it, Cadence."

She didn't speak.

The miles flew past in the thick darkness.

"I need sleep." He needed a whole lot more than that, but he'd take what he could get. Some crash time on a lumpy bed, and he'd be good to go again at 0600.

He wouldn't be such a bastard to her. Once he had rest, and the desperation driving him ebbed—

"You think you know me." Her words were so soft, he wasn't even sure they were real at first. "But you don't."

Stiffening, Kyle glanced toward her.

"And I don't know you."

They didn't speak again, not until they were pulling up at the side of the little motel on the edge of town. Big rigs lined the full lot, and when they went inside to the front desk, the kid with acne on his cheeks apologetically told them, "Sorry, folks, we only have one room left."

That so fucking figured.

But it wasn't the first time he'd needed to share lodging with his partner. It wouldn't be the last, either.

Only I've never been this close to Cadence.

So close to what he wanted.

"Are you sure there's nothing left?" Cadence demanded, voice sharp. "I called earlier and was told that the rooms would be held for us."

The boy's Adam's apple bobbed. "You were supposed to be here sooner. It's almost midnight. I couldn't keep holdin' the rooms—"

"It's fine." Kyle cut through the boy's stumbling words and swiped the key from him. "Just tell me where the room is."

"Room two-oh-seven. Corner room on the l-left." He glanced at Cadence, grimacing. "Sorry, ma'am. Those truckers come in heavy some nights."

He was sure they did. The bell over the door gave a small jingle as they exited the office. Kyle grabbed Cadence's small overnight bag and his own larger one from the back of the SUV. They headed up the narrow stairs to the second floor. Voices and the whir of traffic drifted in the air.

He opened the door to room 207, then stepped back so Cadence could go in first.

She didn't go in.

"What's wrong?" A demon was riding him that night, forcing him to keep pushing her when he knew he should back the hell off. "You aren't scared of staying alone with me, are you?" A deliberate challenge.

Her head tilted back so she could stare into his eyes. Despite the strength she seemed to project so well in the field, Cadence was a delicate woman, barely five foot five, and built along slender lines.

He was so much bigger, his body rougher, and he'd often thought before—

I'd have to take care with her.

He'd imagined the two of them together many times. Harmless fantasies.

Weren't they?

"Why would I be scared of you?" Cadence brushed by him. "I mean, sure, there's the fact you're acting like a jackass…"

He was. Kyle sucked in a sharp breath. *It's this place. The memories.* He was striking out at the person closest to him. *Stop.*

"I'm trying to make allowances, seeing how personal this is for you."

He put their bags near the small closet and went back and secured the door. Right. Like that flimsy lock would really keep anyone out.

"But don't push me much more, Kyle."

She stood glaring at him, in the middle of the worn motel room, her hands fisted at her hips.

His gaze slid over her. That woman was sexy.

Her left eyebrow rose. Just the one. Only Cadence did that move. "Because you are being such a jackass, you can take the floor." Her smile held a wicked edge. "Hope you enjoy your sleep." Then she turned away and marched into the bathroom.

He waited for it. Yes, she slammed the door.

When the shower roared on moments later, he tried real hard not to imagine Cadence naked under the blasting water.

Tried. Failed.

Unable to stop himself, he stalked toward the door.

Cadence.

She was right. He *was* being a jackass, and he needed to cool off. Only being so close to Cadence didn't exactly make him feel cool.

More like I'm burning alive.

That had been the problem from the beginning. The awareness between them, an awareness Cadence was determined to ignore.

He wanted her naked. Wanted her screaming in pleasure.

The fleeting glimpses he'd caught, the hints of emotion in her eyes—*she wants me, too.*

Only she wasn't acting on that desire, and if she didn't act, neither could he.

His hand rose. Touched the chipped wood on the door. "Cadence."

No response. She wouldn't hear him over the roar of the water. "Look, I'm sorry."

His voice was a little louder, but there was still no response from her. Not that he blamed her.

"I want what you can't give."

It was for the best she couldn't hear that.

He turned away. Cleared his throat. "I need some air." Still talking to a woman who couldn't hear him. Yeah, he was skirting crazy that night. "Cadence!" Much louder now. "I'll be right back."

He wanted something to take the edge off for him.

Maybe a trip to Striker's would be just what he needed.

***

Cadence stood in the bathroom, her hands gripping the edge of the sink. The shower blasted beside her as she stared at her reflection.

Kyle's words echoed in her ears.

I want what you can't give.

Her chest ached.

Story of her life.

***

Two hours had passed, and there was still no sign of Kyle. Cadence glanced outside through the small blinds, making sure she didn't see their rented SUV below. Since the vehicle wasn't in the lot, it meant she had a little more time.

She reached for her phone and quickly pressed the number for her contact.

"I know there are clocks in Alabama," came Danielle Burton's annoyed voice about two seconds later.

Cadence almost smiled. "There are, Dani, but we both know you weren't sleeping."

Danielle Burton was *the* source for intel at the bureau. The agent hadn't been cut out for fieldwork—at least, that was Dani's story—but no one could deny she was a master when it came to information retrieval.

"Okay, fine, I don't sleep," Dani said. True. Dani had suffered from insomnia for as long as Cadence had known her. *Our FBI training days.* "But you do. Or you *should* be sleeping."

"I need information, Dani."

"Of course, you do. Why else would you be calling me at almost two in the morning?" A long-suffering sigh. "I'm already running those missing-persons reports for you. If Ben hadn't pulled me away to track a serial in Connecticut, I would've had 'em already."

Cadence's fingers pressed into the side of the phone. "There's one specific report I need right now."

Silence. "I know where this is going, but are you sure you want to go there?" Dani would know exactly what Cadence was talking about.

Cadence glanced through the blinds once more. "It relates to the case. I'm not just digging through his past."

More silence. Dani could say far too much with silence.

Cadence let the blinds snap back into place. "E-mail me the case file, okay? I need to read it. *All* of it." She'd only read the case summary before—gotten the bare bones of his sister's abduction. Now, she needed to know all of the dark details.

"It's already on the way." Dani was nothing if not fast. If the file was coming, then she was also still at their main office in Virginia. Not at home. Working—at two a.m.

Ghosts chased Dani, too. *They chase us all.*

"But be careful, Cadence." Dani's voice was more subdued than normal. "When you dig into someone's past, you won't always like what you find."

That was why she buried her own past.

"His sister vanished here, Dani, and he's..." *Different. Harder.* She didn't say that. "He needs closure." That was true enough. Maybe there was something in the file—something, anything— that could help them.

"Don't say I didn't warn you."

Cadence could easily picture Dani in her mind's eye, and she was sure her friend was sitting back in her chair, shaking her head. Maybe rolling her eyes. "You warned me."

"I'm still working on gathering the intel on other missing persons. I'll send you everything I've got ASAP."

Ah, now she was back to business. That was Dani.

"I narrowed the search just like you told me. Females, traveling alone, no bodies ever recovered."

Those had been her search specifications, and because of Kyle, she had made sure the search went back fifteen years.

She believed in being thorough.

She ended the call, opened her laptop, and found Dani's e-mail waiting for her.

Maria McKenzie. Cadence opened the file with a click. Date of birth—May 17. Cadence hunched over the laptop.

Maria had been so young.

Cadence clicked on the attached images. Maria's face filled her screen. A beautiful girl, with hair a shade lighter than her brother's but with eyes just as blue.

Beautiful, and lost.

Cadence started clicking through the file.

Date of disappearance—August 23.

She'd seen the date before, back when she'd been vetting her new partner. But that date hadn't meant anything to her, not over a year ago.

The date certainly meant something now.

Her breath froze in her lungs. What. The. Hell.

He should have told me.

No wonder Kyle was reacting this way. Going hard-core on her in the field. His sister had vanished fifteen years ago, *exactly* fifteen years ago, to the date of Lily's own abduction. *Two a.m.* Cadence's gaze slid to the clock as a shiver went over her. Lily had been abducted at two a.m. on August 23.

What are the odds? Kyle had asked her that question.

Now she knew…*no odds are that high.*

She also understood just why her partner seemed to be breaking apart on her.

He was reliving the nightmare from his past.

As soon as he'd found out about Lily's disappearance, it must have made Kyle relive the nightmare of his sister's abduction. He was *still* reliving that nightmare, and she wanted to help him. Wanted to give him some peace.

But there was no peace to offer. Only another victim, one who could still be alive…or who could already be dead by the perp's hand.

***

The FBI was in Paradox. Little Paradox. And that FBI agent, the one leaning over the bar and glaring at those around him—

I know you.

Kyle McKenzie was back in town. The guy must think he was some kind of big shot. His face was sure splashed in the papers often enough. A profiler, hunting dangerous killers.

But you've never caught me. All these years, and you've never even come close.

Sharon handed the agent another beer. She was talking with him. Crying.

Like the bitch really cared about Lily. No one had cared about her. *No one but me.*

He eased toward the back door. The FBI agent wasn't even looking his way. He wanted to smile. Wanted to laugh.

But he held it back, because he didn't need to draw any attention to himself.

Then he was outside. The hot night air hit him as he glanced toward the back of the building. Lily's parking spot was empty.

It would stay that way.

He headed for his own vehicle. The cops weren't out hunting through the woods then, so it meant he had time to go and visit his favorite girl.

He knew Lily would be happy to see him.

She'd better be.

If she wasn't, then he'd hurt her. Sometimes, even good girls had to be punished.

He climbed into his car, then saw the agent come out of Striker's. The man's body was tense. Angry.

Emotion seemed to roll from McKenzie.

The agent jumped into his SUV. Hurried from the lot. Never even glanced over at him as he waited in the dark.

I'm right here.

The FBI agents thought they were something special. They weren't. They had no clue about what was happening in this town. What had been happening, for so long.

It's time they knew. It was time the whole world knew.

The Bayou Butcher. The Valentine Killer. Those bastards were the ones getting the attention. They couldn't even come close to his power. They were in his shadow. Always would be.

McKenzie pulled away.

He hesitated. Lily was waiting. He needed to go to her. Touch her. Remind her that he was there for her.

But the agent with all the rage boiling just below his surface…

I need to watch him.

He cranked his car. Followed behind McKenzie.

Lily had never realized he was behind her. So many hadn't. Folks just didn't bother to look back. Would the agent be any more aware?

He turned on his radio and got ready to enjoy the hunt.

***

Kyle braked in front of the motel. The No Vacancy sign flashed. He stared up at their room, trying to see if the light was still on. He'd thought the beer might take the edge off for him.

It hadn't.

And to make his mood even worse, he'd run into Marsh at the bar. The cop had seemed a little too interested in Cadence and her dating status.

Hell. Now he had that cop sniffing around Cadence. Not that she'd be interested in a guy like that. Marsh was too rough. Not her type at all.

But what the hell is her type?

He headed up the stairs.

The blare of a car's radio reached his ears. He turned, frowning, but all he could see were taillights as they disappeared down the road. Taillights and the lingering beat of hard, driving music.

He finished climbing the stairs and hesitated when he reached room 207. He lifted his hand, thought about knocking, then realized—*hell, it's my room, too.* He'd been gone plenty long enough. Cadence should have been finished with her shower and dressed by that point.

Though she really hadn't needed to dress on his account.

He unlocked the door and found the room dark inside. The only light spilling in came from the weak bulb just outside the door.

He eased into the room, trying to be quiet. For her. A quick twist of his wrist locked the door. Then he stood a moment, trying to let his eyes adjust to the darkness, before realizing a small glow drifted from her laptop. She'd left the laptop open, just a few inches, and it sat on the small desk near the TV.

As for Cadence—he could see the outline of her body in the narrow bed.

I want to be in that bed with her.

But she sure hadn't been issuing any invitations to him.

He eyed the floor. There was a pillow down there and what looked like the lump of a blanket. Talk about giving a guy a hint. His lips hitched up in a grim smile.

He'd take the hint. For now. But one day Cadence might just be asking for more.

Begging for it.

Ah, nice fantasy.

Kyle headed into the bathroom. When the door shut behind him, he flipped on the light and looked at his reflection. Stubble covered his cheeks, the lines near his mouth seemed deeper. But his eyes—

Rage.

He knew he had it inside. Building, twisting him. But he would contain the fury. He'd kept it contained for years.

He could keep doing it.

Being back in this place, fifteen years to the fucking day—his hands fisted.

Fifteen years.

I don't need a babysitter.

His sister's voice drifted through his mind as Kyle squeezed his eyes closed.

His response played through his head just as easily. *Yeah, well, Mom says you can't take a trip like that by yourself. So guess who's going shotgun?*

She'd rolled her eyes even as her fingers had toyed with her necklace. The half-moon necklace that he'd given Maria on her birthday. She'd loved that necklace. Worn it everywhere. *Not you, bro. I'm eighteen. This is my chance to do what I want. I have to start college in a few weeks. I need this, okay?*

She'd wanted her chance at freedom. He understood that. He'd even understood when she said—

You know what they're like. They suffocate me. You.

They had. His parents had always kept tight tabs on their children. Because of *who* they were. Rich, powerful, one of the most influential families in Boston.

I'm eighteen now, and I can do what I want.

He'd just shook his head at her.

It's not like I'll really be alone anyway. A sly twist of her lips. She'd dropped the necklace and the charm fell back to her sternum. Frowned at him. *My boyfriend's gonna meet me on the trip. Trust me, if you come, you'll only get in my way.*

Only there hadn't been a boyfriend. She'd just been telling him that story.

There'd just been Maria.

Then there'd been…nothing.

***

"I'll kill you…"

Cadence's eyes flew open at the low snarl. Her heart was racing, and battle-ready tension had slipped instantly through her whole body as adrenaline spiked her blood.

"I know what you did."

She was reaching for the gun she'd placed on the nightstand when she realized the low snarl she heard was Kyle's voice.

"*I'll kill you…*"

Instead of grabbing the gun, she flipped on the lamp. A small pool of light spilled into the room, and she saw Kyle's tense body.

He was on the floor. Chest bare, the blanket she'd given him shoved to the side. His eyes were closed and his body twisted, shaking.

Nightmare.

Apparently, Kyle killed people in his nightmares.

That's a lot better than what happens to me.

Cadence slipped from the bed. Eased down onto her knees next to him. "Kyle, wake up." She made sure to keep her voice low and soothing.

He didn't wake up.

But his movements seemed to become even more frantic.

"I *know*," Kyle growled. "You'll pay."

"Kyle, it's just a dream." Sweat covered his broad shoulders. Dampened his hair. "Wake up." Her voice was louder.

When he still didn't respond, Cadence reached out to him.

Mistake.

He grabbed her wrist and yanked her toward him. Kyle rolled, twisting their bodies, and when Cadence sucked in a sharp breath of surprise, she found herself flat on her back, with Kyle above her, holding her down with his body.

His fingers were chained around her wrists, pinning them to the floor.

His eyes were open. Blazing. On her.

"What the hell? Cadence?"

His lower body was pressed to hers, his legs between hers as his hips thrust against her.

She stared into his glittering eyes, too aware she only had on a thin pair of jogging pants and a loose T-shirt. Not sexy, but...

The clothes sure didn't seem like very much protection right then.

"You were having a bad dream," she told him. Why was her voice a whisper?

He blinked. Kyle seemed to realize exactly where he was and what he was doing.

But he didn't let her go.

Did she want him to?

No.

His hold tightened on her wrists.

"You seemed upset." Her voice was coming out far too husky. Seductive. She didn't mean to sound that way. "I was trying to wake you up."

"I'm up."

Yes, he was. *All* of him. The hard ridge that pressed against the juncture of her thighs was growing longer, bigger, with every passing second.

He leaned closer toward her. "Why aren't you telling me to get the hell away from you?"

Because…she had a few dark secrets of her own.

Rough, hard, wild. Pinned down by Kyle.

That wasn't supposed to happen. Cadence licked her lips and tried to make her voice sound stronger. "Get the hell away from me." Those were the words he wanted her to say.

Only she didn't want to say them.

What she wanted to say…

Kiss me. Make me only feel you. Strip me. Make me scream.

That wasn't what an FBI agent was supposed to say to her partner.

The things she wanted weren't what she was *supposed* to feel.

"You don't mean it." He seemed surprised by her words. "I can tell."

Her voice had been hungry with a need she'd denied for so long.

"But you said it, so I'll fucking do it."

He released her. His body slid away from hers.

She didn't move at first. Just tried to calm her racing heart-beat and pretend she hadn't been moments away from having sex with Kyle.

Hot, hard sex, right on the floor.

The way I like it.

Kyle didn't know that. He thought she was restrained, too controlled.

She kept that mask on for a reason.

Cadence sucked in a deep breath. She could almost taste Kyle on her tongue.

No, she wanted to taste him.

She sat up, then hurried to her feet.

Kyle rose, much slower, and studied her with his head tilted to the side.

"I don't know you as well as I thought."

She'd tried to tell him that before.

His gaze went to the bed. To the rumpled covers, then back to the floor.

Cadence cleared her throat. "Do you always dream about killing someone?"

His shoulders tensed. Then he focused his attention back on her. "Do you always like it rough?"

"No." Her control was back. She could play this. "I was worried about you."

"You wanted me."

Yes. "You had just woken up, Kyle. You were confused." She turned away, glancing quickly at the clock on the nightstand. Four a.m. They could get a little more sleep. They needed more.

Before the hunting started again the next day.

"Tell yourself that if you want, Cadence. Tell yourself whatever you need to believe in order to get back to sleep."

Her eyes narrowed. So much for helping him. Next time, he could suffer in his dreams.

She climbed back into the bed. Jerked her covers up to her chin. Tried to ignore the fact she still wanted him. Her breasts were tight, aching, and need twisted through her.

There was a rustle beside the bed. The groan of wood. Kyle was lying back down.

Good.

She closed her eyes.

Her heartbeat wouldn't slow down, and Cadence was far too conscious of every movement he made. Every whisper and slither of sound. Tomorrow night, she'd make absolutely certain they had separate rooms. This wouldn't be happening again.

"I wanted to kiss you." His voice was a low rumble. One she seemed to feel against her skin.

Her eyes squeezed closed even tighter.

"Why do you fight what we both want?"

She was afraid that if she gave in, he'd see the secrets she kept. Kyle was observant, smart—and dangerous.

So she tried to be reasonable. "We're partners. The FBI doesn't exactly approve of fraternizing."

"Fuck the FBI."

Her hands fisted in the covers. *I'd rather fuck you.* No, that was *not* the way she should be thinking. Not at all.

"This is about you and me," Kyle told her. "*You and me.* And I'm not waiting forever."

She'd never asked him to wait for her.

Cadence opened her eyes and saw the spill of light she'd forgotten to turn off. Her hand snaked out and reached for the switch on the lamp.

They were plunged into darkness once more.

The darkness made it easier for her to breathe, to ask, "Who was in your dream?"

The floor groaned as he shifted position.

"Kyle? Who was it? Who were you killing?"

One of the perps from their cases? One of the serials they hunted?

"When you tell me your secrets," he said, his voice still that deep, dark rumble, "then I'll tell you mine."

***

"Lily…"

Her name drifted from the darkness.

"Lily…"

She couldn't feel her hands, not anymore. At first, her fingers had burned, then she'd felt pinpricks shoot through them.

Now…nothing.

Her feet were the same way. She couldn't even wiggle her toes. She'd tried, over and over again. But she couldn't do it.

She could only lie there, her body heaving helplessly, with the gag in her mouth and the blindfold over her eyes.

"Did you miss me?"

Something stroked her cheek. *Him.* He was touching her. Watching her.

She flinched, trying to jerk away.

"Oh, Lily, you don't need to be afraid of me."

She was. That voice, drifting to her in the dark, she knew it was the voice of a monster. *I want to see my baby.* Her little girl. She wanted to see her so badly. To kiss her.

A sob choked in her throat. *Please let me see my baby.*

She tried to tell him, but her parched and swollen tongue wasn't working either. And the gag stopped any sounds but groans and grunts from slipping free.

I need my baby. She was always there to fix breakfast for Carrie, always. She made pancakes with little smiley faces, just the way her daughter liked them. Then they walked to school together.

The world was a dangerous place, so she always walked her daughter to school.

The world was dangerous.

A soft touch feathered over her left cheek. After a desperate moment, Lily realized what he was doing. *Wiping away my tears.*

"Are you thirsty, my Lily?"

She managed a nod.

"I'm going to take off your gag, so you can drink some water. I'm going to take care of you, Lily."

No, he was going to kill her. She wouldn't believe his lies.

The gag was sliding away and a glass was being pushed to her lips. The water spilled over her mouth, onto her swollen tongue, and at first, she started to choke because she couldn't swallow.

"Easy, let me help you." That dark voice. Then he was massaging her throat, helping her to swallow.

The water went down.

"I can be good to you, Lily. Very good."

She drank greedily, desperate for the water. Maybe he wasn't going to kill her. If he was giving her something to drink, it meant he wanted to keep her alive and strong. Didn't it? Maybe she'd be set free. Maybe she'd see Carrie again.

They'd have pancakes. They'd walk to school.

His fingers tightened around her throat, cutting off her air. The water poured from her mouth.

"I can also be cruel, my Lily. So cruel."

She couldn't breathe. Couldn't fight him.

Carrie...

His hold eased. "You will determine how I act. Good girls get rewarded, Lily, but bad girls..."

She sucked in deep gulps of air, her whole body trembling.

His mouth brushed over her ear as he said, "Bad girls get punished. Don't make me punish you, don't make me..."

CHAPTER FOUR

"We're losing time," Kyle said as he stood in front of the assembled officers. The FBI was in charge of the case now, and every officer in the room knew it. Kyle and Cadence had started a task force, and the others were following their lead.

Unfortunately, so far, that lead had taken them nowhere.

"In a missing-persons case," Cadence said from beside him, "every moment counts. Over twenty-four hours have passed since Lily's disappearance—"

"What does that say about the odds of her coming back alive?" Officer Jason Marsh asked as he leaned toward Cadence. Marsh was sitting in the front row, his body tense.

Kyle narrowed his eyes on the guy as he replied, "If you don't find a missing person within the first forty-eight hours, then the chances of finding the person alive decrease dramatically."

Heather swallowed. "How dramatic are we talking?"

Cadence hesitated, then said, "Less than fifty percent."

And what she didn't say...but what Kyle knew...after seventy-two hours—well, most of the agents stopped looking for a live victim at that point.

Instead, they looked for a corpse.

"Lily Adams has a daughter who is waiting on her mother to come home." Kyle stepped back and advanced toward the area map that he'd attached to the wall behind him. A small red flag marked Lily's abduction site on that map. Yellow indicated the areas that they had already searched. "We need to bring her home."

"But if the dogs aren't turning up a scent, doesn't that mean Lily might not even be in Paradox any longer?" Heather Crenshaw asked, her voice soft and a bit uncertain. "He could have taken her anywhere."

Yes, he damn well could have. "Nearby counties are being searched but we have to do our jobs." His gaze swept the assembled group. James watched him with a steady gaze. "We have to make sure that we've covered every possible location in the area."

"You're the natives," Cadence said. "I told you this before… you *know* the area. Look at that map. Where haven't we been? Where could the abductor take Lily? An isolated spot that we're missing. A place where—"

"No one would hear Lily scream," Kyle finished, voice rough. Heather flinched.

"The storms are coming," Kyle added. "The weather will work against us even more. *Now* is the time to be out there."

Jason Marsh had titled his head. His eyes were on the map.

"It wouldn't just be an outdoor spot," Cadence continued. She walked through the small room, her body sliding through the line of chairs. Her gaze met each officer's, held, then moved to the next. "She's not out in the open. She's in a contained spot, in a place that the perp can control."

"Like a cabin?" Heather said as a furrow appeared between her brows. "But we've been searching them…"

"What about a cave?" Jason Marsh asked. He rose from his seat. Headed toward the map.

A cave?

Marsh tapped the map. A location about twenty miles away from Lily's abduction site. "Most outsiders don't even realize we got the caves up here."

Kyle sure as hell hadn't known about them. And he'd been to this town before. He'd *searched*, and never learned about them.

Marsh rolled his shoulders as he studied the map. "The caves have been used plenty over the years. Indians used 'em for some rituals, Confederate soldiers hid in them and stored weapons in there. Hell, the story goes that even some of Jesse James's men stayed in them once, when they were running from the law. The caves stretch for miles and miles. The areas I know about, anyway."

Miles and miles. "You're taking me to those caves." Because from what Kyle was hearing, they sounded like the perfect spot for the killer.

Marsh scratched his chin. "You wouldn't have to worry about hunters finding her in those caves. Hell, you wouldn't have to worry about animals getting to her, either. Not in there."

"The caves are dangerous," James said, stepping forward with a hard shake of his head. "There was a cave-in there a few years back. Geologists said the whole place could collapse at any moment. Sending men in there—"

"I'll take the risk," Kyle said. No hesitation.

"So will I," Cadence added. He'd known she would say that.

James exhaled and gave a slow nod.

"And I'll lead you." Marsh had straightened his shoulders. "I'll show you the area, and if Lily is there, we'll find her."

Damn straight they would, but Kyle wasn't about to let the task force lose focus. He pointed to the map once more. "Anniston, you keep a team searching near the south ridge area. Officer Crenshaw, you keep interviewing the folks from Striker's. Someone knows something, someone saw *something*."

They would all keep working. And they would *find* Lily.

I just want to find her alive.

***

"How come tourists aren't flooding to these caves?" Cadence asked Jason as they headed deeper into the woods and toward the entrance to the caves.

Kyle kept steady pace with them, not about to be left behind. He knew Cadence was worried about him, but he had this.

He finally fucking had this.

I'm going to find you. He was going to find the man who'd taken Lily—the same bastard he believed had taken his sister, and he would make the guy pay.

Cadence had asked him, *Who were you killing?* In his dreams—his nightmares—there was one person Kyle killed again and again. *The man who took Maria.*

"Captain was right about the caves being dangerous. We had some geologists come in a few years ago. They did some tests, said it wasn't safe for folks." Jason came to a stop before a heavy slab of stone. "Up in Kentucky, they have Mammoth Caves. Mammoth stretches for over a hundred miles."

Kyle damn well hoped the caves in Paradox weren't as vast. If they were, more than just three folks needed to be out there.

"How far do the caves stretch here?" Cadence asked as she approached the slab.

As Kyle got closer, he realized there was darkness behind the slab. Twisting vines, grass, and what looked like a dark window.

The entrance to the caves.

"At least fifty miles, according to the geologist." Jason pulled a flashlight from his backpack. They'd all taken the time to stock up some packs before they left the station. "But most of the tunnels are unstable, so they didn't go too far down them. Just estimated." He glanced back at Kyle and Cadence. "They were from Auburn University. They measured for days, then said we needed to keep folks away, that it was too dangerous inside."

Yet they were all about to head right into the window of darkness.

Jason eyed them both. "Guess I should've asked sooner, but have you two ever explored caves before?"

Kyle stared back at him. "A time or two." More than that, but they didn't need to go over his history right then.

"So I guess you don't have any problem with tight spaces, huh, Agent McKenzie?" Jason asked.

"No, I don't, *Officer* Marsh."

Jason gave him a hard smile. "Actually, it's *Detective*."

The guy was getting on his damn nerves. And if he sent one more longing glance toward Cadence when they had a fucking job to do—

Cadence rolled her shoulders. "Let's get moving."

Jason offered him a faint smile. "At least you left your suit behind. Good thinking."

Screw off. Kyle headed forward, the hiking boots he'd picked up helping him to move easily over the rougher terrain.

Then it was Jason's turn to hurry to keep up with him and Cadence.

Sunlight trickled just inside the cave's interior, showing them a long, narrow tunnel.

"Like I said," Jason murmured, "I hope you don't mind tight spaces."

Kyle glanced at Cadence. Had she flinched?

No, not her…

Had she?

Cadence reached into her pack and pulled out a small light. The light was attached to a length of elastic. She slipped the elastic band onto her head, then adjusted the strap so it fit securely. The black strap blended with her hair, and she hit the button on the front to illuminate her way. "Let's stop wasting time, boys. Jason, take us to the areas you know first."

No, Cadence didn't sound afraid. He'd seen her stare down killers. She rarely ever felt fear.

That he knew of.

Jason took the lead, heading forward in the tunnel. Silence followed as they trekked deeper into the darkness.

Soon Kyle saw more openings, twisting paths leading from the main tunnel. Heavy stalactites sprouted from the ceiling, while thick stalagmites grew from the bottom, some nearly meeting in places.

The caverns were old. Very, very old.

"A small stream flows just ahead. Watch your step," Jason advised without glancing back.

Kyle was already watching his and Cadence's steps. His own headlamp swept the area. He'd secured it moments after Cadence adjusted hers. There was no sign anyone had been in the area anytime recently.

No sign of anyone at all.

"Is there another entrance?" Kyle asked.

"Not that I've found," was Jason's answer.

"With fifty miles to cover, maybe you just haven't found it yet." Cadence moved easily over the stream. She had on tennis shoes. Jeans. Her hair slid over her shoulders. "Maybe there's a lot you haven't found."

Just as she reached the edge of the stream, her tennis shoe slipped.

Kyle lunged for her.

But Jason beat him. "I've got you," he told her, curling his hand around hers.

Holding her a little too tight.

Cadence pulled away. "I'm good."

Kyle hated that cop.

"Yes," Jason agreed softly. "You are." Then he pointed to the right. "This way, it will take us deeper inside the caverns."

Kyle didn't want this to be a waste of time. He wanted to find something, anything.

His head turned to the left. To the right.

He saw only rocks. The heavy walls of the caves.

Nothing to guide him.

Nothing to help him.

Deeper they went. Another chamber opened up, heavier with stalactites, bigger.

"I call this place the ballroom." Jason pointed inside, to the right. "It looks like they're dancing."

Sure enough, the rocks were twisted, seeming to form the outlines of two figures, wrapped tightly together.

A trick cavers used. Naming chambers, describing the shapes they saw so they could remember where they were.

"From the ballroom, you head back out, cross the stream, and go straight down the corridor." Jason was staring at Cadence. What else was new? "Remember that."

"We've got it," Kyle flatly assured him.

They went about ten more feet.

The path split. Two dark tunnels.

Which way to go?

"This will take you to a few more chambers," Jason said, pointing to the right. "It's easier to navigate."

"The left," Kyle said.

Jason frowned. "Why? It's gonna be harder."

"If he's hiding Lily here, he wouldn't put her in a spot that was easy to find." No, the killer would go deeper into the caves. He'd take the path others wouldn't.

Jason nodded. "I haven't ever been far in there. We need to be careful because there was a cave-in when the geologists were up here." But he was turning. Going into the tunnel on the left.

Kyle's light swept into the interior. He saw the heavy veil of rocks, where it looked like part of the ceiling and wall had fallen in.

Gingerly, the group made their way past the rocks.

"If our guy brought Lily in here…hell, I don't see how he *could*," Marsh muttered. "It's hard enough for us to maneuver, without having to worry about pulling in a body, too." It was cooler inside the caves than it had been outside, the stifling heat gone, and there was a heavy stillness.

As quiet as a tomb.

Two more paths cut away from the tunnel.

"Statue of Liberty," Cadence murmured.

Frowning, Kyle followed her gaze. His light connected with hers and shone on the rocky image. One that sure enough looked like Lady Liberty holding up a torch.

"Right or left at the statue?" Jason wanted to know.

Kyle wanted to split up. Wanted Jason to head left while he and Cadence went to the right. They could cover more ground, faster, that way.

"What's that?" Cadence asked. She went to the right.

Where more rocks had fallen.

The cave-in had reached this area, too.

His headlamp lit the scene as Cadence crouched down. She was reaching toward a stone that had been bleached white.

That's not a stone.

"Is that what I think it is?" Jason asked as he pressed close.

Kyle's breath sawed from his lungs. What Cadence was near looked like a human femur.

Bile rose in his throat.

He'd known Cadence was looking for a dump site, but to find the remains—"It's not her," broke from him, a hard growl of denial. *Not Maria. Not Maria.* The mantra repeated in his head.

"Are there more?" Jason demanded in the same instant as he headed toward Cadence.

Carefully, Cadence pushed aside the rock. "Yes." Soft. Sad.

Kyle advanced. Saw that—*fuck*—there were more. Old, tattered clothing covered the bones. "Is there a necklace?" His voice rasped out the question. *Maria always wore her necklace...her half-moon...*

"I can't tell," Cadence said softly, sadly. "There are too many rocks."

That's not my sister. He didn't *want* it to be Maria. Beautiful Maria, reduced to this. *No.*

"Call it in," Cadence ordered Jason.

He scrambled for his radio. Tried to make contact. When it didn't work, he yanked out his phone. "There's no signal here!"

No, Kyle hadn't really expected there would be. They'd traveled down as they headed deeper and deeper into the caverns.

Cadence was still crouched on the ground, studying those bones.

Kyle's muscles had locked down. Could that be his sister? Christ. *Don't be Maria. Don't be.*

It looked like the remains were covered by a dress. A woman. A woman who'd been hidden down in this giant tomb. If it hadn't been for the cave-in, would she still be hidden?

Jason bent down next to Cadence. Kyle frowned at him. The guy needed to get out of there and get some backup for them.

"There's something on her," Cadence whispered as she bent forward.

Her. Kyle's breath was cold in his lungs

"A wire?" Jason said, voice rising. "It is! Looks like it's pinning her down." He reached for the wire.

The fool *reached* for it.

"No!" Cadence and Kyle shouted at the same time.

But it was too late. Jason had pulled on the wire. He glanced up, eyes wide at their shouts, as the detonation began.

A trap.

Jason had taken the bait.

Kyle grabbed for Cadence, locking his arms around her and yanking her back even as Jason lurched forward, surging desperately for escape. Jason shoved against Cadence and Kyle, knocking them to the ground as he ran.

Then an explosion blasted through the chamber, an explosion that had the ceiling collapsing and the walls falling in on them.

Kyle held Cadence as close as he could.

As the rocks hit him.

CHAPTER FIVE

Darkness. A perfect black that made Cadence wonder if she was dreaming. Or dead.

Then the pain came, and she knew she was still alive.

"Kyle?" She whispered his name, afraid that if she spoke too loudly, she might start another cave-in.

Something heavy was on top of her, heavy and warm. Not rocks.

"I'm here."

He was on top of her.

His body curled over hers, shielding her.

She felt the rustle of his breath on her cheek, but she couldn't see him. The darkness was too perfect and complete.

"Are you okay?" she asked softly. Cadence could still hear the faint tumble of rocks.

"Yeah. You?"

Her back ached. The back of her head throbbed, and she could feel the wetness of blood on her legs, but... "Yes, I'm fine." Nothing she couldn't handle.

"There are rocks on me," he told her, keeping his voice low. "Give me a minute and let me see what I can do."

Then he was pushing up, moving away from her in the darkness, and she heard the clatter of stones as they fell off his body.

Her heart was drumming too fast in her chest. The air was thick with dust, and when she inhaled, the air seemed strangely stale.

Cadence fumbled, trying to find her headlamp, but it was gone.

Lost in the rubble?

"Don't move," Kyle told her. "I'll find a light."

That had to mean his headlamp was gone, too. Every caver knew...*always carry three lights*. It was the rule for facing the darkness. They'd all come in with three lights each. But those backup lights were in their bags.

Bags she hoped hadn't been buried.

At least the sound of falling rocks had stopped.

"Jason?" she called quietly.

There was no answer.

He could be unconscious. He could have been separated from them by the cave-in.

Or he could be dead.

"I got my pack," Kyle said. Then in the next instant, a glow of white light spilled from his flashlight. He swung the light around, and it hit her.

"Fuck, you're bleeding."

She scrambled to sit up.

His fingers reached out and brushed against her temple. She winced. Yes, that was where the throbbing was the worst. She grabbed his hand, stopping him. "Don't, I'm okay."

"No, baby, we're far from okay."

He'd just called her *baby*. Since when?

The light swung away from her. Made a slow circle around the space.

The corridor they'd entered was covered with rocks. Big, thick chunks went from the ground up.

They were sealed inside.

"Jason isn't here," Kyle said.

No, he wasn't. It didn't mean he'd survived the cave-in. He'd been running toward the exit, desperate to get out. Had that been his mistake? Had he been crushed beneath those rocks?

"The SOB rigged the place. When anyone touched the bones—" Kyle said.

"The cavern would close," Cadence finished. An explosion. One perfectly placed to seal prey inside.

Fumbling, Cadence pulled out her phone. Jason hadn't gotten a signal down there, but maybe she would.

No. It figured their bad luck would hold.

Fighting to keep her voice calm, she asked him, "Do you have a signal on your phone?"

Silence. Hell. She knew the answer.

Her fingers slid across the surface of her phone. Light flashed. "At least my flashlight app works." But then she turned the light off almost immediately. They'd need to conserve the light until they were rescued.

They *would* be rescued.

"Someone will come looking for us," she said, keeping her eyes on Kyle and his light. He was just a few feet away now, slowly going around the length of their prison. The light swept up high, then down low. She knew he was looking for any other way out of this place.

I hope you find it.

"When we don't check in," Cadence continued, "Anniston will send out a team to find us."

The team would have to dig through the rubble to get to them. How long would it take?

More rocks tumbled down, and Cadence scrambled toward Kyle.

He grabbed her, pulling her close. "It's not stable enough in here."

She choked on the rising dust.

"The ceiling and the walls are gonna keep falling on us."

They *were* falling, rolling down, and she and Kyle had to jump back.

"There's a hole over here," he told her, shining his light down and to the left.

The chamber seemed to be shaking. So much for a moment of safety.

"I don't see it," she whispered. Her hands had a death grip on his arm. *We're being buried alive.*

That was what was happening to them. The rocks and dirt just kept coming.

She could barely breathe.

"There." His light hit the narrow opening. *A hole. Yes, it's just a hole.* Small and dark, and it was on the opposite side, away from the tunnel they'd used before.

They dodged rocks, rushing to the narrow opening. Cadence held out her hand, and felt the faintest stir of air from that darkness. *A way out.* Maybe.

She stared at the hole, measuring it.

For her, it could be a way out.

But what about Kyle?

"Your shoulders are too wide," she whispered as her heart seemed to freeze in her chest.

"I can make it." His voice was grim. "Just go through first."

The shaking in the chamber was worse. There was a terrible, echoing groan from up above them.

"Go, now!" Kyle barked.

Not without him. "I'm not going to leave you to die!" If he didn't get out of the chamber, he'd be crushed.

"I'm not dying," he promised. "Neither are you."

Then he grabbed her and shoved her through the hole.

She shot straight through, sliding fast, tumbling to the hard ground on the other side. Cadence jumped right back to her feet. The glow of the flashlight was shining. Kyle was coming. He was—

"I'm too big."

The bastard had known that all along. A sob choked in her throat.

"The rocks are coming too fast." He groaned, and she knew he'd been hit. "That chamber might not be stable either. Go."

"Not without you." She hurried back to the hole. "Dammit, come on!"

"Get out. Bring back help!"

She wasn't going into the darkness without him. She pressed her hands to the rocks near the hole and found that some were loose. If she shoved hard enough, the hole might open more.

Or it just might send all of the rocks tumbling down, completely sealing Kyle inside the other chamber.

Burying him.

"Come in backward," she ordered him.

"What?"

"Put your legs through first." His shoulders were the widest part of his body. "Put them through, and come in as far as you can." *I'll pull you through the rest of the way.*

"Cadence…"

"*Do it! Dammit, just do it!*"

He tossed his flashlight to her. Then he was pushing his legs through. Sliding through, inch by inch. It was tight, so very tight, near his hips, but he slid through, bringing more of his body into the space with her. More, *more*…

His shoulders were wedged in the opening.

It sounded like hell was falling in the other chamber.

She licked her lips and spoke quickly. "On three, I'm going to pull you. When I do, you shove back as hard as you can with me. Got it?" She was very much afraid the opening would fall when those loose rocks gave way. They would only have an instant of time to make this work.

"Got you, baby."

She could barely hear him over the rumble in the outer room. She prayed he could hear her as she said, "One. Two. *Three!*"

Cadence grabbed him and yanked back with every bit of strength she had as the caves shuddered all around them.

***

"They're looking for you, Lily."

She was shaking.

No, the bed was shaking.

Everything was shaking. The world had started to shake for her a few moments ago, but then the trembles had stopped.

They'd started again now, terrifying her. *What's happening?*

"You shouldn't have made that call when your car stopped. Curtis wasn't going to help you, anyway. He was too far gone."

The blindfold was still on her. No gag.

"Because of that call, they found out too much. They're too close now."

If someone was close, then she should scream.

But he told me what happens to girls who scream.

She kept her lips pressed tightly closed.

"I was there to help you, Lily. I was all you needed that night."

He was touching her, lightly rubbing his fingers over her cheek, and she tried so hard not to flinch.

But she couldn't help it.

He laughed.

"We should've had time to play." He pressed a kiss to her lips.

She choked back bile.

"We would've had so much fun." His fingers were over her breasts. Lightly stroking. "I would have *made* you enjoy yourself."

Then his fingers were gone, and the knife was back at her throat. "They aren't going to find you."

Carrie...

"You aren't going to make a sound, do you understand? You're going to stay in here, you won't speak. You won't move." He shoved the gag back in her mouth. "Just in case."

The gag was wet. It tasted funny. Like it had been soaked in something.

Her head began to ache.

"Lie still like a good girl, and it will be over soon." Another kiss, this one to her temple.

Then he took off her blindfold.

Light spilled on her. She squinted against the light. It was so bright.

The light came from on top of his head. A light like hikers wore when they were in the woods. It was so bright, making her eyes hurt. She squinted, trying to see his face, but all she could see was that bright light in the darkness. It had been dark for so long. She needed that light.

"When I leave, I'll take the light."

Her heartbeat seemed to be slowing down. *No, don't take the light.*

"You'll stay in the dark. It will be all you have."

It had already been all she knew. For so many hours. Days?

"You don't make a sound, Lily. Remember that. You know what will happen if you scream."

She knew.

"I'll know if you scream, and I'll make you hurt, Lily. I'll make it hurt so much when I was going to let you have an easy end. Just the darkness."

I won't scream.

"Be good for me, Lily."

The knife was gone. The light slowly backed away from her. He backed away.

Then the light was gone.

Her heartbeat, slower now, was the only sound she heard.

***

He'd gotten out of there. Sonofabitch, he'd gotten *out.*

Kyle jumped to his feet. Grabbed Cadence, and held her as tightly as he could.

He crushed her body against his. That had been a damn near thing. The hole had closed, showered by rocks, the instant his head slipped free. He was covered with cuts and scratches and bruises, but he didn't care.

"Kyle, I—"

He kissed her. He'd wanted to kiss her from the first moment he saw her, and with death hanging so close, inches away, he wasn't going to let this moment pass.

His tongue thrust into her mouth. She gasped in surprise, and he took the sweet breath away from her. She'd stiffened in his arms.

No, Cadence. No. Want me, need me, as much as I do you.

Her hands locked around his shoulders. Her nails bit into his skin.

She kissed him back with a wild desperation of desire and passion that matched his.

He'd thought about this first kiss a lot. Considered being suave, charming, starting gently as he learned her mouth.

There was no room for gentleness. Only desperation. They were surrounded by the dark, cut off from the outside world. She was all he knew.

All he wanted.

His kiss became even harder. His hold tightened on her. Her hold on him was just as tight and hard. Her kiss was as wild and frantic as his own. Danger had been too close. Now passion and a need denied too long—both raged out of control.

If this was the way he died, then it would be one hell of a fine way to go.

He never would have thought their first time would be in a cave.

First time, last time.

No. Not the last time. Not for her. He tasted her, savored her, then slowly lifted his head. *Her taste was so good that even in hell, it was paradise.* "When we get out of here, you're mine."

Just so they were clear.

Then he eased away from her because if he didn't, he'd fucking try to take her there in the cave.

The glow from the flashlight hit him in the face. He hadn't even realized she still held it. "When we get out of here," Cadence said, her voice husky, "you'll be mine."

Damn.

But first—*I have to get her to safety.*

Cadence shone the light around them. He was afraid they'd just traded one chamber for another, but no. There was a corridor there. Curved, heading back to the left.

A way out?

They hurried toward it in the same instant.

Kyle put his hand in front of the corridor.

The faintest stir of air slid over his fingers.

A way out. Hope could be a fucking beautiful thing.

They headed into that tunnel and they didn't look back.

***

There was nothing to see. Only the darkness. So total and complete.

Lily's breath came slowly from her nose, as slowly as her heartbeat. The gag didn't taste odd anymore. Actually, she couldn't taste anything.

Couldn't see.

Couldn't taste.

Couldn't feel?

I was going to let you have an easy end. Just the darkness. His words wouldn't stop running through her mind.

He'd told her to stay quiet. She had. If she stayed quiet, then maybe he wouldn't hurt her. Maybe he'd let her go.

I was going to let you have an easy end.

Carrie's image flashed through her mind, a spark of life in the darkness that faded too quickly.

Lily thought she heard the sound of her daughter's laughter, but it was gone in the next instant.

Everything was gone.

Only the darkness remained.

An easy end.

But then, she heard something. Finally, something...

Footsteps?

The faint whisper of a voice.

It's him. It's him testing me. Trying to see if she would stay quiet. Stay still.

The footsteps echoed.

I don't want an easy end. I want my Carrie. She's the only thing I want.

Were those her captor's footsteps? Or could it be someone else? A person who could help her?

Hadn't he said something about someone being close? Her hands jerked in the binds. Her wrists were bloody, so they slipped, just a little, in the rope.

If help were close, somewhere in the darkness, and she didn't call out, then she'd never see Carrie again.

Pancakes for breakfast.

With smiles.

She tried to cry out. The gag swallowed the sound.

Walking to school. Holding hands.

She twisted her body. The small movement seemed to take so much effort. Lily didn't understand why moving was so hard. She tried again, twisting, and her hip slammed into something hard and heavy.

Thud.

She froze, expecting to feel his knife on her skin. Expecting to hear the deep voice whispering, "Lily."

I didn't scream.

She shifted her hip again, moving hard to the right.

Thud.

Again.

Thud.

Again.

***

Cadence froze. "Did you hear that?"

His footsteps stopped. "Another cave-in?" They'd been walking for at least twenty minutes. The corridor had narrowed. Branched off. Twisted. There'd been a few times when Kyle had barely scraped forward in the tunnel.

"I don't think so." Cadence tilted her head as she tried to catch the sound once more. "It sounded like a hammer." A steady thud.

But she couldn't hear it now.

"I don't hear anything," Kyle said. His fingers brushed lightly over her shoulder.

She didn't move, not yet. Kyle was behind her, shining the light.

"We need to keep going."

She knew he was right, but…

Thud.

"I hear it again," Cadence whispered. Was it Anniston and his men? Coming to rescue them? Digging through the rocks?

Thud.

"Hell, I do, too."

They started moving as one then, going forward, following the sound.

Then the corridor opened. Split in two.

One way, she could feel a breeze blowing on her face. Sweet, fresh air hit her and she drank it greedily. It was the way out. Another way to freedom.

The other way, to the left, had been where the faint *thud* had come from.

They should get out. Call in their location. Get backup and *then* investigate the sound.

Cadence knew it was the protocol to follow. The right thing, the safe thing to do.

Kyle had already turned to the left.

"Kyle!"

She grabbed his hand.

"Use your phone," he told her, voice hard. "Use the light from it. Get out of here and get us help."

"We've been over this." Her own voice trembled. "I'm not leaving you, remember? Where one of us goes…"

The other followed.

The thuds had stopped once more.

"Someone else could be trapped down here. Hell, it could be Lily," he said. "I can't just walk away. I leave now, he could kill her before I get back."

They'd both worked plenty of cases that taught them just how valuable time could be. And in this place—this dark pit that reminded her too much of hell—the walls were already unstable. Another cave-in could come. If the thuds were from a victim… *she needs help, now.*

"I can't walk away," he said again.

Neither could she. Cadence hadn't joined the FBI so she could play things safe.

"I don't have my gun."

"I've got a knife," he told her, his voice was low and grim. Determined. "The one that was strapped to my ankle."

Just in case those sounds hadn't come from a victim.

Just in case this was another trap, just like the wire had been.

"Then you go first," Cadence said. The one with the weapon should be ready for attack.

Just as she'd be ready to jump in and fight in any way she could.

They entered the branch on the left.

The fresh air drifted behind them.

***

It wasn't dark anymore.

Lily stopped twisting on the bed. She was so tired.

But it wasn't dark. He'd said she would have darkness at the end.

She didn't have darkness.

She could see Carrie. Carrie with her beautiful, blonde hair. Carrie smiling.

Holding out her hand.

Lily wanted to reach for her daughter, but she couldn't.

She tried to call her name.

A ragged groan slipped past the gag.

Carrie.

Carrie was there, surrounded by light. A light that grew and grew.

Such a beautiful light.

***

Kyle advanced slowly. His right hand gripped the knife while the fingers of his left hand curled around the flashlight. The light shone across the rough walls of the cave, pushing back the darkness. The stone was heavy and sharp and—

A door.

The light fell on the rough, wooden surface of an old door. His breath stilled in his lungs even as he found himself rushing forward. The last thing he'd expected to find in those caverns was a door. He tried to open it. It wasn't a fucking good sign the thing had been locked.

He shoved his shoulder into it. Once, twice, three times, ignoring the stab of pain that pulsed through him, and *finally*, it swung inward.

And revealed another room full of darkness.

There were no sounds from the darkness. No more *thuds*. His flashlight cut around the area. Moving carefully. He kept his body tense, prepared for an attack to come at any moment.

Something—someone—*had* been in that room.

The light drifted over a piece of wood.

Frowning, he started to advance.

"Wait!" Cadence's hand tightened on his arm. "Look down." She had her phone out, using it as a flashlight and shining it on the ground.

In the glow of her light, he could just make out the length of the trip wire.

Fuck.

He'd tried to be so careful. Sweeping out with his light and checking constantly as they escaped through the corridors. When he'd seen this room, he'd gotten sloppy.

You thought you'd found Lily.

His breath slowly eased out and his light left the heavy piece of wood to join instead with Cadence's. He checked the ground carefully.

Kyle had no doubt the wire was rigged to set off another explosion. Positioned just past the door to stop someone from racing inside the chamber.

Or racing out?

His jaw locked.

Thud.

His flashlight flew right toward the sound. He saw the heavy piece of wood again, but his light trailed to the right as he realized—

The wood is part of a bed.

And, fuck me, someone is in that bed.

Her blonde hair was in the circle cast by his light.

His first instinct was to run to her, but he held back. He knew she might not be alone.

Where are you, you sonofabitch?

Cadence's breath caught on a gasp behind him. She'd seen the blonde, too.

What else was there to see? His light cut around the room, slowly. Cadence's began to do the same. But dammit, if someone was hiding in there, he could just move, easily avoiding the lights.

Get the blonde. Get her out.

Why hadn't she responded to them?

His light went back to her. She'd turned her head, and now she stared at them, eyes wide, face pale, with a gag stuffed in her mouth.

"The rest of the floor's clear," Cadence said. "*Let's go.*"

They cleared the trip wire and were at the bed in seconds.

Lily—*yes, it was Lily*—didn't so much as blink. Her hands were tied, the rope binding her deeply and securing her to the wooden bedposts.

He sliced through the rope, freeing her.

Cadence pulled the gag away from Lily's mouth. "It's okay," Cadence whispered to her. "You're safe."

Lily didn't speak. She didn't even blink.

"We're with the FBI," Cadence told her, voice soothing. "We're going to help you."

Lily's eyelashes began to flutter.

Kyle pulled her into his arms. He wanted her *out* of there. When he lifted her, Lily's body was slack in his arms. Her head fell back.

Her eyes closed.

"Cadence!"

She checked the woman's pulse and ran her hands quickly over Lily's body, searching for injuries. "Her heartbeat is too low." Fear threaded through her words. If Cadence was afraid, then he was, too. "We need to get her to a hospital!"

They needed to get her out of hell.

Cadence led the way, shining the light as Kyle carried Lily. "Hold on," he whispered to her. "You're almost home."

Alive. They'd actually found her alive. Lily's heartbeat was too slow, and his was about to burst from his chest.

He followed Cadence's light, watching it cut quickly across the room.

Her light froze, locking on the wall to the right.

To the tally marks carved into the cavern's wall.

There were thirteen marks carved into that wall. Fucking *thirteen*. His heart stopped when he saw those marks and realized just what the hell they meant.

Her light swept away from the marks to the floor.

He eased over the trip wire.

Lily barely seemed to breathe in his arms.

The sound of his and Cadence's breathing was far too loud.

Was the SOB here? Was he watching them in the dark?

Cadence turned. They were outside of the door. They just had to backtrack, go to the fork, and then make their way toward the fresh air.

They were close to freedom.

So fucking close.

Then he felt the trembles shake the ground beneath him.

"Kyle…"

Cadence was afraid again.

"Hurry, Kyle," Cadence said.

He clutched Lily tighter.

"Hurry!" Cadence screamed.

There was another blast. They hadn't stumbled into a trip wire, he knew they hadn't.

Was he watching?

Trying to kill them all?

Kyle started running, with Cadence right in front of him. The light bobbed and weaved, and rocks bit into his shoulders as he forced his way through the tunnel toward freedom. Behind him, the sound of falling rocks roared.

Faster, faster…

They were at the fork.

Cadence's light hit the right tunnel.

Safety.

If the cave walls would just last.

But the shaking, the reverberations, were everywhere.

The light began to weaken.

"Straight ahead!" Cadence yelled. "We're going to make it!"

There wasn't any other option.

He could taste the fresh air. His hold tightened on Lily. A rocky outcrop slammed into his side. He pulled her closer, shielding her head, making sure he took any impacts.

Then he heard it—the rushing sound of water. Thundering.

Like a waterfall.

Yes, fuck, yes…he could even see the flow of water in the cave, could see *light*.

His feet slipped in the water. It wasn't a trickle of a stream, not like before.

It was deeper.

A few more steps, and he saw it. A wall of moving water, right before him.

Cadence glanced back at him. There was blood on her beautiful face. What looked like the dried tracks of tears. "There's a ledge," she said, voice rising to be heard over the blast of the falls. "Stay close to the rocks. We can walk around the falls."

He shifted Lily in his arms. She felt cold, and she still hadn't spoken. Carefully, he followed Cadence's orders, moving as gingerly as he could. One step. Two. The ground was wet and covered with thick, green mold. He didn't want to risk crashing into the water with Lily. He didn't know how deep it was, and he wasn't even sure Lily *could* survive a plunge like that.

One step. One slow step. Not running anymore because they were free.

Almost.

Inch by precious inch, they went.

Water sprayed against him, soaking his clothes.

They were skating around the rocky edge.

Every heartbeat seemed to echo in his ears, even as the falls thundered around him. The sunlight was bright, banishing the darkness of the caves. Lily was in his arms. Alive. *Free.*

We saved her.

He searched the area and found a safe spot for Lily. Then he put her down as carefully as he could.

"Lily?" Cadence bent over her. "Lily, open your eyes, *look at me.*"

Lily wasn't stirring.

Kyle yanked out his phone. A signal. Hell, yes! He called for help.

Cadence was holding Lily's wrist. Kyle saw the flash of her eyes, heard the harsh inhale of Cadence's breath. "There's no pulse."

She'd been alive. Back in the cave, Lily had said—

"*Nine-one-one, what is your—*"

Cadence's hands pushed against Lily's chest. Started chest compressions.

"This is FBI Agent Kyle McKenzie. Get a lock on my phone. We've got Lily Adams. We're next to some damn falls."

Cadence kept working. Talking, whispering, "Stay with me, Lily. Don't go. Don't leave your daughter. Carrie needs you."

"There's a search party in the area!" The operator's voice cracked with excitement. "They're looking for you. Detective Marsh called in the accident."

What fucking accident? It had been a trap. A deliberate attack by the SOB who'd taken Lily and all the other women.

"They're searching for you right now."

"Her heart isn't beating." The words were torn from him. "Get an airlift out here. Get *help!*"

Lily Adams had survived hell, and he didn't want her to die just when she'd been brought back into the sunlight.

***

Bastard.

He watched them from the cover of the trees. They'd made it out. They had *Lily*.

But Lily was dead. He saw the way the female agent was working on her. Lily lay there, sprawled, her eyes closed.

Gone.

She wouldn't be able to tell.

The agents should have died in the cave. He'd planned so carefully, to make certain any visitors would never get out once they'd stumbled in.

To make sure Lily would never get out.

The falls crashed behind the agents.

The female agent was still pressing her hands into Lily's chest. Trying to save a dead girl.

There was no point in that.

No point…

Lily was gone. *You lost her, too, McKenzie. How does that make you feel?*

He smiled. At least Lily hadn't been a total loss. And McKenzie wasn't a freaking hero anymore. The big agent who saved the day.

You lost another girl, McKenzie. You didn't bring down the killer. You won't get the spread in the papers for this.

All you'll get…is death.

***

"Come on, Lily," Cadence urged as she kept up the chest compressions. "Stay with me!"

Kyle crouched beside her. Help was coming. Would it get there in time?

He reached for Lily's hand. So cold and limp. His fingers curled around hers. Held tight. "Carrie needs you," he told her. Cadence's voice had been low. Beseeching. His was hard. Demanding. "Do you want to leave your daughter on her own? Because I don't think you do."

Cadence pushed down.

"I think you want to get back to her." How much time had passed?

Cadence was frantically checking Lily, working to bring her back.

"Don't leave your daughter, Lily," he told her. "Don't let that bastard win. Get back home to Carrie. Get back—"

Footsteps rushed toward them. Kyle's head jerked up.

Cadence never stopped working on Lily.

The search team spilled toward him. He saw the familiar uniform of two EMTs. Captain Anniston and a battered Jason Marsh were running with them, as Heather Crenshaw and Randall Hollings trailed close behind.

"I've got a heartbeat!" Cadence yelled.

Kyle realized that he'd lifted his knife at the sound of those stomping footsteps.

His attention flew back to Lily and Cadence as hope pushed through him once more.

But the EMTs shoved him back as they surrounded Lily. As they kept fighting to make sure that she lived.

His gaze lifted. Tracked up the falls. He couldn't see the entrance of that damn cave.

We got her out. And we're going to fucking find you.

CHAPTER SIX

The hospital was bright. Too bright and white, and after being in those caverns, it almost hurt to be surrounded by so much light.

Kyle sat in the cracked chair, his eyes locked on the door leading back to the ICU.

Cadence had brought Lily back. Lily's heart had still been beating when she was rushed away in that ambulance. But even though her heart beat, Lily hadn't opened her eyes. She hadn't come back to them fully. Not yet.

A coma.

The docs said Lily had been drugged. An overdose. They were trying to bring her out of the coma, but, so far, nothing was working.

"Mister..." A quiet, shaking voice reached him, pulling Kyle's gaze away from those doors. He looked to the left, and saw the girl, Carrie, staring up at him with her wide, tear-filled eyes. "Did you save my mommy?"

She'd been at the hospital, along with Lily's mother, Martha, before they'd arrived. James's orders.

In case Lily didn't make it, he'd wanted the family to be able to say their good-byes.

I haven't saved her yet. "I helped bring her home," he replied carefully.

She looked down, lip quivering. "I want to see Mommy."

Dammit. There was something about a little girl crying. It felt like she was squeezing his heart—no, crushing the thing—between her small hands.

The ICU doors opened with a whoosh of sound.

Cadence marched out. The blood had been washed away from her hands and face. She'd changed into scrubs, ditching her torn clothes. A small, white bandage covered her temple.

Her gaze met his. Kyle realized he was holding his breath.

Tell me she's going to make it. Tell the kid her mother is going to make it.

Cadence's gaze dropped to the little girl. She swallowed.

"How is she?" came from James as he rose to his feet. The captain had been keeping a silent vigil near Kyle.

Kyle's back teeth clenched. *Don't ask that fucking question in front of the kid.*

The guy should know better.

"Stable," Cadence said. "For now, she appears to be stable."

That was good news, right? Stable sounded real good to Kyle.

A doctor appeared behind Cadence. Called for the family.

As they surrounded him, Cadence headed toward Kyle and James. "They think she'll recover. Her heartbeat is growing stronger, and her brain activity..." Her voice was low, just for them. "The doctor thinks she'll wake up."

"When?" He wanted to know just who had taken Lily. What the bastard had done to her in the darkness.

"Maybe tomorrow. It's hard to say." She pushed back her hair. "We need to talk, privately."

Away from the family rushing toward the ICU doors.

James motioned to the cops who'd been waiting a few feet back. Heather Crenshaw and a bruised Jason Marsh stepped forward. "Stand guard, got me?" James demanded of them.

They nodded. Jason's gaze cut to Cadence. He looked like he wanted to speak, but Cadence had already stepped away.

She, James, and Kyle slid into an empty hospital room. Cadence shut the door, sealing them inside.

"Preliminary exams are showing there's no sign of rape," Cadence said.

Thank Christ.

"She's got lacerations on her wrists and ankles, no doubt from the ropes, but Lily appears to have no other physical trauma."

"Except that the bastard drugged her," James snapped as he ran a hand over his gleaming head. "Tried to kill her."

"We were close." Cadence clenched her own hands into small fists. "He didn't want her making it out of those caverns."

He hadn't wanted any of them getting free.

"He set his traps," Kyle said, and there was rage rumbling in his voice at just how close they'd all come to dying. "He tried to bury us alive." The trip wire in the Statue of Liberty chamber had been set to bury anyone who'd been lucky enough to find those remains.

He remembered his first glimpse of Lily. Her stark eyes, unblinking.

The darkness. His light had cut through the dark.

Thirteen tally marks.

"As soon as he got clear of the debris, Jason called in backup." The lines on James's face were even deeper. He looked as if he'd aged ten years in the last two days. "We couldn't get through the rocks, and we were trying to find a way to you."

"You didn't know about the entrance behind the falls?" Kyle demanded in disbelief. *Someone* should have known. James had been in that area far too long *not* to have known.

But James shook his head. "No one goes up to those falls, not since a runaway killed herself there." He swallowed as a flash of pain appeared in his eyes. "Those falls aren't good. People stay away—"

"But the entrance—" Cadence interrupted.

"I lived in this town my whole life," James said flatly, "and I didn't know you could get to the caverns behind those falls. Death Falls. Hell, that's what the kids up here call them. If you go too close, they'll pull you to your death."

Lily's abductor had known about that entrance. The killer had *known*.

"We found remains in those caverns," Kyle told him. "In the Statue of Liberty chamber." One body, but there could be more. Eleven more. They had to get Dani to broaden her search. The killer had left those marks on the cave wall for a reason.

Counting off his prey.

"We saw her. When we went searching for you two, we found the—the bones." James's Adam's apple bobbed and sweat beaded his upper lip. "I got a team on the way, coming in from the next county. They're gonna get her out. We'll find out who she was."

Not Maria.

"The geologists are coming up, because—" James paused, sucking in a breath.

"There could be more bodies," Cadence finished. She was only saying what they all thought.

James nodded. "But I don't know if we can get to them. Those explosions made the place even more unstable. Even when we were in the first chamber room, rocks were falling on us. I don't know if I can risk men to find..."

Dead bodies.

It was exactly what the killer was counting on. He'd hidden all the evidence, destroyed it, and made the place so dangerous that others would hesitate to enter his domain.

"We'll start fresh tomorrow." James rolled back his shoulders. His gaze darted from Kyle to Cadence. "You two did it. You saved Lily Adams. We can count this damn case in the win column."

They hadn't been too late this time.

"Now, you both look like shit, so go back to your hotel. Get some sleep."

Sleep was the last thing on Kyle's mind. Adrenaline had his blood pumping, his whole body feeling jacked up with electric current. "He's still out there." The case didn't count as a win for him until the killer was stopped.

Dead.

"We'll find him." James seemed certain. "But you two aren't gonna be any good to me until you get some rest."

Cadence's gaze flickered to Kyle. Unlike her, he hadn't cleaned up yet. Blood and grime covered him. Kyle figured the captain's assessment of looking "like shit" had to be pretty accurate for him.

"You saved the girl." James's eyes were on Kyle, piercing in their intensity. "This time, it ended differently."

Kyle nodded.

"Get your rest. You deserve it. Those caves will be there tomorrow."

Would the killer? Or when he realized that Lily was gone, would the SOB try to vanish in the wind?

Doesn't matter if you run, I will find you.

He wouldn't give up. Not until he stopped the bastard.

The captain hurried away from them.

Kyle stared into Cadence's eyes. "There were thirteen marks."

She gave a small nod and reached for her phone. A few seconds later, Cadence said, "Dani? Dani, how's that search coming? Because I need those results, *now*." A pause. "Based on what we found in those caves, we think there might be a lot more women missing than we first suspected."

Not just missing. *Dead?*

He remembered the flash of white in the darkness. The human bone. The tattered dress.

Please. The desperate thought, the prayer, slipped from him. *Don't be Maria.* Because he'd clung so long to that one hope—the hope that he'd find his sister alive.

And not that he'd stumble over her bones in the middle of hell.

***

"Agents!"

The check-in clerk rushed from the motel as soon as he saw Cadence and Kyle arrive. The kid's wide-eyed stare flew over them, lingering a bit on the blood covering Kyle's shirt.

Yeah, it's blood. Deal with it.

"I heard on the news about what you did." The kid shook his head. Looked like he was staring at movie stars. "You saved Ms. Adams!"

Word traveled fast in small towns. Especially when that word was constantly being pumped through the local news.

"Here." The kid thrust two room keys at them. "I saved the two rooms for you, just like you asked, Ms. Hollow. Right next to each other."

Kyle frowned. He didn't want two rooms. One was all he needed that night.

He'd made Cadence a promise.

He wasn't backing out.

We're out of the darkness, Cadence. You're mine.

He'd warned her.

"If there's anything you need"—the kid's voice shook with eagerness and excitement—"you call me. *Anything.* Anytime."

"Thank you," Cadence murmured. "We'll keep that in mind."

They passed the boy.

"What was it like?" he called after them in the high-pitched, breaking voice that showed both his excitement and nervousness. "In the cave?"

"Dark," Kyle threw over his shoulder. "It was damn dark." They climbed the stairs, leaving the desk clerk behind.

Two rooms. Two keys.

Cadence had them both.

At the top of the stairs, she paused. "Looks like the second room is right next door."

Not close enough.

She handed him the key.

He caught her fingers. "You know that's not the way it will work."

He'd wondered if she would do this. If she would just pretend the intimacy in the caverns had never happened.

He wasn't going to let her get away with that. There wasn't going to be any boundaries between them.

"You need to get cleaned up," she said, her gaze not quite meeting his. "I need to check in with Dani again."

Bullshit. The woman was just trying to slip away from him.

But he didn't want to take her with blood and dirt on his skin. He wanted flesh to flesh. Wanted all of her.

"I'll get clean." Five minutes, ten, tops. "Then I'm coming for you."

Her eyelashes lifted and her gaze finally met his. Her golden eyes were wide, her emotions hidden. "Do you really think this is a good idea?"

This? Them, fucking until the pleasure left them too exhausted to do anything but crash? Sounded like a great idea to him.

He bent toward her. Wanted her mouth again. He'd been denied it for too long. "I think if I don't have you tonight, I might go insane." She'd been what got him through the darkness.

Her hand tugged away from his. "Go get your shower, McKenzie. Maybe it will cool you off." She turned for the door.

He didn't move. "Since I've been burning alive for you from the day we met, I doubt a shower is going to help much."

Cadence's fingers shook as she shoved the key in the lock. That small shake had him tensing. Cadence was nervous. Good. If she was nervous, then it meant she was as aware of the desperate tension as he was.

Cadence didn't look at him. "If you cross some lines, there's no going back." Her voice was husky.

Her voice had always reminded him of sin in the dark. His fingers slid over her shoulder. She stiffened. He didn't stop touching her. *I'll touch you plenty more.* "Who says I'm interested in going back?"

Not when what he wanted was right in front of him.

She hadn't opened the door. Hadn't pulled away from him.

But she also hadn't confessed her own need.

Tell me you want me.

How long had he been needing to hear those words from her?

"Why?" Her soft question.

"Because I need you more than I've needed anyone." Blunt and hard and so true. "And baby, you need me, too." Need. Desire. Lust. Control could only last for so long.

His hand skimmed down the curve of her spine. He felt her small shiver. "You aren't saying no, Cadence." She wasn't telling him to go screw himself, wasn't saying it had just been a wild moment in the dark.

Her breath exhaled slowly. "The doors in these rooms connect."

His heart slammed into his chest.

Cadence glanced over her shoulder. "Back in the dark, I told you. *I'll have you, Kyle.*"

He was about to explode. Just from the sexy, husky purr that was her voice.

"So I guess there's no going back for either of us," Cadence whispered. The faintest smile—sensual temptation—curled her lips. "See you soon." Then she slipped inside her room.

And shut the door.

***

Only a pair of jeans covered him. Kyle stared at the thin door connecting his room to Cadence's.

He could hear her on the other side of the door. The soft rustles of movement. The light pad of her feet.

The shower hadn't cooled him down, not even close. The hunger and lust had just built inside of him, growing even stronger with each passing moment.

The need was so strong, he was almost afraid...*I don't want to hurt her.*

He'd never felt this way before. His control was ragged, adrenaline pumping too fiercely through him, and he wanted Cadence. Naked. Spread. Wanted to be in her so deeply that the pain twisting inside him was finally swallowed by the pleasure he knew she'd give him.

Just a door separated them.

He didn't open the door.

Get your control. Don't hurt her.

He wasn't sure he'd be able to go easy with her. He'd always planned a long seduction for their first time. Gentleness. Orgasms that lasted until they both trembled in exhaustion.

This wasn't about gentleness. Seduction.

He felt too raw. Too wild.

"I know you're there." Cadence's voice drifted lightly through the door.

He'd known she was there, too. Standing on the other side. He'd followed the sound of her footsteps, tensing as she grew closer to him.

The door was all that protected her from him right then.

Did Cadence have any clue about the demons he carried?

Once I have you, I won't be able to let you go.

She was the first thing—the only thing—he'd cared about since he'd lost his sister. He wasn't even sure when Cadence had gotten to him.

I need her.

He'd have her.

"What are you waiting for?" Cadence asked, her voice stroking right over him.

He put his hand to the door. His knuckles were scraped, from the damn rocks, but they'd been scraped plenty of times over the years.

From fights.

Battles.

A life Cadence didn't know about.

She never has to know.

He'd left the darkness behind.

Hadn't he?

His hand flattened on the wooden surface.

"Good night, Kyle," came her voice. Whispering.

Her footsteps eased away.

She was leaving him.

No. He yanked open the door.

She spun back toward him, eyes wide. She wore an old FBI T-shirt, one that slipped to the tops of her thighs.

Her bare thighs. Those long, perfect legs. How many times had he imagined having those legs wrapped around him?

"I—I thought you'd changed your mind," she said.

The faint stutter threw him off. This wasn't the confident woman who'd said *I'll have you.*

There was hesitation in her eyes as she studied him. The faintest edge of fear.

She can see who you really are.

But it was too late to turn away, too late for either of them. The sensual promise was there, and the lust pushing all sane thought from his head wasn't going to let him walk away from her.

"Get on the bed," he ordered, voice guttural. So much for suave. But he was pretty much just lucky to be managing speech right then.

She should tell him to fuck off.

Heat flashed in her golden gaze, making her stare molten.

She turned away from him and headed for the bed. When she climbed on the mattress, her ass tilted in the air—fucking sexy, heart-shaped ass—and he saw the silken edge of her black panties.

He was on her in the next instant.

The mattress sagged beneath their weight. He caught her in his arms, twisted her, then trapped her on the bed beneath him.

"I wanted…to be different…with you…" He barely managed to growl out the words. They were the truth. In his fantasies, he'd seduced her. Spent hours enjoying her body and the sounds of pleasure that came from her lips.

But his control was nonexistent. All he knew was raw lust. A desperate craving for her that was driving through him.

Black silk. That was what he'd seen. He wanted to rip the silk away and find wet, hot, pink flesh.

Wanted to taste that flesh.

He would.

"I don't want you to be different." Her wrists were held by his.

He kissed her. Let the hunger rage out of control as his mouth took hers. He'd thought she tasted good before. He'd been wrong. Her taste was phenomenal. Sweet, hot, better than any wine he'd ever had. Making him drunker than any wine.

Making him crave more.

"Next time." His words were whispered against her lips. "I'll… go easy…" He'd try to. He'd seduce. He'd—

"Why?" Her head tilted back. Her hips surged against him, riding the hard arousal thrusting against her. "I like you this way."

His control shattered.

If she liked this…

He'd make her love what came next.

His hand pushed between her spread legs. Felt the dampness already coating her panties. Then he ripped them away. The rip of fabric seemed too loud in the darkness.

It made him even wilder for her.

Kyle pushed his way down her body. Spread her legs wide. Knew he had to taste before he took.

When he put his mouth on her, Cadence's body arched. He locked a hand around her hips, stilling her and forcing her closer to his mouth.

He'd thought her mouth was heaven. Her sex—*yes*. Even better. Even. Better.

He licked and wanted more. She was gasping now, pushing her hips against him, and he wasn't stopping. He wanted deeper. Wanted more.

Wanted everything Cadence had. Everything she'd *ever* have.

Her nails sank into his shoulders. He liked the sting of pain.

He liked it even better when she came against his mouth, gasping his name.

Tasting her pleasure was the best rush he'd had in years.

When the trembles eased from her body, he pulled back. Gazed up at her.

Her eyes were wide, gleaming. *Still hungry.*

Staring at him, she lifted her shirt. Tossed it aside.

Her nipples were tight. Pink. So perfect.

He slid between her legs. He still had on his jeans, the fabric stopping him from sliding deep into her.

She reached for him.

He caught her hands. Pinned them on the bed.

He liked the faster pants of her breath.

He hadn't expected this from her. Cadence liked it when he took her control away. It turned her on. Anything that turned her on—

He loved it.

His mouth took her breast. He let her feel the score of his teeth. The blood seemed to be boiling in his veins, and he knew he couldn't wait longer to take her.

He'd waited too long already. His tongue licked. Sucked.

"Kyle!"

His name was breathless, desperate.

He yanked for the protection he'd shoved in his back pocket after he'd jumped from the shower. He ditched his jeans and had his cock at the entrance of her body in seconds.

All that wet heat. Just waiting for him.

He held his body still, even though all he wanted was so close. "No going back," he told her. The words were a promise. A warning.

He thrust into her and was lost.

Control was gone. Thought was gone. There was only Cadence. Beneath him. Around him.

He grabbed her silken legs, opened her wider. Thrust deeper.

His heart thundered. In and out, in and out.

Her sex squeezed him. Tight. Heaven. Too good.

He couldn't last.

Couldn't—

Cadence cried out beneath him.

He wanted to roar.

Instead, his mouth took hers as he erupted, a flood of release stronger than anything he'd ever felt before.

A release that left him gasping, desperate—and ready for fucking more.

More was what he'd have.

Kyle wasn't going to stop, not until he'd taken everything Cadence had to give him.

Every. Damn. Thing.

***

The ringing of a phone woke Kyle. He stretched and realized he wasn't alone.

Cadence was curled next to him.

Naked, tangled in the sheets with him. Exactly where she was supposed to be.

The phone rang again. The sound was faint, drifting to him through the connecting door he'd left open.

Carefully, he slid from the bed. Cadence kept sleeping.

He stalked toward his room. Found the phone he'd left on the bed. A quick glance showed that the call's ID had been blocked. What the hell?

Maybe it was James. Had to be.

Who else would be calling at four thirty in the morning?

"McKenzie," he said, answering the call even as his body tensed. He knew a call at this hour couldn't be bringing good news.

A whisper came over the line. A click of sound.

"*Kyle...*" The voice was distorted, far away.

His brows pulled low. "This is Agent McKenzie."

"*Kyle, save me.*"

His grip almost shattered the phone. "Who is this?"

"*Help me!*" The voice had risen to a scream. "*Kyle! Kyle! I want to go home!*"

Ice crystallized in his veins. Staticky, distorted, but he *knew* that voice. There were some voices a man never forgot. "Maria?"

She was screaming on the phone now, her words no longer intelligible.

"Maria!" he shouted.

But she didn't answer. There was only silence on the other end of the phone.

"Maria?" His voice was low, lost, even to his own ears.

There was no answer. The line was dead.

Frantic, he tried to call the number back. It just rang and rang and rang.

"Kyle?"

His head whipped up. Cadence, wearing her FBI T-shirt again, stood in the doorway. She turned on the lights.

He could see the worry on her face as she asked, "What's happening?"

"*She's not dead.*" His voice was a rasp.

Cadence stepped toward him. "Who isn't dead?" There was a strange note of hesitation in her voice.

"Maria." He had to get a trace on the call. Had to pinpoint the location. "It was Maria's voice on the phone." He was staring into Cadence's eyes when he said his sister's name.

Shock rippled across her face even as she shook her head. "Kyle, that's not possible."

She still didn't have hope. Even after they'd *saved* Lily, she still couldn't hope.

"I know my sister's voice." She'd called him. She was hurting. Maria needed him. "She's *alive.*"

***

"He'll be coming soon, Maria," he whispered as he tossed the phone into the woods. It would be found, eventually. "But the agent won't find you."

Maria had been his too long. There was no going back for her.

He slid into the driver's seat. Turned up the music. Music silenced the screams and he hated the sound of screams. You could drive right through town, your radio blaring, a girl in your trunk screaming, and no one would hear.

They'd just pay attention to the music.

Not the screams.

It shouldn't have been time to find new prey. Not so soon. Hunting now wasn't right.

Lily should have stayed with him longer.

As long as Maria had stayed.

He turned up the radio. The driving sound seemed to beat in his blood. Loud, so loud…

Not like in the caves. When he had silence with his girls. That perfect quiet.

Soon, he'd have his new prey within his sights.

The agents would be so fucking lost, so busy, they'd never even notice his attack.

And too late, they would understand just how powerful he was. He'd outsmarted the FBI. He'd hunted for years…and they'd only discovered the truth…

When I let them.

He was the one who should get the glory. He was the one with the power. It was time everyone realized that fact.

CHAPTER SEVEN

The burner phone was lifted and carefully placed in the evidence bag. Early morning sunlight drifted through the trees, glinting like the fingers of a ghost in the woods.

The phone had been ditched just twenty feet from Death Falls.

Cadence shook her head. Twenty feet. After their discovery of the entrance to the caverns—the entrance behind the roaring water—guards had been stationed at the perimeter. Someone should have seen *something* when the phone was ditched.

No one had.

"He wanted me to know she was still alive." Kyle stared down at the evidence bag. "The bastard has had her, all this time."

Even in the rising heat, Cadence shivered. She didn't think Kyle was right about what was happening in Paradox. Fifteen years was a long time to hold a victim prisoner. She'd heard of it happening, just a few times, but the perp didn't usually take other prey when he had a living victim.

He only took a new woman when the other victim died.

The thirteen tally marks had been carved on the wall for a reason. "Kyle, are you absolutely sure it was your sister's voice?" She wasn't sure. She'd just caught the end of the call. Heard his shout. Seen his fear.

Kyle leveled his stare at her. The same stare had burned with passion hours before, but now, it was almost like she was looking into the eyes of a stranger.

Part of him had shut down. He was too focused now.

Obsessed.

With a ghost.

"I'm sure," he said, certainty cracking the words.

Cadence shook her head, even as she handed the evidence bag to the tech next to her. With word of Lily's rescue, reinforcements had arrived courtesy of the FBI and the task force that was forming to capture Lily's abductor.

Lily's abductor—the man they suspected had taken and killed eleven other women.

"It's been fifteen years." She tried to keep her voice emotionless. "You said yourself the connection wasn't good. It could have been some kind of recording, a trick to make you believe you were talking to your sister."

"She called my name." A muscle jerked along his jaw. "She was begging for me to help her. To take her home."

"Maybe that's what he told her to do. Maybe..." It had to be said. "Maybe he's already got another victim. Maybe he *made* her call you, got her to pretend to be Maria."

Kyle stalked toward her, closing the small distance. "Why?"

"So you'd lose your focus. So you'd make this investigation just about her." It hurt to tell him these things, but they had a case to work. Eleven cases. "So you wouldn't be able to do your job."

When emotions were involved, the job always suffered. And the obsession Kyle had? *You can't catch the killer when you're like this.*

Their boss and Dani were both flying down to Paradox. Geologists and an excavation team were already trying to make their way into the caverns.

This killer hadn't just splashed his way into the media. He'd exploded.

Paradox was about to come under a serious deluge of non-stop attention.

"I can do my job," he gritted. "I've always done it."

She knew he'd never stopped looking for Maria. That was who Kyle was. If their positions were reversed...

I'd do the same thing.

Which made it even harder for her to say, "I think he's screwing with you." Blunt words.

He shook his head. "He took her."

"Yes, he did." She believed it with every fiber of her being. There were too many signs pointing to the killer. Lily's abductor and the man who'd taken Maria—Cadence definitely thought they were one and the same. "When Lily wakes up, she's going to give us a description of the perp. We're going to post his picture everywhere. We're going to track him." She waved behind her, to the caves. "They're going to get inside that sick freak's torture chamber." What was left of it. "We're going to find a fingerprint. DNA. Something we can use in there. We are going to *get* him."

"Maria—"

"If we get him, then we find out what happened to Maria."

Kyle stared at her. No, glared. "I know her voice."

She licked her lips, hurting for him.

"I never forgot her voice." He glanced away, as if he couldn't meet her stare any longer. "She was crying, then she was screaming."

Cadence had to touch him. "Kyle." Her fingers curled around his arm. It wasn't enough.

"I should have been with her. If I'd gone on the trip like I was supposed to, she'd be with me now."

"You can't change the past." Hadn't she wished her own past would be different, again and again? "You didn't hurt her."

"I could have saved her. I didn't." He pulled away.

"We can't save the world." He should have known that truth by now.

But he kept walking, heading toward the excavation team.

"Sometimes," Cadence whispered after him as she felt the ghosts from her own past slide around her, "we can't even save ourselves."

***

The agent had taken the bait.

You won't find her.

It must be absolute hell to spend so much time searching for what he'd never have again.

A life lived like that might just drive a man to the edge of sanity.

He would enjoy watching Kyle McKenzie fall into madness. The great agent. The hunter of killers. *You're nothing compared to me.*

The bastard deserved to suffer.

And you will.

He planned to make Kyle McKenzie suffer more than any other man had.

McKenzie had started them all down this path.

McKenzie's name was the one that had ripped through too many nights. Maria's big brother. The hero.

You think you've lost everything? Not even close. Not yet. But you will.

It was time to prove that McKenzie wasn't as damn smart as he thought he was. McKenzie didn't deserve the fame and the attention in the papers.

McKenzie was nothing. *Not compared to me.*

When the FBI agent crumbled, he would be there to watch.

He'd be smiling the whole time.

***

"What are you doing?"

Cadence stiffened at the question. She'd shut the office door for a reason, but it looked like Detective Marsh had ignored the not-so-subtle cue for privacy.

She glanced over her shoulder and found him lounging in the doorway.

A few scrapes lined his cheek. A bruise skirted under his jaw. Otherwise, it looked as if he'd escaped the cave-in without any serious damage.

He stepped into the room. Left the door open behind him. "I was worried about you." His voice had dropped. All warm, southern charm. His brown eyes glinted with his emotions. "I tried to crawl back to you." He held up his hands, and she realized he did have more injuries. Cuts, lacerations, bandages. His hands had been ripped raw. "But I couldn't get through. I ran out, got help, and we were going to dig our way to you. We weren't going to stop, not until you were out."

But they'd gotten out on their own. Brought Lily to safety.

"I didn't leave you. Don't think that." His voice roughened.

Cadence shook her head. "I didn't think you had. The stones fell so suddenly, Kyle and I were afraid you had been hurt. Killed."

Jason shook his head. "It takes more than a bit of darkness to take me out."

He was standing right in front of her. Staring at her with far too much intensity in his eyes.

"*Jason.*"

The cry was sharp, annoyed, and coming from the open doorway.

Cadence glanced over and saw Heather Crenshaw glaring at them.

"We're needed back at the caverns," Heather told him. "Captain said for us both to go."

There was something in her voice, her gaze.

Heather's stare cut to Cadence.

Jealousy.

So Heather and Jason were more than just partners on the force.

"On my way," Jason murmured. But his eyes drifted back to Cadence. "I'm glad you're safe."

"I wish the same could be said for all his victims," she told him. Dani should be sending an updated missing-persons list to her at any time. Cadence needed to start matching victims to those tally marks. Because as soon as she understood the victims, then she could better understand the killer.

"If there are more bodies in that place," Jason said, beside Heather now, "getting them out is gonna be hard. We can get to the one in the Statue of Liberty chamber, but any others..." He exhaled on a rough sigh. "You're talking months of work. Maybe years, if it's even possible."

The cave-in had been so complete.

The killer had intended to cover his tracks. And he had.

"It's a good thing I don't give up easily," Cadence said quietly.

He glanced back at her. "I don't either."

Then he and Heather were gone.

Cadence booted up her laptop. The Wi-Fi in the office was perfect. One good point for Paradox. She immediately opened her e-mail because Dani had told her that the files were incoming…

They were. As she scrolled through the information that Dani had sent to her, Cadence's heartbeat felt too heavy in her chest.

Twelve names were listed, including Lily's. Twelve women. Four states.

Alabama.

Georgia.

Twelve old missing cases. *But when you add Lily Adams to that list…*

Thirteen. A perfect match to the tally marks that had been carved into the dirty cave wall.

"Did you get the intel from Dani?" Kyle asked as he came into the room.

Cadence didn't look up at him. Right then, she couldn't take her gaze off the screen. "Yes."

Tennessee.

Mississippi.

The disappearances had been over such a vast amount of time. Across state lines.

The dots hadn't been connected before. No one had put these women together.

She tapped on the keyboard. Her fingers were trembling.

Their cars had all been found, abandoned. These women had never been seen again.

According to the police reports, the women had gone missing at night, estimated at times between midnight and three a.m.

Her cheeks went cold as she read through the case files. The cars of the last two women taken—Laura Lassiter and Wendy Crighton—had been found on the side of the road, their gas tanks empty.

She'd been right when she thought the perp had done this before. Cadence just hadn't realized how many times he'd committed the same attack.

She scanned the next victim file. Elizabeth Jennings. Elizabeth Jennings had disappeared after leaving her shift at St. Mary's Hospital in Clydale, Georgia. Her car had been found, with a busted radiator, on the side of an old, two-lane highway.

Elizabeth had never been seen again after that.

Kyle came to stand behind her, reading over her shoulder. She tensed, hypersensitive to him, but she didn't glance back. Right then, there was no way she could take her gaze from the laptop.

Another e-mail from Dani popped up on her screen. As she read it, her icy cheeks flushed.

I went back twenty years, just to be certain. Maria McKenzie was the earliest match I found.

Finally, she had to glance up. Glance *back* at Kyle. His jaw was locked. His eyes glittered.

"She found them," he said, but he didn't sound like himself. She'd never heard such an empty, hollow tone from Kyle before. Kyle was passion and fire. This...this wasn't him.

She stood and reached for his hand because she had to touch him right then. "It's all preliminary, you know that. Right now, we're just dealing with links, with cases that match up." They'd have to dig deeper for more conclusive proof, but it was sure looking like a serial killer was at work.

A perpetrator who hunted women, who got them alone on dark, empty roads. He disabled their vehicles. He timed their abductions to fall in the dead of night, when no one would be around to offer help. He took those women. And no one ever saw them again.

Just. Like. Maria.

"The cases fit. The pattern is there." In her behavioral sciences classes at Quantico, Cadence had always been told to look for the pattern.

She'd go back, study all of the victims, learn who they'd been, but first...*Kyle needs me.* After that call last night, a direct taunt from the killer aimed straight at Kyle, she had to make sure her partner was in control.

That he was safe.

Sane. Because Cadence feared that the killer was trying to play a game with Kyle. A very deadly, twisted game.

She swallowed and told him what she'd learned from those files. "Three years after she vanished, another woman was taken."

Three years.

Long enough for everyone to have forgotten Maria McKenzie. Everyone but her brother.

Her hand was still on Kyle's. "After that, roughly a year later, another woman was taken. That's the way it appears to have been since then, over and over, nearly a year passing in between disappearances."

"*Why the hell didn't someone know?*" He pulled away from her.

"He went across state lines. Four states." She wanted to touch him again, but instead she balled her hands into fists. "Right now, right this *minute*..." He *knew* this. He knew the caseload authorities faced. "There are as many as one hundred thousand active missing-persons cases being investigated." So many cases and not enough investigators.

Details, patterns weren't noticed. They slipped through the cracks.

"He took Maria." Kyle gave a hard shake of his head. "He took her and the others."

He. The perp they hadn't profiled. The serial killer they were just recognizing for exactly what he was.

"You said yourself," she whispered. "Same city. Same abandoned vehicle. *Same date.*"

"He came back to where he started." His voice was hollow, but his eyes burned with blue fire.

The killer had hunted again, in the place where the abductions had first begun.

"You're sure she was the first?" he asked, his voice rasping.

Not 100 percent sure, but… "I can get Dani to keep looking, but she's already gone back twenty years. Maria's case was the first to match with the others."

His hands had fisted. "The first is special."

She could feel his pain. She *hated* it.

"That's the spiel, isn't it? With the first kill, something breaks in the serial—"

"Or is born."

"He liked it." That hollow voice hurt her. "He liked what he did to my sister, so he did it again and again, and no one stopped him. No one *cared.*"

She had to touch him. Cadence grabbed his shoulders, unable to hold back anymore. "You care. I care." Her breath was coming too fast. Her heart racing too hard. "We're here. We're going to stop him."

Did he even hear her? See her?

She shook him a little, tightening her hold on him. "He came back here for a reason. His first kill was here, for a reason." He needed to think like an agent and think past the grief and rage. "Why, Kyle? *Why did he come here?*"

She needed him to say what she already knew.

His breath heaved out. "Paradox has meaning for him."

The first kill was never random. Nothing about it was.

"That's right," she whispered. "It has meaning." Then she whirled away from him and yanked down the map of the United States attached to the wall. She grabbed a pen, started circling cities. All of the cities in Dani's files. The abduction sites.

Her palm was damp around the pen.

It slipped from her grip even as she put a star on Paradox. A star, because the city was nearly perfectly in the middle of the abduction sites on the map. "This could be his home base. He could still be here, Kyle." The phone call that Kyle had received meant the perp had to be close enough to watch them.

"With Maria." The words seemed torn from him.

She stilled. *Fifteen years.* "No." Her voice was sad, soft. "He doesn't still have Maria."

Not after fifteen years.

Not after all of those other victims. In her experience, a killer only chose a new victim to take when—

When the other one was dead.

His chin lifted. "We only found one set of remains. If they aren't—they *aren't* hers, so we don't know—"

"Kyle," she began softly, sadly. "You have got to—"

"Fucking have hope, Cadence!" He was the one to grab her, to hold on tight now. "I need it. Let me have it."

It seemed the noise outside of the office had quieted. Had the cops heard his cry?

His breath rasped out.

He wasn't hurting her, had never hurt her, but he wasn't letting her go, either. "This is the first break I've had on Maria's case. The first one." His forehead dropped, pressed to hers.

She needed to call their boss. She could catch Ben en route to Paradox. Cadence had to brief Ben on the developments. When he found out the intimate link Kyle shared in this case, Cadence knew the director would order him off the case.

I can't do that to him. She knew Kyle needed this.

"We're following the leads we get," she said carefully. "We'll work up a profile. I won't give up." *Not on Maria. Not on you.*

After a moment, his head lifted. The blaze had died down in his eyes. More control had come back. Good. But she still had to warn him. "You have to be careful, Kyle. Don't let your emotions take over. The killer is focusing on you. He wants you in his game." That would be dangerous, for them both.

As they searched for the other victims, as they learned more about the perp, the case would become even harder for Kyle.

His control would fray.

Fray and fray until—it broke?

"We work together. We're a team," she reminded him.

His hands fell away from her. "I'll remember that."

Those weren't the words she needed to hear. She needed more of a promise, but he had turned away. Moved to study the information on her computer.

Cadence glanced away, still trying to calm her racing heart. She looked to the left. The blinds were open. She'd forgotten about them.

Jason Marsh was watching her. Staring straight at her.

He'd seen the intimate interaction between her and Kyle. Had he heard them, too?

Marsh gave her a small nod, and then he turned away.

Cadence straightened her shoulders. She had a job to do. She would do it—the way she always did.

Start with the victims.

They were what mattered. In a case like this, victims held meaning to the killer. She would learn about the perp through them. Learn all of his secrets.

Every. Last. One.

***

Cadence stared at the victim board she'd painstakingly created. She'd put up pictures of the twelve still-missing women—the women they believed had all been abducted by the same perp. Twelve missing. One recovered—*Lily.*

So many faces. Smiling images. Happy.

They'd had normal lives once. Hopes. Dreams.

Then they'd vanished.

Time to become them, for a few precious moments.

She'd already spent much of the morning poring over their files.

Emma Black. Twenty-two. A girl with dreams of becoming a singer in Nashville. She'd graduated from Ole Miss, then followed her dreams to the country music capital. Only she'd never arrived in Nashville.

Her car had been found, abandoned, on a Mississippi highway.

According to the report, her convertible had run out of gasoline.

Did you get out of your car and start walking? Did he come to you, drive out of the darkness, and offer to help?

She could see the image in her mind, so clearly. Emma with her dark-red hair, blue eyes, afraid.

Shelly Summers had been twenty-five when she vanished. She'd broken up with her boyfriend, said she was going back to Florida to be with her parents.

Shelly's car had been found over the Georgia border.

The cave, the darkness, the gag...he'd done that to Shelly, too.

Held his victims prisoner in the darkness. Taken them in the darkness.

Always in the dead of night.

So they couldn't see him?

Why didn't he want his victims to see his face? What was he hiding?

And was it about hiding...or did he just like the dark? Did the night hold special meaning for him?

The women were all attractive. Different hair, different eyes, but all physically fit. Ages had varied, from Maria's eighteen to another victim's thirty-three.

"None of you had records," Cadence said to the women who stared back at her. "Not so much as speeding tickets." No trouble with the law. No trouble at work. All the women had been described as good, dependable.

Until they'd vanished.

They were good.

They were all women who'd never caused trouble. Women who were likely to go along with whatever a police officer said if he pulled them over on a long stretch of road.

Her heart started to pound faster. It wasn't the physical traits linking the victims. They were too different. If it wasn't physical traits, that meant—

Behavior?

"Cadence."

She glanced back. This time, Kyle filled the doorway. "I just got the call. Lily's awake."

***

"I don't remember." Lily Adams had bruises on her jaw, bandages around her wrists, and lips that wouldn't stop quivering.

Her mother sat beside her, carefully stroking her hand. "It's okay, baby," Martha Lansing whispered.

Lily shook her head. Her gaze drifted from Cadence to Kyle. "My mom said you two saved me. Thank you."

The woman was breaking her heart.

Cadence eased into the empty chair closest to Lily. "Can you recall any details of your abduction?"

Lily swallowed. The soft click was almost painful to hear. "I was working at Striker's waiting tables."

"What happened after Striker's?" Kyle asked her, keeping his own voice low and calm. Since Cadence could practically feel the tension rolling off him, she was impressed he held himself in check that much.

After the phone call he'd gotten, the guy's control had to be razor thin.

The perp wants him that way.

The killer was taunting Kyle, bringing him into a battle that wouldn't—couldn't—end well.

She had to stop the killer. She wasn't about to risk Kyle.

"I don't know." Lily's voice was raspy. So weak. Her gaze drifted to her bandaged wrists. "I don't remember what happened to my hands or my hip." Her lashes lifted. "My left hip is fractured."

"You banged it into the side of the bed, again and again."

Cadence stiffened at Kyle's words. They weren't supposed to *tell* the victim specific details yet. It would just compromise her ability to recall on her own. "Kyle…"

"*You* saved yourself, Ms. Adams," Kyle continued, not backing down at the warning he had to hear in her voice. "We were leaving the caverns, almost out, but you kept banging, swinging out with your hip to catch our attention. You brought us to you."

A tear leaked down Lily's cheek.

"Lily, baby, it's okay," her mother murmured, voice cracking.

"I don't know who took me." Lily wet her lips. "He could be anyone. He could come for me again."

"You're going to have a guard with you," Cadence said. She'd used some favors to call this one in. She didn't want someone local watching Lily. A local man would know those caverns. A local man could be their killer. *A local cop?* Despite the interviews and alibis, she wasn't ready to rule that one out. Not yet.

"What kind of guard?" Lily asked as her eyes darted to the door.

"A US marshal is out there right now. He's going to be staying with you, twenty-four-seven, while we keep investigating this case." He'd be coming in the room soon enough; she'd just asked Malcolm Williams to stay outside while she and Kyle spoke with Lily first. "Marshal Williams will make sure you stay safe." *Alive.*

Lily's mother turned her head to look at Cadence. "Are you going to be able to catch the bastard?"

"We'll do everything we can," Cadence said.

"Yes," Kyle swore. "We're going to catch him."

Her stare cut to him. *Don't make promises we may not be able to keep.* He knew they weren't supposed to promise victims.

The machines near Lily were beeping too quickly. The doctor had warned them not to stress Lily too much. Cadence pulled out her card. Placed it on the small nightstand. "Your memory might come back to you." With the drug dose she'd been given, there was no guarantee of that. The perp had known *exactly* what he was doing when he gave her the lethal mix of Rohypnol and chloroform. "If you remember anything about the killer or your ordeal, call me."

A weak nod from Lily.

Cadence rose. Kyle followed behind her as they advanced toward the door.

"I didn't scream."

Cadence felt goose bumps rise on her arms. She looked back at Lily.

She seemed so small in the hospital bed.

Lily shook her head. "You found me," Lily whispered. "But I didn't scream."

"No," Cadence said. "You didn't. We heard the thuds from where you were hitting the bed." She'd had a gag in her mouth, so, of course, Lily hadn't screamed.

There's something more here.

"I didn't scream," Lily repeated. Another tear tracked down her cheek. She gave a slow nod, as if reaffirming she'd done the right thing.

Done as she'd been told?

Cadence pushed open the hospital room door. US Marshal Malcolm Williams waited outside.

"How is she?" he asked, dark eyes glinting.

"Breakable." That was the word that came to mind. No— *broken.* "Protect her, Malcolm. If anything happens, if anything makes you nervous…"

His eyes held hers. She'd known Malcolm for years. He was a good man, a great marshal. "I'll take care of her."

She knew he would.

Kyle shook his hand.

Malcolm entered the hospital room.

"She's not going to be able to help us," Kyle said, voice rough as they walked down the hospital corridor.

"He made sure she couldn't." Actually, he'd tried to make sure Lily died. The dosage of Rohypnol and chloroform hadn't been intended to knock her out. He'd wanted to kill her.

A very near thing.

They hurried into the elevator. The doors slid closed, sealing them inside.

Cadence was too conscious of Kyle next to her. She glanced at him and found his bright gaze on her. "Are you all right?" Cadence had to ask him.

A grim nod. "I know he's fucking with me. We can *use* that, Cadence."

She didn't want to use him. "I don't—"

"As far as we know, he's never reached out to any of the victims' families before."

He was right. They'd had Dani check in with the families—*nothing*.

"He called me," Kyle continued as his eyes stared deeply into hers. "He let me hear Maria."

He wasn't giving up on the idea that he'd actually talked with his sister. And right then, she couldn't push him to see the truth. Not when she hadn't heard the call herself. *Maybe I'm wrong.* For him, she wanted to be. Cadence cleared her throat. "What does he hope to gain by contacting you?"

"Attention," Kyle's curt response. "He wants us to know who he is—and what he's done."

She didn't think it was just about attention. Not with Kyle's sister being so directly involved. It almost seemed more like a *competition* to her. A challenge, the killer versus Kyle. But she didn't say that, not yet, because she needed to learn more about her victims first. Instead, Cadence told him, "I've got a profile developing. You and I need to compare notes and see what we have on this guy."

"*He's going to take someone else.*"

Cadence narrowed her eyes as she studied Kyle. "Another abduction so soon doesn't seem to fit. From what I can tell, he's taken a victim once a year." Except…he started the one-a-year pattern three years *after* Maria vanished. Why the gap? Cadence didn't know, not yet, but she would figure it out. Just as she would figure out the killer.

"And he's kept the victim. We messed up his schedule. We changed his rules." He ran a hard hand through his hair. "I've been building a profile, too."

Kyle had his own background in behavioral science. He was good—damn good—at developing profiles. Only he didn't work like Cadence. He focused on the killer from the word *go*.

She started with the victims.

"He'll need to take another woman." Kyle was adamant. "He won't let a year pass before another abduction. He can't. You saw that cave. The total darkness. The way he bound Lily. The guy is all about control. When we took Lily, we took his control away. He's gonna need that control back. Want it back." A hard pause. "The best way to get it back will be to take another woman."

She didn't want Kyle to be right.

The elevator doors opened with a ding. The dark parking garage waited for them.

Cadence's shoes tapped over the concrete. She headed for the SUV.

Kyle caught her hand, stopping her. "Trust me."

She frowned. "I do." He was her partner. She had to trust him with her life.

Last night, she'd trusted him with her body, too.

"I know what I heard on the phone last night. I'm not crazy. Fuck, I might be obsessed, but not crazy."

"You're an FBI agent." She tried to make the words light because the tension in the air was far too thick. Suffocating. "They wouldn't have let you in the bureau if the shrinks thought you were crazy."

"There are ways to get past the shrinks."

That wasn't the response she'd expected.

"Whatever happens, *trust* me. Don't ever stop, okay?"

She managed a nod. Her heart drummed in her chest.

"You can count on me, and I want to make sure I can count on you."

What was that supposed to mean? She'd never given him any reason to doubt he could trust her.

"What I have to do…" His gaze searched hers. "The things that are coming might not be what you expect."

He was making her afraid. She glanced around the garage. They seemed to be alone. She edged closer to him, keeping her voice low as she said, "Kyle, stop this. We're hunting the killer. We're going to catch him."

"I know that could have just been a recording last night. You were right before, when you said that." The words held no emotion, but his grip on her was tight. "A recording from ten years ago, hell, maybe fifteen. It didn't have to be now." The faint lines hardened near his eyes. "I replayed that damn call in my mind, again and again. She didn't respond to anything I said. The words they played…"

Her chest ached.

"But it *was* her. He hurt her. Tortured her. She was begging for me." His gaze blazed down at her. "I'm going to make him beg."

No, no, that wasn't an agent talking.

It's the victim's brother.

"Kyle, we have badges for a reason."

He pulled her deeper into the shadows, caging her with his body against the concrete wall. "Do you think a man who abducts, tortures, and kills a dozen women—a dozen we know about—should keep living? What if some dumbass DA screws up his case? What if he escapes? What if we stop him, only to have the guy get loose and do it again?"

"You aren't a killer." She'd been afraid of this. Deep inside. "You help people. We *stop* the killers."

"I will stop him." His lips twisted and the smile made her even more nervous. He'd never smiled with an edge so cruel before.

This isn't Kyle.

This was the Kyle the killer wanted him to be. Pushed beyond control. Beyond the limits of the law.

"We'll stop him," she said, desperate to get through to him. "Together. We'll put him in a cage, and make sure he can't ever hurt anyone else."

But the cruel smile stayed on his lips.

"Stop it!" The words ripped from her, and she said just what she'd thought. "This isn't you!"

"Maybe you're finally seeing who I am." His head bent. His mouth pressed to hers. Hard. Hot. "Maybe part of you likes who I am."

The darkness in him.

"I'm seeing more of who *you* are," he whispered against her lips.

A car horn sounded in the distance, echoing through the garage.

The elevator doors dinged from just a few feet away.

Cadence pushed against his chest. After a moment—a moment that seemed too long—he stepped back.

"We need to get to the station." Her voice wasn't steady. Neither were her knees. "Finish the profile."

He stared back at her.

"Kyle…"

His hands fisted. "I wasn't always like this."

No.

"I wish you'd met me before."

Two nurses walked from the elevator. The women barely even glanced their way.

"I didn't need to meet you before," Cadence said as she tried to make her voice even. "I know you now." She trusted *him*. "Let's go do our job, let's stop him the way we're *supposed* to handle perps."

They didn't hunt to kill. They hunted to save lives.

Kyle nodded.

But as they left, he didn't meet her stare, and unease deepened within her.

***

The task force filled the interior of the station. Cops, deputies from the county, the local district attorney. The county's coroner was even in the back, nervously wringing his hands. They'd all come in for the profile reveal and the update on Lily Adams.

Kyle stared at the assembled group, letting his gaze sweep around the room. First they were informing these personnel, then he'd handle the media.

One fucking step at a time.

He and Cadence had finally worked up a joint profile, one reaffirming exactly what he'd thought before.

The SOB will hunt again, soon.

Cadence wasn't certain of that part, but he was.

They'd taken away the perp's toy, and he'd want another. He was probably already searching for his next victim.

When Kyle stood, silence stretched across the room. Some of the deputies were young, so young, barely looking like they were old enough to drink. *Every* man or woman in the room who wore a badge had been checked and alibied out before being able to join the task force.

Kyle hadn't wanted to take any chances.

Alibis can be faked. That knowledge sat heavily in his gut. No, he didn't want to take chances, and so far, all of their stories were checking.

That didn't mean he trusted them, though. The only person he trusted 100 percent was Cadence.

Jaw locking, he said, "I want you patrolling the highways."

Cadence rose and handed out prepared files to those gathered in the station.

"Our killer hunts after midnight, but before dawn. He sticks to unpopulated roadways like old highways or the untraveled paths most folks wouldn't stumble across. He disables the victims' vehicles." Time and again. "He makes his victims vulnerable. Then he goes in to save them."

"Save them?" This came from Jason as he flipped through the file he'd just been given. "How the hell is he saving them?"

Of course, he wasn't. "He offers them a ride. Gets them to unlock their cars so he can get close."

Then he took them.

"He had Lily Adams in his car within two minutes," Kyle said.

Two fucking minutes. That had been the length of that damn phone call.

"He's fast, methodical, and very, very good at covering his tracks."

Cadence returned to his side. "No prints were found on Lily's vehicle. The perp may have been wearing gloves when he approached her. Or he could have wiped the car down *after* he took Lily."

Now more folks were flipping through the files.

"Thirteen women." Kyle threw out the number and waited for the gazes to lift back to him.

He wanted them focused on what he was saying. They all needed to be searching the roads. They needed to know what—who—they were searching for.

"Once a year, our perp goes out and abducts a woman. He's hunting in Alabama, Georgia, Mississippi, and Tennessee. We're alerting authorities in all of those areas so they can be searching, too."

There were mutters then. Did the men and women realize what a large target zone they were facing? Too bad. But maybe he could narrow things a bit for them. "He likes hunting down here, probably because it's his home. He feels comfortable here."

Silence, the uncomfortable kind.

Yeah, I'm fucking saying the killer could be right here, in your town. He could be the guy who works at the diner. The man who runs the repair shop. He could be here.

"Lily is the only victim to have been recovered at this point." Lucky number thirteen. They'd yet to identify the woman in the Statue of Liberty chamber. "The others were never found.

But based on Lily's encounter…" The memory of his sister's voice, pleading for help. "We don't think he kills his victims right away."

"Jesus Christ," Jason said. The guy looked shaken. "Just how long does he keep them alive?"

"We don't know that." Kyle wished he did.

"It's possible." Cadence's voice carried easily through the room. For an instant, he thought he heard a slight drawl in her voice, but it vanished as she continued, "It's possible they stay alive for the full year. When the year is over, he kills them, and hunts again."

Jason scrubbed a hand over his face. "Twisted freak."

Heather Crenshaw shifted in her chair. "Could any of the victims still be alive? Are we *sure* he kills them?"

The ME hurried forward. Dr. Hank Crane was in his sixties. His cheeks were ruddy, his eyes watering, and his hands moving in a nervous rhythm. "We know the remains of one victim are in my lab. I can't ID her, not yet, but based on decomposition, I'd say she's been dead for at least eight years."

"That's one body," Heather said, swallowing. "What about the other ten?"

"They could be buried in the caverns. They could be hidden somewhere else," Cadence said.

"Or maybe they're still alive?" Heather pressed.

"The odds of that are low," Cadence told her. "This man, he's what we'd view as a collector. He sees a woman he wants and he does anything necessary to get her. He keeps her, breaks her, and when he's done with her, he kills her." She pushed back hair that had fallen over her forehead. "He dosed Lily Adams with enough drugs to kill her. She *was* dead for five minutes while we waited for rescue personnel. He didn't want Lily to escape, and I don't believe he let any of the other victims escape, either."

Then Cadence stepped to the side and pointed to the photos covering the wall behind them. "When it comes to his prey, our perp is very particular."

"Those women don't look a thing alike," one of the deputies muttered.

"It's not how they look. It's how they act." Cadence squared her slender shoulders. "These women never caused trouble with the law, they weren't late on their taxes, their acquaintances all described them as being good friends, easy to talk with. Folks who knew them said these women liked to help others."

"They were good people," the captain said, frowning. "They didn't deserve this."

No one would deserve this.

"How would the guy know this stuff?" Jason demanded. "Some of these women were just passing through town. There's no way he could have so much information on a stranger."

"He could've gotten the information if he talked with them." The obvious answer. Cadence delivered it softly. "If he sat with them for a few hours in a restaurant. If he overheard them talking with someone else. I believe this man is very, very good at figuring people out. At seeing what makes them tick. He realized very quickly that these women would be the perfect prey for him, so he took them."

"Perfect prey?" Now this came from James. "What does that mean?"

"It means these are women who were likely to respond quickly to his commands. Women who weren't going to argue, weren't going to question." Her voice was smooth, emotionless. "These women would want to survive, and they'd follow his orders if it meant freedom waited for them."

"Wouldn't most people react that way?" Heather wanted to know as her fingers tightened around the file in her lap. "To survive, hell, wouldn't we all do just about anything?"

Kyle knew she was right. When it was your life on the line, you'd do any damn thing.

"I pulled the school records for the victims," Cadence said. Cadence was always the thorough one. "In school, these girls never had so much as a warning in their discipline files. They followed the rules, they were—"

"Good," Kyle finished. He knew it was what the killer wanted. "He takes the good girls for his collection."

"And he figures this out," Heather asked with both fear and confusion sliding over her face, "just by talking to them for a while? That's what you're saying? The guy knows who they really are that fast?"

"Our perp is highly intelligent," Cadence said, voice calm and clear. No fear flashed on her face. "I believe we'll find that he's well educated, and that he might have even spent time studying psychology. He knows people. He knows these women. I think he approaches them and asks them questions. He learns from their own words and actions whether they would be the type of prey he wants."

"He's looking for control." Kyle knew the SOB wanted to control everyone and everything around him. *That's why you called me, isn't it? To prove you were the one with all the power. But guess what, asshole? I'm taking that power away.*

"What happens," James asked as he rolled his shoulders, "when the victims aren't...good? What if he makes a mistake? No one is damn good all the time."

No, they weren't. Most folks had a darkness inside.

I do.

"The profile is showing"—Cadence's voice was calm and cool, still with no emotion as she talked about life and death—"that our killer is extremely dominant. When he takes the women, he exerts complete control over them. He keeps them in darkness, controlling one of the most vital things to them—light. He binds them, imprisons them, and it's by his will whether they live or die."

"But what happens when they break his rules?" James still pushed to know.

"He punishes them." Simple. Stark. "If the girls break his rules, he could kill them. If they stop being what he wants, what he thinks them to be..." She licked her lips. It was her first sign of nervousness. "I believe, in his mind, the victims would lose value."

Twelve victims.

"We're looking for a man who is physically fit." Cadence cleared her throat and continued with the profile as the gazes of those gathered drifted to the victims. "He would have to be fit in order to carry the victims, to get them through the caverns. The man is probably in his midthirties or early forties and Caucasian."

"*Is* he a cop?" Jason demanded. Kyle had known the question would come up. It had to. "Or was the guy just tricking Lily?"

This was where they had to be careful, because they didn't know yet. Kyle inclined his head toward Jason and revealed what he could, saying, "The killer would have chosen a dominant profession for his career, one in which he was in charge. He could be a cop, could be in the military. We're still developing his background." He exhaled slowly. "But there is one thing I believe, one thing we all have to be ready for. This man will be hunting again, soon. We need you out on the roads. We need you to be vigilant. We don't want another woman taken."

It was why they were going to the media next. They wanted word to spread, because the guy had a kill zone stretching across four states.

If a woman found herself on a long, lonely stretch of road and she was approached, they wanted her to exercise extreme caution.

"He's hunting again, and if we don't stop him, another woman could vanish."

CHAPTER EIGHT

Cadence stared at the entrance to the caves. Darkness was falling, the setting sun casting a red glare across the sky.

A crew had been doing excavation work all day long, and had barely made any headway. The hours kept crawling by, and they had gained damn little ground.

"It's too risky," Dr. Aaron Peters told her, shaking his dark head. The geology professor had come up from Auburn University, rushing to get to the scene. He'd been the lead on the cavern exploration years before, and the man who'd ruled them too unstable for the public. "Every time we try to advance, more of the ceiling falls in on us."

She exhaled slowly. "There could be bodies inside those caverns. Victims. There are families out there, waiting to hear about their daughters." Would this be their grave now? Forever?

"I'm not saying it can't be done." His voice was grim. In his late thirties, Dr. Aaron Peters had high, sharp cheekbones, and a slightly rounded chin. His green eyes shone in the waning light. "I'm just saying it's going to take time."

"That's not exactly a luxury we have," Kyle said as he came to stand with them.

In those caverns, the killer could have left clues behind, something that would help them to track the man.

"If we rush, we risk hurting the *living* men and women who have to go inside." Aaron's jaw locked. "I'm not risking the living for the dead."

Kyle's arm brushed against Cadence. "Dr. Peters, how far did you explore when you were up here five years ago?"

Aaron's gaze darted to the cave. "Not nearly far enough. She's got secrets, plenty of them."

"You didn't find the exit behind the falls?" Cadence asked him.

"I did, but we'd had a surge of storms then. The water was so high that the entrance was *covered*. You needed to swim through in order to gain access, and that wasn't something most folks were going to do." A shrug. "So I didn't tell the locals about it. Didn't see the point."

"Was there anything else," Kyle said, "that you didn't tell the locals about? Something you didn't see the point of them knowing?"

Aaron's shoulders stiffened as he focused on them. "I didn't see bodies, if that's what you're asking, Agent. I didn't see some poor woman being held inside a chamber. I saw caverns. Stalactites, stalagmites. Miles of caves I wanted to search, but they were too damn unstable." Anger pulsed in his words. "Now, if you'll excuse me, I have a crew waiting on me."

Cadence lifted a brow. "I don't think he likes you very much."

"Tell me something new." He rolled back his shoulders. "You heard the ME. The victim had been dead for eight years."

"Yes, but that doesn't mean her body had been in the cave the entire time. Five years ago, she might not have been inside." She turned away from the scene.

He caught her arm. "Lily was inside."

She tensed at his touch. His fingers seemed to burn her skin.

"You and I both know he could've had the others here. He could've been holding a victim in that chamber when the professor and his students came to explore."

"She didn't scream," Cadence murmured.

"He gave her that order. He could've given the same order to the others. A victim could have been right there, and she was too afraid to call out."

She glanced at him from the corner of her eye.

"Hell, the professor fits the profile," Kyle snapped.

Yes, he did. She'd realized that quickly enough, and she'd already gotten Dani to start digging into the man's past.

"You want control?" Kyle continued. "He's got it over every one of his students, *and* he knows this area."

"But he was at the university when Lily was abducted." She shook her head. "I already checked."

She was actually double-checking that alibi. One of his students had backed up Peters.

She wanted more than just the word of the guy's coed. "There's nothing else for me to do here today," Cadence said, not with the night falling.

"He hunts at night."

She hadn't wanted to believe the man would hunt again, not so soon, but Kyle had convinced her. Now she was afraid of what the night would bring.

"Maybe he's gonna start a pattern now," Kyle said. "Fifteen years, it could be a cycle for him."

That idea was the best one they had at the moment. But they needed to discover *why* the killer had seemingly come back full circle. She glanced at her watch. If the perp was going back to the beginning and starting his same hunting cycle again… "The second abduction happened in Tennessee, just over the border outside of a city called Maverick."

"Then I think we need to take us a little road trip."

Hitting the road, searching. It would be better than waiting in the darkness.

***

Shouts and laughter filled the bar. A little place on the edge of Maverick, the bar, with a glowing sign that simply said Dale's, sat nestled off the main highway, surrounded by thick pines and not much else.

Shirley Wayne had gone into that bar nine years ago. Her boyfriend had broken up with her, left her alone…she'd run out of the bar, jumped in her vehicle, and had never been seen again.

Would the perp really come back here?

Maybe.

Cadence studied the busy bar scene, her gaze darting over the crowd. Wayne's boyfriend had been the owner of the bar back then, and he still was.

Dale East was big and had a shaved head, with plenty of muscles stretching his shirt. He stood just behind the bar.

Cadence made her way toward him. Kyle was a few feet behind her. When the bartender looked up, Cadence flashed her ID. "FBI. I need to ask you a few questions."

His gaze immediately slid toward the door marked "Staff."

Great. The guy probably had plenty of less-than-legal activities going on. Right then, they didn't concern her, unless those activities related to Shirley.

"It's about Shirley," Cadence added as Kyle closed in beside her.

Dale frowned, his gaze coming right back to her. "Who?"

"Shirley Wayne," Kyle gritted. "Your ex-girlfriend. The one who went missing nine years ago."

Dale's forehead cleared. "Oh, her." He shoved a beer toward a guy at the end of the bar. "She didn't go missing. That girl couldn't handle the breakup. She went running home to her mama."

"Her mother died two weeks after Shirley was last seen in Maverick. No neighbors ever reported Shirley coming back to the area, and she wasn't at her mother's funeral." Cadence had made a point of checking these details. She'd wondered why it took over six months for someone to file a missing-persons report on Shirley, and now she knew. With the mother's death, there had simply been no one left to realize she was gone. A distant relative had eventually been notified that Shirley's childhood home was being foreclosed upon, and it had only been then that someone finally noticed—

Shirley's gone. The perp had taken a perfect victim. One that no one had seemed to miss. The thought made Cadence's heart ache.

But she wasn't about to show weakness or the grief that she felt for Shirley's lost life. Cadence carefully put her ID away. "We have reason to believe Shirley fits a pattern of abductions."

His bushy brows lowered. "You're shitting me."

"No," Cadence said very clearly, "I am not shitting you."

Dale grabbed a cloth, swiped over the bar top. "Shirley was crying when she left. Running for the door." His fingers whitened around the cloth. "I called after her, told her not to drive like that—"

"But she did," Kyle finished.

Dale nodded and stared down at the cloth. "Abducted." He shook his head, as if he just couldn't grasp it. "Shirley?" He swallowed. "We didn't work. I liked to party—hell, still do. Shirley wanted me to settle down. To have a family." He tossed the cloth away. "I always thought after all these years she was somewhere with the family she wanted so badly."

It was possible Shirley was currently on the ME's exam table. "Did anyone ever give Shirley any trouble?"

His jaw had hardened. "No, no, everybody liked Shirley. She was—fuck, she was one of those people that was always smilin', you know? She just didn't like me drinkin' so much. Said it reminded her of her ex, that jerk Jake Landers."

Cadence made a mental note to run down Jake Landers. "Did she have any contact with Mr. Landers?"

"He was in jail, so, no, she didn't. She didn't want anything to do with that loser." His chin lifted. "Shirley was too good for him. Too good for me." He swallowed. "*Missing? All this time?*"

Pain rumbled in his words.

"Do you remember anything else from that night?" Kyle asked Dale, his expression tight. "Was there anyone here who was paying too much attention to Shirley?"

A hoarse laugh came from him. "I don't remember. She was pretty. Like you." He jutted his chin toward Cadence. "Men always look at pretty women. Always want 'em."

Cadence pushed her card toward him. How many cards had she given out over the years? Always the same routine. Always wondering if one witness would call her back with the break she needed. Only she never got the calls she needed. "If you remember anything, call me, okay?"

He swiped the card. "That why you're here? You wanted to see what I remembered?"

"No," Kyle said, his voice hard. "We're here because the same perpetrator is hunting again, and we want to stop him." He pointed to the news blaring on the TV right behind the bartender.

"Maybe you should turn that up. You might fucking save a life." Anger snarled in the words.

Frowning, Dale turned back to the screen where the reporter was detailing the abduction of Lily Adams and the manhunt currently underway for the man who'd taken her.

Dale turned up the volume. "Authorities are cautioning women who are traveling alone The perpetrator may be assuming the identity of a law enforcement officer. If you are approached…"

Cadence turned away from the TV. Her elbow bumped into the arm of a dark-haired waitress. A woman who was staring up at the screen. "Sorry," Cadence murmured.

The woman—Christa, according to the slanting tag pinned on her shirt—kept staring at the TV. "Someone's taking women?" Her hold on the tray tightened. "That's—"

"Christa, hurry up!" Dale shouted. "I got people waitin' on those drinks."

Christa's face flushed with embarrassment. "S-sorry!" She immediately hurried to obey.

Cadence glanced around. No one else was paying attention to the news.

They were too busy dancing. Drinking.

Making out.

So much for the warnings reaching their target audience.

She saw Kyle's gaze. Realized he was thinking the exact same thing.

"No wonder he has such easy prey," Kyle muttered. "No one here even knows to be cautious. That's damn well changing." A band was playing in the corner. Blasting out lyrics that rolled with a twang. Kyle jumped up on the stage. Grabbed the microphone from the singer. "I want your attention!"

His voice echoed through the room.

"Who the fuck are you?" one man shouted out as he weaved toward Kyle.

Kyle lifted his ID. "I'm the fucking FBI, and I want you to listen!"

More curses. Obviously, the crowd wasn't impressed with his badge.

"There's a killer hunting, possibly in this area." He pointed toward the TV. "We believe he abducted a woman from Maverick before, a woman who left *this* bar, and he might do it again."

She saw some of the women glance nervously at each other.

"If you're a female, and you're traveling alone, do *not* open your car to any strangers. He disables vehicles, isolates his prey, and then he comes in to help them." Kyle's gaze took in the women surrounding him. "We think he pretends to be law enforcement so his victims feel secure. It lets him get close enough to take them."

"Then what?" a man called out, holding tight to a redhead.

"Then they vanish." His voice was flat. "So pay attention. Stay on your guard—and you might just stay alive."

***

The sonofabitch agent had gone to Maverick. *He's tracking me. Following in my footsteps.*

He eased back into the corner. He'd picked the most shadowed place in the room. A deliberate choice. He always chose the spot that would let him watch others—even while the location helped to keep him concealed.

The agents hadn't spotted him yet. In the dim interior of that bar, even if they looked his way, they'd just see a man with baseball cap pulled too low over his brow. They wouldn't get closer to him.

He wouldn't give them the chance to get closer.

Time to act.

McKenzie had just jumped down from the stage. The guy was stalking toward Cadence, his face grim.

He caught her arm. Pulled her close.

A little too close for a partner's hold. A little too intimate. Too possessive.

Interesting.

Kyle led Cadence to the back of the bar and pushed her inside the staff room.

The agents never glanced his way. But then, the bar was packed. Bodies pressing tightly together. Finding him would have been like finding a damn needle in a haystack.

That's why I picked this place. It was always easier to hide in a crowd.

People started talking again, mumbling. Some of the women looked nervous. Hell. But some of them…

Some of them were already heading back onto the dance floor. Already laughing and flirting once more.

That was the thing about fear. Unless the experience had happened to *you*, it was often easy to gloss over it. To think it never *would* happen.

How wrong they were.

"Another drink?" He glanced up and saw the dark-haired waitress, Christa, standing over him. Her smile was hesitant.

She knew he was a good tipper.

"Nah, I think I'll cut out soon." He pulled the brim of his hat down a bit lower. "Got to be safe while I'm driving."

Her smile widened a bit more. Christa didn't like the drunks. She was just working there to help pay off her mom's hospital bills.

Christa was good to her mother.

Good.

When she went to move his empty bottle, his hand slid out and his fingers caught hers. "I want you to be careful tonight, Christa." He'd been coming to this bar for a long time.

Off and on for ten years.

He liked to visit the places that offered him fond memories.

"I will be."

"Is your car out back?" He injected a note of concern into his voice. His voice had always been a gift. He could adopt any accent, any pitch, any time he wanted. He'd played around in the drama club back in high school. The girls had loved it when he ditched his twang and used an English accent on them.

He'd always had an easy time with the girls.

"It's across the street. I have to leave a little early, and I didn't want to get penned in by the customers."

He rubbed his thumb over her wrist. So delicate. So perfect for his ropes. "Then I guess I'll see you next time."

A little nod. She pulled away from him. Christa never liked to touch the customers too long. She didn't get too friendly with anyone. She was like Lily in so many ways.

Christa hurried away.

His gaze slid back to the staff door. Just what was Kyle doing in there with his partner?

Maybe he should take a look. If Kyle was following in his steps...*then how about I follow in yours?*

He tossed a generous tip down on the table and rose. Kyle had come after him. Now it was his turn to go after the agent.

***

"They're making it too easy for him," Kyle snapped as he paced the small confines of the storage room. Boxes. Booze. "Did you see them? They didn't even care about what was happening."

"Some of them did. I noticed one of the waitresses—Christa— she stopped to watch the news. She was listening." Cadence's voice was cool. Easy. Always the voice of reason.

He didn't want her so reasonable.

He didn't want to be the only one who was so screwed up.

He whirled toward her. "This is one bar. One. He could be in any of a hundred other places just like this. Only we're not there, telling those people to be on guard."

She caught his hands. Held them tightly. "You have to let it go."

His back teeth ground together. *She sees too much.*

"You weren't there when Maria was taken. You couldn't tell her to be on guard, I get it. But Kyle, this is destroying you. *Let the past go.*"

"That's easy for you to say." The words were an angry growl that he hated, but couldn't stop. "You never lost someone you cared about, you never saw—"

Her eyelids flickered. She dropped her hold on him and stepped back. "I've seen plenty."

"On the cases, from a distance. It's never been personal for you."

She'd turned away. He was a damn asshole. He hurried after her. "Cadence…"

She swung toward him. Her cheeks were flushed. Eyes glittering. "My mother."

He stilled.

"You want to know why I'm in the FBI? My mother. I became a doctor for her, too, but it wasn't enough. It was *never* enough."

Kyle didn't know what to say.

"I was ten when she died. Ten when the man came into our house. My dad was gone, out on a deployment. Mom and I were having a girls' night. Painting our toenails. Doing those silly things a girl does with her mother."

Her words were painful, and he wanted her to stop. He tried to reach for her, but she backed away.

"She knew something was wrong. Glass shattered. I remember the sound so well. It came from downstairs. She told me to get under the bed. To stay quiet."

Oh, fuck. No wonder she'd gone white when Lily had said…

I didn't scream.

"He never knew I was there. He came in, and he hurt her while I was hiding under the bed. When I crawled out and found her"—Cadence's words came faster. So much faster—"there was blood everywhere, but she was still alive."

"You tried to save her." His hands had fisted. How had he been so wrong about her?

"I didn't know how to save her."

The puzzle that was Cadence fell into place. "You became a doctor so you would know how."

"And an agent so I could *stop* the killers." Her shoulders straightened. Her chin lifted. "So don't tell me I don't understand. I do. I *get* it. I also understand that if you don't let the past go, it will destroy any chance you have for a future. For a life."

He was staring at life. At the one thing that made him feel.

She spun away from him. Reached for the door.

His palm slammed down against the wood, sealing them inside. He bent his head over her, inhaling her sweet scent. Flowers. "I'm sorry."

He turned her toward him. Cadence. She'd given him the best damn night he'd had in forever, and what had he done? Not

SCREAM FOR ME

even talked to her about it all day. Been driven by the killer. "Last night—"

"Maybe we shouldn't talk about last night."

"No, we should. That wasn't some fluke." Standing there, so close to her, he wanted. Ached. Craved her. "That was the best sex I've ever had." Because it had been with her. "I want more. I want you."

Whatever kind of chance she'd give to him. He'd been wrong about her. She still didn't know the real him, but until she found out about the darkness that haunted him so much, he would hold tightly to her.

So tightly.

Maybe then she'd never be able to slip away.

He pressed his lips to hers. He wasn't sure how she'd respond. Part of him expected Cadence to shove him across the room.

Instead, her tongue licked against his lip.

His cock jerked in reaction.

The kiss deepened. His tongue slid into her mouth. Cadence was the one thing that calmed him, that centered him.

What would I do without her?

The thought, dark, sinister, twisted through him.

I won't be without her.

He kept kissing her, tasting her, as his hands and mouth became harder on her. But Cadence liked the rough edge they shared. He knew. He could feel it in the tightness of her nipples. The arch and thrust of her hips against his.

He wanted her naked again. Beneath him, above him, any way he could get her.

Soon.

Kyle forced his head to lift. His breath came out in a heavy pant. "Cadence."

He heard the shuffle of footsteps. Coming from just beyond the back door of the bar. *Someone watching…*

In an instant, he was at the back door. He yanked it open and ran into the night.

His gaze swept to the left. To the right.

A couple was stumbling away from Dale's, arm in arm.

He started to call out to them, then saw they were headed for the taxi waiting near the edge of the street.

His heart slammed into his ribs. He should have been watching the bar, not getting so tangled up in Cadence.

But tangled up is where I want to be.

"We should stay until the bar clears tonight, just in case," Cadence said as she stepped out into the night.

Yes, just in case.

His gaze slanted to hers. They'd stay. When they were sure these people were safe…

I'll have my time with you.

***

He shuffled back into the bar, making sure to keep his head down. The conversation between the agents had certainly been interesting.

There were far more layers to the agent and his lovely partner than he'd realized.

Far more.

The phone call to Kyle had done exactly as he'd hoped. The agent was unraveling.

A dangerous situation for McKenzie.

But if McKenzie thought the game was finished, he couldn't be more wrong. Things were just about to get interesting.

You think you're the badass who can catch all the killers? You never caught me...and you never will.

So much for Maria's hero. In the end, the hero wouldn't be remembered.

But I will be.

***

Christa Donaldson knew she was holding her steering wheel a little too tightly. Her car's headlights cut through the darkness as she hurried back toward her mother's place on the ridge. The sitter had only agreed to stay until two a.m. She was running late, and if she didn't get there soon—

The car sputtered.

Her gaze flew to the dash. Plenty of gas. Plenty. But the car's temp was too hot. The gauge needle was heading straight to the H.

She immediately reached forward and turned on the heater, getting the hot air to blast toward her. An old, temporary trick that a high school boyfriend had taught her.

The car sputtered again.

A trick that isn't working.

The sound of her breathing was far too loud in the interior of the car.

Then the car started to slow down.

"No, no, no." This couldn't be happening. The agents, *this* was what they'd warned her about.

The car's engine died. The vehicle barely coasted to the side of the road.

She fumbled, reaching for her phone.

The flash of headlights lit her as a car pulled up behind her.

CHAPTER NINE

Christa screamed when the light rap sounded at her window, and her fingers flew out, frantically making sure she'd locked the door.

"Ma'am?"

It was a woman's voice.

She squinted as she craned her head to see in the darkness.

"I'm FBI Agent Cadence Hollow," the voice told her. "We met at Dale's earlier tonight."

Tears stung Christa's eyes. She remembered the agent.

"Is there a problem with your vehicle?" Cadence asked, raising her voice.

Christa rolled down the window as fast as she could. "It just stopped." Tears wanted to choke her. "It stopped."

The other agent, the handsome man with the hard eyes, stood behind Cadence. "Are you okay?" he asked her.

She nodded. "I just want to get home."

The two agents shared a look. "Don't worry. We'll make sure you get there."

***

Sonofabitch! The agents had followed Christa. How had they known he wanted her? *How?*

Christa's car had stopped, just where he'd wanted. She'd been alone. Such perfect prey.

But the agents had been there.

Now they had Christa. He watched from the darkness, every light in his vehicle out.

Christa's car door was open, the light spilling onto the ground. In the pool of illumination, he saw Kyle pull out his phone.

Calling for backup.

The agent would figure out what had happened to Christa's car.

Not the gas this time. He'd made the radiator overheat. Giving her enough time, just enough, to get where he needed her to be.

He'd even been out there, waiting for her.

But she hadn't come alone. The agents had been tailing her.

Dammit.

His jaw ached as he clenched his teeth. Christa had been so perfect. He'd *needed* her.

He reversed, moving slowly, keeping his lights off.

Part of him wanted to floor the vehicle, to get out of there as quickly as he could.

The agents would hear him. They'd chase him.

He wouldn't be caught.

He turned the car, headed quietly down the narrow dirt road, a road that would cut through the hills and forest and send him out far away from the agents.

And Christa.

Perfect Christa.

He'd had his eyes on her for years.

So many years.

But she'd been in Maverick. She'd had to wait until it was time to hunt there again.

The agents are screwing up everything. This wasn't the way things were supposed to happen. The pine trees and the darkness wrapped around him as he drove. Drove and drove as the rage built inside of him.

He needed his prey. He was empty. Alone. He needed her.

Maria...

He needed his perfect girl. Maria had been his first. He'd thought he could never have another girl who would be as good.

Kyle McKenzie had been there. Coming back to the town. Searching. Always looking.

But you couldn't find her, could you? So close, but so far away.

Kyle had joined the FBI. Started tracking others. *Did you forget about me?*

It had seemed that way. Three years...

The urges within him had grown again. But he'd realized he had to be more careful. Then, one night, he'd found himself on another dark road. With another girl. A girl who could have been all he needed, too.

Three years. That night, the rush had been just as good. Just as strong.

The power had flooded through him as he'd taken her.

He'd surrounded her with darkness. Locked her away. Held the ultimate sway over her life.

After that girl, he hadn't tried to hold back. When the urge came for another—he took her.

A new girl, a new year. The same rush.

He taught his girls. They learned to obey him. If they didn't obey, they suffered.

Some learned faster than others.

Some...didn't learn at all.

The car fishtailed off the dirt road, cutting once again into the highway. He jerked the wheel, bringing the vehicle under control. He had to play this cool.

He passed the bright lights of a gas station, and almost missed the blonde who was hurrying out of a red sports car.

He slowed his vehicle.

The blonde disappeared into the gas station.

The girl, the blonde…she might not be perfect, she might not be what he wanted—

But the agent took my girl.

So he'd have to make do.

Because the urges within him were too strong to deny. He would show the FBI. He would show them all.

They can't stop me.

***

"How did you know?" Christa whispered. She was standing to the side, watching as the tow truck settled in to haul her car away.

Kyle saw that she was still shaking. She'd been terrified when they first approached her. Terrified, with good reason.

Christa had been prey tonight.

"Cadence knew." His stare slid to her. She was huddled with some local cops, talking quietly. No doubt telling the men to keep their eyes open as they continued patrolling.

They had a killer in the area.

When they'd left that back room and headed into the main bar area once again, Cadence's attention had focused on the waitress. The one with the nervous hands who jumped so quickly to obey Dale's instructions.

Cadence had made a quick call to Dani, and they'd pulled up Christa Donaldson's background information almost instantly. No speeding tickets. No jail records. A model citizen.

When they'd questioned Dale again, he'd told them about Christa's mother.

A good girl. They'd followed her because Cadence wasn't wrong when it came to victim profiles.

Never wrong.

The patrons in the bar had been pairing up. They'd actually seemed to have gotten the message about not leaving alone.

Christa had slipped out alone, with her shoulders hunched.

"Why me?" Christa asked, voice breaking.

"You're his type." The bastard *had* gone back to the beginning. Back to his location pattern. He'd lost Lily, and Kyle had known the killer would have to strike immediately again. They'd headed straight to Maverick and were prepared to stay as long as it took for the killer to strike. They hadn't had to wait long. Part of Kyle was surprised how little they'd had to wait. Because they hadn't delayed their search in Maverick, Christa was alive.

But now he wondered…since he hadn't been successful in Maverick, did that mean he'd go on to the next city? Hit again, as soon as he could? If so…

We'll be ready for you.

But they weren't giving up on this county yet. The perp had been there, and he'd lay odds the guy had been *in* that bar. *Did he see us? Was he there when Cadence and I went inside?* So many people had been crammed into that place. Too many faces.

"Christa." Cadence came toward her, moving quickly, easily, over the broken road. "Did you talk with anyone tonight? Anyone who might have asked you some personal questions? Anyone who wanted to know a little too much about you?"

Christa's hands were clenched in front of her. "No." She hesitated. "Well, just my regular."

It was so dark, she probably wouldn't be able to read his expression, but just in case, Kyle made sure to control his emotions. "Your regular?"

She nodded. "Yeah. The guy's been coming in for years."

"How many years?" Cadence asked before Kyle could.

Christa rubbed her hands over her arms. "At least five. I mean, as long as I've been there."

Could the guy have been going back, visiting all of his abduction sites?

Yes. Killers liked to head back to those locations. The sites comforted them, gave them a rush of power.

"What does this regular look like?" Kyle was too conscious of his thundering heart as he waited for her answer.

"He's got dark hair, dark eyes. He's big. Not fat, but built."

"His age?" Kyle had to fight to keep his voice level.

"Probably in his thirties. Maybe in his forties. It's hard to tell. The lighting in Dale's is crap. And the guy usually wears a ball cap." She rocked back on her heels.

"Does he have a name?" Kyle asked her instead of answering.

"Billy?" The name sounded like a question. "He always pays in cash."

He would. The guy wouldn't want to leave a trail behind.

"You told me I could go home." Christa's voice thickened. "My mom had a stroke. She needs me. I *have* to get home."

"We'll get you to your mother, but Christa, we're going to need you to talk with some cops first thing in the morning. To get a sketch going of your regular."

How long would it take to get a good sketch artist in town? He'd make a call to the FBI office. They'd get a guy there by dawn.

"I want to see my mom first. Before anything else. She *needs* me," Christa said again.

Fair enough.

He led Christa to his car. Opened the back door. Christa slid inside, the tears drying on her cheeks.

When he looked up, he saw Cadence hadn't moved. He hurried back to her. "What is it?" Her instincts about Christa had been dead-on. Cadence had saved the waitress's life that night. But she didn't look pleased.

Her body was tense, her posture almost afraid.

"He didn't get her," she whispered. "So who will he take?"

He glanced down the dark, stretching road.

And wondered if the killer was hunting right then.

***

"Shut the fuck up!"

The bitch wouldn't stop screaming. He had his radio on, but it wasn't drowning out her screams. And the cops—

They were everywhere.

She was still screaming.

He'd told her to be quiet.

She hadn't listened.

Still screaming.

Another cop car passed him.

Could the guy hear her screams? *No, no...*

The patrol car kept going.

He started breathing again. This wasn't working.

He pulled off the road. Cut his lights. The old diner was closed, had been for at least two years.

He eased in behind the building.

Her screams were even louder now.

He shoved open his door. Hurried to the trunk. Yanked it up.

The bitch sprang at him. Jumped right for him. He grabbed her, trying to choke off the screams.

When his hands pressed on her windpipe, the screams stopped. Silence. That perfect silence of death. Only…the rush wasn't there.

He didn't let her go.

She wasn't what he wanted. Wasn't good enough.

His head was pounding. His hands shaking. She'd had a car similar to Maria's. The bright, flashing red. The red that had first caught his eye.

But this one didn't understand her role. She wasn't supposed to fight. She was supposed to obey. To follow all of his orders.

He kept squeezing her throat.

She never screamed again.

***

Sunlight was just cutting across the sky when Kyle opened the door to the motel room. Another cheap motel, complete with faded carpeting and a sagging bed.

One room.

This time, it had been by request.

He shut the door behind Cadence.

"We did it."

She glanced up at his words.

"We didn't arrive too late. We *saved* Lily. We saved Christa."

A faint smile trembled on her lips.

He took two steps and had her in his arms. Held her tight.

Cadence. He'd thought she didn't have hope. Too late, he was realizing she was *his* hope.

His mouth took hers. He lifted her higher, holding her fully as he carried her weight easily.

Her legs wrapped around his hips.

They wouldn't have much time. Just a few hours to crash before they reported in at the local police station.

More questions. More searching.

But for that moment, that one moment—

I have her.

He pulled his mouth from hers. Began to kiss a hot path down the curve of her neck. Her legs tightened around him.

She likes this.

He licked. Lightly bit her silken skin.

Her hands fumbled, pushing between them, trying to get his shirt out of the way.

He wanted to rip his clothes off, shred hers. Wanted to be *in* her.

Would it be as good as before? Was that even possible? It had to be the adrenaline kick he'd had after surviving the cave-in and finding Lily. No way could the sex have really been that mind-blowing.

No fucking way.

They fell onto the bed. Rolled. Cadence came up above him. Stared down at him with eyes that glowed with an emotion he couldn't name.

Lust was there, yes, desire, but something more lurked in those golden depths. Something he couldn't make out.

"This is a mistake," she whispered.

"Then it's the best fucking mistake I've ever made."

She smiled then.

His heart stopped.

Her hands went to his zipper, pulled it down with a hiss that seemed to vibrate through him. She shoved the pants away.

Her fingers curled around the aroused flesh that thrust so eagerly toward her.

Her head bent.

"*Cadence.*" If she put that mouth on him—those full red lips—he was gone. "Be careful, I don't know..." *How long I can last.*

"Let's see how far I can push." She didn't seem afraid. She never did.

She put her mouth on him.

Fuck.

His eyes wanted to roll back in his head. She licked and sucked and had his hands fisting into the bedcovers.

"Enough." He couldn't hold on, not anymore, and when he exploded, he wanted her with him.

Cadence rose above him. Straddled him with the legs that blew his mind. She'd ditched her pants. When? She still had on her shirt. No panties, though, because he felt warm, wet flesh press against him.

He parted her folds. Pushed two fingers into her and enjoyed the flush covering her cheeks.

When they were in bed, it wasn't about being agents.

It was about—

She's mine.

"I'm clean." His voice was a snarling rumble he should have hated. Hadn't he sworn he'd give her seduction this time? Gentleness? "No diseases, nothing." He wanted to thrust into her, to feel that hot flesh all around him. "Are you—"

"I'm protected." Her breath panted. "No diseases."

He'd never gone bare. With her, it was all he could think about.

Staring into her eyes, unable to look away, he thrust into her. *So tight.*

He knew he couldn't last. Not in that sensual heat that was driving him mad. His hands locked on her hips. *Holding her too tightly, go easier, be careful.*

He couldn't stop.

He lifted her, brought her back down. Thrust in and out. She was rising on the bed in perfect tune with him. A frantic rhythm that *couldn't* stop. Faster. Harder. Deeper.

The bed was thudding into the wall. Release was seconds away.

Cadence had to come first. He needed to feel—

"Kyle!"

Her delicate inner muscles clenched around him. Pleasure flashed across her face. The most beautiful thing he'd ever seen.

When his release hit him, he knew he'd been wrong. The first time with her had been good. The second had made him an addict. No one else would ever do.

No one else was Cadence.

***

He'd made a mistake.

He stared down at the small house, the place sheltering Christa.

A sheriff's car waited out front. A man in uniform had been stationed at her door.

There was probably another deputy inside.

Mistake. He'd realized it as dawn came calling.

The agents hadn't noticed him at the bar, but Christa had seen his face. He'd visited her too many times. *She knows me.*

The agents would have questioned her. They would have asked who she'd talked with that night. Who showed her too much attention.

She would have remembered him. His stupid fucking good tips. He'd given her the tips so she'd feel more comfortable with him. So she'd talk more. Tell him about herself.

He'd learned about Christa.

But in turn, she'd learned about him. Christa knew what he looked like.

The agents would want Christa to work with a sketch artist. He knew the drill. Christa would tell them all she knew.

In a few hours, his picture would be on every television in the Southeast.

He'd worked too hard to lose everything.

"I'm sorry." Christa wouldn't hear those words. She'd never have a chance to hear them. Things shouldn't have ended this way for her. He would've taken care of her. Enjoyed her.

Savored sweet Christa.

But she had to die. *Now.*

Before the agents came back for her. Before the sketch artist arrived.

Before everything was destroyed.

The door to her house opened. A man in a sheriff's uniform came outside. He talked to the deputy.

They hurried down the steps, moving toward the waiting patrol car.

This was it.

Another vehicle pulled up. Sweat trickled down his back. He knew that vehicle. Agent McKenzie was already on the scene. There was no more time to waste.

McKenzie was *there*.

So was Cadence.

His breath whispered out. He didn't like doing this. It was wrong.

Christa appeared in the doorway. Her shoulders were hunched. Through the scope on his rifle, he realized she was pale.

Christa hadn't slept well.

Lovely Christa.

This wasn't the way it should have been.

His finger pulled back the trigger as the sheriff turned and reached for her.

Then he fired.

***

Blood bloomed on the sheriff's chest, a thick circle even as the crack of gunfire echoed around them.

Shot.

Christa screamed and lunged toward the sheriff.

"No!" Cadence yelled.

But it was too late.

Christa was trying to help, but she should have run the other way. Gone back inside. Been safe.

The second shot hit Christa. So did the third.

Cadence could hear Kyle yelling, swearing. His gun was out and he was trying to get to Christa. But Cadence was closer. She'd been just a few feet from the sheriff.

Cadence dove for the other woman. She curled her body around Christa's and tried to pull her to safety.

Then she saw the wounds.

One hit had been to Christa's head. A shot that had torn across the right side of Christa's skull. The second shot had gone in her chest.

"Christa, *stay with me*." The same words she'd given to Lily, but Christa's wounds…

She won't make it. Cadence knew there would be no saving her.

Christa's eyes were already closed.

She was already gone.

Cadence heard the thunder of footsteps. She looked up. Kyle was running toward the line of trees on the northwest side. Running without backup.

The sheriff started to wheeze.

"Go after him!" she yelled to the deputy. The guy, fresh faced, ghost white, clutched his gun and nodded.

But he didn't move.

"Agent McKenzie needs backup!" She eased Christa onto the ground and crawled to the sheriff's side. Oh, Christ, what a mess. "Go after Agent McKenzie!"

She yanked out her phone and called for backup. Then she put her hands on the sheriff's chest. Sheriff Henry Coolidge, aged fifty-two. A grandfather of four. His newest grandbaby had been born just three days before. He'd shown her a picture of the little girl last night.

She'd run a check on him, as she did all the folks she brought in on the investigation.

"Henry." His name whispered from her.

His lips moved. He was trying to talk. Choking.

She knew what the wheezing sound meant. His lungs were filling with blood. If she didn't work fast, he was dead.

The deputy's footsteps thundered away.

Finally going to give Kyle the backup he needed.

While Cadence got to work trying to save the man before her.

***

Kyle raced through the trees, his heart pounding in his ears. The SOB was *there*. He'd come out into those woods, and he'd eliminated Christa.

She saw your face. She knew you.

Fuck, but he hadn't thought the guy would shoot her. The profile indicated the perp was an up-close, intimate killer.

But when a man was desperate, he could do anything.

Kyle reached the incline, the perfect spot where the killer had been. Grass was bent, as if the man had been crouching there for a while. Kyle even saw the indention of a shoe print. He'd get techs out to make a cast of the print.

You screwed up. By hunting this way, you left evidence behind.

Then he heard the growl of an engine. Kyle's head snapped up. "Agent McKenzie!"

Kyle ran toward the growling engine, not slowing for the deputy. His legs pumped, faster and faster.

Branches cut into him, slicing over his arms and face. The growl was starting to fade away.

He broke from the woods and stumbled into the road. It was a tight, curving road. He raced into the curve, and saw the back of a car, wide and dark. Then the car was roaring away.

No.

He yanked out his phone. As soon as his contact at the sheriff's office answered, he barked. "Lock down Highway Thirty-One! Get troopers and deputies out there!" His breath sawed out of his lungs. "We need an APB out for a black vehicle." What the hell kind had it been? Similar to a cop car. "Looked like a Dodge Charger. Heading west on Highway Thirty-One. The suspect is armed and dangerous and should be approached with extreme caution."

If they could get the car, put up the roadblock in time...

Then we've got you, you SOB.

***

Cadence stared down at the body. She was in what passed for the morgue in Maverick, a small county office that was chilled and smelled too strongly of antiseptic.

Christa Donaldson was in front of her. Covered by a thin, white sheet.

Christa's mother had come out, seen her daughter, and collapsed. She was in the hospital then.

The doctors weren't very optimistic about her chances of recovery.

Sheriff Henry Coolidge was still alive, mostly, anyway. When she'd left him at the hospital, he'd been attached to more machines than she could count.

On scene, she'd helped the EMTs insert an endotracheal tube into his lungs to help him breathe. That tube had saved his life. Now, if he could just get off the ventilator, Henry might pull through and be able to see his grandkids again.

But Christa would never see anyone.

"I'm sorry," Cadence whispered to her. Like Lily, Christa had given her hope, something she didn't have much of. A victim who'd been saved, only to be gunned down in front of her.

The door squeaked open behind her. Cadence stiffened, wondering if it was the ME. There were other questions that she'd need to ask him.

"I know you don't like the dead bodies"—Dani Burton's voice was soft—"so want to tell me why I find you hiding in here with her?"

Cadence turned. "What are you doing here?"

She was so glad to see her friend. She had to blink a few times because the antiseptic made her eyes watery. *Must have been the antiseptic.* Great. Now she was even lying to herself. *The case is getting to me.* Seeing a familiar face, the face of someone who knew her so well, had Cadence feeling a rush of emotion.

Dani's black hair was pulled back, secured at her nape, and her dark coffee-cream skin glowed, even under the horrible fluorescent lights. Dani was a beautiful woman. She was so pretty that people often underestimated just how smart she was.

Dani used that underestimation to her advantage, all the time.

"We'd just touched down in Paradox when we heard about what was happening over here." Dani let the door close behind her as she approached Cadence. Dani's dark gaze drifted to the victim. "How old was she?"

Cadence pulled in a steadying breath. Dani had said *we'd just touched down.* It meant the boss, Ben Griffin, must be there, too. Backup. With the way this case was going, she and Kyle needed more FBI agents in their hunt. "Twenty-nine."

Dani's lips thinned. "He just couldn't let her go."

"She knew him. The perp had been at her table, talking to her the night before." Deputies were at the bar right then, questioning all of the waitresses, trying to get the names of any people who'd been there the night before. "She was going to talk with a sketch artist this morning."

Dani shook her head as her gaze lingered on the sheet-covered figure of Christa Donaldson. "Doesn't seem right, does it? She got away once. It should have been enough. Nobody should have to face a monster twice." Her gaze came back to Cadence. "Some men just can't let go."

Some men were more monster than anything else.

"The roadblocks haven't turned up anything," Cadence said as she ran a tired hand over the back of her neck. "The car hasn't been spotted again, but with all the woods and cabins in this part of the country, the guy could have just stashed the ride somewhere and taken another one."

If he'd been smart, and she sure thought the killer was. He would have planned ahead. Had another vehicle waiting just in case he'd been spotted at Christa's house.

Kyle did spot you. Spotted him, but had been unable to stop the perp.

"I'll run a check," Dani said with a decisive nod. "Get a listing of all the cabins and rentals in a thirty-mile radius of the crime scene. We can search them all."

With Dani's skills, they'd have the information yesterday.

Dani's gaze drifted over Cadence. "You realize you have blood on you?"

Dried blood, staining her shirt. "It's the sheriff's."

Dani's eyes widened. "Just how close were you to the guy?"

Not close enough to protect him. "*I* worked up the profile on him. I should have realized how desperate he'd be if he knew a witness had seen him."

"This woman's death isn't on you."

"Isn't it?"

She sure felt like it was.

Her gaze slid back to Christa. *I'm sorry.*

Before Cadence could say anything else, the door flew open again. A young deputy with flushed cheeks stood in the doorway. "Agent Hollow!" His voice cracked on her name. "W-we found someone else…"

***

Patrol cars were parked haphazardly in the old diner's parking lot. Men in uniform rushed around the scene.

Cadence advanced slowly. *This woman's death isn't on you.* Dani's words seemed to echo in her mind.

They weren't just talking about one woman's death any longer.

Cadence slipped behind the diner and saw the body.

Another victim.

The blonde was on the ground, her arms spread beside her. Fully dressed, except for one high-heeled shoe that had slipped off her foot.

The ME crouched beside her.

Cadence pulled on her gloves. She schooled her expression and bent near the victim. She could easily see the bruises on the woman's throat. Carefully, she tilted the blonde's head. More bruises were behind her ears.

"Her eyes are bloodred," said Kathy Warren, the chief—okay, *only*—ME in Maverick. The young doctor was in her midthirties and had short black hair. Kathy lifted one of the woman's eyelids so Cadence could see for herself.

She didn't flinch at the sight of that blue eye stained red. Cadence had stopped flinching long ago. When the killer had been strangling the woman, blood had been forced into the sclera, the white portion of the eye. A classic sign of strangulation.

Cadence studied the body's rigor. "She hasn't been dead long."

"No, she hasn't," the ME agreed softly, sadly.

Just a few hours. The killer had been denied Christa, so he'd chosen another victim.

"You weren't what he was looking for," Cadence whispered to the dead woman.

The ME glanced up, frowning.

Cadence turned away from the body. *Strangulation.* She could see the act so easily in her mind. A woman, screaming—and a man's hard hands stopping those screams forever.

The perp had picked the wrong woman.

Cadence slid off her gloves and reached for her phone. Kyle needed to know what was happening. Because it sure looked like their killer was losing his control. He was breaking his own patterns.

Becoming even more dangerous.

***

No one at the bar remembered Christa's regular customer. The bar had been dark, too crowded. The guy who'd sat in Christa's booth hadn't stood out to any of the staff.

A crime tech was dusting for prints at the table. Only the table had been washed down, and cleaned too fucking thoroughly, just after closing time.

Kyle shoved open the bar's door. Stalked outside into the blinding sunlight.

The Dodge Charger had vanished. His witness was dead. The killer was still on the loose.

And he's going to hunt again.

His phone vibrated in his pocket. He yanked it out. "McKenzie." The word growled with frustrated fury.

"We've got another body." Cadence's voice was soft where his had been snapping.

Another body.

"A blonde female was just found behind an abandoned diner." She rattled off the address. Her voice sounded hollow. "Can you meet me there?"

"Is this *his*?" Their perp didn't kill and dump a body so quickly.

He also hadn't shot a victim, not until that morning. *Not one we know about.*

"She was a single woman, traveling alone, killed during the night when our killer was in the vicinity." Voices murmured in the background. "Until I learn otherwise," Cadence said, her words still soft and completely lacking emotion, "I'm thinking it's him."

He hadn't seen Cadence, not since she'd raced away with the ambulance and the sheriff.

There'd been so much blood then.

"Cadence." He walked away from the building, hunched his shoulders. "Are you okay?" Her voice worried him. Yeah, Cadence was controlled, but this was different. *She's too cold.*

"I hadn't felt hope in a long time," she said, her words even softer now. So soft he had to strain in order to hear it. "It's hard to find something, then to lose it immediately." She cleared her throat. "I'm at the scene. Meet me here?"

"On the way." On the fucking—

The line was dead.

He rushed for his vehicle. Another body. If the kill at the diner was his, then the perp could be breaking down. Losing control.

It would explain why he'd gone after Christa with his gun. The gun wasn't his weapon of choice, so maybe he'd misfired. Hit the sheriff first, then finally managed to eliminate Christa.

A perp who lost control was sloppy. He'd leave evidence behind. *Like the shoe print.* Size twelve. Men's. An uncontrolled perp would be easier to catch.

A man like that was also much, much more dangerous. Unpredictable. The pattern of his kills could change.

There would be no dormant time for him, no cooling down between kills.

A bloodbath could be heading their way.

Kyle jumped into the vehicle. Punched the address in his GPS and hoped he wasn't about to start following a trail of bodies.

***

Kyle stared down at the blonde as a tech took her picture, cataloging the scene behind the old diner.

The woman's hair was blonde, falling just below her shoulders, and she was young. It looked like she'd been as young as Maria had been when his sister vanished.

Her hands were beside her, palm up.

She looked weak. Broken.

"Asphyxiation," Cadence said as she stood behind him. "There's petechial hemorrhaging in both eyes."

He hadn't seen the victim's eyes. Hadn't gotten close enough to touch her. "How long did it take for her to die?"

Cadence's breath rasped out softly. "Her windpipe was crushed. She would have died within a few minutes."

Strangulation was all about control. He'd worked a serial case hunting a strangler months before. Controlling the breath that your victim took could be the ultimate power trip.

They already knew their perp wanted power.

"If this is our guy, why didn't he take her?" Why kill her and dump her so soon? That wasn't his MO.

"There's bruising on her hands."

"She hit him?" Maybe there was DNA.

"Based on the pattern"—Cadence's voice was thoughtful—"I think she was pounding on a hard surface."

Like a trunk. "Pounding and screaming," he muttered.

The screaming would explain the strangulation.

Cadence glanced at him. "*If* this is our guy, he would've been looking for a victim, been pissed because he lost Christa."

"Your girl drove a red convertible," Dani said as she walked toward them. She had a tablet in her hand, was scrolling through the information there. "It was just found, at a gas station about five miles away."

"When my sister vanished, she was driving a red convertible." Had the guy seen her, seen the car, and remembered?

"He took her," Kyle said, certain now. "But she wasn't what he wanted." She hadn't listened to his orders. He'd had to pick the girl too fast. *Did that mean you didn't have time to screen her? To see if she'd be good enough?*

"Hold on, Kyle." Dani shook her head. He noticed she didn't look directly at the victim. Danielle never did. The victims always made her too nervous. She wasn't usually in the field. She stayed safely shut in her office. Behind all those locked doors at the bureau. "We need more evidence before we start saying this girl is *his*."

Kyle's phone vibrated. He yanked it from his pocket. Glanced down.

Blocked caller.

The breath in his lungs became icy. "Cadence." He snapped out her name right before he took the call.

She glanced at him, her left eyebrow rising.

"Who the hell is this?" Kyle demanded.

Cadence's eyes widened.

Laughter rasped across the line. "You know." A dark, rasping voice.

His voice.

"We need a trace on that call," Cadence said to Dani. "We need it *now*."

"Do you feel hunted?" Kyle asked him. He knew he had to keep the guy on the line as long as possible. Dani was already working frantically, typing on her tablet and talking to her crew at Quantico. They'd need to ping cell towers and trace the signal. He had to buy as much time as he could. "We're closing in on you. I *saw* you today."

"I let you. Just like I let you find that poor girl behind the diner. The woman you're standing over right now."

Fuck. *He can see me.* He mouthed the words to Cadence. She eased back. Went to talk with the cops in the area. Then he saw them all spread out.

They'd start searching.

"I don't buy that she's yours," he said, but he did. "This isn't the way you kill."

"You think you know me." The words were mocking. "But Agent McKenzie, you don't know anything."

"You take your victims, you keep them. You didn't keep her."

"She wasn't good enough."

Sick prick.

"My girls have to be just right." His voice never rose over a low rasp. "I thought the little blonde might work, but she wasn't like the original."

Maria.

"I know you, Agent. The man who takes down the killers… you like to see your name in the papers, don't you?"

He didn't give a shit about the press. "I'm going to take you down."

"Maria's hero," that rasping voice mused. "How quickly you forgot her."

"I *never* forgot!" The rage surged within him.

"Now no one will forget." Satisfaction was there, thickening the words. "They will all know what's been done. All know that no one can stop me."

Bullshit. Kyle would stop him.

"You haven't asked to talk with her." The words faded into a whisper. "Don't you want to hear from Maria again?"

What he wanted was to kill that SOB. "It's hard to talk with a ghost."

More laughter. "Why do you think I killed them all? You only found one body in those caverns."

Kyle's shoulders tensed. How the fuck did he know that?

Cadence had disappeared into the trees. Dani was still close. "Not yet," she mouthed to him.

They didn't need the cell tower pings. The SOB was right there. Kyle's gaze swept the line of trees. The rolling hills. So many places to hide.

"If they die too quickly, then what's the point?"

"You killed this one fast enough," Kyle pointed out. The scent of death was heavy in the air.

"That bitch wouldn't stop screaming, so I stopped her! You don't follow the rules, and you get punished."

"Bullshit," Kyle called. "You get off on killing, so you do it. That's why you shot Christa."

"Christa wasn't the first one I aimed for."

"The sheriff's gonna make it." *He'd better.* "Your aim was shit."

"Yes." A surprising admission. "I wasn't trying to hit the sheriff, either."

He tried to remember who'd been close to the sheriff.

"You took my girl away," the voice told him, rasping now. "So I'm going to take *yours*."

Cadence had been the only other person close to the sheriff. His blood had splattered on her.

His heart slammed into his ribs. *I can't see Cadence.* She'd vanished into those woods.

The killer waited in those woods.

"No, no, you're fucking *not!*" Kyle snarled into the phone.

Dani's head jerked up.

"*Let me go.*"

That voice. Maria's voice.

"*I want to go home. Kyle, I want to go home!*"

Tears choked her.

Then all he heard was silence.

"Kyle?" Dani touched his arm. "Kyle, the call is coming from somewhere in a five-mile radius. We couldn't pinpoint it any better than that."

The phone's screen cracked. He tried to ease the pressure of his hand, but couldn't. "Cadence." It was all he could manage right then.

"She's searching for him now."

"He wants Cadence."

Dani stumbled back.

Kyle's fingers slid over the broken phone's screen. With one touch, he was calling her, even as he raced for the woods. For the last spot he'd seen her.

Cadence's gun had been out when she went into the woods. She was a federal agent. Trained. She could handle herself.

Answer the phone. Answer…

***

Cadence advanced slowly. She kept her gun up as she swept the area. From what she'd heard, it had sure sounded like the perp was watching Kyle at the diner.

Even with binoculars, he'd have to be close.

Where are you?

The land slanted upward. Four deputies had branched out, searching with her. She kept trying to find the telltale glint of metal in the brush. The flash of a lens on the binoculars, but she didn't see anything.

Insects buzzed around her. The heat of the Tennessee summer had her T-shirt sticking to her skin.

Her phone vibrated, shaking in her pocket. She fished it out with her left hand. "Hollow."

"*He's after you.*" Kyle's voice. Shaken. Furious. Harder than she'd ever heard before. "The sonofabitch told me that he wants you."

She retreated a few steps, putting her back against the broad base of a tree. Her eyes kept scanning the area. "I haven't caught sight of him."

"Come back down here. Fuck, come on *now*, Cadence."

"This is what I'm trained for. I have my vest on and I've got my gun." She wouldn't give in to fear. "He can see me regardless, and if I start rushing out of here now, then I might just make myself more of a target." It would be better for her to lie low and search for the perp. *You're hunting me? We'll see who gets caught first.*

"Then I'm coming to you! Where the hell are you?"

"About fifty yards northwest of the diner. There's a tree here, a pine that's been stripped of bark." Like it had been struck by lightning.

"*Stay* there. I'm coming." She could hear him running. Hear the hard rasp of his breath.

She also heard a twig snap, to the right of her.

Cadence whirled. A deputy stood about twenty feet away. "Sorry, ma'am. Didn't mean to scare you." A deep drawl accented his words. He inclined his head. The glaring southern sun was behind him, and his long shadow swept forward. A wide-brimmed hat drifted low over his forehead and he wore a pair of sunglasses. He began to retreat from her. "No sign of him in this area. I'm heading on up to check near the top of the slope." The rising sun was behind him, pushing shadows over his body so that she couldn't see his face clearly.

Cadence had to squint against the bright sunlight. She had her gun aimed toward the guy's chest even as her left hand still clutched the phone to her ear. "Keep your radio on," Cadence ordered as she slowly lowered her weapon. "If you see anything, you call me."

With a quick nod, he turned away.

Her gaze fell down his body.

"Cadence, Cadence, *you better still be next to that tree.*"

The deputy was wearing brown hiking boots.

Hiking boots.

She frowned. He shouldn't be wearing those boots. The other guys hadn't been. She'd noticed with a quick, cursory glance that the other deputies were all wearing the usual black boots customary for officers in this area. Not hiking boots.

You wore hiking boots when you knew you would be climbing. The deputies today hadn't known they'd be searching the woods, not until she'd given them the order.

"Deputy!" she called out.

He didn't look back. The guy headed into thick patch of brush.

"*Deputy!*" Her cry sent birds flying into the air.

If she waited for Kyle, the man would be gone.

He *could* just be a deputy. One who'd come prepared with hiking boots. But why ignore her call?

Just a deputy…

Or he could be their killer. "I'm moving," she said, clutching her phone with her left hand even as her grip on the gun remained steady. "Heading up the slope."

"What?" Kyle's bellow burst in her ear. "Don't! Just stay where you are until I'm there. Dammit, I'm your backup. Wait for me."

"Following a suspect."

"No, Cadence. *No!*"

She wasn't a helpless victim. If the SOB turned on her, she'd shoot him straight in the heart.

She hurried forward.

"I'm almost to you, Cadence, *stay* there. Just stay!"

She hadn't become an FBI agent so that she'd hide and wait for someone else to protect her.

She burst up onto the slope. Cadence saw the back of the deputy. "Freeze!" she shouted.

The phone fell to the ground. She gripped the gun with both hands, her left coming up to steady the weapon as she took aim.

The deputy froze. His back was still to her. "What's the problem, ma'am?"

"Turn around!" She wanted to see his face. Needed to see it. The wide hat covered his hair.

Slowly, the man turned. His weapon was drawn.

"Drop it!" Cadence yelled.

He hesitated.

"Drop it or I shoot."

"Ma'am?"

He dropped the weapon.

She advanced. Cleared the brush enough to realize…

This man wasn't wearing hiking boots. He had on the regular black shoes of the deputies. The breath left her lungs in a hard rush. *Not him.* "Where's the other deputy? The one who just came this way?"

"I didn't see another deputy. This was my search zone." His voice was shaking. His eyes wide and nervous.

Probably because her gun was aimed at his heart.

"*Cadence!*" Kyle rushed to her side. "What the hell is happening?" He already had his gun out, and aimed at the deputy whose whole body was now trembling.

"It's not him," she whispered. "There was another man, dressed as a deputy. He had on hiking boots." Her gaze darted to Kyle as she lowered her weapon. "He was right here."

A muscle jerked in Kyle's clenched jaw.

She glanced away from him. Let her gaze sweep the line of trees stretching as far as she could see.

The killer was playing with them.

She was tired of his game.

CHAPTER TEN

The FBI unit director was pissed.

Special Agent Ben Griffin marched back and forth in Sheriff Coolidge's small office. Since the man was still in the hospital—recovering, thankfully—they'd taken over his space while they were in Maverick.

"What the hell is happening here?" Ben demanded. "A witness is *dead*. On our watch. Do you know how this is gonna look to the press? *In* the press?"

Kyle didn't really give a damn how it looked to them.

But the killer cares. Kyle knew he did. The SOB had brought up the papers. *You want the attention, don't you?* He'd hunted fifteen years in secrecy, but now he was trying to catch as much attention as he could. Shooting a sheriff. Dumping a body at the diner. *You want all eyes on you.*

And they were.

"This perp is jerking us around," Ben snapped. "He's slipping right through our fingers."

He'd been in those woods. Killing close to Cadence.

Ben's steely blue gaze pinned him. "You know you should be off the case."

Kyle lurched to his feet. "The hell I should!"

Ben waved that away. "It's too personal. The connection to your sister, the way this fellow is calling you. You can't be objective."

He wasn't going to be shoved to the side on this one. "It's *because* of my connection that you need me. He's not going to contact any other agents. He won't. He's pulling me in because he likes screwing with me."

"It's a dangerous game," Ben said. His stare focused on Cadence. She sat in the chair just a few feet away. "One that could wind up hurting someone."

Ben had already been briefed on the phone calls. He knew everything the perp had said. Everything he'd threatened.

"I'm not afraid of him," Cadence said, lifting her chin.

"I am," Dani muttered from her position behind the desk. She was tapping frantically on her laptop.

Ben glowered at Cadence. The guy had trained her, even worked as her partner before his promotion. Sometimes when he looked at Cadence, there was an intimacy in his stare that put Kyle on edge.

Had they been lovers?

"You're never afraid when you *should* be," Ben muttered to Cadence. "That's part of the problem. The guy said he was targeting *you*. He was going to take you out. If he'd been better with his gun, you wouldn't even be here now."

Ben's attention turned back to Kyle. "Don't you see the risk we're running? You're already emotionally involved. He's using that. Getting you twisted up so you can't effectively hunt him."

"All he's doing"—Kyle kept his voice flat, cold, because now wasn't the time for emotions—"is making me more determined to stop him." He gave a grim nod. "He's slipping up."

A furrow appeared between Ben's dark brows.

"He's too confident, cocky, when he talks to me. He said he knew we'd only found one body in the Paradox caverns."

Ben's gaze narrowed. "We didn't release any information about the remains to the press."

No, they hadn't. Cadence had been very, very careful during the press conference.

But when they'd briefed their task force in Paradox, he and Cadence had told *them*.

"He's involved in the investigation," Ben said.

Yes. "You know it happens. Killers insinuate themselves in the investigation all the time," Kyle said. The perps did it to keep tabs on the investigation—and because they liked the rush of thinking that they were outsmarting the authorities. This perp was all about competing with the authorities. The guy wanted to show them all just how strong he was.

"He was wearing a deputy's uniform today," Cadence said and she rolled her shoulders, as if pushing away a heavy burden. "He got everything right about the outfit, except for his shoes."

The bastard had gone hunting for her, but when he'd approached her in those woods, he must have realized Cadence had already been alerted.

She'd been waiting with a gun. *So you had to back away, didn't you?*

"I checked all the deputies after I met up with Kyle. They were accounted for. This guy slipped into the perimeter, and I'm guessing he's done it before."

"He could have walked right into the Paradox station," Kyle said. "Passed by the officers there just as easily as he did today."

With a hat pulled low to hide his face. The right clothes, a badge. The badge would get you anyplace.

A lesson the killer had learned.

"The press is calling him the Night Hunter." Ben barred his teeth in a grimace. "You know how I hate those fucking names. You give a serial a name, you give him power. Fame. They just kill all the more."

Dani stopped talking and slanted a fast glance at Ben. "He killed two girls in the last twelve hours. I think we're safely in the 'kill all the more' zone already."

She went back to typing.

Ben went back to studying Kyle with that narrowed gaze. "You heard your sister's voice again. In the second call."

A slow nod.

"Is it a recording or the real deal?"

"There's too much static, I can't tell for certain."

Ben wasn't backing off. "You tell me the truth 'cause you know I'm damn good at catching a lie. Do you think your sister is still alive? Even after all this time?"

Kyle could feel the weight of Cadence's stare on him. "I want to believe she's alive."

"That's not an answer," Ben snapped, sounding aggrieved. "Do better."

"The killer wants me to think some of the girls are still alive. He all but said they were."

"Killers lie," Cadence stated as she pushed back her hair with a tired hand. "It's what they do."

When they weren't killing.

"There could be other bodies in those caverns." Cadence's voice was cautious. He knew she didn't want to tell him that his sister was dead.

Even though that was precisely what she thought.

"Or someplace else," Ben added. "The guy's hunting grounds sure stretch far enough." Then Ben scrubbed a hand over his face.

"You know how I caught the FBI's attention? Back when I was a cop, hitting the streets of Brooklyn?"

Kyle shook his head.

"I was running down a cold case. A little girl, five years old, who'd vanished from a shopping mall. Every year—every single year on July seventh, the parents came to the station, looking for their little girl. Hoping we had some news. Hoping we had something." His gaze had turned to the past. "When the date started rolling around, the other cops would get nervous. They'd all but told those parents they weren't ever getting the girl back. It had been seven years. Hell, you know what the odds are on a recovery like that."

They all knew the grim stats.

"I got cold case duty, I read through the files, and I thought, 'Hey, why not?' Why not just go back and see if any witness remembers anything else? Why not try to give the parents something new this time?" He swallowed. For an instant, his gaze seemed haunted. "The girl was playing at a park when she vanished. I had a list of the parents who'd had their kids there that day. I started on the list. The first two didn't remember jack. When I went to question them, their kids were running behind them, playing, and I could tell they just wanted me to get away from them."

They hadn't wanted to head back into the nightmare. He'd seen that behavior time and time again. The only way to cope? Pretend it hadn't happened.

"The third guy I visited wouldn't open his door more than a few inches for me."

Kyle tensed.

"According to the notes in the file, he'd been plenty cooperative during the initial investigation. He'd even been the one to identify the suspect, a male in his late forties, wearing a red pullover." Ben's lips tightened. "We never found the suspect. But when I was at that guy's house, standing on the porch trying to get in, you know what I saw?"

No, he didn't.

"I saw a girl's bike propped against the side of his house. Now, see, the man didn't have a little girl. He had a boy, one who'd been Sara's age, but no girl. Sure, the bike could've just belonged to the kid's friend, but the place felt off to me."

Even Dani was watching him now. Her fingers had frozen over her keyboard.

"No matter what I said, I couldn't get the guy to let me in his place, so I finally left. I left, but I came back and started watching the house. That night, he hurried from the house, with two kids with him. A blond boy and a blonde girl, a girl who would have been Sara's age."

Ben rubbed at the faint scar under his chin. Kyle had always wondered about that scar.

"I called out to him because I wanted a better look at the girl, and that was when he pulled the knife. He put it to her throat, and he told me that no one was taking his family away from him."

Silence.

Dani shook her head. "What did you do?"

His fingers fell away from the scar. "I took his fucking family away. He sliced me, but I took him down. Got those kids back to the police station. The girl—"

"She was your missing Sara," Cadence said.

He nodded. "Gone seven years, presumed dead. But very much alive."

Kyle was getting the message. But seven years and fifteen—

"And the blond boy?" Ben continued as his eyes stayed locked on Kyle. "Turned out that guy wasn't his father. The boy had been taken twelve years before. Stolen right out of a hospital in D.C." He exhaled slowly and never looked away from Kyle. "Now, I'm going to ask you again, McKenzie, and I want a real answer. Do you think that was your sister on the phone?"

His hands had fisted. "It was her voice."

"Is she alive? Or is he screwing with you? What does your *gut* say?"

Hope wouldn't die. Not until he saw his sister's body. "Yes, I believe Maria is alive." He looked at Cadence. "I won't ever believe otherwise, not until I see her body." The brutal truth. He wouldn't give up, he'd do anything necessary, until his sister was found.

Found either alive…or dead.

"That's what I needed to hear."

"Why the hell did you need to know that?"

Cadence watched him with worried eyes.

"Because," Ben said, shrugging, "if you thought he'd killed your sister, then I'd have to worry you were just hunting him with the sole purpose of killing him. I needed to know you'd try to bring him in alive." A pause. "We need him alive. I've got at least ten missing women and their family members are just like you. They won't stop searching, not until they know…one way or the other."

Then his gaze went to Cadence. "Are we all clear on this? A kill shot is our last resort with this guy. We want a live capture. We need it."

"I'm clear," Cadence said, her voice soft. "Don't worry."

"I do because if the perp does come for you—and it sure looks like he might—*you* take him down."

"Take him down," she repeated with a faint nod, "but just keep him alive."

"That's the plan."

Dani whistled. "Guys, I've got something."

Their attention immediately shifted to her.

"We've got a hit," Danielle said, her voice cracking with excitement. "I found an owner of a Dodge Charger, a guy who lives about twenty miles from Christa Donaldson's place. The search was easy, because the car links to Jake Landers."

"Shirley Wayne's jailbird ex," Cadence clarified to Ben's questioning look.

When Dani looked up from the screen, her smile was cold. "Jake Landers is ex-military, aged thirty-seven, and he has plenty of arrests on file. The first came over fifteen years ago, when the guy got drunk and put his girlfriend in the hospital for two weeks."

Talk about fitting the profile to a T.

"Seems he didn't like the fact she wanted to breakup with him," Dani continued. "Our guy has a real problem letting women go."

So did their perp.

"At least three women filed restraining orders against him over the years. The man sure has a problem with the concept of rejection."

Or giving up what he wanted.

"What's the address?" Kyle asked as he checked his weapon.

"Forty-five Old Mills Road."

Hell, yes.

He headed for the door. Cadence was right by his side.

Ben hurried behind them. "Remember," the boss directed, "*alive*."

That was the goal.

But one way or another, the guy would be stopped.

***

The cabin sat in the middle of the woods, its small roof sloping, the porch sagging, and wood near the door rotting.

"This is it," Kyle said as the glanced at Cadence. They were lead on the approach, heading in first with local backup right behind them. Backup that had been screened, cleared. No one was slipping by in a deputy's uniform this time.

Cadence nodded, but her gaze, when it found his, was hooded. "Kyle, if this is his place, there could be trophies inside."

Serial killers often kept mementos close to them.

"Can you handle that?" she asked him, worry threading through her voice.

"I can handle anything." He wondered if that was the truth. When he'd thought the killer was targeting Cadence, hadn't he been so desperate to save her that he'd run blindly into those woods? Not stopping when Dani shouted for him. Not stopping for anything, until he could see her.

They had men spreading out in the woods around the cabin. Securing the perimeter. The only road in was already blocked.

It was time to see what waited in that cabin.

He ran forward. They'd gotten a warrant easily enough. In a case like this one, the small-town judge sure hadn't been about to say no to the FBI. When he reached the door, Kyle shouted, "FBI!"

There was no sound from inside.

He didn't want to give the guy any chance to hide or destroy evidence, so he kicked in the door and rushed in, staying low, while Cadence covered him with her gun.

The smell hit him almost instantly. The stench of decay. Rot. Flesh.

She was waiting for them. Tied to a chair, her head sagging forward. Her red hair trailed over her, concealing her face.

Not bones. Flesh.

"Fuck," he bit off.

The bastard had kept a trophy *right in front of him.*

Cadence approached the body cautiously.

"How long?" Kyle demanded.

Cadence's breath came heavily. "We need the ME to be sure."

Bullshit. Cadence knew bodies. She'd even spent time at a body farm last summer, a place that should have sent her spiraling into nightmares but hadn't.

"A week," she whispered as she bent over the woman. "I think she's been dead for about a week."

That would explain why their guy had gone out collecting again. He'd lost—killed—his girl.

He had to find another.

Kyle backed up, his gaze taking in the area. The small kitchen. The closet-sized bathroom to the right side. This section of the cabin was clear. To the left, a small, snaking hallway led to darkness.

The floor creaked beneath his feet as he advanced down the hallway.

He could hear the soft rustle of Cadence's steps behind him.

His fingers curled around the doorknob. It looked like this place only had one bedroom.

He turned the knob. The door swung open easily, but there was no light inside the room.

Was the killer waiting in there?

He crouched low as he entered, not wanting to present a target. His flashlight swept the room.

An old bed. A small desk. A wooden chair.

Nothing else.

No *one* else.

His hand flew out, searching along the wall near the door. Then his fingers were flipping the light switch.

The bulb flickered, then pulsed with light.

No, the guy wasn't there. Just the body he'd left behind.

Kyle turned toward the desk again, then realized there was something on it.

Cadence had already seen it. She was staring down at the desk's surface, the gun gripped tightly in her hand. "It's him," she whispered.

Yeah, the body in the other room had pretty much confirmed that.

He crossed to her side, and realized she was looking at sketches. Nearly a dozen of them. Painstakingly detailed, charcoal sketches.

Of the missing women. He recognized their faces.

His gloved hand pushed aside some of the sketches.

Maria. His sister's image stared up at him. Not a smiling, happy Maria. Not the vision of her that he struggled so hard to keep in his mind.

This Maria was afraid. Her lips were pressed tightly together. Her eyes wide.

Fuck, fuck, fuck.

"Kyle!" Cadence grabbed him and pulled him back. "Focus on me, Kyle, got it?"

He blinked and realized that a haze of red—fury—had covered his vision.

Cadence tapped the small transmitter on her ear. The transmitter linked her to everyone in the search group. "He's not in the cabin, but we have an affirmative. This *is* our perp. Keep searching the woods and get the dogs out here."

Kyle's heartbeat thundered in his ears. His gaze slid back to that picture. Maria. His Maria.

She wasn't a trophy for that bastard. *She was* my sister.

"There will be something here with his scent on it," Cadence told him. "We'll check the whole place."

He knew they would. They'd search every crevice for clues. They'd run down the paper used in those sketches. Figure out where the guy had gotten his charcoal. They'd tear his life apart and take him down.

Kyle's gaze held Cadence's. He choked back the rage and gritted out, "If he's running, if he's hiding out there, we *will* find him."

***

The dogs raced through the woods, searching even as the sun began to set. Kyle ran right after them, not about to be left behind, because they had a scent.

The dogs were barking, so excited they were nearly dragging their handlers, and they'd found their prey.

You won't get away.

They'd found clothing in the cabin. A man's shirt, size large. Some hiking boots, size twelve. The dogs had the scent, and now they had *him*.

They crested a small rise, then dove into a thick patch of pines. Their handlers were fighting to keep the dogs in check. They had him.

The dogs stopped. They were pawing at the ground.

At the loose dirt.

The handlers pulled them back. Two deputies started to carefully brush away some of the dirt.

"Stop!" Kyle's voice snapped out. He could see the remains already.

The flash of white bone. The piece of cloth that one of the dogs' paws had caught.

"Another victim?" a female deputy asked.

He wasn't sure. The scent the dogs followed should have belonged to Jake Landers.

But if Jake Landers was in the ground…

Then who has been killing?

***

Cadence stretched, her spine aching as she finally stepped away from the exam table. She'd been working with the county coroner for most of the night.

First on the redhead they'd found tied in the cabin.

Then on the second set of remains brought in by the deputies.

She studied the files that she'd prepared one more time. There was no denying the evidence on the female victim.

"Why did he just leave her in that house?"

She glanced over at the coroner's voice. Kathy Warren had been incredibly thorough during the exams. All business. Now, Cadence saw the faint moisture at the corner of her eye as Kathy glanced at the remains.

"I don't know," Cadence said.

Kathy swallowed. "I used to work in Nashville. Started in the ER. I saw plenty of murder cases come across my table up there." Her breath blew out as she pulled off her gloves and tossed them in the disposal. "It was the kids who were the hardest. Seeing what people can do to them."

That was the hardest for Cadence, too.

"Why'd he leave her there? Why'd he just let her rot?"

Sometimes, people shouldn't ask questions, not when they really didn't want to hear the answers. Cadence pressed her lips together, but Kathy just waited. The faint ticking of the clock on the left wall sounded incredibly loud. Cadence finally said, "Maybe he didn't want to let her go."

Kathy flinched.

Cadence tossed away her own gloves. The team would be waiting for her upstairs. She strode from the room before Kathy could ask any more questions the woman would be better off not getting answered.

The morgue doors swung shut behind her. She climbed the stairs slowly. The morgue was located in the basement of the sheriff's office, so it only took her a few moments to make her way to the FBI's temporary home.

They'd made copies of the sketches. Pinned them to the walls. The originals would be checked very thoroughly to see if any prints had been left behind. To see if the paper itself could be traced, the type of charcoal used tracked down.

The FBI labs would go over every inch of those sketches. If there was a clue to be found there, they'd discover it.

"Agent Hollow!" She paused and glanced over her shoulder. The coroner was breathing quickly, and she had a file in her hands. "Just got the dental report back on the male."

Cadence took the file. "Thank you." The twist in her gut told her this wasn't going to be the news the task force wanted to hear.

She opened the door and headed inside. Dani looked up from her computer. Ben frowned at Cadence. Kyle didn't look her way. He was still staring at the sketch of his sister.

She cleared her throat. After a moment, Kyle glanced up and then over at her, blinking, as if he'd just stepped out of a daze.

"We have an ID on the remains that were dug up." Her breath eased slowly from her lungs, feeling cold. She rolled her shoulders. They were tight with tension that wasn't going away.

She opened the file. The tension got worse as she read the results. Her stomach knotted. Before she could speak, Kyle said—

"Landers?"

That was what she'd feared—and it was what the report showed. Cadence nodded. "Yes, Landers has been identified from his dental work." Her gaze scanned the file. His ID had been confirmed from two sources. Dental records and from an old knee surgery he'd had years before. The bones—the only things remaining—were definitely Jake's.

"How long has he been dead?" The question was Ben's. He was tapping his fingers on the table, a gesture that from anyone else would have indicated nervousness. With Ben, it meant he was trying to connect the puzzle pieces.

"Quite some time," she murmured. And this was where things were going to get even worse for their investigation. She'd determined this part herself during the exam. "At least four years."

Kyle swore.

Cadence wet her lips, which felt far too dry. "I'm waiting for more testing, but I believe his body was moved recently, that it was put out there in those woods. The clothes we found in the cabin were put there for us. I think the scene was staged." A trail for them to follow. "The killer wanted us to know Jake Landers wasn't the perp." She closed the folder.

Ben's hands flattened on the table. "He wanted to make sure he got the credit. He wanted us to know *he'd* taken all those girls."

Time to tell them all the rest. A last minute report wasn't needed on this one. She knew all the details. "Dental records also helped us to ID our female vic," she said, rubbing the back of her neck. The muscles there had clamped down, squeezing too tightly. "She's Judith Lynn, originally from Tampa, Florida. She was headed up to Chicago."

"Four years ago," Kyle said.

Right. Judith was one of the victims Dani had pulled for them. Back in Paradox, her driver's license photo was on their victim board.

And in Maverick, her sketch was just to the left of Kyle. His gaze cut to the sketch, then back to Cadence.

She's not missing any longer. Four years. Cadence suspected that Jake Landers had been killed right before Judith's abduction. He'd been killed and his cabin and land had been used by the man who would later dump Jake's body in the woods.

Cadence pushed a copy of her report—and the coroner's file on Landers—toward Ben. "She never made it to her aunt's place, and she's been listed as missing since then."

Kyle squared his shoulders. "You've finished examining her body."

Not really a question, but she still softly said, "Yes."

"She disappeared four years ago," Kyle repeated. "So how long has she been dead?"

This was the most painful part. "Based on the decomposition and the presence of insects…" It was the insects that could tell them so much about the time of death.

She saw Dani shudder.

Cadence cleared her throat and said, "The ME and I both agreed Judith Lynn was killed approximately six days ago."

"Fuck," Ben snarled.

Exactly.

"Four years," Kyle said, hands clenching. His eyes had darkened, his cheeks flushed. "He kept her alive for all that time, and killed her *now*?"

She nodded. "There were signs on her body to—" Cadence broke off, hesitating. God, she hated telling him this. She feared that when she described the things that had happened to Judith, Kyle would picture those same things happening to his sister. "There were signs to indicate long-term abuse." Broken bones. Malnutrition. Severe vitamin D deficiency.

Cadence fully believed Judith Lynn had been held prisoner every day since her abduction. She also believed, based on the vitamin D deficiency, that the woman had been held in darkness.

In the caves?

"Why kill her now?" Dani barely whispered the words. Shocked horror was etched across her face. "After that long…"

"Maybe she did something to upset him." Only the killer could tell them for sure. "Maybe she broke one of his rules."

I didn't scream. Lily's voice replayed through Cadence's mind.

"Or maybe he just got tired of her," Kyle growled. His words were hard, biting. "He wanted someone new."

"He already had someone new," Cadence said. She walked toward the sketches and pointed to the woman with the heart-shaped face and big, wide eyes. "Melanie Myers disappeared a year after Judith." She moved the pictures, lining them up as best she could, in order of disappearance. No, not disappearance. Abduction.

She lightly touched the images that came after Judith. "He had Melanie. He had Bridgette Chambers." A square jaw, oval-shaped eyes. "He also had Fiona Slater." High cheeks and a long curtain of hair. "He had them, and he still took Lily Adams."

"He takes one girl a year," Ben said as he ran a rough hand through his close-cropped hair.

Cadence nodded. "Now we know he doesn't always *kill* the girls." At least, not right away.

Four years. *Why couldn't we have found her three weeks ago? Why couldn't someone have found her?*

And who would die next?

"Where's the guy going next?" Dani rose and headed toward the sketches. Her question seemed to mirror Cadence's own fear. "He's following a pattern now, right? Paradox, Maverick, so next up is—"

"Deerfield," Cadence told her. Deerfield, Georgia.

"We've already got cops patrolling there," Kyle added, still in the emotionless voice that was *not* him.

Ben nodded. "They pulled in patrols from two other counties over there. When I checked an hour ago, they were patrolling the back roads and sending out public alerts on every news channel." He glanced over at Dani. "There have been no reports of abductions or abandoned vehicles from the area. If there were, trust me, we'd be on our way to Deerfield."

"Maybe we penned him in here," Dani offered. "We've got all the search units in the woods. The guy *could* still be here."

Yes, he could be.

"If he had a place here and in Paradox"—Kyle blew out a hard breath—"then what's to say he didn't have a place in Deerfield, too? The guy might have a base in each state he hunts."

He could, if he didn't want to transport the victims. But more bases meant more risk. With more locations, there would be less control. The perp would always have to worry about someone finding his hiding spots. Finding his victims.

Had Jake Landers found him? Is that why he wound up dead?

Cadence thought that might just be the reason.

Kyle's head cocked as he studied Cadence. "How did Landers die?"

"A gunshot wound to the chest." The same way Christa had died.

It made sense. Landers had been a big, muscled guy. Taking him out in any close combat manner wouldn't have been easy. To make sure you got the job done, why not use a gun?

"Could they have been partners?" Dani asked as she turned away from the sketched. "I mean, teams work together. We've seen it before."

Yes, they had. Too recently for comfort.

But Cadence wasn't buying the team angle on this one. "I pulled his records. Jake Landers was doing a stint in jail when Judith Lynn vanished."

Dani seemed to absorb that. "So while he was in jail, someone made use of his place."

It looked that way to Cadence.

"Then he came home," Ben continued, picking up the story, "and found someone waiting on him."

With a shotgun.

Ben shook his head. "We shouldn't completely rule Landers out yet." He glanced over at Dani. "Tear apart his background. I want to know the guy's whereabouts for every disappearance, not just Judith Lynn's."

Cadence had been planning to request the background check, too, just in case.

It pays to be careful.

And sometimes, it paid to take risks. "There's something I want to try."

Kyle's gaze had strayed back to the images, but at her words, he frowned, glancing over at her.

She braced herself for the explosion she knew was about to come blasting her way. "At this point, I think we should work under the assumption that one or more of these women may still be alive."

Dani sat down, hard. Maybe she hadn't sat. Maybe her knees had just given way. Cadence had her own knees locked.

Doggedly, Cadence continued, "Our priority isn't just on stopping the killer. It's on bringing these women in alive." They'd already been prisoner for far too long.

If they were alive.

Keep hope. Keep it for Kyle. Kyle, who watched her with his haunted eyes and grim, determined expression.

"Just what is it you want to try?" Dani asked, sounding very, very wary.

Her friend knew her well. Too well.

"If we don't find him soon, we know he *will* take another woman." Maybe he'd go to Deerfield, or maybe not. Since he'd realized that they were following his pattern, then he might try to change on them again.

We have to try to control him. We can't just follow the trail of death he leaves for us.

Kyle stalked toward her. "Cadence." He knew her well, too. The hard glint in his eyes said he knew exactly where she was going with her plan.

She kept her chin up. "He told you that he wanted to take me."

"Cadence, *no.*" Fury ripped through his voice.

She tore her gaze from him. Focused on Ben. She'd need his approval, not Kyle's. "So I say we give him exactly what he wants."

Kyle's hands locked around her arms. "Are you crazy?"

No. She was desperate. "I'm a federal agent. I've been trained to handle myself in any situation that develops. No matter how dangerous." She made herself glance into his blazing eyes. "The way I figure it, I might be our best bet right now. The guy's leading us around, and the bodies are piling up."

"So you want to give him another body?" His voice was a low, deadly rumble. He'd leaned in even closer toward her. "I'm not risking you."

This would seem cruel to him but… "I'm not yours to risk."

He blinked. One slow blink. Then his hands fell away from her.

She sucked in a bracing breath. "He was in those woods. I *know* it was him." The deputy with the wrong boots. "He wants to take me, then I say let him. Wire me up, get a lock on me, and use me as bait. He takes me, and you follow." She trusted the team. She trusted Kyle.

Even if he was staring at her with rage smoldering in his eyes.

"You follow," she said, forcing the words out, "and I'll take you to whatever hole he's hiding in. Then, hell, maybe some of the other victims will be there or—"

"Or we have the guy in custody," Ben cut in, the Brooklyn snapping in his voice and giving the words a hard edge, "and we *make* him tell us."

Yes.

Either way, they'd stop chasing him in the dark.

"Let him take me," Cadence said, "and then we can take *him*."

CHAPTER ELEVEN

It was the worst fucking plan he'd ever heard. Kyle glared at Cadence. She stood there, with shadows under her eyes, her skin too pale, her body too fragile, and the woman was willingly offering herself up as bait for the killer.

"He didn't keep his last victim long enough for anyone to trace her," Kyle said. The words were like razors, slicing across his throat. Cadence wasn't looking him in the eyes.

Look at me.

"He killed the blonde, Valerie Tate." They'd found her ID still inside her abandoned convertible. "And he dumped her body all in the same night. What if he does the same to you? What the hell then?"

Silence. He realized he'd shouted the last question at her. So much for playing it cool.

But this was Cadence's life. It wasn't about playing anything.

"He said he aimed for you at Christa Donaldson's place. He said he was trying to kill you." Kyle's control had splintered. He couldn't stand the thought of Cadence in jeopardy.

"He was lying to you."

"You don't know that!"

"I know he was trying to jerk you around. I know that if he just wanted me dead…" She licked her lips. "He could have shot me in the woods. We both know he probably had the chance."

Fuck.

"What I know," she said, "is how to be the victim he wants." Cadence's voice was soft, such a contrast to his. She was controlled. Certain. So very certain she could jerk around a killer.

He was certain she'd die.

"I can get him to keep me alive, Kyle. I can make this work."

She had her theories, profiles, but they could be screwed to hell and back in an instant. "He's not just jerking the FBI around, he's jerking *me* around." Kyle's words weren't for the others in the room, only for her. Just like his fear was for her. "If he wants to hurt me"—and he knew that was exactly what the bastard wanted—"then he'll kill you his first chance."

And he'd leave her body for Kyle to find.

If that happened, Kyle knew he would be lost.

But Cadence was shaking her head. "We can draw him out. I can do this." Her lips lifted in a faint smile, one that showed no humor. "It's not like this is the first time I've faced a killer."

He knew that.

"Better me than a civilian out there. Another sister or friend who vanishes."

His hands were tight fists.

Cadence turned away from him. Focused on Dani. "I know you have tracking devices you can use."

He saw Dani nod, but worry had tightened her face. "Plenty. You could pick your poison."

"We'd need several," Ben said. *The bastard is considering her plan.* "Just in case one gets disabled, we'd want backups on her."

"This *isn't* happening," Kyle thundered at them. "You can't."

Cadence whirled back around to face him. "Do you want her back?" Some color had come into her face. A flash of red on her high cheekbones.

"Yes," Kyle gritted. But he didn't want to risk Cadence.

"If any of the women are alive, he could panic right now. We're searching for him, and he knows it. Hell, he already broke pattern with Christa's death. *If* they are still alive, maybe he'll decide it's better to eliminate them."

"Or to eliminate you." His voice was flat. There was too much danger to her, she had to see that.

"I'm giving you a chance to get her back." In her golden stare, he saw stark determination. "He *told* you that I was on his list. That means he's already got me in his sights. We use that, okay? We don't wait for me to be prey."

"Making you bait is supposed to be better?"

She shook her head, sending her dark hair sliding over her shoulders. "We just make it easier for him. If we can get him to come for me, then we can get him."

If she died, Kyle didn't know what he'd do.

"Dani." Ben's voice. Calm in the storm. "I think we need to give these two a few minutes alone."

Kyle couldn't look away from Cadence.

He heard footsteps. Dani and Ben heading for the door.

Kyle didn't move. Neither did Cadence.

The door closed with a soft click behind the other agents.

He wanted to put his hands on her, but he didn't trust himself. Wasn't sure what he'd do if he touched her.

Pick her up, run away with her. Get her out of here.

"This is the chance you've always wanted," Cadence told him as a faint line appeared between her brows. "This is your hope. Why aren't you taking it?"

He'd never wanted to trade hope for her. She meant too much to him.

Her hand reached out. Closed around one of his clenched fists. Her touch seemed to scorch right through him. "I trust you to find me, Kyle."

Something seemed to break inside of him. "Don't." The word was more growl than anything else. "Maria trusted me, too, and I failed her." He'd *lost* her.

I can't fail Cadence.

"I do trust you." She came closer, and her body brushed against his. Her hand tightened around his fist. "You'll be able to trace me. I'll lead you to him. With the FBI's resources, we can close this case before anyone else gets hurt. No other women have to be hurt. They don't have to die by his hand."

Her mouth was inches from his.

What he desired most was right fucking there. "I want to take you away." A brutal confession. "I want to just grab you and take you as far away from this hell as I can."

Her smile was sad. "That's not who I am."

No. She wasn't the kind to run, not even from the monsters who hunted with their deadly intensity.

"We protect, that's what we do." The line between her brows smoothed away. "I'm not scared."

She should be.

Cadence leaned up on her toes and pressed a light kiss to his lips. "Whether you agree or not," she whispered, "I'm doing this."

Hell.

He moved in an instant, locking his arms around her, yanking her harder against him, and kissing her with the desperation that pumped through his veins like acid.

He couldn't control Cadence, but the woman controlled him. The thought of her in danger had his heart racing, fear rising in his chest.

If the plan didn't work—if she didn't come back—darkness seemed to wrap around his mind. *She will come back to me.*

His hands sank into her hair. He tilted her head. Kissed her with a desperation that should have alarmed them both.

Cadence had said she wasn't scared.

Not of the killer.

Not of him.

She will be.

Her nails bit into his shoulders. She pulled him closer as she kissed him with the same frantic need.

Even as a knock sounded at the door.

The damn door was shut for a reason.

I want her naked.

Actually, he just wanted her.

Cadence pulled away. Her breath rushed out. Too fast. Panting. "I trust you," she said again.

The drumming of his heartbeat wouldn't slow.

The knock came again. Someone out there was pissing him off.

"I told you." Kyle barely recognized his own voice. "Maybe you shouldn't."

The door swung open just as Cadence slipped from his arms.

"Well?" Ben demanded.

We needed more time.

Only they were working against the clock. He got that.

Cadence's chin was up. Her shoulders squared. "Tell Dani to get the trackers ready. We're doing this."

***

He knew who he wanted, and he wasn't going to settle for anyone else. Not this time.

He'd tried to settle before, but it had been a fucking disaster. The blonde woman hadn't been right. Even her death had been a waste for him.

No release. No pleasure.

At least the screams had stopped.

He knew they'd searched the cabin. Found Judith. Judith had been good. She'd learned quickly. Been so eager to please.

Until the end.

She'd broken then. Kept crying for her family. Kept begging for death.

So he'd given it to her.

The cops had also found Landers. The asshole. He'd never understood how women should be treated.

He knew all about Landers. The guy had been sent to the pen, and he *shouldn't* have been released so soon. But there'd been a slipup. Landers had gone free, and the guy had stumbled right into his cabin and found Judith.

He liked to keep his girls separated. He focused on them, one at a time, so he needed that second location. The cabin had seemed perfect for him.

Until Landers appeared.

When he'd shot the bastard, just as the guy's hands had gone for the ropes binding Judith, the man's blood had splattered all over her.

But Judith hadn't screamed.

Good, even then.

He didn't think Cadence would scream, either. She'd said she stayed quiet before, when she'd been under the bed.

Listening to her mother die.

She'd stayed quiet.

He liked the quiet.

Needed it.

Craved it.

He just had to find the perfect way to get to Cadence. He'd need to separate her from the others. Separation. Isolation. That was how he worked.

He'd been close to her in the woods.

But she'd been on guard. Too ready to attack.

That wasn't the way he liked his prey.

His prey should be weak. He was the strong one. The one meant to always survive.

He would have to wait for the right moment. There would be no more desperate hunts, he'd learned from his mistake. He could be careful. He could be cautious.

He could wait for her.

She *would* come to him.

***

"He's not going to walk right up to you," Dani said as she bent over Cadence's wrist and adjusted her new watch. "You know that, right? He's not going to offer you a ride in his car. Not going to sweep you away on a dark road."

"I know," she said, sighing. Like Kyle, Dani was definitely not on board with the plan. "I've got a pretty good idea of how this will work."

Dani paused, then she glanced up at Cadence. The watch around Cadence's wrist was a GPS tracker. It would send her location back to Dani every five seconds. Dani always kept her tech toys close, so Cadence hadn't been surprised when Dani had brought out the equipment.

Having it so close saved them time.

"You think so, huh?" Anger pulsed beneath Dani's words. "What happens if this grand plan of yours goes wrong?"

Cadence lifted a hand and stroked the earring on her right ear. Another tracking device. Hidden so easily in plain view. "I've got you keeping tabs on me, what could go wrong?"

"Plenty," Dani snapped. "Maybe he takes you to a place where I can't get your signal. If he goes underground again, if there are caverns or caves near here that he uses…" She shook her head. "I'm not sure the signals will transmit back to me. I could lose you."

Cadence wasn't going to let fear hold her back. *Judith was alive a week ago.* She had to offer herself. Had to be bait for the killer. "If the transmission stops, then you follow the last signal. Every five seconds, remember? You follow it and you'll get close enough to find me."

"Why?" Dani demanded, voice low. "Why are you doing this? For him, obviously, I get it. I see the way you keep staring at Kyle."

I see the way you keep staring. She'd have to watch that. "The women could be alive. I'm doing this for them."

"Not just for them," Dani argued immediately. "Tell that to someone who doesn't know you that well."

Fine, she was doing it for Kyle, too. "If it were your sister, would you want her left with him? Left for all of those years while he tortured her, again and again?"

She wasn't even sure how Kyle was keeping it together. After he'd found out about Judith, she'd expected more of a reaction. *Alive.* For four long years.

They hadn't told Judith's family the news yet. Cadence knew it would devastate them.

"You have your gun?" Dani asked her, not answering Cadence's question.

She lifted her arm, revealing the holster.

Dani's breath huffed out. "And a backup? You have your backup, right?"

"Strapped to my ankle." Her right ankle had a gun strapped to it. Her left, a knife.

"Two transmitters are in place on you now." Danielle's breath exhaled slowly. "A third is on the way. It's shipping from Quantico and should be here in a few hours." Her right eyelid twitched. "This had better work, or I'm gonna kick your ass when I see you again."

Cadence nodded. "Fair enough."

Dani backed away from her. "You know I can take you out. I did it plenty of times in training."

When she wanted, Dani could be vicious.

She moved to stand near the small window, one that looked over the line of trees in the distance. "So," Dani's musing voice began. "When did you start sleeping with him?"

Yes, she'd figured her friend would pick up on that.

Dani glanced over her shoulder. "The guy's looked at you like he wanted to eat you for months. He *still* looks that way, but something's different."

It was. "In Paradox."

"You know you won't be able to keep working with him. Not when Ben finds out."

She thought the guy already knew. "Why not? You and Ben seem to get along just fine."

Silence. Dani's lips were parted, her stare startled.

Cadence almost smiled. "Did you think I didn't know about you two?" Her friend wasn't that good at keeping secrets.

"We don't usually work in the field," Dani said, but her words were halting. "You and Kyle, with this case—"

"I don't know what's happening with us. I don't know if there's a future or if there's only now." She couldn't think past the moment. "We'll figure it out after we stop this asshole."

"The Night Hunter."

So the media kept calling him. Since he only hunted at night, the news folks thought they were being clever.

The moniker would just feed the killer's ego. Make him think he was larger than life.

He already thinks that.

Cadence adjusted her watch. "If we're set, I want to check in with Kyle. See if he's heard anything else from the police captain over in Paradox." She headed toward the door.

"Ben doesn't."

Her words had Cadence pausing.

"Ben doesn't look at me the way Kyle watches you. When he stares at you, it's like nothing else matters."

At those words, Cadence's heart beat a bit faster. Her hands wanted to tremble, so she made sure that Dani couldn't see them. Sometimes, she did catch a look in Kyle's eyes that was…intense. No, consuming. She'd never had another man look at her with that kind of need.

But Dani was wrong. Something else did matter. Someone else.

Cadence opened the door and hurried into the bustle of the station. The watch on her wrist was no bigger than any other watch, but it felt too heavy to her.

Only the FBI agents knew about her plan. They didn't trust the locals not to leak information. Accidentally or even on purpose, they couldn't be trusted with the plan Cadence was putting into motion.

Not yet.

Her gaze searched the station's open area, but Kyle wasn't there. She turned, heading down the hallway that would lead to the back offices. Kyle and Ben had disappeared that way before.

"Are you looking for me?"

Kyle sat at a desk inside the last office. His gun was on the desk. His jacket behind him.

She entered the small room. Closed the door.

His gaze rose to pin her. "Are you set?"

"Yes." Mostly.

"I told you this was fucking crazy, right?"

Her jaw locked. He'd mentioned that a few times. He wasn't changing her mind. Why risk innocent civilians if the killer already wanted her?

He rose from the chair. It rolled back with a squeak of its wheels. "I get it, okay? I know what you're trying to do." He came toward her with slow, deliberate steps. "Part of me is grateful because it *is* a way to draw him out."

With every step he took, her heart pounded faster.

"But I don't like it." Grim. Hard. "I don't fucking like having you in his sights at all."

Hadn't she been in his sights ever since she'd gotten off the plane in Paradox? "Our job always puts us in the path of killers. I told you before, if I wanted safety, I wouldn't have joined the FBI."

He was just a foot away from her now. Plenty close enough to touch. She wanted to touch him. She knew the plan that was coming. She was supposed to head back to Paradox. Go back out to those caverns. Make sure she was seen moving around in the open, on her own.

Kyle would follow her, slowly. He'd stay in her vicinity, just as Dani would. Ben was remaining in Maverick a little longer, running down a few more leads.

It was time for the next stage to begin.

Only she wasn't ready to walk away from Kyle.

Her hand slid down. Found the small lock on the door. The click seemed incredibly loud in the narrow room.

His gaze held hers.

"Kiss me before I go," she whispered.

His hands flattened on either side of her head, pushing against the door frame. His mouth lowered, paused just above hers. "When this is all over, we won't go back to the way things were."

She'd told Dani she didn't know their future.

"I had you, and I can't let that end. I *won't*," he said, the words dark and rumbling.

She wasn't ready to let go of him either.

His lips brushed over hers. The faintest of touches. Not what she needed.

"I had you all wrong." He growled the words against her lips. "I thought I knew what you wanted."

She kept her secrets close.

"It's not gentleness. Not just a lover in the dark."

His mouth pressed harder to hers.

Lifted.

"What you really want is to lose that control you keep so closely. To let go. To *burn*."

She was burning right then. Her breasts ached, the nipples tight peaks. Her hips were pushing toward him, toward the thick bulge of arousal pressing against her.

"You make me burn, Cadence. You make me crave."

His mouth wasn't on hers. His lips were on the curve of her neck. His tongue rasped over the skin. She felt the faint edge of his teeth. Then he was licking, sucking that sensitive flesh.

She held back the moan trying to break from her. She didn't want anyone in the hallway to hear her.

"I want to take you every way I can for as long as I can."

Heat pooled in her sex. She knew her panties were getting wet.

"And I will." Kyle's mouth came back to hers. His lips were open, and his tongue thrust into her mouth. *Yes*. This kiss was what she wanted.

Only it didn't stop the ache she felt.

The kiss made it so much sharper.

Footsteps sounded in the hallway. Voices called out just beyond the door. She lifted her hands, wrapped them around Kyle's broad shoulders, and pulled him closer.

She loved his taste. Talk about craving.

But he was lifting his head again. Dammit. Putting those inches between them that she hated. "You make sure you come back to me, baby." A hard order. "You make *damn* sure."

She would.

"I *won't* let you disappear."

Then he kissed her the way she'd wanted—completely, totally, sending her heart thundering and her body trembling because there was power and passion and so much need in that one kiss.

She'd be coming back for this. For him.

The bastard out there wasn't going to stop her.

If there weren't others a few feet away, if she didn't hear them coming toward the door—

Kyle's hand slid down her body.

His fingers were over her breast. Stroking.

She jerked against him. *Feels so good.*

She wanted his hand even lower. On her sex.

In her.

Not now. Not here.

If she didn't stop soon…

Her hands pressed against his shoulders.

Their eyes met.

"Come back to me," Kyle demanded.

She nodded.

He let her go.

***

Time for me to be bait.

The killer was keeping close tabs on the FBI. He could be watching her, right then. But just in case he didn't have her in sight at that moment, she knew exactly where to go in order to draw him out.

The caves.

The caves were special to the killer. Those tally marks had been left in the cave with Lily because the killer had been marking his territory. He felt safe there, so he'd left a record of his victims.

They'd found the remains of one woman there. If there were others, then the killer would feel compelled to go back…

And he'd find me.

Since the FBI team suspected the killer was closely monitoring the investigation, Cadence had made a point of informing all the local officials that if they needed her, she'd be back at the caves. She'd even told a local reporter that she was focusing most of her attention on the dark caverns to learn more about the killer.

She'd put out the bait, now the killer just had to act.

"It's not exactly easy to move several tons of rocks." Dr. Aaron Peters gazed at the entrance to the caverns. He didn't look like a buttoned-up professor anymore. Dirt stained his cheeks and hands, and his jeans were ripped in a half-dozen places. He shook his head. "Every time we advance, it seems like we wind up taking five feet back. The place is too unstable. Those detonations—hell, we're lucky the explosions didn't create a fifty-mile sinkhole. The bastard could have destroyed *everything*."

Dark clouds swirled in the air above Cadence and Aaron, blocking out the evening sun. Wind pushed against her cheeks.

"My team can't stay down there during storms like the ones coming. It'd be too dangerous."

She knew they couldn't. The local weatherman had been predicting the severe surge of storms for days. Now the storms were almost on them.

"I heard about what happened in Maverick." Aaron's voice was lower now. Sympathetic. "Is the sheriff gonna make it?"

"I think so. He was stable when I left." She'd never forget the gurgles he'd made as he lay on the sidewalk, drowning in his own blood.

Aaron turned away from the caverns. Focused totally on her. "What makes somebody do this? I mean, how do you get so messed up that you keep women as your prisoners in caves? That you shoot sheriffs and kill without hesitation? Why do you do that? *How* do you do it?"

Her gaze slanted toward him. Cautiously, she began to explain, "There are lots of different theories." The wind had kicked up even more, tossing her hair. "Some folks think serials are born bad. That's the nature idea. You're born evil, and no matter what happens, you're meant to grow up and kill."

It sounded like the wind had started to howl.

"Others say it's all in the environment. Events that shape people into becoming who they are. Things happen. They twist good people and turn them into—" *Monsters.* "Killers." She paused, intent on gauging what sort of reaction he might have at her words.

Aaron just shook his head, as if he couldn't understand how a person could be so twisted. "But becoming someone like this?" His lips twisted in a grimace. "Why?"

A flash of lightning lit up the sky behind him. "We believe this individual is a collector, of sorts."

"When I was a kid, I collected rocks, not people."

But their killer *did* collect people. "He's not quite like you." Their perp wasn't like anyone she'd ever met or profiled before. For most of the serials she encountered, the kill was the end goal for them. They received satisfaction—fulfillment—from the act of killing their prey. But this guy actually kept his victims alive. Multiple victims, seemingly alive at the same time. Death wasn't the end goal for him.

Control was.

"How do you do it?" Aaron wanted to know as he narrowed his eyes. "How do you go after these guys without the nightmares driving you crazy?"

Behind him, Aaron's team and the authorities on hand were leaving the caverns. Securing the area.

How do you do it?

Late at night, she wondered the same thing. "I put them in cages. I lock them up. When I know the killers are off the streets, I sleep much better." Not the total truth, but Aaron didn't need to know about her nightmares.

Thunder rumbled in the distance.

Aaron turned away. "All right, guys!" His voice rose. "I'm calling it for today! Let's get out of here before the first storm comes through!"

The local weatherman had predicted the line of thunderstorms would roll in just before sunset. They were supposed to last all night.

The storms would slowly make their way up to Maverick, Tennessee.

The wind and rain would wash away any recent evidence the killer had left behind. Now they even had Mother Nature working against them.

She glanced toward their makeshift parking lot. Search teams who'd been in the woods were already piling into their vehicles. Getting ready to go home.

She headed for the line of trees. Voices floated behind her. Aaron, talking to his team.

She knew the path led back to Death Falls—the falls that had offered her freedom before, when she'd been trapped in the darkness.

Her steps were fast as she hurried toward them. The woods were silent, the voices of the men soon disappearing behind her. The trees swayed. Lightning lit up the sky in hot flashes every few moments.

Then the thunder of the falls reached her. It seemed louder, stronger than it had been before.

She stopped and stared at the water. It was beautiful, but when she saw it, Cadence could only think of death.

The name of the falls was damn fitting. Swallowing, she glanced away from the thundering water. Cadence looked to the left. The right. She was sure the killer had used this exit from the caverns. Sure he'd come here, over and over.

Awareness pushed through Cadence. There had been no sound to alert her to someone else's presence. But…

I'm not alone.

Cadence spun around, her gun out and aimed in an instant.

The gun was pointed just a few inches from Aaron's face.

He blinked. "I was just making sure you were okay." His cheeks flushed. Even in the weak light, there was no missing the bright red. "I saw you come over here by yourself. You don't want to get trapped up here during a storm. The water there"—Aaron inclined his head—"it gets rough pretty quick. One misstep, and you could be in trouble."

She lowered the weapon. Lowered it, but didn't holster it. "Sorry."

He took a few quick steps back, putting some distance between them. "The crew's leaving. You heading back with us?"

For now, she was.

More thunder rumbled.

Or was it just the falls?

She stepped toward Aaron.

His hands had clenched into fists.

Her own body tensed.

"I know what you're thinking," he said. "What you're *all* thinking."

Lightning flashed over him.

"I was here, just a few years ago, I should have seen something." He shook his head. "But I swear, I didn't. I searched those caverns as much as I could. I searched in the area where you found Lily. *There was nothing.*" His breath heaved out. "I keep wondering—dammit, did I miss something? Could I have stopped this?"

Rain began to pelt down on them.

Aaron swore.

They both began to jog back to the base, back to the waiting cars.

She knew guilt ate at him.

It ate at her, too.

For her mother.

For all the victims she hadn't been able to save over the years.

They stopped at the cars. She had an SUV of her own now. She'd picked the rental up on her way out of Maverick. Aaron waved to her once she was at her vehicle, then he headed over to join his group.

"Dr. Peters!" She called out his name over the rising storm. The rain drove down in a hard blast now. Her hair stuck to her; her clothes were already drenched.

He looked back, water streaming down his face.

"It doesn't do any good," she called out to him. "To think about the coulds." On all the things they both could have done differently. On what could have changed. "Just focus on what you can do now."

He stared at her a moment longer, then gave a hard nod.

Maybe her words would make it easier for him to sleep at night.

Maybe not.

They didn't usually help her. It seemed all she could ever think about was the *coulds* in this world. She'd just given him advice she'd never be able to take on her own.

***

They'd all run away. Leaving the caverns. The woods.

Fleeing the storms that promised to beat so hard and long against the town.

There would be no searches that night. No one stumbling where he or she shouldn't for the next ten hours or so.

He watched Cadence's SUV disappear around the bend. She was on her way back to the motel. Back to the little place at the edge of town.

Only McKenzie wasn't with her. Not yet.

Not. Yet.

It was a terrible mistake for the agent to make.

***

She'd driven about ten minutes when her windshield wipers stopped working.

Cadence's hold tightened on the steering wheel. The rain battered down in a torrent that just wouldn't stop.

She couldn't see a damn thing.

There were more curves up ahead. Twisting, sharp curves. Drops at the edge of the road.

I can't see them.

She pushed on the brakes, trying to carefully guide the car to the right-hand shoulder of the pavement. Her heart was pounding in her chest, so very fast. The damn wipers.

228

The others had pulled out of the parking area first, leaving the base before her. *That was what I wanted. I wanted to be prey.*

She knew this growing fear churning in her stomach. This was exactly how the others had felt when they'd realized they were stranded.

Only it was still early. Barely past nine. The killer didn't normally hunt at this time.

He also doesn't normally shoot his prey, but that's exactly what he did to Sheriff Coolidge and Christa.

The glow of headlights lit up her vehicle from behind. Cadence checked her weapon. Pulled in a deep, steadying breath.

Had that been a car door slamming? It was so hard to be certain. The rain was so loud.

Cadence turned, trying to see through the driver's-side window.

Someone rapped against the window.

She jumped. Dammit, she was an FB-freaking-I agent. This was her plan.

And she'd jumped.

She'd also curled her fingers around her weapon. There was a shadow on the other side. She couldn't tell much about the person.

"*You okay?*"

She caught the faint words, barely, and realized…*That's a woman's voice.*

Cadence rolled down her window. Rain and wind rushed inside her rented SUV.

A woman stood there, pale, too thin, shaking, in the storm. She had a small umbrella clutched tightly to her. "I saw you pull over," she said, frowning as she peered into Cadence's car. "Are you okay?"

Cadence made sure to keep her gun out of sight. "I'm fine. Just some trouble with my wipers." The rain might ease soon and then she'd be able to drive again.

The Good Samaritan frowned. "Do you…do you want me to call someone for you?"

"No, thank you." Cadence forced a smile. "I have a phone. I'm fine." *You need to get out of here. Hurry home. Lock your doors.*

But the woman wasn't moving. "I—I saw on the news." She bit her lip. "It's not safe for you to be out here. Why don't you let me give you a ride?"

"I'm good, but thank you." Cadence turned on the car's interior light and pulled out her FBI identification. "Thanks for stopping."

The woman, who had dark-brown hair falling heavily down her back, reached for the ID. She held it a moment, and after a quick scan, handed it back to Cadence.

Then she just turned and walked away. The woman didn't say another word.

"Okay," Cadence muttered. Not weird at all. She rolled up her window.

The car's headlights were still on behind her. But the lights were moving as the woman began to pull away.

She started to put her ID up, then she realized…

There was a piece of paper stuck to the ID. Her interior lights blazed down on the small scrap of paper. And the words that had been written there.

Help me.

Cadence shoved open her car door and leaped out, but the woman was already driving off.

No!

Cadence jumped back in her vehicle and yanked out her cell phone. She had the sheriff's office on the line instantly. "This is FBI Agent Cadence Hollow. I'm on County Road Four, and I need assistance. I'm in pursuit of a—" Hell, she hadn't even been able to make out the vehicle in the downpour. "A possible victim" was all she could say. She rolled down her window and shoved her head out. It was the only way she could see. She took off after the woman.

Help me.

Cadence was sure going to try.

She let the phone fall from her fingers as she tried to keep her vehicle on the road, and see what curves waited up ahead.

***

"Agent Hollow just called!" Heather Crenshaw ran up to Kyle as he entered the Paradox police station. "She said she's out on County Road Four. There's a victim who needs help!"

He immediately whirled back toward the front door and out into the rain. The wind was pushing harder now, gushing fiercely and howling.

As he ran for his vehicle, he yanked out his phone and tried to get Cadence.

She didn't answer.

One of the perp's victims? Had she found him?

Danielle was hurrying toward him, clutching an umbrella. "What's happening?"

Heather had already made it to her patrol car.

"We're going after Cadence," he said grimly. Cadence and her victim.

***

Her phone was ringing again, but Cadence couldn't take her hands off the wheel to answer. She was driving too fast, the curves were too sharp, and she could barely see.

She kept shoving her head out the window, staring into the night, trying to find the black edge of the road.

Who was that woman? *Doesn't matter. She needs me.*

You didn't turn away from someone who needed help.

You never did.

Cadence saw the next curve coming up toward her.

She slowed down, went into it—

And never saw the vehicle that slammed into her. She only felt the impact. Heard the horrible crunch of glass and metal.

And heard her own scream.

CHAPTER TWELVE

Cadence's voice mail picked up. *Again.*

Kyle shoved his foot down on the accelerator. The vehicle cut through the night, sending rainwater spraying in its wake.

"She didn't say the victim was related to the Night Hunter," Dani said as she sat beside him, her body as tense and alert as his own.

They slid into the curve. His headlights fell on the wreckage.

His heart fucking stopped.

He knew that SUV. When Cadence had left Maverick hours before, she'd been driving that vehicle.

Now it sat on the side of the road, its headlights cutting through the rain, the driver's side door hanging open and the passenger side of the vehicle completely smashed in.

He braked and jumped from his own vehicle.

"*Cadence!*" He yelled her name as he reached the crumpled SUV. Dani's footsteps clattered behind him. An air bag had deployed on the driver's side, an air bag that now looked like a deflated flag. Cadence's phone was in the front seat. Her purse. Her gun and holster. Her FBI ID. All still there.

And a note…

The rain beat down on him as he bent into the vehicle to read the note.

Help me.

"There's blood." Dani's voice shook as she shone her light at first the steering wheel and then at the open driver's side door.

"And no Cadence." *The plan. The plan.* His jaw locked as he spun to face Dani. "Get the tracking system up!" Their prey had taken the bait.

They'd better not fucking lose him.

Or her.

I'm coming, Cadence.

She trusted him. He wouldn't let her down.

***

Her head hurt. The pain was what brought consciousness back. The throbbing. The nausea. Cadence opened her eyes. She lifted her hands, trying to touch her aching head.

Her hands slammed into something.

Dark. Why is it so dark?

She stretched out with her hands, searching. The surface above her was cold, hard metal, but ridged in places.

She realized she was moving.

Her breath froze in her lungs then. The perp had kept his word. He'd come for her.

He'd taken her.

The woman. How the hell did she fit into the mix? Cadence and Kyle had both been so sure they were looking for a man who worked alone.

Cadence tried to stretch down, reaching for her ankle. Her knife wasn't in the strap on her left ankle. No gun on her right.

He'd taken away her weapons.

***

Kyle found the gun first, tossed away, and when he found the gun, he found the knife.

Cadence's backup weapons.

The SOB had made sure she was defenseless.

No. The thought immediately snapped through his head. Cadence was trained in self-defense. He'd seen her take down guys twice her size.

Only her blood had been in the vehicle. Cadence was hurt. *How badly?* Would she be able to defend herself when she was hurt?

His phone hadn't rung. Shouldn't the SOB be calling to taunt him?

Police lights lit up the scene, some swirling in a sickening blur from the patrol cars braking nearby. This was a crime scene, and they were all treating it as carefully as they could.

"Kyle!" Dani's shout.

He ran back to her side. She was in his vehicle, her tablet out as she tried to connect with Cadence's tracking signals.

Dani looked up with a cold smile. "We've got her."

Hell, *yes.*

***

Her weapons were gone, but her watch wasn't. A frantic grab assured her the earrings were in place, too. So was the small pin, the third tracker, that had been attached to the back waist of her jeans.

Come find me.

The vehicle slowed.

Cadence sucked in a low breath. She knew what was going to happen next. When the trunk opened, she'd see the man who'd abducted all of those women. She'd finally have a face for the monster.

Except…

When the trunk opened a few minutes later, when the rain and wind poured in, she didn't find herself staring up at a man.

The brunette was before her. The brunette with the sad eyes. The pale skin.

And the gun in her hand.

Help me.

Cadence had thought she was looking at a victim.

So damn not.

Cadence prepared to lunge at her, gun or no gun.

"He wants you inside." The words were a whisper. The gun trembled in her shaking grasp. "If you try to get away now…"

Cadence had to strain to hear the words.

"He'll kill me."

Cadence wondered just *who* this was as she stared up at the brunette.

***

"He's using dirt roads," Dani said as she directed him after Cadence's signal. "Cutting right through the woods."

The roads weren't easy to follow because the storm was washing them away.

The vehicle lunged forward. The wheels spun, losing traction in the thick mud.

"Left up ahead. Then straight. He must have a cabin in these woods, a place he's using."

A place they hadn't found in their searches.

Two cop cars were behind him. Randall Hollings was in the lead patrol car. Heather Crenshaw was rushing after them.

Faster, faster…

"Her signal isn't moving anymore," Dani whispered. "Wherever he was taking her, she's there."

They weren't. Fuck. He shoved the accelerator down harder, just as part of the road seemed to fall away.

***

Cadence didn't move from the trunk. Her hair was soaked, her clothes clinging to her, but she didn't move. "What's your name?"

The woman glanced over her shoulder. "We have to hurry. He wants us inside."

"Were you driving the car?"

A nod. Sad. "I'm s-sorry." Hoarse. "Please…don't make me sh-shoot you. Y-you have to…come inside."

"Did he take you?"

The gun jerked in the woman's hand. The bullet blasted out, burning a path over Cadence's shoulder.

"I'm sorry!" The woman gasped out. "I—I didn't mean to do th-that!"

"It's okay," Cadence whispered. *No, it's not. She freaking just shot me.* Cadence climbed from the trunk, trying to move as carefully as she could. Her gaze tracked across the area. She couldn't see any kind of landmarks. Just trees swaying too hard in the storm.

They'd driven up as they traveled. She'd felt the incline and she could see the trees slanted, drifting below her.

The gun shoved into her back. "Just…walk st-straight ahead. Please."

It sounded like the woman was crying. Cadence started walking. "You didn't answer me before." She ignored the blood dripping down her arm, and the throbbing in her head that seemed to get worse with every step. "Did he take you, too?" The brunette was the right age for his victims, and Cadence tried to run through all of the images in her mind. Could she be Bridgette or Melanie? The hair color could have been dyed. The woman's face was so thin and pale. Ravaged.

"Push through the bushes."

Heavy bushes were in front of her. Cadence pushed through them, and saw only darkness.

Not another freaking cave.

It was.

Goose bumps rose on her arms. "This connects with the other caverns, doesn't it?" Jason had said the caverns stretched for at least fifty miles.

"Go inside." The woman's voice was even weaker now.

Cadence stepped inside.

Her captor—*victim*—followed her. The bushes seemed to spring right back into place, sealing them in the thick darkness of the cave. A darkness that deepened with every step.

"How can you see?" Cadence whispered.

"I've been d-down here…" The words broke. "A very long time. I don't n-need to see anymore."

Those words made her heart hurt.

Cadence stopped walking. Screw going farther. This woman's safety took priority. Cadence would get her out, then she and Kyle would come back to hunt for the others in this cave. "I can help you," she said to the woman. "Let's go now. Let's get into the car and I can take you to the police station."

"No!" Her shout echoed through the cave.

There was fear in that denial. So much fear.

"Y-you can't h-help me," the woman said. Softer once more. "B-but you can…take my place."

Cadence stiffened. When she'd first started the case, she'd believed that the killer abducted a new victim when he killed his previous prey. But to discover that the victims were actually help-ing him…*I didn't expect that.*

She should have seen it. Dammit. She should have seen it.

"Now, walk. Please."

"I can't see in front of me. I need a light."

"The l-light's gone. You learn that."

She didn't plan to learn anything.

But Cadence put one foot in front of the other. She walked in the darkness. The gun was still behind her. It pushed into her back every few moments. She could try to take the weapon away from the woman, but in the struggle, Cadence couldn't be sure the gun wouldn't go off.

The plan was to save the victims. Not kill them.

She walked. One foot. The other. Her eyes couldn't adjust to the perfect darkness. There was no seeing. Just an endless night.

Her arm throbbed. Her head ached.

She walked.

***

The tires were spinning in the mud.

"Fuck, fuck, *fuck*!" Kyle snarled as his hands slammed into the steering wheel. He jerked the gearshift, pushing the vehicle into reverse.

The SUV heaved back.

The lights shone ahead of them. The road had been washed away. If he tried to advance, the vehicle would just get trapped again.

"There's got to be another way to her," he said, fury and fear knifing through him. They were losing too much time.

Time that Cadence didn't have.

Dani was pulling up aerial maps on her tablet. "We need to go back, about two miles. Looks like there's another turn we can take back there. As long as"—she exhaled slowly, the sound ragged—"as long as the road is still intact."

Not a road. His gaze narrowed on her tablet screen. Another damn dirt trail. "If it's not?"

She glanced up at him, the screen's light shining on her worried face. "Then we go back to the highway. We circle around. It will take maybe forty-five minutes that way."

Going by the time Cadence had made the call to the station, she already had at least a forty-five-minute head start on them.

He yanked out his phone. Called Heather. "Reverse the team," he ordered. "We're hitting the trail two miles back."

They would get to Cadence, even if he had to get a fucking helicopter out there to take him in to her.

***

"How long have you been with him?" Cadence asked. She couldn't stand the silence. The dark.

"Always," was the soft answer behind her.

"That's not true. *How long?*"

Stockholm syndrome. The words beat through Cadence's head. This woman had been held by her captor for so long.

"I don't remember anything...before him." Stilted.

"You're lying." Her words weren't angry, because this woman *was* a victim. Cadence kept her voice calm and steady. "You remember."

A light was up ahead. A faint, flickering light.

Her breath heaved from her lungs. "Is that him?"

"Don't scream," was the whisper from behind her. Shaking. "He doesn't like it when you scream."

I didn't scream. Lily's words.

Cadence swallowed and kept walking toward that light. A candle? "Do you know Maria?"

Silence.

"She was taken fifteen years ago. Blonde hair. Blue eyes. She has a brother who's been looking for her, all that time."

Still nothing. Just the faint scrape of the woman's shoes on the stone floor. The press of the gun into Cadence's back.

The light flickered again. She could see a curving entrance near the light.

"There have been others who were taken," Cadence said, determined to keep talking. Determined to make a connection with this woman. "Did you know Bridgette, Fiona, Judith—"

A choked sob came from the woman.

You knew her.

"We found Judith's body," Cadence said. "I don't want you to wind up like her. Let me *help* you."

"Can't..." The barest of whispers. "He's here."

She realized the scrapes she'd heard in the tunnel hadn't come from the woman's shoes.

They were farther back. Closing in on them.

They were coming from *him*.

Cadence started to turn around, but the woman shoved her in the back, sending Cadence stumbling toward the light.

The light was a candle, barely an inch high. The flame was sputtering because it was about to go out, and when it did, she'd be in the darkness again.

"Give me your hands," the woman said.

Cadence lifted her hands. The watch was a reassuring weight. *He's coming.*

Metal clicked around her wrists. Handcuffs.

"Don't scream," was the whisper once more.

Then the woman was backing away.

A creak of sound reached Cadence's ears. Like a door opening. Or closing.

The flame sputtered out. Darkness.

"Hello?" Cadence called. The drumming of her heart was so loud. She lifted her hands, testing those cuffs. The woman had put them on too tightly. They bit into her wrists.

A familiar scraping sound reached her ears.

A sound that was very, very close.

He's here.

Just as she had that thought, a bright light hit her right in the face, temporarily blinding her.

"Hello, Agent Hollow."

She didn't recognize his voice. It was low, rumbling. Almost mocking.

She squinted against the light. She wanted to *see* him, but the light was on top of his head. A headlamp. Just like the caving light she'd used before. No, not just a headlamp. She could just make out the bulk of the helmet on his head. Because of the helmet, no light actually fell on him. He was a shadow. Cadence saw the rough outline of his body, but little else.

About six foot three.

Wide shoulders.

"You know, of course, Agent Hollow, that you won't get out of this place alive."

His words chilled her.

"Actually, I'm planning to walk right out pretty soon," she said.

He laughed. Her goose bumps got worse.

"It's a maze down here," he told her, still in the same voice. "You probably thought you were walking straight ahead, but my girl was guiding you. I trained her well. She knew just where to walk. I taught her the path. One wrong step could have led to your death. If you were to run out, you'd just get lost. You'd die in the dark."

"Sounds like you plan for that to happen anyway."

Keep him talking.

"Why are you so interested in the victims?"

His quiet words caught her off guard. He hadn't moved. That bright light kept blaring on her.

"Why do you want to know what they feel—what they think—so badly?" he said.

"It's the victims who matter." If she ran for him, would she be able to take him out? Her body tensed as she prepared to attack. "They're always the key."

"You want to know so much about them." His words were considering.

I'm here with him. Actually here with him. Kyle, hurry the hell up! She could feel the man's evil in the room.

This place seemed to hold the taint of evil and death in the air.

"You want to know what it's like to be the victim, and now you will."

The light came closer.

Cadence didn't back up. Where would she go? "Where's Maria?" she demanded. "Where's Bridgette? Where's Fiona?"

"Fiona." He drew out the name softly, with relish. "You just met her."

The light vanished.

She blinked, seeing red spots dance in the darkness.

Hard hands grabbed her. Yanked at her. She was shoved back. Her body slammed into rocks. Her cuffed hands were yanked up. Pounded into the side of the cavern.

She heard her watch shatter at the impact.

***

"We lost the initial signal."

Kyle felt his heart stop. "You've got three transmitters on her. Use the other two."

Silence.

Silence wasn't fucking good. "Dani?"

"The other two stopped sending signals about ten minutes ago. I'm sorry. They were linked to a different satellite system, and she must be in an area they can't reach."

The thick mud tried to suck the wheels down into its greedy grasp. He shoved down the gas pedal and the vehicle surged forward. "She hadn't moved?" As long as she hadn't moved after the last transmission, they'd find her.

Coming, baby. Coming…

"No. She was stationary."

Stationary. As in not moving. But she couldn't be dead. *Not dead. Not. Dead.*

"ETA?" he demanded.

"Ten minutes."

Stay alive ten minutes, Cadence. Stay fucking alive. Just ten more minutes.

***

"You didn't scream." His breath blew against her cheek. "You know better than that, don't you? You were the girl under the bed. The one who knew not to make a sound."

How does he know about that? Cadence's stomach clenched as the worst memory of her life was shoved back at her. Her chest ached, pain swelling within her as she remembered her own silence.

And her mother's cries.

"Let's see if you can keep quiet now. The longer you stay quiet, the longer you get to live."

One hand held her wrists pinned. The other hand was around her throat. She thought of Valerie Tate, just tossed away at the old diner.

Valerie hadn't stayed quiet.

His fingers squeezed lightly. That was when she realized her captor was wearing gloves. Thick, rough gloves that chafed against her skin.

"Remember, not a sound," he whispered.

He let her go.

Cadence slowly lowered her hands.

The bastard dug into my life. He found out about my mother.

The killer had profiled *her*.

"Fiona!" he called softly.

There was a faint rustle from about four feet away.

The light came on again. Only this time, it fell right on Fiona. She didn't even blink when the light hit her. Her face was blank, empty. Just like a lifeless doll.

"Fiona, you did a very good job," he said.

She gave the faintest of nods.

"It would have been easier if she'd just gotten into your car, but having her follow you worked just as well." A pause. "How *did* you get her to chase after you so quickly?"

He doesn't know about the note.

"Fiona?" he prompted when she said nothing.

"I got her," Fiona whispered. "I proved myself, didn't I?"

"Oh, yes, you got her. But you haven't proven yourself yet. Come here, Fiona."

She shuffled toward him, the brightness growing around her as she neared the light.

Cadence didn't move.

"You said she'd take my place," Fiona mumbled, rubbing her arms. "Can I go? I want to go."

"Not yet. You have to do one more thing first."

He'll never let you go! Cadence wanted to scream those words, but she bit them back. She understood how to play this game.

Then she saw the knife in the light. The knife he held in his gloved hand. "First, you have to drive this into the agent's heart."

Fiona froze. "She can't take my place then."

"You'll prove yourself to me. Prove you will always obey me. That you love me." No emotion or accent filled those dark words.

Cadence's body tensed as she prepared to lunge at him.

That sonofabitch. This was how he exerted his ultimate control. He turned his victims into killers.

"Take the knife," he told Fiona. "Shove it into her heart."

Fiona shook her head. "I can't." Tears clogged her voice.

He lowered the knife. His other gloved hand came up. Curled around Fiona. Brought her closer to him.

Cadence couldn't see his hands clearly. Couldn't see Fiona clearly as the light focused—*on me.*

"When you first saw me, you were thinking about charging me, Agent Hollow. Fighting me. Killing me," he said as the light shone onto her. "Know that if I die, no one will ever find the others."

The others—alive or dead? She didn't let the question slip free.

The longer you stay quiet...

"I said she'd take your place." His voice had changed, softened. He was talking to Fiona once more. "I meant that."

"Thank you!" Hope filled Fiona's words. A hope that was painful to hear. "I want—"

When a knife sinks into flesh, it makes a wet sound that is both unmistakable and horrifying.

Cadence heard that sound in that instant. Then she heard the gurgle. The desperate gasp that came from Fiona.

"No!" The word was ripped from Cadence.

She sprang forward, her cuffed hands up.

She caught Fiona. The woman's body came at her, and they fell to the ground in a tangle of limbs.

Fiona was shaking so hard. Cadence tried to ease her to the side. Tried to search for a wound.

The light hit the handle of the knife. The knife embedded in Fiona's chest.

"Now you take her place."

His footsteps scraped away.

She understood. Too late. *If they won't kill for him, then they die for him.*

Fiona's hand locked around Cadence's wrist. "Help."

There wasn't anything she could do. Not with her hands cuffed. In the darkness.

Just then, she heard a *creak.*

It was the sound she'd heard before, when she was first pushed toward the flickering candle.

A door. Only it wasn't closing this time.

"I'll be back." His voice drifted to her.

"Home," Fiona begged. "T-take me."

"I will," Cadence promised. "I will." Without his light, she couldn't see the wound anymore. Could only curl her fingers around the knife's handle. If she took out the knife, she could do more damage to Fiona. The blood would pump from the woman even faster. She had to leave it in place. "Help's coming." Kyle would be there. "We'll get you to a hospital. We'll get you home!" She didn't want the words to be a lie. You weren't supposed to make a promise to a victim, not one you couldn't keep. You weren't supposed to. "We'll get you home," Cadence said again.

"I'm sorry."

"Don't be sorry. Just live, okay? *Live.* Fight and stay alive, and we'll get out of here."

"No." His voice drifted to her, but sounded more distorted. *Because he'd shut a door and sealed them inside?* "You won't."

CHAPTER THIRTEEN

He saw the abandoned car. The trunk was still up.

You put her in there, didn't you, you bastard?

Kyle shined his flashlight on the trunk, then he searched the ground. The storm was in full force, blowing so hard that Dani staggered beside him.

"They're in the area," he said. The car was still there. If the guy had rushed away, he would have needed the vehicle. The question now was...

Where exactly?

His light swept the scene. Twisting pines wrapped around the woods. If Cadence had gone through those trees, maybe she'd been led toward another cabin. A place like the one they'd found in Maverick.

He ran forward, his boots sticking in the mud. *The mud.* His light was shining on the ground then because he'd just seen the telltale sign of tracks in the mud. Tracks that didn't head toward the pines, but instead toward a thick patch of bushes, a patch that had to be at least five feet tall.

Some of the bushes were broken. Bent. From the storm? Or from someone passing through them?

He grabbed for them even as he heard the sound of car doors slamming behind him. Their backup.

"Here!" he yelled. His hand had just shoved through those bushes and touched nothing. Absolutely fucking *nothing*.

Dani helped him to yank those bushes aside. The yawning entrance of a cavern stretched before him.

Dani's hand reached out and locked around his arm. "Our girl's in there."

"Get lights!" he barked to the others. "As many as you can find! And rope!" They'd have rope in the back of their police cruisers. If this tunnel snaked out like the others had, they'd need to be able to find their way back outside.

"What if he's set this place to explode, too?" Dani asked, having to shout to be heard over the storm.

The perp probably had set his traps. But the threat of an explosion wasn't keeping Kyle back. "Watch your step!" he yelled to the others. "Every move you make, check! Look for trip wires. Look for any sign of a trap. We know how this SOB works."

Kyle grabbed a flashlight. Checked his weapon. Then, because he couldn't hold back any longer, he headed into the darkness.

With every step he took, he prayed Cadence was still alive. Trading her life for his sister's—

I won't do it.

He wanted Maria back, but he wasn't about to give up the woman he needed more than air.

***

Help's coming. The bitch's words replayed through his mind as he ran through the tunnel. He wanted to go back to her. Wanted to play with Agent Hollow some more.

She'd done so well at keeping quiet.

Until he'd stabbed Fiona. Then Agent Hollow had cried out. She should be punished for that. She'd broken the rule.

He'd planned to leave her in the dark. The dark made his prey afraid. It was the silence and the darkness that broke them so quickly.

Then he'd heard…*Help's coming.* That was what she'd whispered to Fiona. He realized what a fucking fool he'd been.

Cadence had been too confident. Too certain. He had to get out of there. Had to check to see where McKenzie was.

He can't be here.

As soon as he was sure Cadence's words were a lie, he'd be back for her.

He'd finish what he'd started.

***

"Are any of the others alive?" Cadence asked as she bent over Fiona. Her fingers were at the other woman's throat. Feeling the pulse struggling to beat.

Fiona's breath wheezed out.

"Are the others alive, Fiona?"

"Jud…"

Judith isn't alive any longer.

"Are others in these caves? Are more girls here?"

She felt the slow shake of Fiona's head. Her pulse was even weaker beneath Cadence's fingertips.

I have to get her help.

Cadence surged to her feet. She walked forward, with her hands out, movingly blindly in the darkness.

Trapped.

The blackness was so complete. Not a hint of light.

Every ragged breath seemed magnified.

Her hands scraped against rocks. The side of the cavern. She started walking around, moving her hands up and down as she tried to find an exit. A way out.

Wood.

Her breaths were even louder now as she slapped her hands against what she prayed was a door. But there was no knob on the door. Just old, rough wood. She shoved against the door.

It didn't budge.

Again and again she hit the door. Pounding.

Then Cadence remembered…

Thud. Thud.

The sounds that had drawn her to Lily in the dark.

Lily had been trapped. Desperate. But she'd kept hitting out, kept making the *thuds* that had led Cadence and Kyle to her.

Cadence hit the door again and again.

She wasn't just imagining what it was like to be a victim anymore.

She was one.

But Kyle was coming for her. She'd guide him to her location, the same way Lily had pulled them in.

Cadence lifted her bound hands and rammed them into the door.

Again and again.

She didn't care if the sounds alerted her captor. If he came back in, she'd attack him with everything she had. Cadence was *not* going to just wait in the darkness, not just sit in the silence like a good little girl while Fiona died.

She drove her hands into the door.

I didn't scream.

Cadence did. She screamed as loudly as she could.

***

Kyle froze when he heard the sounds. Pounding, like a hammer. Echoing. Sound traveled so well in the cavernous darkness.

Cadence.

He lowered his light to the ground. Made sure no trip wires were in place.

Then he fucking ran toward the sound.

The others were right behind him. Dani, who *never* went in the field but had stayed with him for Cadence. Heather and Randall. Two more cops trailed in the rear. They knew just how close they were to their prey.

His light hit a door. Old, wooden, with heavy slats running its length. "Cadence!"

The pounding stopped.

He saw a thick, metal latch and shoved it aside. It groaned as it slid free.

Then he shoved open the door.

His light hit Cadence—and the blood covering her. She stood just a few feet from the door, frozen like a statue.

"Baby." He grabbed her, pulling her close, his hands running over her desperately.

He couldn't find her wound.

"Fiona," she whispered. "We have to get her out!"

He turned. Dani had already found the other woman. Her flashlight bathed the still figure on the floor. The figure with blood soaking her shirt, and a knife still stuck in her chest.

Dani reached out a tentative hand. Touched the woman's throat.

"She's still alive," Cadence said, speaking quickly, desperately. "We can help her."

"She's dead." Dani's soft voice told them.

A hard sob choked in Cadence's throat. "It's *Fiona*! She just wanted to go home!" Then Cadence yanked away from him. "He's still here! He was just *here*! We have to find him!"

They were going to find the SOB. No, *he* was. Cadence needed to get to safety. "Dani, take Cadence out of here. I'll keep heading through the tunnels. I'll find the bastard."

"No!" Cadence's shout. Then she didn't wait for him to argue. She lunged away from him and ran through the door. Heather hurried back, but she moved too slowly. Cadence grabbed the flashlight from the woman's hands and fled deeper into the caverns.

"Cadence!" The echo of his shout reverberated as he raced after her.

She didn't stop at his call.

Was she even looking at the ground? The bastard had planned to cover his tracks before. Why not this time?

"Cadence! Look out for trip wires!"

She didn't slow. He saw the light bobbing as she ran.

He kicked up his speed, getting closer and closer to her.

He reached out his hand, but before he could grab her, she fell, tumbling down, face first, and he knew she'd tripped on something.

Kyle expected the explosion to rock through those caverns at any moment.

He expected hell to come calling and he threw himself toward Cadence. He'd protect her with his body. Maybe she'd make it out alive.

Only no explosion came.

A sob broke from Cadence. "I found them."

Her light had fallen to the ground, too, and its beam focused in the middle of the tunnel, on the object that had tripped her.

A skeleton.

No, not just one skeleton.

His own light flashed down the tunnel.

One.

Two.

Three.

The bones stretched in the darkness. A deadly trail.

The victims were now found. Bones. A graveyard in the dark.

But where was the bastard who'd done this to them? Where?

Kyle pulled Cadence to her feet. Held her close. She was shaking against him. Trying to jerk free. "He's here! We have to go after him!"

Kyle locked his arms around her. "Reinforcements are coming. We'll search the tunnels. Every damn space in here, I swear." He breathed the words against her ear.

She didn't stop struggling. "He's getting *away*! Dammit, you wanted to stop him."

He shook her. Hard. "I want you." Fuck, didn't she get that? "I want you safe. I want you out of here."

She didn't even have a gun. She was going to run blindly through the darkness? Where the killer could be waiting with his booby traps any moment?

No.

He wanted the bastard. But...

Not at the price of her life.

Footsteps rushed toward them in the darkness.

Keeping a tight hold on Cadence, he whirled, shining his light on their company.

Heather. Randall. They were both out of breath. Both gasping.

His hold tightened on Cadence. "You did your job, baby. You found another lair."

The tricky bastard. This made three kill sites. Three. Talk about confidence.

"This place connects with the other tunnels," Cadence whispered. "Fiona said it all connected."

Then they'd search until they'd covered every possible inch in the caverns. But they weren't going in blind. It was what the killer wanted. For them to chase after him so he could spring another trap.

Not happening.

"Get Cadence out of here," he said as he forced his hands to release her. He didn't want to release her. He wanted to hold her tight. To make sure she was okay.

She needed to be checked out. She'd been in a car crash. Who the hell knew what that bastard had done to her after that?

"I don't want to go," Cadence said as she dug in her heels. "I can help."

"You already have." They'd set up guards at the entrance to that hell. No one would get out that way. "We're going to send teams searching through here. We're going to find every secret the bastard has."

So many of those secrets were right there. Their bones laid out in a macabre grave.

Is Maria there?

He slammed the door on that thought. He wouldn't go there. Not yet.

He had to hold onto his control. Not let the rage and fear break through.

Cadence needed him.

He needed *her*.

"Come with me," Heather said softly. "It's okay, Agent Hollow." Her voice was low, soothing.

"Fuck that," Cadence snapped back. "Nothing's okay. You've got a sick, twisted SOB out here. He's been hunting his victims for over fifteen years. Nothing's going to be okay until we have him tossed in a cage, because he won't stop, not until then. He won't stop!"

"Cadence…"

She choked back a sob. "I couldn't save Fiona." She lifted her hands. The cuffs glinted. "If I took the knife out, she would've bled out faster. He left me with her, and there was nothing I could do."

She was breaking him. Cadence backed away.

"I can get the cuffs off you, ma'am," Heather said, still in the soothing voice. "Come with me. I have something we can use in my car."

"I was supposed to save her," Cadence whispered.

"Please, ma'am," Heather pushed softly.

Cadence moved toward her. Her steps were wooden. Slow. But she left Kyle.

Cadence glanced back. "Screw his rules," she said. "Screw him."

Kyle didn't move. He just stared after her until she vanished with Heather. Then he forced himself to speak. "There are bodies here," he said to Hollings. "We're gonna need an evidence-and-retrieval team down here." Not just local guys. Ben would make sure they had the best team they could get. He'd fly them in.

"Is he here?" Hollings whispered.

Kyle stared down the darkened tunnel. "Get the ropes because we're about to fucking find out."

***

There were too many lights outside. Bright lights flashing from the police cruisers. Headlights turned on high. Searchlights.

Local county officers were running around, desperately trying to secure the scene as the rain continued to pound them.

"Chaos," Cadence whispered as she rubbed at the goose bumps on her arms. This would be just the type of scene the perp wanted. He could slip right out with all these people here. All he'd need was a cop uniform. Or maybe even the clothes of an EMT.

"Agent Hollow?" The EMT frowned at her as Heather pushed her toward the ambulance. Heather had gotten the handcuffs off, as promised, then she'd started yelling for medical help.

I don't need help.

"Agent Hollow," the EMT insisted, "I need to examine you."

"I've got a concussion. I don't have blurry vision, no memory loss. No shaking. I'm *fine*."

His gaze slid to Heather.

"We understand why you did it," Heather said softly. "It's okay, Agent Hollow. She came at you, you must have needed to defend yourself."

Cadence blinked. "What are you talking about?"

Heather licked her lips. "The woman in the room with you. The woman you killed."

"I didn't kill her!"

"You were alone with her. The knife was in her chest. Her blood was on you."

Oh, hell. "My fingerprints are going to be on that knife, too," Cadence threw out as her head throbbed. "Just mine because the SOB was smart enough to wear gloves." He was so much smarter than the average predator and that was why he'd been able to get away with his kills for so long. "But I didn't kill her. I tried to save Fiona!"

"Fiona?" Heather's voice trembled and her eyes widened. "You mean Fiona Slater?"

"She was working with him." She raised a hand, rubbing her eyes. "No, not working with him. That's not what happened. She thought if she helped him bring me in, she'd be free. That I'd take her place." Only that hadn't been the killer's plan.

If Fiona had killed Cadence, then the SOB would have kept her alive. *Because he would have proven he had ultimate control over her.*

But when Fiona had refused...*he took her life away.*

"That's why you stabbed her?" Heather asked, her face solemn. "She was working with—"

"He stabbed her because she wouldn't kill me." Her voice was brittle. "Fiona was desperate to be free. Desperate to get her life back, but she wasn't going to kill another person, no matter what he wanted. When she didn't do it, he drove the knife into her heart and left her there with me. Left her to die." She looked down at her hands and realized they were covered with blood. No wonder Heather's eyes held so much suspicion. "I thought I might be able to keep her alive long enough for help to arrive."

If only.

"I didn't take the knife out." Her words were wooden. "That would have just made her bleed out faster. The knife stayed in, I tried to keep her calm." Every breath Cadence took seemed to hurt her. "She just wanted to go home." Her shoulders slumped as the rain pelted her. "I couldn't stop her."

Fiona Slater was finally free.

Cadence looked back at the entrance to the gaping cavern. The bushes had been shoved aside. More men armed with bright lights were slipping inside.

Some were coming out.

"Every man here..." Cadence fixed her stare back on Heather. "Take their pictures. Get their IDs. Check them all."

Heather's brows climbed. "Didn't he run away through the tunnel?"

Had he? Or had the guy just been waiting for his moment to escape? "He blends. He slips away." Nausea was rising in her throat. She couldn't seem to stop weaving on her feet. "Every man here. Get a record of everyone."

Heather nodded and hurried away.

"Agent Hollow?" The EMT pressed. "I need to examine you."

She turned to look at him. His shoulders were narrow and he was small in height, barely around five foot five.

"You're not *fine*." He emphasized her word. "With a concussion."

"You know that," she muttered. "I know that." The killer didn't. Her knees buckled.

The EMT caught her and pulled her into the back of the ambulance.

***

He'd counted six skulls. Six gleaming skulls in the darkness.

Six victims.

And one glittering necklace. A silver chain. A half-moon hung from the chain, a moon encrusted with small diamonds.

The necklace lay in the dirt, right next to a skull.

He couldn't take his gaze off the necklace.

Maria. Blood pounded in his temples. He sucked in deep gulps of air even as a hard tremble ran the length of his body.

"Agent McKenzie?"

He'd been reaching for the necklace. His hand fisted. "Tell the techs to use every care here. These are *people*." Not bones. Loved ones.

Women who'd been beautiful in life. Happy.

His light swept away from the necklace.

He made himself advance carefully through the maze of caverns, using the rope to make certain he didn't get lost in the endless night. His light swept ahead. No trip wires. No sign of anyone up there.

His light hit on the outline of wood. Just like the wood that had blocked the chamber Cadence had been held in.

Another door. A very old one.

"I heard that back during the war," came the voice of Hollings behind him, "Confederates had secret gunpowder rooms hidden in the area. They stored guns and weapons, trying to keep 'em out of Union hands."

Their hideaways had been left behind, the perfect prison for their perp to use.

A long, heavy bar slid across the front of the door. A bar designed not to keep people out.

But to hold someone *in*.

He wrapped his hand around the bar. Was another victim inside? He pulled it back, and the old metal groaned.

When the door opened seconds later, he was holding tight to his gun and his light.

His light swept the interior of the chamber, landing on a bed, a bucket...

"Agent McKenzie?"

He turned at Hollings's hesitant voice. His light hit the man, and the video camera in his hand.

"A camera. It was right here," Hollings said, "half in the wall."

He kept them down here, and he watched them.

The sick SOB.

"We're gonna need Dani." The camera wouldn't be able to transmit too far. Not down here with all the rocks. They had been going down as they walked. He'd felt the incline.

The man would want to see his prisoner. Watch her all the time.

Kyle stalked out of the room. Hollings was with him. Fuck, the rope didn't have any more slack. There were no sounds of other footsteps behind them.

Or in front.

To keep searching, they were going to need more help.

He wasn't ready to give up.

The camera…the room…

He'd seen hell. So had the women the perp had taken.

Hell was a small, five-by-eight-foot chamber. A room with no lights or windows. A room smelling of human waste and decay.

A room with no hope.

Only death.

Deep inside, Kyle knew the room had been the last thing his sister had ever seen.

I'm going to kill you, bastard. I don't care about doing what's right. You're not going to see the inside of a cell. You won't fucking get off that easily.

A calm settled over him. Chilling him.

The death wouldn't be easy because the SOB didn't deserve easy.

He deserved to suffer, as all his victims had suffered.

Kyle would make sure he didn't get an easy end.

***

"Looks like we've recovered the remains of six victims in those caverns." Ben Griffin's voice was soft. "Seven, counting Fiona."

Cadence flinched at his words. She hadn't even realized he'd been next to her. She'd been sitting there, her eyes glued to the entrance of the cavern.

Fiona Slater had just been brought out. Judith had already been secured inside a black body bag. The growing sunlight peeked through the remnants of the clouds and fell on the bag.

Fiona was free.

"You did a good job, Cadence."

Good job, her ass. Cadence pushed to her feet. The dizziness was mild this time. She only staggered a little bit. She dropped the blanket that had been wrapped around her shoulders and squared off with Ben. "He got away."

Ben shook his head. "They're still searching the caverns."

"He left the minute the FBI arrived. As soon as he realized what was happening, he was gone." She waved toward the scene. "He was one of the ones who just walked right out of the cavern."

Ben frowned at her.

"He's authoritative. He knows the area intimately. He's domi-nant. Smart. He's...*one of us*. He's working the case because I'm betting he was tipped off the minute the authorities started clos-ing in on this place." Her words came, faster and faster. "The rea-son no one has ever been found? He knows what the authorities are gonna do *before* they do it."

"Cadence." His voice was so calm. It made her want to scream. "Cadence, you need to go back to your motel. Get some sleep. You recovered *eight* victims."

"Fiona Slater was alive seven hours ago. If I'd really done my job, she would still be alive right now." A brutal truth. One that would haunt Cadence the rest of her life. "Her death is on me."

Ben's fingers locked around her shoulders. Ben. He'd always been a good friend. But one tough, demanding boss. "It's on him,"

Ben gritted out. "Not you. It's on that sick prick who gets off on torturing women."

"It's not about torture." She saw that. Torture was a means to an end. "It's control. He controls everything. He makes them into what he wants them to be."

If they didn't live up to his expectations...

He eliminated them.

Ben's hold on her tightened. "Cadence, did you see his face?"

She shook her head. "It was too dark." That consuming darkness had been all around her. Then...*his light.* The blinding light had come from his helmet. The echo of fear beat through her, but she pushed it back. Cadence remembered that light. Remembered him. "I know he's approximately six foot three, maybe four. Broad shoulders. Strong."

"If you didn't see his face, you can't say he's one of the men here." He leaned toward her. "We can't accuse the local cops. Do you know what kind of media nightmare that would be? You didn't see him. You were concussed. Trapped in the dark. Hell, take the win, okay?"

The win? Where was the win? Was the win the woman in the body bag?

"We can give those eight families closure now. They can finally bury their daughters."

They'd rather be hugging them. Welcoming them home. She swallowed, trying to ease the tightness in her throat. Cadence tore her eyes off Ben and looked over his shoulder. Kyle stalked from the cavern. When he saw them, his eyes narrowed.

"I'm not sure." Her voice was soft, weak, because there was no proof to back up what she had to say next.

She only had the push in her gut. Instincts.

The hope that had been born when she realized Fiona Slater had survived for so long.

Hope that hadn't died with Fiona. Hope that was too stubborn to die now. They'd had *two* live victims.

"I'm not sure they are all dead." A whispered confession just to Ben. She'd whispered her words to Ben because she was afraid to give those words to Kyle.

There had been thirteen tally marks on that wall. Lily was one mark. The remains they'd found in the Statue of Liberty chamber were another.

Judith made three.

The fourth tally mark? That would have been poor Fiona.

And they'd found six skulls tonight.

That leaves two more victims. One tally mark could belong to Lily.

But what about the last mark? Where is she?

"He kept them separated," she said softly. "Isolated. Three containment areas we know of…" What if there were more?

The number of spots spoke of his confidence. His absolute control.

At first, he'd probably kept his prey in one location.

Here.

This was where he'd kept the skeletons. The presence of the bones indicated this spot was special to him.

But he'd branched out as his confidence grew, as the years passed and no one stopped him. No one but Kyle had even realized he was hunting.

No one but Kyle.

And the killer had *called* Kyle. Directly taunted him.

She frowned as she gazed at her partner. He was stalking toward her.

"We found a recording device in one of the chambers." Kyle's voice was cold. Distant. But his eyes were blazing with fire.

Ben released her and turned to face him.

"I think he watched the women. Used infrared filming. He wanted to see them in the dark."

Why was the dark so important to him?

The dark... "He controlled the light," Cadence said. She'd been trapped in the darkness. Not able to make a sound. He hadn't wanted her to scream.

Why?

There was silence in the caves.

Silence in the isolated cabin.

Darkness. Silence.

That *he* controlled.

"We missed it," Cadence said as a burst of adrenaline pumped through her.

Dani had just left the caverns. She hurried toward them, her eyes wide and haunted.

Dani had gone back into the field...*for me.*

When she reached their group, Dani wrapped her arms around Cadence and held her tightly. "Don't ever scare me like that again," she gritted.

Dani had scared her once, years before. When she'd been stabbed fifteen times in the chest and left for dead by a perp. Dani had survived the attack, barely.

Her blood had coated Cadence's fingers as surely as Fiona's had.

But Dani had *survived.*

Only she'd never quite been the same. All the psych evaluations had said she wouldn't be able to handle the pressure of fieldwork.

She should have left the FBI.

She hadn't.

Ben had just made a new job for her. One that kept her safe. Until now.

Dani had lain in the hospital bed for weeks. Her eyes shut. Trapped in her own body. Unable to speak or move without help.

A prisoner.

Every muscle in Cadence's body locked. "He's doing to them what was done to him."

Dani pulled back, frowning at her. "What do you mean?"

"We need to do a search, pull medical records. This man may have even been blinded temporarily. He wasn't able to communicate with others. He was hurt and now he's doing the same thing to his victims." Controlling them, as he'd been controlled.

Kyle's eyes narrowed.

"We need to go back." Cadence tried to figure out the time line. "It would have been before Maria's disappearance. Probably several years before." Her heart was pounding because now, she *saw*.

The victims had been the key for her. She'd seen what they'd seen. Heard what they heard.

What the killer had heard.

"We're looking for a car accident. On an old highway." The victims had vehicles abandoned on old highways. The SOB had come after her car with such intensity. There was a pattern, a reason, behind everything he did. "He was probably hurt in the wreck. He would have stayed in the hospital for a long time. Weeks, maybe months."

He kept his victims for a long time.

Years?

"You can find him, can't you, Dani?" she pushed.

Dani nodded. "I can search through accident reports. Check the databases for hospitals in the area."

"All four states," Cadence pressed as Kyle and Ben watched her in silence. "All from his kill zones. Don't overlook any of them."

Dani nodded.

"The guy was smart. He deliberately crossed state lines, deliberately spread out the abductions into different jurisdictions so that it would be harder for law enforcement to connect his crimes. But we know what he did, and we can find him now." This was it. This was how they would figure out the perp's identity. Then there would be no hiding for him. No pretending.

No blending in.

They'd have him.

"Our crime team from Quantico is flying in," Ben said, but his voice was considering. He went with her hunches, always had. No, not a hunch. *Profile.* She was certain. "They'll search the caverns. The professor from Auburn said he'd have his team out here at first light."

She could hear the approach of more vehicles. The professor was already arriving?

"I think there's more video equipment in those caves," Kyle said. His voice was still off. Too unemotional to match the discoveries they'd made. One of those skeletons could be his sister's, but the man was acting like ice water poured through his veins.

This wasn't the man she knew.

Cadence tried to slide closer to him.

He stiffened, then backed up a step.

Cadence's breath caught. He'd never withdrawn from her before, and that small move hurt.

"A signal wouldn't go far, not down in a place like that," Kyle continued in his wooden voice. "So he must have a base room down there. If there's more equipment…"

"We'll find it." Ben's voice held plenty of emotion. And confidence. "We've got the equipment and the manpower coming in. Every damn secret he has down there, we'll discover."

"But you don't think *he's* there," Cadence said. She'd caught what Ben said—and what he hadn't. "You don't think he's hiding inside."

"I think our boy had an escape plan in place, but I don't think he'll run forever." Ben gave her another nod. "I told you, you did well on this one, Cadence. Now get back to your motel room before you collapse." His voice hardened. "'Cause if you don't get some rest soon, I'll make those EMTs take you to the hospital."

She started to shake her head.

Ben pointed to Kyle. "Take her to the motel."

Kyle's jaw locked. Cadence was sure he didn't want to leave the scene.

"You both need time to rest, and this scene is covered, okay? I'll supervise every move until you get back."

A car door slammed. "Cadence?"

It was Aaron. Shouting her name. Running toward her and looking incredibly relieved when he saw her face.

"I can't believe…" He stumbled to a stop. "I'm so glad you're all right!"

He was tall. Just around Kyle's height of six foot three. His shoulders weren't as broad as Kyle's but with the right coat in the dark, they could appear stronger.

"You didn't mention the caverns tracked this far over," she said to him.

Dani and Ben were both regarding him with suspicion.

But Kyle just looked on with those glacial eyes of his. Blue flames in ice.

That's not Kyle.

"I didn't know!" Aaron jerked a hand through his hair, causing it to jut out at rough angles. "I never explored this far!"

"Marsh told me stories have circulated up here ever since the Civil War." Kyle's voice was as cold as his eyes. She wanted to shake him. To make the real man come back out. "Confederates hid weapons up here."

"And gangsters used caverns as speakeasies. Yes, yes, I know, but *finding* these places, after all this time, it's next to impossible." Aaron's breath heaved out. "If I'd known, I would have told you! I didn't! No one on my team knew about this area!" He gave some fast nods. "But I'm here to help you. *Anything* I or my team can do—"

"Don't worry," replied Ben's certain voice. "You'll help us plenty." Ben's gaze met hers. He understood. She could see it in Ben's stare. Aaron was on their suspect list. To be watched, questioned, and certainly not trusted.

"Take her back to the motel," Ben told Kyle once more. "We'll meet back up at noon and see what's been discovered."

She expected Kyle to argue. Instead, he took her hand in a grip that was too light. As if she were too delicate. Or as if he didn't want to touch her at all.

He led her away from the others. Opened the passenger side door of his vehicle. Giant streaks of mud covered much of the SUV.

She didn't speak, not until he was in the vehicle with her. Not until the others were shut out and they were on their way back down the mountain. "Kyle?" She hated the hesitation in her own voice.

The fear.

"When I found your car, I thought you were already dead," he said. There was still no emotion in his voice.

She had to break through his ice. "You saw the tracking device, though. You found me." *You kept your promise.* She'd known he would come for her.

"How did Fiona die?"

She glanced out the window at the swirl of the trees. "When she wouldn't kill me, he killed her."

"That's what I thought."

How could he sound so cold?

"But what if she *had* gone after you, Cadence? Would you have killed her in order to save yourself?"

She hated that question. Deep inside, she wasn't sure of her answer.

Fiona had suffered so much.

"The plan didn't fucking work." The words sliced like ice. No, like a knife. "I could have walked into that chamber and found you on the ground, with a knife in your chest."

She glanced back at him. His knuckles had whitened around the wheel.

"Kyle..."

"What do you think I would have done then?"

She had to be careful. The ice was a lie, a protection to keep the fire inside him from raging out of control. "Our job is about risk."

"Fuck the risk. *What do you think I would have done?*" The words were a lethal whisper.

Before she could respond, he said, "I can't lose you. I *won't.* I'll do any damn thing necessary to make sure you're never in his sights again."

***

They'd found his girls. Soon, they would be brought out of the darkness. They'd be identified. Their families would be contacted.

The FBI would keep searching. The unit director was there now, a self-important jerk who was barking orders. He wanted everyone to be careful.

The guy was afraid traps were inside.

But he hadn't put traps in this area. He hadn't thought the FBI would be coming to this spot. This was *his*.

No one should have found it.

The bitch had been tracked. He shouldn't have taken her. He should have just killed her.

He *would* kill her.

He had unfinished business. He should have stuck to his original plan.

His original victim.

By letting Lily go, by letting her live, everything had unraveled. She'd been chosen, she was the one who had to join him.

Or else she had to die.

He wasn't going to lose all he'd built. The FBI was supposed to see how powerful he was. That was the point. He'd gone too many years with no one knowing, no one realizing all he'd done.

Time is running out. The world needed to know about him.

While others had their names splashed in papers. The Valentine Killer. The Bayou Butcher. Twisted freaks who didn't understand the value of a perfect victim.

He understood. He was better than all the others. So different. He deserved the attention. The FBI—everyone—had to recognize just how great he was.

How weak they were.

He wasn't going down easily. The end would come, but the end would be on *his* terms. Just the way he'd planned.

He'd faced the darkness. He controlled the darkness.

After all this time.

I am still in control.

The others were just prey. It was time he eliminated them.

One by one.

Lily, my love. I'll start with you.

CHAPTER FOURTEEN

"You're not supposed to sleep when you have a concussion," Cadence said softly.

Kyle was in her room. His back to her.

He wouldn't look at her. "Then just rest." He seemed to grit out the words.

His back was so tight. His shoulders tense.

She stepped toward him. Reached out her hand.

He spun toward her in an instant, his fingers locking around her wrist. "You don't want to do that."

"Why not?" From where she stood, it looked as if the man needed her. Perhaps far more than he realized.

"If sleep isn't good for a concussion, then what I want to do to you sure isn't either." The words were a growled warning.

A warning she ignored. "Kyle."

He pulled away from her. Dropped her hand. "Get in the bed, Cadence. Don't sleep. I'll stay with you. Make sure you just rest." He turned his back on her. *Again.*

Resting wasn't what she wanted.

"I need to wash away the blood." Samples of the blood had been taken by the techs. Now she wanted to scrub herself clean. To get the smell of the caverns off her.

His shoulders tensed. "Your clothes are evidence. I'll need to bag them. Send them to the lab."

She glanced down at her torn clothes.

"Do you need help in the bathroom?" he asked.

"No," Cadence said as she moved away from him. Whatever wall he was trying to put up between them, she wasn't going to allow it. They'd come too far for that distance now.

"I don't want you risking your life for me." His words were a low rumble that stopped her at the bathroom door. "You think I don't know what you were doing? You went in there, you put your life on the line, for me."

She braced her hands on the door frame. "The victims needed me." *I'm sorry, Fiona.* What if she'd recognized the woman when she first appeared at Cadence's window? What if…

"What if you'd died for me? For a sister who's probably been turned to bones for these last fifteen years?"

"Kyle!" She whirled toward him.

His jaw was clenched as he turned and stared at her with glittering eyes. "I saw her necklace. The half-moon charm I gave her when she turned eighteen. It was with the bones. I saw it when I was searching in the caverns."

Cadence didn't remember seeing a necklace. Just skulls. Femurs. Death.

"I didn't touch it. I just saw it." His shoulders rolled back. "She's gone. You could have been, too."

She hurt for him. Cadence wanted to wrap her arms around Kyle and just hold him.

He shook his head and retreated a step from her. "Take your shower. If you need me, I'm here."

"What about what you need?" Cadence demanded. She wanted to scream at him. To break through to him. "Dammit, Kyle, *talk* to me."

"What I need?" The words were so low, she strained to hear them. "I need him. Dead. In front of me."

That wasn't an agent talking. That was a grief-stricken, revenge-driven brother.

"That's what I'll have."

She knew the words were a vow.

***

Danielle Burton stared at the entrance to the caverns. She didn't want to go back inside. Ben was already in there, leading a group of local authorities. Searching deep into what she thought had to be the entrance to hell.

The bones were being brought out. Slowly. Carefully.

The FBI's forensics team had arrived moments earlier. As soon as Cadence had vanished the night before, Ben had ordered the team be brought in.

She wondered if he'd expected to find Cadence's body.

Dani wasn't sure she wanted to know the answer.

Then Ben appeared, striding from the caverns. His broad shoulders and handsome face were covered with dirt. He was walking fast, and his eyes shone with excited intensity.

He found something.

"Tapes," he said as soon as he got close to her. "DVDs, CDs. We hit the freaking mother lode in there."

Her breath blew out lightly as she tried to keep her expression blank. "You know what will be on those tapes." There was only one reason for the perp to have kept them.

They were his trophies. The moments of his victims, recorded. Kept.

"I don't want Kyle seeing them," Ben said and some of the excitement faded from his gaze. "Not until you have a chance to view them first. See who's on there. See what happened to them."

Sometimes, she hated her job. "There aren't any more survivors?"

"Not down there. We reached the cave-in wall, what I think is the cave-in, anyway, from the explosion at the last site."

"If you reached the wall, then how'd he get out?" But she knew. Heather had already told her about Cadence's orders to photograph and get the name of every man at the scene.

He just walked right out. He was beside us.

Ben nodded, obviously reading her expression. "The SOB is playing with us. I'm tired of playing."

She didn't think the guy was playing "with us." She thought he was jerking Kyle around, and from what she'd seen, it appeared the agent was close to breaking.

Been there, done that.

"Cadence can go over the tapes with you. She'll know what to look for."

Terrible plan. It would be like making Cadence face her own hell, over and over again.

But...*Cadence knows the victims.* Dani swallowed. Some days, she wasn't sure how Cadence stayed sane.

"I have to go in to the police station," Dani said. She was surprised her voice came out sounding so normal. She didn't feel normal. It was one hundred and ten degrees out there, and she had goose bumps. "I need to run the medical records check, and I can't do it out here."

The signals were shit. They'd sure gotten lucky they'd been able to trace Cadence as far as they had.

He nodded. "I'll bring the evidence tapes in to you myself." Ben turned to leave.

"Why did you lie?" She had to ask. It had been bothering her since Maverick.

Ben stiffened. He glanced over his shoulder. "I don't know what you mean."

Since she'd been sleeping with Ben for over a year, Dani had gotten to know him pretty well. Well enough to be able to tell when he lied to her. "That story about the kids who were missing for years—the one you fed Cadence and Kyle—why'd you do it?"

He moved to fully face her, the faint lines near his eyes deepening. "What makes you think it was a lie?" His head cocked. "You haven't been digging into *my* files, have you, Dani?"

Not yet. It sure was an item on her to-do list now. "You've had nightmares."

He blinked.

"You scream out, 'Kill me, not the kids!'" The words haunted her.

His lips thinned. "In my nightmares, I don't get to the kids in time," he said, stepping closer to her. Close enough for her to feel the brush of his body against hers. "In reality, I fucking did. I got those kids. I saved them. I told that story, a story I don't tell many people, because I know just how close to the edge Kyle is." He pulled in a ragged breath. "My job is to make sure he doesn't go over the edge until we close this case."

***

The shower had stopped. It had stopped a good five minutes ago, but Cadence hadn't come out of the bathroom yet.

Kyle glanced toward the bathroom door. "Cadence?"

He took a step toward the closed door, then stopped. Behind the door, he knew what waited. Cadence. Naked, wet.

No, he didn't need to get close to her right then. Someone else—Dani, Heather—should have been sent to watch her at the motel.

Not me.

A rap sounded at the motel's door.

Frowning, he glanced over his shoulder. He sure as hell wasn't expecting anyone then.

And as far as he knew, neither was Cadence. This was her room. No one would know he was in here with Cadence.

He checked through the small peephole and saw the detective, Jason Marsh.

Eyes narrowed, Kyle yanked open the motel room door. He made sure his body blocked the entrance. "What do you want, Marsh?"

Jason blinked. "I wanted to see Cadence."

"She's in the shower." Let him assume whatever the fuck he wanted.

The guy's jaw hardened. "I was going back to the station. I just wanted to stop by and make sure she was all right."

Wasn't that nice of him?

Kyle tilted his head as he studied the guy. "She's not going to sleep with you."

Jason's mouth dropped open in shock, but he recovered fast and said, "Look, man, I was—"

"We both know what you want, and it isn't happening." Jason had made it clear what he wanted the first night in Striker's.

"I was *worried* about her," Jason snapped.

"I don't remember seeing you at the caves," Kyle said as he studied the man before him. "If you were so worried…"

"I was there! Dammit, I was searching, just like the rest of you!"

He didn't remember seeing the guy. His gaze raked Jason's face. "How'd you get that scar? Looks like it almost took out your eye." Cadence's theory pushed through his mind. *The killer had spent time in darkness.*

Jason rocked back on his heels. "Car accident when I was a teen. And yeah, I almost lost the eye, but that's ancient history."

Kyle wasn't so sure. "You knew where the caves were. You took us right to the body." Suspicion was tight inside of him. This guy just came right up to Cadence's room? Who the hell did he think he was? "You took us there. Then you left us when the walls caved in."

"I went for *help.*" Marsh's cheeks flushed. "If you don't believe me, ask Anniston! I called the captain as soon as I got out, and I told him that you were trapped down there! You should be thanking me, not—"

"What's going on?" Cadence's voice. Worried.

He hadn't even heard the bathroom door open.

Kyle glanced over his shoulder. Her hair was wet, her pale skin scrubbed clean, and she wore a terry-cloth robe.

She needed more fucking clothes on then.

Jason shoved Kyle aside as he stormed into the room.

Wrong move.

"Your partner is accusing me. Hell, I think he believes *I'm* the Night Hunter!"

Cadence's gaze sharpened on Jason. "Are you?"

"What? Hell, *no.*"

Kyle grabbed Jason and spun him around so the two were eye to eye. "Where were you last night, when Cadence was taken? Just where the fuck were you?"

His hold was unbreakable as he trapped Jason in place.

The man's face mottled with fury. "Where were *you*?" Jason tossed right back. "You're her partner! Shouldn't you have been with her?"

He wanted to break the bastard's arm. Actually, that sounded like a damn good idea.

"I was at Striker's!" Jason shouted as Kyle's hold tightened. "Ask the waitresses! They saw me. I was there until I got the call to join the search for Cadence!"

Easy enough to check. Kyle planned to do exactly that.

He shoved the man aside. No, he shoved the fool right back out the door.

"I could write your ass up for assaulting an officer," Jason threw at him.

Kyle's brows climbed. "Let's see how that shit works out for you," he dared.

Jason's gaze tried to cut over Kyle's shoulder. Back to Cadence? "I'm sorry about what happened to you. This dick"—he pointed his index finger toward Kyle—"isn't gonna stop me from saying that. I thought you were damn brave to face off with that perp, and if you need me, if you need anything…" He gave a nod. "You call me."

Kyle imagined driving his fist into the guy's face. Hearing the crunch of bones.

"Thank you," Cadence said. "I will."

Jason gave a jerky nod, then he was gone, hurrying down the steps to the parking area.

Kyle slammed the door after him and yanked the flimsy lock back into place.

Then he felt Cadence's fingers on his arm. He didn't turn to her, not yet. Instead, he grabbed for his phone and had Ben on the line in seconds. "I want you to run another check on Jason Marsh's background." They'd checked before, but they damn well needed to do it again.

"What's happened?"

He's too interested in Cadence. Too focused. He cleared his throat. "Cadence has a new theory on injuries the perp may have sustained. Dani's checking, but—tell her to look at Marsh's background. He fits." He quickly explained about Marsh's accident.

Do you like the darkness, Detective?

A huge part of him wanted to race out of that door and go after Marsh but…

Cadence came too close to death.

He couldn't leave her now.

"I'm on it," Ben assured him. "That guy won't move tonight without me knowing exactly where he's at, every second."

That was exactly what he wanted to hear. Kyle ended the call and tossed the phone onto the small nightstand.

"You think I can't see what's happening to you?" Cadence demanded, her voice low. "Kyle, you're ripping apart right in front of me."

Fifteen years' worth of grief was ravaging through him, twisting up with the rage and fear of nearly losing Cadence.

His eyes squeezed shut. The useless movement didn't stop the vision. He saw Cadence, bathed in his light. Blood on her face. Fear in her eyes.

If Cadence died, he would truly be lost.

I love her.

No, it was more than love. Too hard and dark and dangerous for love. Too consuming.

She was his drug.

His breath.

His fucking everything.

"Talk to me," she whispered.

Grief and rage and fear twisted inside of him and made it damn hard to think. All he could do was feel.

I can make her feel, too. But maybe he could be careful. Maybe he could show her.

He turned in her arms and found her staring up at him with the eyes that had always seen straight through him.

"I need you," he said, pushing the words out. Those growled words were more true than she'd probably ever realize. "I can be careful."

She pulled him toward the bed.

This room. This bed. Her.

He'd touched heaven here.

Then found hell waiting in the dark.

"Lie down," Cadence told him.

Kyle slipped down onto the mattress. The bedsprings groaned beneath him. He wanted fury and flesh. Desperate passion. A release that left him hollowed and hungry.

But he couldn't hurt her.

Wouldn't.

She let the robe fall to the floor. There were bruises on her flesh. The sight of the darkened blue and brown marks made him even angrier. He wanted to kiss that skin. To take all of her pain away.

"Don't see the pain," she said.

Her voice had his eyes rising to her face.

"It doesn't matter."

It mattered to him.

"You. Me. This minute. That's what I want you to think about," Cadence told him.

She slid onto the bed. Her silken thighs straddled his jeans-clad legs. He'd changed while she showered. He'd cleaned himself, then hurried back into the adjoining room to be with her.

Always, he wanted to be with her.

She bent toward him. Pressed her lips to his. "I knew you were coming for me."

"I should have been there sooner."

Her fingers sank into his hair. She tilted up his head. Made him look at her. "Let it go."

He blinked, not sure.

"Let the guilt go. She didn't blame you for anything, and neither do I."

Then her mouth was on his. Sweet, full, her lips pressed to his as her tongue dipped into his mouth.

Her hands were between their bodies. Opening the snap of his jeans. Pulling down his zipper.

It was wrong. She was hurt.

Need.

He kissed her back. Harder. Tasted her as his tongue thrust inside her mouth.

Then his hands were between their bodies. His fingers pushed between her thighs. Careful. So very careful. He eased his index finger into her sex.

She moaned into his mouth.

Her scent, her body, was all around him.

Life. That was what Cadence was to him. His hope, his chance. His life.

A second finger pushed into her.

He wanted to lift her. To roll and pin her beneath him. To taste every secret she had.

To lick her until she screamed.

I can't. I have to stay gentle. No more pain for Cadence. No more.

She caught his hands. Pushed them away.

He tensed.

She took his cock in her hands. Her silken, soft hands. Stroking him, base to tip. Again and again. The blood heated beneath his skin. Pounded through his veins.

She rose onto her knees and positioned his cock at the entrance to her body.

His hands lifted.

Threaded with hers. Held hers.

A faint furrow appeared between her brows.

He thrust into her, not the driving, consuming thrust he wanted to take. Slow, easy, and he watched her expression for any sign of pain.

Only pleasure whispered over her face.

She started to push up on her knees.

"No." His whisper was rough.

He was afraid too much movement would jar her. *Be careful. Be careful.*

His flesh swelled even more within her. He arched his hips, pushing deeper.

She pushed down, a gentle glide of her hips.

Her fingers squeezed his, tighter.

He stretched her completely, feeling every inch of her sex. She was so hot. Wet. Perfect. A sensual heat that had his jaw clenching.

"Have to…" Her breath panted. "I need to move."

She rose up onto her knees.

Slid back onto him. His flesh pushed through her heat. Drove deeper.

His right hand stayed twined with hers.

But his left moved, going to the juncture of her thighs. Then down, to press against the sensitive flesh that waited. "Don't move, Cadence." She needed release. But she wouldn't have pain.

He wouldn't allow her pain.

His fingers stroked over her. His cock stayed in her.

Her eyes on him.

His fingers on her.

Stroking. Caressing.

When she came, her delicate inner muscles clamped his length, milking his release from him because he couldn't hold back anymore.

He exploded within her, even as he kept his hips locked down against the mattress. His release pulsed through him, jetting into her. Cadence whispered his name, her breath heaving, as she leaned forward, pressing her chest to his.

He wrapped his arms around her. Held her.

Her heart thundered against his chest. Or maybe it was his own heart. Right then, it was too hard to tell the difference. Too hard to tell anything but how much he loved holding her.

He pushed back her hair, held her against his chest, and didn't pull his cock from her. The damn thing was still half erect, and growing more so by the moment. He didn't want to move, though. He wanted to stay part of her.

"Don't go to sleep." His voice was gruff.

"I won't," she said softly.

The bedside lamp was still on. The light seemed harsh then, but she might need the light to help her stay awake.

"I know she's gone." He hadn't meant to say the words. Kyle felt Cadence stiffen. "I want to kill him." He confessed his dark wish even as his fingertips skimmed lightly over the delicate curve of her spine.

"Kyle…"

"I *will* kill him." She should know the truth about the man with her. "I'm not planning to bring him in alive."

It was easier to confess to her when he didn't have to stare into her eyes and see just what she truly thought of him.

But some monsters didn't belong in cages. They belonged in hell.

He felt a hot splash against his shoulder.

It took him an instant to realize—*Cadence was crying.*

Cadence didn't cry.

His hold tightened on her.

"I wanted to save her," she whispered.

"So did I." Maria, Judith, Fiona, Christa—he wished they could have saved *all* of the victims.

He hadn't been able to do that. He could do one thing, though. He could stop the perp from taking another woman. From destroying another family.

That he would do.

"From here on out, where you go, I go." Kyle's words were flat. His fingers kept sliding over her spine. "If he thinks he'll get to you again, he's wrong. He'll have to come through me first." That was exactly what Kyle wanted. To face off with the man who got off on imprisoning women in the darkness.

His phone rang then, and Kyle tensed. Would it be the SOB, calling to taunt him again? Another burner phone, another tear-filled plea from his sister?

When he'd found the camera in the caverns, he'd realized he'd been listening to his sister's recording during the calls.

Once she had begged for him.

The phone rang.

But she was far past begging for anyone then.

On the third ring, his hand slid over to the nightstand. He picked up the phone. "McKenzie."

"Kyle!" It was Dani's voice. Excited. "Kyle, I did that check, just like Cadence said. People who'd been in car accidents who went into the hospital." It sounded like a door shut behind her. "I got three hits. *Three.* All on men in this town right now."

Cadence sat up, frowning.

Kyle turned the phone on speaker so she could hear better. "Three? Who are they?" he demanded. But he already knew one…

Cadence had been right all along. To know the killer, you had to learn about the victims.

"The geology professor, Aaron Peters. He was hit by a drunk driver when he was twelve. The guy had to stay in the hospital for almost three months after that. He was in a coma, and the docs weren't sure he'd ever wake up."

Cadence's breath caught.

"Ben told me about Marsh, so I focused on him fast. Seems he was in an accident when he was sixteen. He was driving with his twin sister, Caroline. His sister died at the scene. The guy couldn't go to her funeral because he was in the hospital. He had a brain injury, and it took days for the swelling to go down."

The cop had just been at the motel. Was it to check up on Cadence, or for something more?

"Who's the third man?" Cadence asked carefully.

"I had to dig farther for this one. It was over thirty years ago. Happened just over the state line in Tennessee. James Anniston was hit head-on."

"The captain?" Cadence asked, surprise sharpening her voice.

"Yeah, he wasn't hurt too badly, though. He was pinned in the car overnight, had some stitches and was sent home from the hospital a few days later."

Excitement still hummed in Dani's voice. "Ben's rounding them all up now. I figured you'd want to be in on the questioning."

Damn straight.

"We're on our way to the station," Kyle said.

But…Anniston? Anniston was trying desperately to *find* the women. He'd been the one to call Kyle back down to Paradox.

The other two, yeah, they were the right age. They were the ones with access to the caverns. The ones who seemed to know the area best.

"The tapes are here, too," Dani added, the excitement slipping away from her voice.

"Tapes?" Cadence asked as she frowned down at the phone.

"Dozens of them. Ben thinks the girls are on here."

Their lives. Their deaths.

Cadence's gaze rose and held Kyle's. "We're on our way," she repeated, her voice soft.

The call ended.

Cadence didn't move. Neither did Kyle.

"They're leads," Cadence said, with a slow nod. "We'll talk to Marsh, Peters, and Anniston, and see if we can get one of them to break."

Break the way the bastard had made his victims break.

***

Dani shut the door to her temporary office. Ben had commandeered the space for her so she could work in peace.

She'd already set up her equipment.

Now it was time to watch those tapes.

The chair squeaked when she sat down. Dani leaned forward and cued up the first video.

Static crackled across the scene. Almost instantly, the blinding white of that static gave way to darkness.

The cave?

There was a faint click, as if the camera had been adjusted—and suddenly she was seeing things in the faint tinge of infrared.

She could see the rough outline of a bed. A woman was on the bed.

"*Please...*"

The softest of whispers.

Dani leaned toward the screen as she narrowed her eyes. Her breath was coming too quickly. Her heart racing.

"I—I want to go home..."

The woman's hands were bound.

And there was a man standing right over her.

The man had navigated that room. He'd turned on his camera. Then he'd gotten close in that perfect darkness.

He just stood there. Watching the woman. Listening to her soft cries.

"Look at the camera," Dani muttered. "Come on, bastard, look this way."

But he didn't. His back was to her. His whole focus was on the woman. The woman who whispered, "*I don't like the dark...*"

***

Three suspects. Three men who were swearing their innocence.

There were two interrogation rooms at the Paradox police station. One room currently housed a tense and too quiet Aaron

290

Peters. The second room contained a pissed Jason Marsh, a man who was currently being guarded by two fellow cops.

And their third suspect? James Anniston waited patiently in the conference room.

"He didn't argue," Ben said as he stood with Kyle and Cadence right outside of the rooms. "Just told me, 'Get me cleared and back on the case.'"

Cadence glanced over at Kyle. She knew he thought Anniston was innocent.

At this point, Cadence wasn't nearly as trusting. "Kyle, give Ben your gun before we start the interviews."

His blue eyes narrowed on her.

Cadence lifted her chin. This was a deal breaker for her. Kyle was ready to kill, she got that, but it wasn't happening in here. She wasn't going to let him shoot an unarmed man, even if the bastard was a twisted SOB who belonged in a hole in the ground.

She loved Kyle too much to let him throw his life away.

Even as that thought raced through her mind, Cadence actually took a step back. *Love?* When had that happened?

Ben cleared his throat, bringing her back, even as his brows climbed. "Uh, something I should know here?"

Very, very slowly, Kyle pulled out his weapon. Then he gave it, grip first, to Ben.

Ben frowned at Kyle. "I can trust you, can't I, Agent?"

Kyle had already turned away from him.

Cadence squared her shoulders.

Time to figure out if one of these three men was a killer.

We'll start with Anniston.

Kyle opened the door to the conference room.

CHAPTER FIFTEEN

"I wasn't hurt in that accident." Anniston's voice was gruff, his gaze faraway as he seemed to revisit his past. "I don't know what that little lady of yours found, but I barely had any scrapes. They kept me in the hospital just as a precaution." He rubbed his jaw. "The other driver, now, she was hurt. I could hear her, calling out for help, but there wasn't anything I could do."

His fingers dropped to the table. Drummed. Stilled. "I was a seventeen-year-old kid. She'd hit me. Came right out from nowhere. I was scared as shit. She was dying, begging for help, and I was pinned in the car. I wasn't strong enough to get the metal off me, and I couldn't do anything but sit there and wait for her to stop calling out to me."

His ragged breath filled the room.

"When my eyes opened the next day, the first person I saw was a cop. He was there, telling me everything was gonna be all right." His lips twisted. "He was a damn liar, of course, but he was trying to help me. I knew then I wanted to save people, too. I didn't want to ever hear anyone begging for help again."

Cadence didn't let her expression change at his words. The killer she was after seemed to crave silence, and Anniston had just confessed he didn't want to hear victims begging for help. "What was it like for you, hearing her cries?"

He swallowed and his Adam's apple bobbed. "It was hell, Agent Hollow. As close to hell as I ever want to get. There wasn't a damn thing I could do for that poor woman, no matter how much she pleaded with me." The echo of pain flashed in his gaze.

Cadence kept her eyes on Anniston's face. "When Maria McKenzie vanished fifteen years ago, why didn't you initially believe she was the victim of foul play?"

His stare cut to Kyle. Kyle stood just to the left of the table, watching them both carefully. Guilt was etched across the captain's face. "We'd never had something like that happen around here. She was an eighteen-year-old girl, supposed to be meeting up with friends on a beach trip. Hell, I figured they were following each other—that when her car stopped, she just hitched a ride with them or a boyfriend. I was sure she'd turn up after a few days."

"She didn't." Cadence's voice was flat.

"No, she didn't." He gave a sad shake of his head. "I kept looking for her." His words were directed at Kyle. "You know I never gave up. I kept her picture up in my office."

Cadence had seen the picture on the missing board.

"But the years slipped away, and there was never any news." He ran a hand over his grizzled jaw. "When Lily went missing, I knew there was a link. The car, abandoned, *just like hers*. I called you. I *knew*."

From the corner of her eye, Cadence glanced at Kyle. There was no expression on his face. Like her, he knew better than to give away his thoughts or emotions during an interrogation.

She glanced down at her notes, not that she needed them. She wanted to buy herself time to think a bit more. "You never married. Never had a wife. A family." She glanced back up at the captain. "Why is that?"

"My job was—*is*—my life. I know you think it's not much, being the captain in a Podunk little town, but what I do matters to the people here." His shoulders straightened. Pride shone in his eyes. "It matters to me."

Time to change tactics. "You lived here your whole life."

"Yes, ma'am."

"Then why didn't you ever think to search the caves for Maria? For Lily? You had to hear the stories about them, you had to know."

"I did search them for Maria," he gritted and those rumbling words had Cadence tensing. "I didn't see anything. You know how they stretch—"

"Yes," Cadence interrupted, locking gazes with him. "I do. I know just how far they stretch because I was there. I watched a woman die in front of me. A woman who only wanted to go home. A woman who'd been held in your 'Podunk little town' quite possibly for the last four years."

He swallowed again, then his breath rasped out. "If I'd known…"

"You would have saved her? Because you want to save people?"

Kyle stalked closer to them.

"You fit most of our profile," she told Anniston simply. "You know the area. You were here when the first disappearance happened. You've been involved in the investigation since day one."

"I'm in my forties."

"The original profile was for a man in his thirties, but that was assuming the killer started killing when he himself was younger. You're still fit, certainly still strong enough to easily navigate through the darkness of those caves." She leaned toward him. "Is that what you do? Do you enjoy taking women into the darkness? Showing them just how much control you truly have over them?"

She searched his eyes. Could she be staring at a monster? Some people thought evil could be seen. It couldn't. There were individuals in this world who were born actors. They showed only what they wanted you to see. The darkness inside of them might not appear until it was too late.

Anniston held her stare. He didn't flinch. Didn't look away. Didn't even sweat. Completely confident.

In control.

"You have to investigate me," he said with a nod. "I understand. Rip into my past. You'll find I have alibis for the disappearances. All of 'em. I was working cases. Hell, I *knew* Lily. Don't you think she would have recognized my voice if it had been me on the road with her?"

"Not if you had disguised your voice, I don't think she would have." Cadence's immediate reply.

Anniston exhaled. His attention turned to Kyle. "Investigate me. Do what you both have to do, but I'm telling you, it's a waste of time. The SOB is out there. He's probably rushing across state lines right now. You're losing him while you question *me.*"

Still no sweat. No tremble of his fingertips. Just a voice vibrating with growing impatience.

"We are investigating you right now," Cadence told him as she gauged his reactions. "We're pulling up all the work logs from your station, and comparing them with the disappearances."

A ghost of a smile, so confident, slid across his face. "Good. Then you'll clear me within the hour." But then that smile faded. "Only maybe I can make that faster for you." His hands twisted in front of him. "Remember how you said the killer had to be fit, strong?"

She remembered their profile clearly.

He lifted his hands. Cadence could easily see the faint tremble. "I'm taking early retirement in three months. Just waitin' for the paperwork to go through." Sadness drifted through his words. "Your agent accessed the accident reports because those are out in the open. She wouldn't have been able to get into my recent medical history."

Cadence sat back, her gaze sweeping over him.

"I had the stroke five months ago. The trembles still come in my hands, I still get weak on the right side of my body." He shook his head. "I'm not the man you're looking for because I *can't* be him right now. I'm not strong enough." There was almost… shame…in his voice. "My own body turned against me. Docs said that if I didn't slow down, I could have another stroke, one that might just kill me."

"Christ." Kyle expelled a hard breath. "Why the hell didn't you tell me?"

James's chin jerked into the air. The trace of shame vanished and ragged pride glinted in his eyes. "Because what's happening to me doesn't matter. The victims—they are the ones who matter." His gaze cut back to Cadence. "You were sure right on that one, ma'am."

***

Cadence's hand curled around Kyle's arm before they entered the interrogation room housing Aaron Peters. "Are you okay?"

Kyle nodded. "He should've told me."

"He isn't a man who likes to admit weakness."

His gaze held hers. "This bastard has destroyed too many lives."

Yes.

He cleared his throat. "When will they identify the bodies?"

Not the bodies. The *bones*.

"The first step is to compare dental records." Something that was already being done. "If there is enough for a match, then the IDs will happen very quickly." Just as they'd happened fast with Jake Landers and Judith Lynn.

Footsteps hurried toward them. Cadence looked to the left. Saw Dani. Dani's eyes were wide. Her lips pale.

"What's wrong?" Cadence asked her as she moved closer to her friend.

"I started watching the videos." Dani pushed back her hair. Lowered her voice. *Because she didn't want Kyle to hear her?* "He recorded the women in the dark. Used infrared." Her lips trembled. "They're crying—begging—for help."

Just as Maria had begged on the calls Kyle had received.

"It's going to take weeks to go through all the footage. I identified Judith Lynn and Bridgette Chambers." Her exhale was rough. "There are so many tapes. God, those women."

Cadence gave a quick, hard shake of her head. She didn't want Dani to say any more, not with Kyle just steps away.

Dani's gaze slid to Kyle. "I haven't seen any of your sister yet." Her voice was a little stronger.

"You probably won't. I think the SOB took those." His words were flat. "He used her tapes to call me. To make me hope she was alive."

"I'm sorry," Dani whispered, sounding miserable.

Kyle inclined his head. "I am, too." He cleared his throat, looked at Cadence. "Come on," he told her. "Let's see just what the hell the professor has to say."

Cadence squeezed Dani's hand, then headed for the interrogation room. Kyle opened the door. As he opened the door, it was like a mask slid over his face. The grief vanished. Only the cold agent remained.

Aaron immediately jumped to his feet. "I didn't do it!" He shook his head, a frantic move. "You've got the wrong guy! It wasn't me!"

His eyes darted back and forth between them. Nervous energy hummed from his body.

Kyle pointed to the chair. "You need to sit back down, Professor." The bite in his voice made the title a taunt.

Aaron gulped and hurriedly sat back down. "I know how this looks. I was in the caverns. I should have found the women, but I didn't see them! I've told you that already!"

Yes, he had. They just weren't necessarily buying his story. They'd sure found the body in the Statue of Liberty chamber easily enough.

"Look, maybe the guy moved them. I had to get permission from the county before I went in with my team. Anniston and all the members of the city council had to approve my request. Word was in the local papers. I mean, hell, *everyone* knew I was heading into the caves back then." Aaron licked his lips. "He knew what I was doing, and he had time to move them."

"You are the expert on the caves," Cadence said, cutting through his words, trying to catch his focus. "You knew about the entrance at Death Falls, but you didn't tell us anything about the entrance on the northwest side of the mountains." The entrance she'd been forced to walk through at gunpoint. "Do you expect us to believe you didn't know about that entrance?"

"I didn't get to explore the caverns fully! After four days of study at the first site, the walls started to tremble."

Had someone given that tremble a little help? The perp, who'd been worried the professor might go too far and discovery things he shouldn't?

"You never heard anything in the caverns?" Cadence pressed. "Did you, or anyone on your team, see anything that made you suspicious?"

He shook his head. His fingers were tapping on the tabletop. "Nothing. I swear, I would have gone to the cops if I had!"

She didn't sit in the chair across from him. Kyle didn't sit either. They both stood and studied the man who was shaking before them.

"You didn't return to your motel room last night." That had been easy enough to check, since the guy was booked at the same no-tell motel she was. "The clerk was watching. He said your crew came back, but you didn't."

He blinked a few times, clearing watery eyes.

She leaned across the table toward him. "Where did you go?"

Aaron surged to his feet. "It wasn't—"

Kyle wrapped his hand around the guy's shoulder and shoved him right back down into the seat. "Don't fucking *move*."

Aaron gulped.

"You were with me at the site. You followed me to the falls." Cadence kept her voice flat. "Were you the one who sabotaged my wipers? You knew I'd have to pull over if they stopped, but you also knew I wouldn't let my guard down if a man came toward my vehicle. So you sent Fiona—"

"No!" He lunged up again. "I don't know any Fiona!"

In an instant, Kyle had grabbed the man and slammed him against the wall. Kyle's forearm shoved under Aaron's chin, pinning him in place.

Oh, hell. "Kyle!"

"Did you take those women?" Kyle demanded, his voice lethal. "Is that why you don't have an alibi for last night? You took Cadence, you wanted to hurt her."

"No." A gasping wheeze.

"Where the fuck where you then?" Kyle snarled.

"Picked up a waitress...named Susannah Jane...We hooked up behind the bar..."

Cadence remembered Susannah Jane. Lily's coworker who had been so concerned.

"Ask her! Please...just ask..." His face was turning bright red.

Cadence touched Kyle's shoulder. "Let him go."

He held the man for a moment longer.

Kyle, let him go.

Grudgingly, he released the man.

Aaron sucked in deep, gasping breaths. A normal shade slowly returned to his face as he gasped. "Freaking...police... brutality..."

They weren't the police. They were the FBI.

Kyle was still crossing the line.

She looked into his eyes and only saw fury. So much for the mask he'd tried to don.

"I don't believe your story." Kyle's words snapped out. "You're the one who closed down the caves, the one who said they weren't safe enough for anyone else to go in. Why? I think you just didn't want someone stumbling into your sick playground."

Even though his chest was still heaving, Aaron straightened his shoulders.

The nervousness of his body seemed to ebb.

"I know about your sister," Aaron muttered.

Wrong thing to say.

Kyle froze.

"You want her killer, and you'll do anything to close her case, even blame me." Aaron shook his head and jutted out his chin. "Screw that. I'm not saying another damn word without an attorney. You *won't* pin this on me!"

Kyle lunged for him.

Cadence yanked him back and hauled him outside before he could rip into Aaron. Or rip him apart.

She had the feeling that was exactly what Aaron wanted. To push Kyle.

To make him lose control.

She slammed the interrogation room door and jerked her hand to get a uniform to stand guard.

Then she pushed Kyle into the nearest empty room. "*Don't* let him push you."

"He was lying."

"We don't know that."

"His body language was all over the place! The man was shaking, sweating. He couldn't make eye contact for shit. He was *lying*."

Her gut said he was, too. "He gave us an alibi. We need to get Susannah in here and find out what the hell is going on."

He gave a curt nod. His whole body was locked tight. She could almost feel the heat rolling off him.

"We'll talk to Marsh, and while we're doing that, we can send some cops to pick up Susannah." Right then, Aaron was at the top of her suspect list, but she wanted to see what Marsh had to say, too.

"Let's go." Kyle tried to pull away.

She just made sure to block his path. "When we're in those interrogations, I could be standing across the table from an SOB who threw me in a dark hole with a dying woman hours ago."

His pupils grew, swallowing the brightness of his eyes.

"You think I don't want to go across that table? That I don't want to shove my elbow into that man's throat and watch him struggle to breathe, just like Fiona struggled?" Her words flew out.

Her control was cracking.

"I *can't*," she snapped. "We have the badge. We have to do this the right way. You have to help me, and I have to help you."

His hand lifted. Brushed against her cheek.

Wiped away a tear.

Then his head bent. He pressed a kiss to her cheek.

The drumming of her heartbeat was far, far too loud. She wanted to grab him and hold tight, but she locked her arms at her sides.

"I'm sorry," he whispered.

Her eyes squeezed closed. "Hold it together, because it's all I can do to…" No, she wouldn't say any more.

He would know, anyway. Didn't he always know?

His lips feathered over hers.

Then his head lifted. "For you," he told her.

She nodded, understanding.

They left the room and went to find Ben. It was time the cops tracked down Susannah Jane.

***

When they finally entered the next interrogation room, Jason Marsh was sweating. But when he saw them, he didn't jump to his feet. Didn't shout a denial of his innocence as soon as he saw them.

He just shook his head. "Look, I've got an alibi, okay? I was at Striker's. I hooked up with Susannah, and I was with her until I got the call to join the search."

Cadence didn't let her expression alter.

"You were with Susannah Jane?" Kyle asked carefully.

Jason jerked his head in agreement. "Yeah, go talk to her, and we can clear things up real damn fast."

Kyle glanced toward Cadence. "That's interesting, because according to Aaron Peters, he was with Susannah last night."

Jason straightened in his chair. "No fucking way."

"Looks like one of you is lying," Kyle murmured.

Jason's fisted hands slammed into the table. "Not me! Dammit, do you think I would have done that to you? I mean, hell, that's not me! I would never have hurt you!"

"You were the one who first took us down into the caverns," Cadence said, not answering his question. It was getting harder and harder to keep her voice calm. Was he the man who'd taunted her last night? The one who'd ordered Fiona to kill her?

"I checked with dispatch," Cadence told him. She had, right before starting the interviews. "They tried to contact you twice last night. You didn't respond."

"I wasn't on duty! I didn't know."

"Then you called back thirty minutes later, asking where the search team was headed." She stared at him. *He was the right size. His background fit.* He was the only one of the three suspects who had actually faced blindness. Temporary, according to his records, a result of the accident that killed his sister. "If you hadn't talked to dispatch by that point, how did you even know a search team had formed?"

"Heather," he bit out. "She called. Left a message on my voice mail. I got her calls before I heard from dispatch."

Ah, yes, Heather. "You and Heather have been involved—"

"The same way you and McKenzie are." His lips twisted. "Sometimes, partners get close." Anger hummed in his voice.

Cadence didn't look at Kyle. Her focus stayed on Jason. "You and Heather are involved, but you were still *close* with Susannah last night?"

"Heather and I aren't serious. Susannah Jane was just there to pass the time."

The man's opinion of women sure seemed low enough to fit with their killer's.

"Was Lily a girl to help pass the time, too?" Cadence asked, pushing in the dark, but wondering. Jason was a good-looking guy. The town was small.

His eyes widened, just a bit. "Lily and I were over a long time ago."

Her breath eased out slowly as another suspicion was confirmed. Linked to the victims. Linked with the caves. Linked with a past that perfectly matched their profile. The guy might as well have a bow tied around him. The blood seemed to pump faster and harder in her veins.

"You have a nice southern accent," Cadence noted, and she let her own drawl slide through. "The more you're in the South, the easier it is to pick up."

Kyle glanced toward her, a furrow between his brows.

"Once you leave…" She let the faint drawl vanish. "You can lose that drawl easy enough."

"Didn't know you were a southern girl." Jason studied her with a hard gaze.

"Until I was ten." Cadence nodded. "Then I moved up north to live with my aunt. That was when I realized I could make the accent come and go anytime I wanted." Her head cocked as she studied him. "You grew up in Chicago until you were fifteen. That accent of yours—I'm betting you use it when you want and drop it when it suits you."

No expression was on his face now.

"Maybe Lily didn't recognize your voice at first because the accent was gone," Kyle threw at the guy. "Once she saw your face, she *knew*, didn't she?"

Jason shook his head. "You got this all wrong!"

"You moved to Paradox right around the time Maria McKenzie vanished," Cadence said. "Just a few months before."

Jason licked his lips and slanted a fast glance toward Kyle. "I didn't know her."

The glance at Kyle had been far too nervous. Cadence's instincts went into overdrive. "You *shouldn't* have known her since she was just driving through town. A pretty girl, in a fancy car. I bet it would have been hard for a girl like that to pass a teen boy, unnoticed."

His shoulders had tensed. "Go talk to Susannah. She'll back me up. Aaron is the lying asshole, not me. He's the one you need to be questioning. He's got family up here, too, in case you didn't know. He's been spending his summers in Paradox most of his life."

"Don't worry," Kyle told him. "We're questioning him, too."

Jason's breath heaved out as he glanced at Kyle. "Look, man, I'm sorry for what happened to your sister. To all of 'em, but I didn't do it. I've been trying to help them, not hurt them."

Trying to help them…

The words seemed hollow.

Goose bumps had risen on Cadence's arms.

A knock sounded on the door behind them.

Cadence backed away from the table. She opened the door. Ben was there, face tense. "I need to talk with you and Kyle."

She motioned to Kyle.

"Find Susannah!" Jason called after them. "She can clear all of this crap up!"

The door shut.

Ben's jaw had locked. "Two suspects…both telling us that the same woman can back up their alibis."

"So one's lying," Cadence said. "Obviously, but—"

"That woman is missing."

"What?"

"I got an APB out for her right now, but she's not at home, not at Striker's, and none of her friends have any clue where she could be." He yanked a hand through his hair. "Her car is still at the bar. No one knows where the hell she is."

"Are there any signs of foul play at the bar?" Cadence asked but there hadn't been, not with the other abductions. *Only with me.*

"I know we've been over this, but"—Ben's breath hissed out slowly as his brows lowered over his eyes—"could we be looking at another team of killers? I know you worked the case with them before."

Cadence shook her head. Ben was talking about the alpha team she and Kyle had helped take down in Louisiana. "The perp used Fiona to help him last night. He wanted to show his total power over her, to prove he could get her to do anything he wanted. If our guy has help, it would be—"

"One of the other victims," Kyle finished for her.

A victim whom he'd brainwashed—*broken*—into believing her only method of survival was to do exactly as he ordered.

"Both of those men just offered up Susannah as their alibis. That can't be coincidence," Kyle said.

"I think we have to consider there could be two people working these abductions." Ben was adamant. "It *could* be happening."

Cadence wasn't buying that theory. "It's personal for him. The way he talked to me last night. The way he's kept the skeletons.

Everything he does is personal." Intimate. "He's not the type to share, don't you see that? This guy is about controlling, collecting. Not sharing with a partner." That was why his only partner would have been a woman. One of his girls.

Susannah Jane...

Cadence's breath exhaled slowly. "Where's Dani?" Dani could pull up Susannah Jane's life in about two minutes for them.

Ben pointed to the room on the right.

Cadence threw open the door.

"*Kill me!*" A woman's voice shouted. "I don't want to stay in the dark anymore. Just *kill me!*"

Dani spun toward her. There were tears in her eyes. A trembling hand rose and froze the infrared image on her screen.

Cadence looked over her shoulder. Kyle had tensed. Damn, she *hated* his pain.

Through clenched teeth, he managed, "It's not Maria."

"No, no, it's not." But she didn't want him hearing any more. Not then. Not when she'd had to fight to stop the guy from attacking their suspects. If he saw too much, heard too much, she might not be able to control him.

Cadence softly shut the door. "Dani, I need you to run a check for me."

Dani swiped away her tears. "Sure. Anything."

Cadence started to speak, but then she frowned as she stared at the screen. The woman. Her long hair. The strong point of her chin. The line of her jaw.

Cadence's heart began to beat faster.

"Susannah Jane," Cadence whispered.

Dani shook her head. "I don't remember a Susannah being on our list of missing persons."

"No, I want you to pull up everything you can find on a Susannah Jane Evers. She's a waitress over at Striker's. She's also the alibi for two of our suspects. And she's missing."

Cadence leaned toward the screen. Her eyes squinted as she tried so hard to see through the darkness.

Dani's chair rolled away with a squeak of her wheels. She started typing quickly on her computer, her fingers flying over the keyboard.

"No Social Security card," Dani muttered. "Nothing turning up on her. Are you sure that's her legal name?"

Cadence stared back at the grainy image. "That's the name she gave us." Cadence reached for her phone. A few moments later, she had the owner of Striker's on the line. He dug through his personnel files for her, and she rattled off the Social Security number he had for Susannah Jane.

"That's not your girl." Dani glanced over her shoulder as Cadence ended the call. "That number is for a Donald Evers, a guy who died in a boating accident about five years ago." She shrugged. "Wouldn't be the first time someone's tried to ditch their past with a stolen ID."

It wasn't just about having a stolen Social Security number. Susannah worked at Striker's, where Lily had been abducted. Where the police had gone to question suspects. Now she was the alibi for two men.

Both men appeared completely confident she would back up their stories.

"Keep digging," Cadence ordered. She knew if anyone could uncover Susannah's past, it would be Dani. "I need to know exactly who that woman was *before* she became Susannah Jane Evers." She glanced back at the screen. "We're going to need those images refined. The guys at Quantico can do some amazing things with their digital equipment." The only problem was that refinement took *time*. Time that they didn't have. "Make sure they know this is a priority for them."

Cadence hurried out of the room. Rushed right past Kyle and Ben.

"What did you—" Ben began.

She didn't stop.

Cadence twisted the doorknob for that conference room and marched inside. "Susannah Jane."

Captain Anniston blinked at her. "What about her?" Then his eyes widened in worry. "No, don't tell me...not another—"

"She's missing."

He swallowed. His hands trembled.

"When did she first arrive in town?"

"About five years ago. She moved in, started working at Striker's."

"Did she have any family?"

"No." He frowned. "What's this—"

Frustrated, she waved away his question. "Was she ever in any trouble with the law?"

"No. She was like Lily." His lips twisted. "Never even so much as a traffic ticket."

"Where did she come from?"

Anniston shook his head. Kyle and Ben had filed into the room. They were standing back. Watching. Waiting. "I think she might have said she was from Orlando. Seems like she mentioned going to Disney World when she was a kid."

Orlando. That would be a starting point for them. "One of our missing women was from Orlando." Dani had pulled her up earlier. Nina. Nina Jones. She'd been missing for eight years.

Could Susannah be another victim?

309

"I want to see her car." It had just been abandoned at Striker's. Abandoned, as if Susannah were a victim.

"Dammit, let me help!" Anniston said, but he didn't lunge out of his chair. Didn't slam his fist into the table. Just sat there, with frustration stamped on his face. "Susannah is good. Just like Lily. I can help!"

"We need to start searching for her," Cadence said as she looked at Kyle and Ben. Searching. "We're going to need cadaver dogs." If her hunch was right, if Susannah truly had once been a victim, she might now be someone the killer wanted to eliminate.

Susannah could identify him. She could bring his entire game crashing down in flames.

***

The Jeep sat, rain and mud splattered near its tires, in the back of the Striker's parking lot. Cadence searched in the vehicle. Found nothing out of the ordinary.

Except for the fact the keys were on the floorboard.

Kyle lifted the keys. Put them in the ignition. The car sputtered to instant life.

"Plenty of gas," he said. "Battery seems fine." He turned on the Jeep's wipers. They flew over the grimy windshield.

Cadence stared at the car. She was missing something. She *knew* she was. When they'd first talked to Susannah, the woman had seemed so worried, so heartbroken about what had happened to Lily.

Lily.

"Who is she?" Kyle shook his head as he turned off the Jeep. "Is it even fucking possible she was a victim? One he let go? Why wouldn't she go to the authorities?"

"She knew he was watching her." A man that controlling would never let her go, not completely. "She knew he was watching." She thought of the police station. Their suspects. "Or she knew he *was* the authorities."

Jason Marsh.

James Anniston?

Anniston's voice whispered through her mind. *Susannah is good. Just like Lily.*

"I want to talk with Lily Adams again."

Kyle rubbed a hand over his face. "You think I haven't been checking in with the marshal you sent to protect her? *Every day.* Lily still doesn't remember anything."

She shoved out a frustrated breath. "Not about the abduction, but she might remember plenty about Susannah." The women had been friends for years. Lily *should* be able to tell them about Susannah. About Susannah's past?

Despite the heat, Cadence felt cold as she stood in the parking lot. The heat surrounded her, but the ice came from within.

Susannah Jane had vanished of her own volition, running away? Or had someone made *sure* that Susannah vanished, because she knew too much?

And…after what she'd seen Fiona do, Cadence realized that there was another option in play. A dark possibility that twisted Cadence's guts into knots. *Could Susannah Jane be helping the killer?*

***

The little girl with the big, blue eyes watched Cadence with worry as she hurried to her mother's side.

Lily Adams shook her head. "I already told you both." Her gaze dipped from Cadence to Kyle. "I don't remember what happened to me." She bent and pressed a quick kiss to her daughter's forehead. "Sweetie, why don't you go play in your room? I'll be there in a few moments."

Boxes were stacked in the house. Moving boxes. Cadence glanced over at US Marshal Malcolm Williams. He stood near the door, the bulge of his weapon barely noticeable beneath his jacket.

"When are you moving?" Cadence asked.

Lily exhaled softly. "As soon as I can. I just don't want to stay here anymore. I can't." Her knuckles were white. "I don't feel safe. Malcolm can't stay here forever." A broken laugh escaped her. "I'm afraid to go out by myself. I don't remember anything about what happened. Nothing at all. But I'm terrified."

"A fresh start could be very good for you." Cadence didn't blame the woman for running. Getting out of a nightmare was hard.

"I'm sorry I can't help you," Lily said, voice shaking. "I wish I could. I watched the news. I heard about…" Her voice dropped as she cast a worried glance toward her daughter's bedroom door. "About the others. I want to help them, their families, but I just *can't.*"

Kyle eased into the chair beside Lily. "Can you tell us when you first met Susannah Jane?"

"Susannah?" Lily blinked, then she smiled, a real smile that lifted her lips and chased some of the fear from her eyes. "She was here a few hours ago. Ever since she came to town, she's always been such a good friend to me."

Cadence kept her expression neutral. "Susannah came by to see you?"

"Yes, she…" Lily pointed to Malcolm. "She told me I was lucky to have my own guard, but I told her he wouldn't always be here." Her voice dropped. "I wish he could be."

Malcolm's face tensed. "I told you, Lily, I'm not going any-where yet." Malcolm "Mac" Williams had once been an Army Ranger, before he'd traded his military life for marshal service. He might be pulling protective duty right then, but Malcolm's true talent lay in hunting. He never gave up his hunt.

Lily gave him a weak smile, then she looked back at Cadence and Kyle. "Susannah said she was sorry for what happened to me."

I'm sure she was.

"Did she say anything else?" Kyle asked her.

Lily rubbed the back of her neck. "She told me that if she could, she'd stop something like this from ever happening again." Lily glanced once more at her daughter's bedroom door. "I told her the only way to do that was to stop the SOB who did this to me."

***

Dani stared at the gritty image. She'd frozen the video on the woman's face. Cadence had sure been looking at the video closely enough, and now that she'd finally found pictures of the woman calling herself Susannah Jane Evers, Dani knew why.

Is that you?

Her eyes narrowed as she leaned toward the computer screen.

Had the woman who begged for death been Susannah Jane? It was possible. There were some similarities, but it in the dark-ness, it was just too hard to tell for certain.

She leaned closer…

A gunshot rang out, the blast deafening.

Dani shot to her feet, her hands automatically going to the holster at her side. She always kept her gun with her, after what had happened to her.

Always keep your weapon close.

She opened the door a crack and inched carefully down the hallway.

"*Where is he?*" a woman's voice screamed.

Then she saw the woman. The woman who looked just like the image she'd scanned a few moments before for Susannah Jane.

Susannah stood just a few feet inside the police station. She had a gun in her hand. A gun now shoved beneath her own chin.

Ben advanced toward Susannah. The female officer, Heather, closed in on Susannah's other side. Heather had her own gun drawn and her face was deathly white.

"Stop!" Susannah screamed. "Stop right there, or I'll shoot."

Dani pulled out her phone. Called Cadence. "Get your butt back to the station," she said when her friend answered. "Your missing girl is here, and she's about to shoot herself."

"You don't want to shoot," Heather said. The woman lifted her own weapon. Put it down on a nearby desk.

Oh, hell. *Don't do that. Don't play hero.*

Heather was confidently heading toward the other woman. "Susannah, it's me. We're friends."

Susannah moved faster than a striking snake. "That's not my name!" She grabbed Heather. Held her tight with a wild strength even as the cop twisted in her grasp. Desperation was giving her power. Susannah put the gun against the cop's head. "I'm Shelly! I was *Shelly*!"

Shelly Summers. The name clicked immediately. A home in Florida. Parents who'd filed the missing-persons report when their daughter had never made it back to them.

"It's too bright in here," Susannah muttered. "I like the dark. It used to scare me. Not anymore."

I'm tired of the darkness. Kill me!

Dani swallowed the lump in her throat.

"Bring him out to me or I'll kill her."

"Bring who?" Ben asked her quietly. Unlike Heather, he hadn't advanced toward the other woman. He also hadn't put down his gun. It was up, and aimed right at Susannah.

"What happened to me?" Susannah—Shelly?—whispered with a shake of her head. "Why did I become like this?" She shook her head once more and seemed so lost that Dani hurt for her in that moment.

"Let me go," Heather said but she didn't fight against the other woman. Maybe she was afraid the gun would go off.

Susannah's hold tightened on Heather. "Bring him out, and I will."

Him.

Dani whirled away from the scene and ran back toward the interrogation room. She threw open the first door. Aaron Peters jumped. His eyes doubled when he saw her gun. "What's happening?"

"Come with me," she demanded.

He hurried to his feet. Rushed outside with her.

"Susannah!" She shouted for the other woman, trying to get her attention. If she could distract her, then Dani knew Ben could make a grab for her weapon.

They needed to take Susannah in alive because she was the key to so much.

The key to everything.

Susannah turned her head at Dani's call. She stared at Aaron, frowning. Then she gave a negative shake of her head. "That's not him. I told you I need *him*!"

Well, she had two more men left to go.

"He hurt Lily." Susannah pushed the gun against Heather's temple. Shoved it hard. "I should have stopped him. Why didn't anyone stop him?"

Dani shoved Aaron away from her. She was so afraid Susannah was about to pull the trigger.

"Why didn't I?" A desperate whisper. "After what he did to me, *why didn't I*?"

The tension was so thick that Dani could feel it pressing down on her.

"Susannah!" Aaron suddenly shouted. "Tell them I was with you last night!"

What. The. Hell. The man was an idiot. He had eyes in his head. The guy had to see what was happening.

Susannah blinked. She seemed to weave on her feet.

Footsteps pounded behind Dani. She looked back. Saw both Captain Anniston and James Marsh rushing down the narrow hallway.

Dani's gaze flew back to Susannah. The woman had taken the gun away from Heather's head. Now she was pointing it at—

Me.

"No," Dani said. Because she knew what was going to happen. With the gun pointed at her, with Susannah's trembling fingers tightening around that trigger—

"Drop it!" Ben yelled.

But Susannah didn't drop the weapon. Tears leaked down her cheeks.

"Don't!" Dani begged her. "You don't want to do this."

A blast shook the station.

Susannah's body jerked.

She smiled as she fell. As her blood spattered.

"No!" James Anniston ran toward her. His shoulder bumped into Dani, jostling her.

James and Ben surrounded the fallen woman. "I had to take the shot." Ben's voice was tight. "She was going to shoot."

The people who'd been frozen before all sprang forward. A thick circle formed around Ben and James.

"Get an ambulance!" James shouted.

Someone was already calling for the EMTs.

They weren't going to be able to help.

"Are you okay?" Aaron said, his voice shaken.

She looked down and realized Susannah *had* been firing. She'd fired even as Ben took his shot. The thundering sound had been so loud because—*two bullets.*

Blood dripped down her arm. "The bullet just grazed me."

She turned, glancing back to see where the bullet had gone.

Jason Marsh was on the ground. Blood pooled beneath him.

Oh, hell, *no.* "Man down!" Dani shouted and hurried toward him.

His eyes were wide, shocked. Blood leaked from his lips and from the hole in his chest.

Susannah was smiling when she died.

Because she'd taken out the man who'd turned her into a monster?

Dani put her hands over Jason's wounds. Others were coming to offer help but his blood was soaking her. Pouring out far too fast. If the bleeding didn't stop soon, he'd be dead.

Cadence, I need you. Cadence would know what to do. She always knew.

Jason's hand rose. Locked around her arm. She glanced at his face.

"Help's coming." She tried to reassure him, even if he was a killer, she tried. "We'll get you sewn up."

The bullet was still in him. It had torn its way through his organs. Where had Susannah even gotten that weapon?

Jason shook his head. "Not…"

"You'll live!" *Lie, lie.* "Just hold on!"

She heard the screech of sirens then. When cops called for an ambulance, the ambulance *rushed* to the station.

Her knees were soaked in his blood. It covered her jeans. Every space of skin on her hands.

"Susannah." His voice was a rasp. "She…okay…?"

Not based on the sounds Dani heard.

Then the EMTs were there. Pushing her back. Loading him on a stretcher.

Susannah had been loaded up, too. They were put in the same ambulance.

"Fuck, you're hurt." Ben grabbed her arm.

She pulled away from him. Stared after those swirling lights.

"Dani!" Cadence was finally there, running toward them with shocked eyes.

"What the hell happened?" Kyle demanded as he rushed behind her.

"Justice." This came from James Anniston. He didn't sound satisfied. Just tired. "Susannah said she was here for the man who'd hurt her. Dammit, she was a victim, too?"

One who had been there, all along.

Her arm throbbed. The lights from the ambulance were vanishing.

"She shot him. She took out Marsh. My own detective." The words were a whisper from Anniston. "My detective…"

Cadence caught Dani's arm. "You're going to need stitches."

Ben was still staring at Dani. "It looked like she was shooting you."

Yes, it had.

"I had to take the shot." She'd never heard Ben sound so shaken. Wait...

Yes, she had. Back when she'd been in the hospital, fighting to stay alive.

"Is Susannah gonna make it?" Kyle demanded.

Ben shook his head.

Anniston swore and stormed back into the station.

They were left there, with the scent of blood and death all around them.

CHAPTER SIXTEEN

"I don't understand." Anniston's shoulders were hunched forward. "She was one of the women he took? But she was here in town, all those years…"

The police station was a crime scene. The people inside were stunned.

Susannah Jane had died en route to the hospital. Jason Marsh had survived until he got onto the operating room table.

Then died five minutes later.

"He kept her for so long that he brainwashed her." It wasn't the first time a victim had turned killer.

Anniston's head lifted.

Kyle sat in the chair near hers, but he wasn't speaking.

"A victim can be held for so long." She hated what could be done to a damaged psyche. "It's a form of Stockholm syndrome. You bond with the captor. The victim has to have that bond in order to survive. The bond can go so far that in order to function, the victim has to identify with her attacker. She has to become like him. Think like him. Act like him."

Kill like him?

Anniston swore. "But she was free, walking around town. She could have come to *me*. I would have helped her!"

Susannah Jane's freedom had been superficial. She might have been walking around the town, but the perp had still held her captive. He'd controlled her completely through fear. "Just because she wasn't still being held in the cave," Cadence said quietly, "it doesn't mean she wasn't still a prisoner. Her abductor no doubt kept close tabs on her. He would have *controlled* her, every aspect of her life."

Anniston shook his head. "I was here. Right damn here for her!"

Kyle's hands had fisted. "You were here, but Jason was here, too. Jason was in the station. He worked for you. If she'd gone to you for help, Jason would have found out." Kyle shook his head. "That wasn't an option."

"Neither was turning on him," Cadence said. "She feared him far too much." Until he'd taken her friend. Until she'd seen it was possible to escape from him.

She'd tried to fight back, but it was too late.

"We're gonna search his place," Anniston said. The lines on his face were so much heavier now. The case—*cases*—had taken a heavy toll on him. "Do you think we'll find more evidence there?"

Yes.

Cadence glanced toward Kyle.

"Is it over now?" Anniston asked.

They hadn't closed the case, wouldn't, until they'd tied up the loose ends. But Jason fit as the killer.

A nice, neat bow.

They still had to go through the videos. Had to ID the remains.

They'd search Susannah's small home on the outskirts of town. They'd tear apart Jason's place.

There was still a lot more work to be done. The case wasn't over, not yet.

Cadence prayed the deaths were, though. "We won't be leaving town just yet."

Anniston nodded. "If there's anything I can do, tell me."

The reporters were already outside, ready for a feeding frenzy. A serial abductor—and killer—who'd turned out to be a cop. This story wouldn't go away any time soon.

No matter how much the town might wish it would.

"Identify with the killer." Anniston couldn't seem to get past that. "I can't believe it's just—"

"There are plenty of theories out there," Cadence told him as she ignored the throbbing in her temples. "Things like learned helplessness."

He frowned at her. "Learned what?"

"Helplessness. It's why battered wives don't leave their husbands. After so much abuse, you learn to adapt your behavior in order to survive."

Was that what had happened to Susannah? An adaption? One that came back to haunt her.

They'd never know for sure, not now.

"We're heading out to Susannah's place," Kyle said as he rose. "We'll keep you updated on what we find."

Anniston stood, too. "Son, I'm sorry we never brought your sister home."

"Maybe we did." He gave a slow nod. "The ME is working to ID those remains. Maybe Maria will get her funeral. Maybe I can take her home."

Cadence wanted to reach out to Kyle. So she did.

So what if Anniston was there to watch? She took Kyle's hand in hers. Curled her fingers with his.

Together, they walked to the door.

"Thank you," Anniston said. There'd been no anger from him. No demands of an apology after he'd been suspected as the killer.

The guy seemed to know just how the cases worked.

Cadence glanced back at him. Anniston was watching them with a steady stare.

"I just wish I could've done more to help you." Anniston spoke again, voice solemn. "Something more. Anything."

They left his office. The cops in the station looked shell-shocked. Heather was swiping away tears on her cheeks. "You never suspect your own," she whispered as they passed by her desk.

Cadence hesitated near her.

"I should have seen." Heather swallowed. "We were so close, and I never knew what he was." Another swipe of her hand over her cheek. "I feel so stupid."

"You shouldn't." Killers were good at deception. The man had spent plenty of time perfecting his craft. Fifteen years.

"Captain Anniston said for me to go home," Heather told them. "What will I do there? Or here?" Her gaze locked where Jason had fallen. "Maybe I should go home."

She turned away from them.

"We need to get over to Susannah's place," Kyle said quietly, "before some reporters hungry for an exclusive bust inside and ruin any evidence."

Cadence could hear the reporters outside the station. They'd pretty much staked out camp there. The story was too juicy to ignore. Especially when a cop was tagged as a serial killer.

They pushed open the station's doors. The questions flew at them.

"Is it true one of the victims *helped* the killer commit his crimes?"

Not just one of the victims. Two had.

"Detective McKenzie, have you found your sister?"

Kyle didn't even slow down. He figured someone had leaked that tidbit to the press.

"Was Detective Marsh the killer?"

The SUV's doors slammed closed. Kyle pulled away from the station.

Silence.

Cadence stared down at her hands. She wished she had been at the station when Susannah arrived.

Could she have saved her?

Maybe.

Or maybe Susannah had just been ready for death.

Maybe she'd been ready since she woke up, locked in a tomb deep within the ground.

"It consumed me," Kyle said.

At his rumbling words, Cadence glanced over at him. His words had seemed hesitant, when he was never the sort for hesitancy.

"Finding her was all I had. It kept me going for years. The thought I'd bring her home."

He drove easily through the twisting roads, following the GPS instructions as they filled the interior of the SUV.

"Then I met you."

He never took his gaze off the road.

"Something else started to consume me."

She sucked in a sharp breath. "Kyle."

"I don't know how you feel about me. But I wanted you to know. Cadence, sometimes I feel like I'm not even fucking alive if you're not near me." His hands had tightened around the wheel. "Love is supposed to be easy, isn't it? Kind and good. The way I feel about you…it's dark. Sometimes, I worry it's closer to obsession."

They were leaving the small town. Heading for the outskirts. Heading to Susannah's home.

"If you want to get the fuck away from me, hell, maybe it would be for the best." He shook his head. "But I'm not even sure I could let you go. I feel like I'd spend the rest of my life—"

He broke off, but she knew what he'd been going to say.

Looking for you.

"I'm not going anywhere, Kyle."

Her hand touched his.

He slanted her a fast glance.

"I'm right where I want to be," she told him. *Beside the man I want to be with.*

"I'm going to let go of the past, Cadence," he promised her. "I know it's time. I want a present. I want a life, with you."

That was what she wanted, too. Hope beat inside of her, warming her when she'd felt cold for so long. Kyle had always been the one to push them forward, to keep hoping for the victims. Cadence had been afraid to hope. She'd seen too much death. Been forced to tell too many grieving families that their loved ones would never come back.

But Kyle had taught her to see past the darkness. No, he'd taught her that even *in* that darkness, hope still lived.

"We'll tie up the loose ends. Then we'll put this town, this whole place, behind us."

A new start. Together.

Cadence nodded. Her breath seemed to ease, and the shadows of the past that had weighed her down for so long suddenly didn't seem quite as heavy.

They didn't speak again during the drive.

***

The beeping of the smoke alarm reached Heather Crenshaw's ears. She frowned, then glanced around the station.

She inhaled and caught the scent. *Smoke. Fire.*

She could hear the crackle of flames.

She raced down the hallway and threw open the door to the small room Dani had been using for her work at the station.

Fire raced around the room. The videos were melting—all of the tapes, the CDs, everything.

Breath heaving, Heather shouted for help. Two other cops ran inside. One had a fire extinguisher. They doused the flames.

But…

The evidence was ruined.

The tapes. The victims. *Gone.*

"What the hell happened here?" the captain demanded as he came up behind her.

She could only stare at the remains and wonder…*what had happened*?

Someone had just destroyed their evidence. But the killer should have already been dead.

And dead men didn't start fires.

***

It looked as if no one had actually lived in the little cabin beside the county line. There were no pictures. No mementos. No little knickknacks inside.

A small, scarred wooden table.

Two chairs.

The den consisted of a brown couch. A TV.

No magazines. No books.

The bedroom was organized in the same spartan way. A double bed. Blue comforter. A chest of drawers to the right.

Susannah's clothes were all hung up, nice and neat, in the closet. No, not Susannah. Shelly. Shelly Summers.

"She lived here for five years, and this is all that's left behind?" Kyle shook his head. He'd never seen a woman live so sparingly. Never seen a man do that, either. This place, there was just—

Nothing.

Cadence glanced above them. "She liked the light."

Frowning, Kyle glanced up and he realized those weren't ordinary bulbs. They were too bright. Too strong.

He went back into the den. The small kitchen. The same bulbs with the powerful wattage were in those rooms, too.

He looked at her front door. Extra locks. He'd had to break those locks to get inside.

"There are just as many locks on the back door."

"She was still afraid of him." So afraid that she hadn't ever gone to the cops. *Until today. When she went in with a gun.*

Cadence nodded, then she went back to Shelly's bedroom. She started opening those drawers. Going through them, one by one.

"It doesn't look like there is anything here." Why wasn't there anything personal in the whole place?

Susannah was dead, and the cabin already felt like a grave to him.

***

"Heather, come out back with me for a moment."

The captain's voice floated to her. Most of the others had already cleared out of the station because the smell of smoke was so strong. The firefighters had come in, making sure no flames remained.

There was no more fire. No more evidence, either.

"Sir." She hurried away from her desk and followed him outside. The fresh air felt so good when it hit her. Heather inhaled greedily.

"I want to know the truth." The captain's voice was gruff. The hard note in it had her whirling toward him. "Did you start that fire?"

Shocked, Heather could only shake her head. "Of course not!" Why would he even question her?

"You were the first one in there. The others told me—"

"I heard the smoke alarm. I ran in there when I heard it!" She hadn't been in there because she *set* the fire.

"You didn't see anyone in there?" His eyes glinted in the setting sun. "*Think*, Heather. We lost all the evidence we had. The FBI agents are gone, and this is on us. On our watch. We already look bad enough to the public. I can't have someone saying Marsh has an accomplice in my station, someone trying to cover up for the man even after he's dead."

He's dead. The pain hit her again, stark and brutal, seeming to drive right into her heart.

"Sir, it wasn't me." She fought to keep her voice steady. "I didn't see anyone. I'm sorry."

If only she had.

"Maybe it was just an accident." He paced a few feet away from her. "The fire department will be able to tell us. They'll investigate. Maybe Danielle's equipment got too hot."

"Maybe," Heather whispered. She wasn't convinced.

Not convinced at all.

He slanted her a long, hard look, then rubbed his chest. Just above his heart, as if he hurt, too. "You need to go home, Heather. Get some rest."

But home was empty. Silent.

Home made her think too much.

She frowned at the hand on his chest. "Captain, are you okay?"

"I'm fine." But he sounded tired. "Hell, I'm heading home. Maybe tomorrow, we'll wake up, and things will be different."

She watched him walk away.

She opened the station's back door. As she stepped inside, the scent of smoke seemed even stronger now.

Heather hurried past the damaged room. She should call the FBI agents. Tell them what happened. When they found out, they were going to be so pissed.

Small-town office screws up again.

***

Cadence's fingers curled around the small business card that had been hidden in the bottom drawer. Her card.

She remembered giving it to Susannah, and hoping—*hoping*—the woman would call her with news.

Only Susannah had never called.

Right then, Cadence's phone began to vibrate in her pocket.

Her left hand cradled the card as her right lifted the phone. "Hollow."

"The tapes burned."

She frowned. The connection was horrible. She could barely hear. "Heather? Is that you?"

"There was a fire at the station. All of the tapes burned." Heather's words tumbled out.

Cadence actually felt her heart stop at that news. *No, no!* If the tapes were burned, then that meant their evidence was gone. Her heart started to beat again, at a double-time rate. Cadence glanced down at the card in her hand. *If only Susannah had called her...*

"I think you should get back here," Heather whispered. "If Jason was the killer, then how could a dead man start a fire?"

He couldn't. But a live killer *could*.

***

Kyle led the way into the station, rushing down to the evidence room. The tapes were gone, but they still had the remains—the bones.

And Maria's necklace.

He pounded his hand against the heavy door that secured the evidence room. "Kyle..." There was a warning edge to Cadence's voice.

He slanted her a fast look. "I have to see it." Every instinct in his body was screaming at him right then.

The door opened with a groan of sound. Morty Adams, the evidence clerk, frowned at them. "Wh-what's happening, agents?"

"You heard about the fire." Not a question.

But Morty nodded. "I—I had to evacuate when the firefighters came in. We all had to leave..."

And that would have meant this room wasn't secured.

If Maria was his first victim, she'd be special. The one he wanted to hold on to for the longest.

"Get the necklace that was recovered from the caves."

Morty's eyes widened and he stumbled back, hurrying to obey.

"You think it was a distraction," Cadence said as her shoulder brushed against his.

"It could have been." A fire to draw away the attention of everyone while the killer went after what he really wanted.

Killers and their keepsakes. Their tokens.

A token from the guy's very first kill…

You'd want it back.

"It could just have been an accident," Cadence said. "You heard what Dani said. Shelly was aiming at Jason."

He wasn't so sure.

Morty came back. Breath heaving. "I-it's gone."

Sonofabitch.

"It was here earlier, I swear it was!" Morty's cheeks flushed dark red. "I showed it to James. We secured it. It was *here*."

Why would James want to see that necklace?

"Someone had to take it while I was outside. During the fire…"

"And dead men don't set fires," Cadence whispered.

Footsteps sounded behind them. Kyle whirled around.

Heather paused on the stairs.

"Where's the captain?" Cadence asked her.

Heather licked her lips. "He…ah…he went home. He hasn't been feeling so good these past few months."

Kyle forced his jaw to unclench. "Shelly—Susannah—she was holding a gun to your head."

Heather flinched, but nodded.

"So you had the same view she did," Cadence whispered.

Another rough nod. "Sh-she shot James."

So they all knew, but what they didn't know… "Was anyone else standing near Detective Marsh?"

"The agent. Dani." Heather's gaze lowered to the floor. Then she exhaled and straightened her shoulders. She glanced back at Kyle. Then Cadence. "And the captain."

Sonofa—

"I saw him running up, right behind Jason. They were both there when Susannah Jane fired the shot."

The captain. The *captain*. The man who'd been free when the fire was set. The man who'd come to see the necklace.

The man who'd huddled so closely over Susannah Jane in her last moments.

"That bullet wasn't meant for Jason." Cadence had turned toward Kyle.

His heartbeat drummed in his ears. "It was meant for Anniston." The man who'd been there, from day one. The man who'd helped him *search* for Maria. The man who'd known every single step that their investigation had taken.

"Heather, are you sure he was going home?"

"Th-that's what he said."

Home.

Kyle glanced out of the narrow window. Saw the darkness spreading over the sky. "I want you to get some officers and go search his house."

Heather's face reflected her growing horror as she understand just what was being said—and what wasn't.

Behind them, Morty swore.

"Do I have the authority for that?" Heather sounded terrified. "He's the captain."

"We have the authority for it," Cadence told her flatly. "If I'm wrong, it's on me. But you get a team out there. Kyle and I will go back to the caverns to see if he's there, back to the site where we found the bodies."

There hadn't been any booby traps there. Nothing to destroy— *his home*? Cadence sure seemed to think that was what the guy had meant.

He took the necklace—was he going to try to return it home?

The hell he was.

"If you don't find the captain at his house, you meet us there." Cadence reached for Heather's arm. "Don't let your guard down for even a moment, understand, Heather? Don't think you can trust him. If he's there, you put him in handcuffs and lock him in a cell until we can get to you."

Heather whirled and ran for the stairs.

"He helped me look for Maria." Kyle's voice was strained. "No one else back then…no one else…"

"Maybe he helped you," Cadence said grimly, "or maybe he just made sure you never found her."

He flinched.

"I think he's going to the caverns. To him, that's home."

There was only one way to find out if she was right.

In the darkness. With the girls. Only they weren't there anymore.

During the interrogation, he'd seemed so controlled. But maybe the facade of control had been just that—a facade. With the recovery of the remains, with Susannah walking right into the police station, his world could be unraveling.

When a killer's world unraveled, no one was safe.

They rushed back up the stairs. Cadence was already calling for Ben. They'd get as much backup on this as they could get.

***

Two dead. Two fucking dead. Ben glared at the bodies. At least the killer was one of the dead.

His phone rang. He grabbed for it, even as he turned and his gaze searched for Dani.

He needed her close.

She could have died.

There was a reason Dani wasn't in the field. It wasn't just about her fear. It was about his. He hadn't pushed her to go back, and he knew it was wrong but—*I need her.*

He glanced down at the number on his phone. "Cadence," he said, "I'm with the bodies."

"James Anniston could be our perp."

Every muscle in his body locked down. He remembered Susannah's face. Her voice. Her eyes.

Not on Dani. On the man behind her.

"The evidence at the station has been destroyed."

Fuck! He'd only been gone an hour!

"The destruction happened *after* Jason was already dead. The tapes were burned and Maria McKenzie's necklace was stolen." His head was pounding. "And you're sure it was the captain? You already had the guy in interrogation."

"Yes, but I wasn't asking the right questions." Intensity hummed through her voice. "We need to bring him in, Ben."

He nodded even though she couldn't see the gesture. If Cadence wanted backup, he'd give it to her. Always. "Where are you?"

"Heading to the site where the SOB held me. I think that's where he's going. Either to destroy more evidence or—"

The line cut out on her. Crackled. Finally came back.

"...Kyle and I are almost there..."

The connection was *shit.* "I'm on my way." He whirled for the door.

Almost ran right into Dani.

He realized she'd heard everything he'd said.

"*We're* on our way," she told him.

Ben shook his head. "You need to get back to the station."

"I'm not hiding anymore."

Dammit.

"I'm not asking you for permission," Dani said.

"I'm the senior—"

"As the director, you should have ordered me back in the field long ago." Her breath blew out. "As my lover, you let me hide. I'm not doing that anymore. I won't."

His jaw locked. As her director *and* her lover, he wanted her protected. Always.

"Now let's get out there and give them backup." She pulled in a shuddering breath. Straightened her shoulders. Hurt his heart. "I won't let you down. I won't let *them* down."

"I know you won't."

He'd make absolutely sure *nothing* happened to her.

***

James Anniston. James fucking Anniston.

Kyle could remember the first time he'd met the man. He'd raced into the station, fear like acid eating away at him.

"*My sister! Please, I need someone to help me find my sister!*"

The cops there had whirled in surprise, concern etched on their faces, but it had been James who hurried toward him.

"*Mister, slow down.*" James had been barely ten years older than him. "*I'll help you.*"

Kyle slammed on the brakes. The headlights stayed on, cutting through the darkness. Shining right at the entrance to the caverns.

Two cops should have been there. Guards to make sure no reporters or anyone else wandered inside the gaping entrance.

They weren't there.

"Where are the guards?" Cadence whispered, her thoughts obviously following his.

He pulled the flashlight from the glove box, then eased from the vehicle without answering her. His boots sank into the mud, thick mud still left from last night's storms. The flashlight's beam drifted around the area.

Two patrol cars were parked to the right. No sign of their drivers. His light swung back to the left. Yellow tape crisscrossed the entrance to the caverns, but nothing else was there.

"We need to check inside," Cadence said as she exited the vehicle and came toward him.

She had a flashlight, too. A flashlight and a gun.

He stared down at her. She didn't seem afraid. She was entering the place that had been her hell with the stoic determination that was just…Cadence.

I love you.

This wasn't the place to tell her. Not the time.

So he just nodded. As he got closer, as the light swept over the tape and edge of the cave, Kyle saw the blood.

Cadence's light joined his. Then he heard her saying into her phone, "We've got possible officers injured at the cavern entrance on the northern side of the mountains. No, no, Ben, we can't wait. We need to head inside *now.*"

It was a lot of blood.

Too much.

Cadence shoved her phone back into her pocket. She lifted her weapon and her light.

They slid under the police tape. Went five feet in the darkness. And found the first body.

CHAPTER SEVENTEEN

It looked like the officer's head had been bashed in. Blood soaked his temples and streamed down his face.

His throat had been cut open.

Kyle swore at the savagery. To bash the man's head like that—to get close enough to easily slice his throat—the captain could have done that. He would have walked right up to the guy. The man wouldn't have even tried to fight back, not until it was too late.

Poor sonofabitch.

"Where's the other officer?" Cadence whispered. Her light cut through the tunnel. To Kyle, the light seemed so weak in the darkness.

"Help."

A whisper floated from deeper within the tunnel.

Kyle tensed. He wasn't sure the voice belonged to the other officer.

One man was dead. Why leave the other alive?

Bait.

Or maybe he was dead already, too, and the perp was trying to lure them into his trap.

"He came back here for a reason." The place hadn't been rigged to explode before, but maybe it was because their perp hadn't been able to set his traps in time.

They'd followed Cadence too soon. Tracked her. Saved her. Before the SOB could destroy the place.

If he'd gotten rid of the evidence at the station, then hell, yes, he could be destroying evidence here, too.

Bait or killer? They had to find out. They advanced with careful steps. Cadence kept her light on the ground, checking for a trip wire, while Kyle shined his beam at eye level, making sure they weren't about to face-plant into another wire.

"*Please.*"

The cry came from the right, from the same chamber Cadence had been trapped in.

Her breath heaved out, too loud in the silence. He could feel her fear.

Kyle didn't want her back in that fucking room.

The big, wooden door was shut. It had been shut before, when Cadence had been trapped. He hadn't thought of explosives then. He'd only thought of getting to her.

Was the place now rigged to blow if he opened the door?

"*Help.*" The voice was even weaker.

A man's voice. The other officer had been a fresh-faced kid who Kyle only vaguely remembered. He'd been young, maybe in his early twenties.

Too young to die.

Weren't they all too young?

Was that him? *Or is it you, Anniston?*

"We're here!" Cadence called out, but Kyle noticed she didn't open the door. "Identify yourself!"

"Officer Bailey. Ken Bailey..." The words were rasping. "*Please...someone has cut me...*"

He was being used as live bait.

But they couldn't leave him in there to die.

Carefully, Kyle pushed open the door. Inch by slow inch. Checking up and down the door's length for a trip wire.

There wasn't one.

He slipped into the room.

And felt a knife shove into his chest.

"*Please…*" A voice grated in his ear. "*Someone has cut me…*"

It wasn't the young cop.

Kyle shoved hard against the SOB who'd just stabbed him, but the man just laughed and twisted the knife.

"No!" Cadence's scream. Then she was there, but she couldn't attack.

Her light had fallen on Kyle and on Captain James Anniston.

"I'm close to his heart," James whispered. "So close. All I have to do is yank up my blade. You think you can shoot me before I do that, Agent Hollow?"

She didn't. Kyle knew it. If she had thought she could take the shot, then Cadence already would have done it.

"He can still survive if I don't jerk my knife any more."

The guy was taunting them.

"You won't shoot," James muttered. "Because you *fucking* love him, don't you?"

Kyle hoped to heaven she did. But it wasn't just about Cadence. If she didn't take the shot, Anniston would still kill him. Still kill them both.

A numbness was spreading through Kyle's body even as his blood soaked his shirt, but he lifted his weapon. Pointed it right at Anniston's head. "I'll…shoot."

Anniston laughed. "Do it, and you'll never find out what happened to that sweet sister of yours."

Fucking bastard.

"I know." Talking was so hard for Kyle. Maybe the SOB had already clipped his heart. The beating seemed off in his chest. "She's gone. Maria's...at peace."

Cadence's light was on Anniston's face. Rage twisted his features as he shouted, "She's not! She's not gone!"

Kyle's fingers tightened around the trigger. This was what he'd wanted. What he'd planned all along.

To kill the man who'd taken his sister.

Even if it was the last thing he did.

With the way he was bleeding, it damn well might be.

James jerked the knife from Kyle's chest. Then he dropped the weapon. Put his hands up. "I can take you to her."

Kyle locked his teeth against the pain ripping through him. He staggered forward and put his gun right at James's chest. Payback.

"No!" Cadence's shout. Her hands were on his shoulders, trying to pull him back.

"You can't kill an unarmed man," James whispered.

Yes, he could.

"That's not the way the FBI works." The bastard was taunting him.

Screw the FBI. This was how *he* worked.

"Kyle, there are still women missing. All of the victims haven't been found." Cadence's voice shook with fear. So did the fingers holding him.

Those victims were dead. He knew it.

"You can't shoot me because I'm not armed." James's voice boomed. His current voice, not the scared imitation he'd done of the young cop. The SOB was one fine actor.

"Don't care if you're armed." Dead was dead.

His hands were still up. "Do you care about the others? If you let Agent Hollow come with me now, I can take her to Maria."

He wouldn't believe this killer's lies. It took all of his strength to stand upright as the blood pulsed down his chest. "She's... dead."

"Judith wasn't." His hands were still up. His eyes glinted under Cadence's light. "Susannah...was alive. I don't like to kill my girls, despite what you may think."

"No," Cadence's voice. "You like for them to kill each other, don't you?"

James's face tightened. "I have to punish the ones who don't obey. If they just followed my rules, then they wouldn't have to get hurt."

"Bull," Cadence snapped at him. "You love hurting them, that's why you keep them bound in the dark. You love having the power over them."

A grim smile curved his lips. "That's true for some. But Susannah lived, didn't she? I let her keep living because she followed my orders. She checked in with me every single day. Always did exactly what I ordered..."

"Until..." Pain pulsed through Kyle. "She came after you... with a gun."

"She lived!" Fury beat in James's words. "So how do you know others didn't, too?"

"You're not going to take us anywhere else in these caverns." Cadence had her gun locked right under her light. Aimed at Anniston. "We're all going to walk out of here. I've got handcuffs in my back pocket. I'm about to put them on you. So get your hands *up* and keep them up!"

Kyle staggered.

"I hope I didn't nick his heart," Anniston murmured, the fury seeming to vanish. "He'll die if I did. Bleed out before help can arrive."

The gun was sagging in Kyle's hand.

"Did you ever find that second guard?" Anniston asked, cocking his head. "Ken Bailey...?" Then his voice rose, changed. "*P-please...someone c-cut me...*"

It was another perfect imitation of the desperate call they'd heard before.

Anniston smiled. "Someone did cut him, you know. Cut him, hid him. If you won't go and find Maria, then maybe you'll want to find him. He's still alive." A pause. "But then, Maria could be, too."

The sick fuck just wanted them to keep walking in his darkness. He had a trap set for them.

"You want us all to die here," Cadence said as she grabbed Anniston's hand. She locked a cuff around his right wrist. Then his left. "But we aren't. You're not getting away with an easy death, no matter *what* you want." Her body was between Kyle's gun and Anniston's black heart. "When you go to prison, the others will know you're both an ex-cop and a freak who got off on torturing women. Just imagine all they'll do to you. 'Cause I'm imagining it."

Anniston laughed. "Your partner is going to be dead in the next two minutes."

Cadence glanced over her shoulder at Kyle.

"Shine your light on his chest."

Cadence's light dipped to Kyle's chest. He heard her sharp inhalation.

"I didn't lie about the stroke, you know. It changed things for me. Made me realize...the world needed to know about the legacy I'd left. I was in the hospital, recovering, thinking about my girls..."

Sick fuck.

"And I opened the newspaper." James's voice had flattened. "There was a picture of you, Agent McKenzie. The big, tough agent who'd taken down another serial. Maria's hero. You were on the cover of that paper. In the news, and I was *trapped* in that hospital bed!"

"You're going to be trapped in a cell soon enough," Cadence promised him.

"No, that's not the end for me." James was still too damn confident and cocky. "I wanted the world to know how smart I was—and how clueless the FBI was." He rolled back his shoulders. "The Night Hunter." It even sounded like a touch of awe was in the man's voice. "That's who I am, who everyone fears."

Kyle didn't fear him. He wanted to kill him.

"I won't be forgotten. Everyone will remember. They'll whisper about me. They'll drive faster down dark roads...*because of me.*"

Big fucking deal.

"*I* got the fame. I'm the one who killed and killed, and no one knew. Now, *they know.*"

So the bastard had started the killing cycle over again. He'd taken Lily in Paradox. He'd called Kyle down first thing, all so he could get attention. Could get his fame before death.

Death is coming.

"I chose my own end." James said. "I'm not going out slowly, my body failing on me. I'll be remembered for my power."

Because it was all about the damn power. Kyle's breath sawed in and out of his chest. He gathered his strength for an attack.

"Do you know why I came back?" James asked.

Cadence's eyes were on the captain. "To destroy any evidence we hadn't found yet."

"Yes." He seemed so pleased. Too pleased. "How long have we been talking?"

How long...?

"*Get out,*" Kyle gritted to Cadence as he understood just what was happening. There didn't have to be trip wires.

Timers.

James wasn't going to let another stroke debilitate him. He was choosing his own death, a death with his girls.

She stumbled away from Anniston.

"One way in," the captain whispered. "No trip wires, but I planted the explosives just the same. You won't be getting out of that mountain entrance."

He was sealing them all inside.

"One way in," Anniston muttered again.

Then the tunnel rocked with an explosion.

***

The blast threw Ben and Dani twenty feet. They'd just reached the mountainside entrance when the explosion hit. A fiery eruption sent the side of the mountain falling down and sealed the entrance.

"Dani!" He screamed her name as he lurched to his feet.

"Here." She was pushing up, wincing, a few feet away.

He grabbed for the flashlight he'd dropped. The light hit her, and he could see the fear on her face.

"They were inside," Dani whispered.

He pulled her to her feet. The rocks were still tumbling down. The area too unsteady to get close.

"He buried them in there."

If there was evidence in that place, more bodies…

Anniston was trying to cover his tracks.

He'd do anything to keep his secrets, even if it meant sending more people to their graves.

"There's another way." He made himself say the words. Because they had to be true. "There's another way inside. All of the caverns connect here. We're gonna get that damn professor, and we're gonna find them."

There had to be a way inside.

If there wasn't, then he'd carve a way in. He *would* get to his agents.

***

Cadence coughed, choking on the dust and soil that had fallen down on her. But…

She wasn't hurt.

The dust and soil also weren't the only things that had fallen on her.

"Kyle?"

He'd grabbed her, even as the explosion had thundered. He'd yanked her close. Thrown his body over hers.

His blood soaked her shirt.

"Kyle!" She twisted, pushing against him.

Where was her light? The chamber was pitch-black.

She fumbled out with her fingers, looking for her gun or light.

Her fingers curled around the rim of the flashlight. Kyle was a dead weight on top of her.

No, no, not dead. Not Kyle.

He couldn't be dead.

She hit the button for the flashlight. The beam flew across the room and caught Anniston's back as he ran from the chamber.

If there's only one way in, then where the hell is he going?

She saw her weapon. Stretched for it. Got it. *Hell, yes.* "Stop!" she yelled as she took aim.

Anniston didn't stop.

She didn't shoot. If she missed him or if the bullet went through him, more rocks could fall.

"Stop him," Kyle growled as he heaved himself off her. "Go."

Cadence didn't run after him. Instead, her fingers flew over Kyle, checking his injuries.

The stab wound was vicious. Too deep. Too close to his heart.

"He can't get away…"

"I can't just leave you!"

"Get help…" Kyle's fingers grabbed hers. "Dammit, *please!* Stop him. Don't let him get away."

Cadence leaned forward. Pressed a hard, quick kiss to Kyle's lips. "I love you."

Then she looked around the chamber. Found his light. Shoved the flashlight in his hand. One for him. One for her. "I'm coming back. We're getting out of here. Keep the light—" *So I can find you.* She was afraid Kyle would pass out before she could return. *Too much blood loss.*

The light would guide her back.

Cadence stumbled to her feet and rushed after Anniston.

He hadn't headed back to the entrance she and Kyle had used. *One way in, my ass.* The guy was rushing even farther down the main tunnel, away from the cave-in.

His light was shining, bobbing.

She raced after him. He wasn't getting away from her. There was no way he'd escape after the hell he'd unleashed on them.

That's your plan, isn't it? To bury us in here. To destroy any remains from your victims and then to disappear.

Only he wouldn't really disappear. A guy like him wouldn't be able to stop killing. He'd go someplace else. Start hunting again.

She wasn't going to let that happen.

Cadence pushed forward.

And Anniston's light vanished.

***

Kyle's fingers sank into the dirt. His chest burned, his blood soaked him, but he wasn't giving up. Inch by slow inch, he dragged himself up.

The light shone beside him, revealing the location of his fallen weapon.

He should have killed the bastard while he'd had the chance.

Kyle, I want to come home!

His sister's cries seemed to echo through his mind as he rose to his feet.

Cadence was gone. Hunting Anniston.

She wouldn't kill the man, though. She'd catch him. Try to turn him in.

I don't want him in a cage.

Kyle wanted the bastard in hell.

He pushed the gun in his holster. Staggered to the wall. The light trembled in his shaking grasp.

One step.

Two.

He held onto the rocks as he advanced.

He knew Anniston had sealed the main entrance to the caverns. He'd heard the thunder of the rocks falling. The SOB wouldn't have retreated that way.

Kyle turned to the left when he eased out of the chamber. His steps were slow. He knew he'd be leaving a trail of blood as he walked.

But he wasn't going to miss the endgame.

He wasn't going to let Anniston win.

***

The tunnel was empty.

Cadence jerked to a stop. Her light swung to the left. To the right. The man couldn't just vanish.

"Anniston!" she yelled. Her voice echoed back to her.

No other sound.

He'd just been there. He was cuffed.

"*Help me!*" A woman's scream. Coming from what sounded like straight ahead.

Dear God, was he telling the truth? What if Anniston had come back because someone else was still in the tunnels? Someone they'd missed on their initial search?

Don't scream. Maybe she'd been too afraid to call out.

Or maybe...dammit, maybe it was Anniston. Using another recording to trick her. Her breath heaved out. She couldn't leave a victim—and she also couldn't let a killer get away. Cadence tightened her hold on her weapon and moved forward.

Anniston slammed into her, leaping from the darkness. He lifted his hands and drove them—and the cuffs—right at her weapon.

The gun discharged as it flew from her fingers.

***

Ben's head jerked up.

"That wasn't an explosion," Dani said, voice definite. "That was gunfire."

Yes, it was. Ben was already running toward the fading sound. It had come from the east, back in the trees. He slipped and fell, but jumped right back to his feet.

Dani was with him, rushing as quickly as she could.

A gunshot. Either that was his team, trying to signal him—

Or Cadence and Kyle were in trouble.

***

Cadence wheezed for breath as Anniston's hands closed around her throat. He'd pinned her against the rocks with his body, and his hands were slowly choking the life from her.

He brought his mouth close to her ear. "Those were Fiona's screams. Before she learned how much I value the quiet, she used to scream. I kept the screams, the pleas—little mementos I liked to listen to."

She kneed him in the groin.

He just laughed, but at least he moved his head away from hers. She tried to shove her hands between them. Tried to go for his eyes.

But he just deflected her attacks.

"I'm glad that I get to kill you. That I get to touch you while you die."

Sick freak.

"You'll have the full experience this way, and isn't that what you wanted?" He pressed a kiss to her cheek. "To know the victim, you have to be the victim."

Her left hand managed to wedge between them. Her nails scraped over his chest.

Red dots were dancing before her eyes, and the throbbing of her blood in her veins was like a desperate drumbeat.

Her light had fallen and the flashes of red—*not enough oxygen, not enough*—were all she could see.

"McKenzie can't save you. He couldn't save her either. I hope he knows. I hope he knows before he dies that he let you down, too."

Kyle needed her. She had to find a way to get help to him. He was bleeding.

A light hit her. Hit Anniston. He froze for a second. A second she needed. Her fingers clenched, grabbing at the sharp object she felt just beneath his shirt.

A half-moon necklace.

Maria's half-moon.

"Let her go!" Kyle's booming voice. Not sounding weak at all. Furious. Enraged.

"Shouldn't you be dead?" Anniston snarled.

Anniston's hold lightened, but he didn't free her. Cadence sucked in desperate gulps of air as dizziness and nausea rose within her.

"I remember the first time I saw Maria," Anniston shouted to him.

Don't listen to him. He's trying to get to you. To screw with your head. But she couldn't say the words. Her throat was swollen, her breath heaving.

"She stopped for directions. I liked her smile, so I convinced her to have coffee with me. She was so pretty. So sweet. How was I supposed to let her go?"

"*Get your hands off Cadence!*"

But he didn't.

"After talking with her for just a little while, I knew how special she was. How good. I kept her with me. She was my first."

"*Let. Her. Go!*"

Cadence wasn't sure if Kyle was talking about his sister or her.

She yanked on the necklace. The clasp broke, but Anniston didn't even seem aware. He thought she was too weak to attack him.

The half-moon spilled into her hand. The jerk should have buttoned up his shirt more.

"*Why?*" Cadence managed to wheeze out the question, but it wasn't because she wanted to know what made this man tick. It was because she was trying to focus his attention back on her. She'd dropped her gun when he hit her. If she kept him distracted, maybe Kyle would find the gun, or maybe he already had his gun.

A partner's job was to protect, to help.

So was a lover's.

Anniston yanked her in front of him, using her as a shield, even as one arm stayed locked tight around her throat.

"I will snap her neck."

She knew the guy would get off on making Kyle watch her die.

How was Kyle even there? With his injury, Kyle shouldn't be on his feet.

Then she saw Kyle's light weaving.

Cadence realized then…*Anniston will also get off on making me watch Kyle die.*

That wasn't something she would allow. Kyle would *not* die.

They were both getting out of this giant freaking grave.

"I wasn't pinned." The words blew lightly over her ear.

Cadence wished she could see Kyle.

She only saw his light.

It was steady now.

"When I was in that car accident, I wasn't pinned. I got out of my car that night. I went to the other driver. She was trapped. Bleeding and desperate. It was just the two of us on the dark road."

A monster had been born then. No, a monster had always lived in him. The beast had just finally come out to play.

"I could have gotten her help. Tried to, anyway. But she was delirious. She begged me to stay with her. Begged me to hold her hand."

Cadence had the half-moon in her hand. She was just waiting for the right moment to attack.

"I stayed with her. I watched her blood soak the seat. I watched her skin become even paler in the moonlight. I watched every moment. It was the most beautiful thing I'd ever seen. At the end, do you know what I enjoyed the most?" He paused for the briefest moment and whispered, "The silence. That's what death is, you know, sweet, perfect silence."

His arm tightened around her neck.

"When she died, I went back to my car. It was so dark and quiet, and I could smell her blood in the air. I loved that darkness. Right then, surrounded by it, *I was death.* It was all me."

No, it wasn't.

"The cops found us about an hour later. I tried to forget her, the beautiful girl in her blood-soaked car. The beautiful girl who begged me in the dark, but I couldn't, and I wanted to see her again. I wanted that *power* again."

The power of life.

Of death.

"Then little Maria came into town. Smiling. Smelling so sweet. Shy and all alone. She was my chance to have death again."

"Fucking...bastard," Kyle's voice rasped out.

The light still wasn't weaving. It didn't seem to be moving at all.

How had he stopped the shaking? The light was a perfect beam. Angled up, hitting their faces.

He's not holding it. The knowledge sank in. Kyle must have found a little ledge or outcropping of rock. The light wasn't giving away Kyle's position. She needed to act, *now*, before Anniston realized what was happening.

Kyle was looking for his moment to attack.

She'd give him that moment.

No matter how much it hurt her.

And it was going to hurt—a lot.

She wished she could see Kyle once more. Just once more.

In case...

"Do you know why I called you?" Anniston asked, the words a hard curl of sound in the dark. "Why I even brought you in on Lily's case? I didn't have to call. You never would have known."

"You *wanted* me to know," Kyle growled at him. The caves distorted his voice, made it sound both close and far away. "'Cause you're...fucking...twisted..."

"The world needed to know!" Anniston yelled. "I have the power, the control! Years—*years*—I did this, and no one knew."

That was what had finally gotten to him. The need to show off his work. The need to show just how smart he was.

Only things hadn't gone according to his master plan. He'd lost his girls.

That's not all you'll lose.

She just had to find the right moment. Just had to distract him long enough…

So Kyle could go in for the kill.

CHAPTER EIGHTEEN

Cadence was afraid. Her face didn't show her fear. Her face was an expressionless mask, bathed in the harsh glow of his flashlight.

It was her eyes that gave her away. The eyes that searched the darkness frantically for him. Even as her gaze told Kyle that Cadence wasn't going to be a victim much longer.

He had his gun. The blood on his hands made it hard for him to hold a tight grip, and his fingers growing numb made aiming a bitch.

He'd still make the shot.

He just had to get Cadence out of the way first.

The bastard held her too tightly. Her breath had wheezed out before. She'd trembled.

You won't kill her.

Cadence was the only thing that made life worth living for him.

"I kept her," Anniston said, the words a sly purr. Taunting. *Bastard, you will die.* "She cried and screamed at first, for so long, until her voice broke. You heard her cries, though, didn't you? I kept them because I liked to remember her."

"Let Cadence go." He felt cold. His knees had already buckled and he was only standing up because his left hand was braced against the rocks near him.

"You were here, when she was so desperate to get away. When she would beg to go home, you were in this town."

Fuck, fuck, *fuck*!

He felt his mind begin to splinter. He wanted to kill the SOB more than he wanted his next breath.

But Cadence was there. Staring back at him with her beautiful face and her frightened eyes.

She knows what I want. Cadence always knew.

Her head inclined in the faintest of moves, as if she were giving him permission.

Permission to shoot her? *No!*

He'd sworn never to hurt Cadence. Cadence mattered. Cadence was life.

Cadence was love.

It was getting harder to hold the gun. If he didn't take out James, what would happen to Cadence? "Let her…go…"

"One day she stopped her cries. She gave me that perfect silence. She started doing everything I wanted. She needed me. She liked the darkness, just as much as I did."

Once upon a time, Maria had enjoyed the dark. She'd loved to sit outside and stare up at the stars. To watch the moon. It was why he'd given her that necklace on her eighteenth birthday.

Maria and her moon.

Why hadn't he gone with her on that trip? Why?

I don't need you to babysit me, Kyle. She'd tossed him the smile that always helped her get her way. *I'm all grown up now, remember.*

"I remember," he rasped.

"I trusted Maria, I thought she was coming to understand what she meant to me." James pulled his arm back even tighter around Cadence's throat. Her hands flew up, her nails clawing into him. He didn't let her go.

356

"I trusted her, but she ran."

"You're *killing...her*!"

Cadence had squeezed her eyes shut.

"I didn't kill Maria!" James bellowed. There was truth in that bellow. Desperation. Insanity. Truth.

"She ran." His voice was softer. "Fall..."

Cadence's hands were trying to reach Anniston's face. She was going for his eyes.

He saw the glint of gold in the light.

"Let *her go*!" Kyle yelled with all the strength he had.

"She chose—*chose*—but it should have been my decision! I'm the one in control!" James bellowed back. "I'm the one who decides life or death. Just like on that road. I decided. I took the glass. I cut her deeper. I made her bleed more. She begged. In the dark, she bled and begged, and I was in control."

Cadence had his sister's necklace. The half-moon. He could see it now. She shoved the sharp edge of the moon into James's left eye.

He screamed and shoved her away.

Cadence fell.

It was the moment Kyle needed.

He didn't feel the pain in his body any longer. Didn't feel the cold. Didn't feel anything but—

Rage.

He fired the gun. Once. Twice. Three times.

James's body jerked like a puppet, and he kept screaming, screaming even as he fell.

Kyle rushed toward him, stumbling. His damn legs didn't want to work right, but then he was over James. He sank to his knees before the man.

"Kyle?" Cadence's voice. She was there, and he just wanted to wrap his arms around her and make sure she was alive and safe.

But first he needed to send Anniston to hell.

The bastard was still alive. Gasping for breath.

Cadence had gotten the light. She lifted it, making the beam fall on Anniston's face.

He was smiling. Even with one eye a bloody mess and three bullets in his chest, he was *smiling*. "She's a doctor. She has to help me."

"Don't even fucking look her way." He grabbed the man's chin. "You look at *me*." This was the man who'd ripped his world apart. Who'd destroyed the lives of so many. "I'm going to be the last thing you see in this world."

"C-can't kill me...I know...way out...only...me...y-you kill me...you...kill *her*."

Kyle had his gun to James's head.

The captain was still smiling.

Get Cadence out. It was the one thought consuming his mind. Cadence had to get to safety. Cadence had to live.

He began to pull the gun away.

"Kyle, I can hear the falls from here."

He realized the mad pounding in his ears wasn't just his heartbeat. It was the thunder of the falls. Death Falls.

James wasn't smiling anymore.

"We don't...need you," Kyle said.

James roared and jerked up. His hand flew out, grabbing for the gun even as his head slammed into Kyle's.

His nose crunched as the bones broke, but Kyle almost welcomed the new surge of pain.

He squeezed the trigger, but no bullets came out.

James laughed. "Which...of us...is...stronger?"

Kyle yanked the knife from his waistband. He'd picked it up before leaving the dark chamber, too. *Always have a backup weapon.* "I am." He shoved the knife into the bastard's throat. Shoved it. Jerked it. Cut his throat wide open.

A gurgle was the last sound James made.

"Why don't you try screaming, asshole?"

James's body jerked.

The blood flowed.

With his eyes open, staring at Kyle, James died.

Welcome to hell.

Cadence's arms wrapped around him. "Kyle…"

He left his knife in James's throat. The half-moon was embedded in the SOB's eye, and the necklace's golden chain gleamed in the dark.

Cadence pulled him to his feet. "Come on. We need to get you help."

He wanted to go with her. He even tried to take a step.

But he couldn't.

He fell right back to the ground, landing hard on his left wrist. It cracked. Broke.

"Kyle?"

The light wasn't on her face, and he wished he could see her clearly. One more time.

He managed to lift his right hand. Managed to touch her cheek. "I…love you…"

Her hand curled over his. "I love you, too."

They could've had a life together. The two of them. Maybe even a kid. He would have liked a girl.

A girl with her smile. Her golden eyes.

Maybe they could have named her Maria.

Yes, he would have liked that.

Kyle knew how bad his wound was. Only rage and fear had given him the strength to get down the tunnel. Rage, blinding fury, and fear. Fear that Cadence wouldn't survive.

But James was dead now, and Kyle's strength was gone.

He didn't want Cadence to watch him die.

"Go to the falls…" She could follow the sound. Find her freedom. "Get…help…"

Cadence shook her head. "I left before because you didn't want Anniston to escape. He's dead, and *I'm not leaving you*."

But he was leaving her. His heartbeat was struggling in his chest. A stutter, a beat, a stutter.

He fell back, his head hitting a stone. *Can't feel it.* At this point, there was only numbness.

He'd miss Cadence. Miss so damn much. Happiness had finally been in his grasp.

"Don't do this to me!" Cadence yelled at him. Her hands were on his chest. He knew where they were, not because he saw them or felt them, but because he heard the sound of fabric ripping as she tore his shirt. "Don't you do this! You fight, Kyle! You fight to live!"

He had. He'd managed to get down the tunnel. Managed to get to her.

"Love…" Had he told her that he loved her? It was so important she knew, and he wasn't sure.

"I love you!" Her words were a scream. "I'm not letting you do this to me! You aren't leaving me! Kyle, you can't! You don't want to leave me in the dark. You don't want to leave me alone!"

No, Cadence couldn't stay in that dark grave with him.

"Falls…" She had to get to the falls. To the light.

"I won't go without you. If you want me to make it, then you have to make it, too."

There was pressure on his chest. So much pressure. He felt it past the numbness.

"If I have to *make* your heart keep beating, I will!" Was she yelling or whispering? He couldn't tell for sure. "Don't leave me!"

"Always…be with…Cadence…" She was his constant.

"Kyle!"

He fucking hated the darkness.

And loved her.

***

Ben and Dani were soaked. They'd run through the falls, headed back into the deep caverns, then heard the gunshots.

Ben rushed after the gunshots, chasing the thunder even as he knew he should be more cautious. The gunshots themselves could send more of the tunnels caving in.

But I've got two people missing.

His flashlight beam bounced as he ran.

"There!" Dani's cry.

He froze. Tracked his beam to the left. Saw the hunched figure of Cadence on the ground. She was crouched over—*Kyle.*

Kyle wasn't moving.

Another body was there, too.

Dani's light hit him—Anniston. A knife handle protruded from the man's throat.

Ben rushed forward.

"Kyle, don't do this," Cadence was saying, begging, her voice was so low and desperate. "Stay with me. Don't leave me in the dark, stay."

"Cadence?" Dani called.

Cadence's head whipped around. The lights caught the tear tracks on her face. "Help him!" Her hands were still on Kyle's chest. "He can make it! The knife sank too deep. But there's no sucking chest wound. His lungs are clear, we just have to stop the blood!"

Oh, Christ. He could see all the blood.

"Go back out," he told Dani. There was no phone signal down there, he'd already tried to get one too many times. "Get the medical airlift out here! Tell them we have an officer down!"

Dani ran back through the darkness, not even hesitating.

He realized Cadence's hand was *in* Kyle's wound.

"Cadence…" He'd never seen her look so lost.

"I need to keep my hand right here. I can feel his life…in my hand."

More tears leaked from her eyes.

His jaw locked.

But she wasn't looking at him anymore. Cadence was pressing a kiss to Kyle's still lips.

Is he alive?

"I'll get you out," she told Kyle. "You won't stay in the dark. I won't stay. We'll get out together."

Ben's light swept back to Anniston. He saw the bullet wounds. The gaping throat. The knife.

What the hell was in the guy's eye?

"He took them all," Cadence's voice was hoarse. "Then he tried to take Kyle. I won't let him do it. I won't let Kyle go."

Ben swallowed the lump in his throat. Then he bent next to Cadence. "Show me what to do." As long as Cadence had hope, he would, too.

"We have to keep his heart beating," she said, still in a hoarse and broken rasp. "The heart has to pump so his brain gets oxygen." Her fingers were moving on his chest, in his chest. *Keeping his heart beating.* "We keep him alive until help gets here."

Ben nodded. "We keep him alive," he repeated.

✶✶✶

It took five men to get Kyle out of the tunnel.

The airlift was a nightmare. The whirring of the blades—that hollow sound would stay with her forever.

He was flown to the nearest trauma unit. Doctors and nurses rushed out to meet the copter.

They made her let him go.

He'd never opened his eyes. Not when they came out of the tunnel. Not when they flew in the air.

Not when the hospital staff wheeled him away.

His eyes stayed shut the whole time. He couldn't see that he wasn't in the dark anymore.

"Cadence…" It was Dani's voice, sounding worried. Scared.

Cadence turned toward her, her movements sluggish. Her fingers had cramped, locked, because she'd worked on Kyle for so long.

Long enough? Please, please be long enough.

"Cadence, I'm so sorry." Dani's arms wrapped around her. Dani held her tightly.

Cadence crumbled.

***

Kyle wanted to see Maria again. Laughing. He wanted to climb into her car and drive down to Florida with her.

I'm all grown up now, remember.

He wanted to stay with her. To be with her. To make sure she was safe.

I want to go home!

Only there was no home. Their parents were dead. Maria was dead.

Kyle pushed through a sudden surge of pain. His chest— someone was carving it open.

That bastard, James Anniston? Was he still there? Still coming with his knife?

Cadence. If James was still alive, the SOB would go after Cadence. Kyle had to fight. He had to get to her. Cadence. He could save Cadence.

He had to save her.

He loved her.

"*Cadence!*"

"He's coming around, Doctor."

The voice whispered, then floated away.

"Do we need to keep him strapped down?"

His arms wouldn't move. He'd get the knife. He'd stab the—

"Since he took out two orderlies, yes," a stronger voice said. "Get the other agent in here. See if she can calm him down."

Nothing would calm him. James was alive. He was going after Cadence. Trying to take her from Kyle.

He couldn't lose her.

"Calm down," that same voice told him—the voice of a stranger. "We spent too many hours repairing you. We don't want you in the OR again."

Footsteps. Rushing toward him.

Darkness. Too much darkness.

They were back in the caverns.

He hadn't killed James.

"Kyle?"

That voice *wasn't* a stranger's. It was Cadence's.

He needed to see her.

But there was only darkness.

"It's okay," she told him. "Everything's okay."

Was she lying to make it easier for him?

"You're going to make it. You're safe. In a hospital. They fixed your chest. Your nose is broken again, and that's why you have the bandages near your eyes. They're swollen, but if you try..." Her voice broke. "Please try, Kyle, *please*. If you try, you can open your eyes for me."

For her, he would do anything.

So why won't my eyes open?

"Anniston's dead, Kyle. He won't ever hurt anyone else. We've got teams gathering evidence from his home. We're clearing the tunnels. We even found the other cop, Ken Bailey. He was hurt, but alive. *Alive.* And the victims' families are going to get the closure they need. Because of *you*. You stopped him."

A sliver of light reached him as his eyes cracked open.

"That's it," her voice trembled. "Come on, Kyle. I want to see you. Don't you want to see me?"

More than anything.

His lashes lifted a bit more.

She was hazy at first, just an outline in a too-bright room. He blinked and then—

The most beautiful woman he'd ever seen appeared before him.

"Hi," Cadence said. She was crying. He didn't want her to cry. She swallowed. "It sure took you long enough."

It had only taken a few moments to open his eyes. It should have probably taken seconds but...

She leaned over him. Her sweet scent filled his nose. "Six days. You were out for six days."

Machines beeped around him. His chest ached.

Cadence's golden eyes narrowed. "Don't ever do that to me again, understand?"

He should be dead. His memories flew back to him. James. The bullets. The darkness. The half-moon necklace.

Cadence. Begging him to live. To stay with her.

She'd been touching his chest. "What did you do?"

"She saved your life." The stranger's voice again. The stranger—a male—came into focus behind Cadence. A doctor, wearing a white lab coat. "If she hadn't been there, you'd be a dead man."

He had been dead, until he'd met her. A corpse of a man walking around and living only in his past.

When his future was right in front of him.

"Just a few minutes," the doctor said, his fingers pressing against Cadence's shoulder. "He won't be able to stay awake long." Then the doctor was gone. Vanishing behind a curtain.

"You're in ICU," Cadence said. "They couldn't move you out, not until you were stable." She licked her lips. "You scared me."

He'd scared himself.

"You might not remember what happened."

"I...do..." His voice was a weak rasp. His throat burned.

Cadence's fingers slid to his throat. Stroked him. "They had a tube down your throat. You were bad, Kyle." She swallowed. Exhaled slowly. "It was very close."

He remembered being in the tunnel. Sinking his knife into James's throat. Jerking the blade. Watching the bastard die.

Then...

Maybe I don't remember it all.

"Love..." It was so hard to push the word out.

She smiled at him.

His chest didn't ache so much then.

"I know you love me." She pressed her lips to his. "And I love you."

He wanted to smile at her.

"You've been in and out for the last few days." Her head tilted. "Once, you even asked me to have your baby."

A little girl with golden eyes.

"Just so you know, you're going to have to marry me before we even *start* talking about kids."

He would marry her, if she'd have him. He'd love her, adore her, for the rest of their lives.

Kyle gathered his strength. Pushed. "Marry…"

Her lips parted in surprise. "Do *not* let that be the drugs talking." Then her hand lifted and she swiped her cheek.

"Don't like…when you…cry." It was getting easier to speak.

"I don't like when you nearly die on me." Her hand dropped.

It *had* been a tear.

"I'll stop crying," she promised as her eyes held his. "If you promise not to scare me like that ever again."

She hadn't answered him before, so Kyle tried again. "Marry… me…"

Cadence nodded. Her slow, beautiful smile spread over her face. "I will."

He was staring at his hope. His future. There was light all around her. No grave. No darkness.

His Cadence.

The ghosts were gone. The killer dead.

He was ready to live again.

With Cadence. Always, with Cadence.

***

Cadence made her way to Death Falls. The rocks were slippery, the water even higher that day.

Divers were in the water. Searching, on her orders.

Kyle was still in the hospital. He wouldn't be released for another day or two.

The remains they'd taken from the caverns had all been identified. Even though Maria's necklace had been found with the bones, *she* hadn't been.

Not yet.

Another diver disappeared into the water.

"Are you sure she's here?" Dani asked as she crept to Cadence's side.

"Anniston said Maria got away. Then he said, 'fall.' I thought he meant that she fell, but he meant these falls." On her hunch, she'd done some digging.

The suicide that had made people so fearful of coming to this place? The rumors of the troubled girl who'd thrown herself to her death, the girl who'd given the place the name of Death Falls?

The girl had died seven months *after* Maria vanished. The only witness to her suicide had been Officer James Anniston. He'd been patrolling when he witnessed the "tragedy."

No one had ever ID'd the girl because her body had never been recovered. No local reports of a missing person had gone out then, so the story had just been brushed aside.

Anniston had said it was too dangerous to search for her. He'd closed the case.

He hadn't wanted anyone finding Maria.

A diver's head broke the surface as he rose. He took off his mask. Glanced toward Cadence.

And nodded.

Finally, Maria would be coming home.

EPILOGUE

His shoulders were hunched as he leaned over the grave. A simple headstone, one just beneath the sweeping limbs of an oak tree.

Cadence stood back, watching Kyle, knowing he needed this time alone.

He'd finally grieved for his sister.

All of the missing women had been identified. He wasn't the only one grieving.

Paradox, Alabama, would be remembered for years to come. The story was still on the news. The police captain who'd kept women prisoners in his darkness. A man who'd found his own end in that same dark hell.

Kyle stood. Squared his shoulders. He'd put daisies on Maria's grave.

He'd told her that his sister had liked daisies.

Kyle turned from the grave. His gaze swept the cemetery until he found her.

She didn't smile. Just waited.

He came to her. His steps becoming faster, stronger, the closer he got to her.

Then he was there, pulling her tightly against him, even as his hand dropped to her stomach.

They hadn't actually waited until marriage to talk about kids. It seemed fate had other plans for them.

She was already pregnant. So much for being safe on the pill. Seventeen weeks.

They'd gone to the doctor's office just hours before and found out they were having a girl.

Kyle had looked at the fuzzy ultrasound and said he could see her perfectly.

She'd never seen him look so happy.

She'd never been so happy.

"Are you ready?" Cadence asked him. There was so much pain in his eyes. His parents had never gotten to see this day. Maria, at peace. But Kyle had. He'd given his sister the justice that she deserved.

His head lifted. He stared down at her. Gazed at her with the brilliant blue eyes that had first made her heart race.

Her tough agent.

Her sexy lover.

The man who'd walked out of the darkness and come into the light, with her.

"I'm ready," he said.

Her hand was on his chest. Above the scar he'd always carry.

A reminder of what they'd survived. A reminder of the life they needed to cherish.

He smiled at her.

She knew life had finally begun.

Their life.

Together.

ACKNOWLEDGMENTS

I owe a huge thanks to all the phenomenal Montlake staff. Working with you all is a pleasure!

Lindsay—thank you for all the insight and your "catches" during the editing process. Kelli—thank you for the brainstorming fun! You ladies push me and strengthen my work, and I love that!

For my romantic-suspense readers—thank you, thank you, *thank you* for encouraging me to write more of my dark and sexy romantic suspense stories. I had such a fantastic time writing these novels, and I hope that you've enjoyed reading the "For Me" books!

ABOUT THE AUTHOR

A southern girl with a penchant for both horror movies and happy endings, *USA Today* best-selling author Cynthia Eden has written more than two dozen tales of romantic suspense and paranormal romance. Her books have received starred reviews from *Publishers Weekly*, and Cynthia Eden has also twice been named a finalist for the prestigious RITA award. Her novel *Deadly Fear* was a RITA finalist for best romantic suspense, and her book *Angel in Chains* was a finalist in the paranormal romance category. She currently lives in Alabama.

More information about Cynthia Eden may be found on www.cynthiaeden.com. You can also follow Cynthia on Twitter at www.twitter.com/cynthiaeden, or you can learn about her books on her Facebook fan page (www.facebook.com/cynthiaedenfanpage).